Equity of Evil

A Novel

- Based on True Events -

by **Rudy A. Mazzocchi**

Twilight Times Books
Kingsport Tennessee

Equity of Evil

This is a work of fiction. All concepts, characters and events portrayed in this book are used fictitiously and any resemblance to real people or events is purely coincidental.

Paladin Timeless Books, an imprint of
Twilight Times Books
P O Box 3340
Kingsport, TN 37664
www.twilighttimesbooks.com/

First Edition, July 2012

Library of Congress Control Number: 2012941877

ISBN: 978-1-60619-237-5

Cover art by Ardy M. Scott

Printed in the United States of America

During an eleven day cruise through the Panama Canal,
my wife Gina settled in one morning on the deck with a good book.
As I strolled by her for the fourth time in ten minutes,
she finally suggested that I
"...go down to the library and find something to read."
My response: "I would rather *write* one than read one."
Her reply: "I think you should!"

Without her initiative, patience and support
through the subsequent three years,
this first novel would not have been possible.

Acknowledgments

Years of dedicated work and research would not have seen the light of day without the inspiration and mentoring of Gerry Mills, who had the patience to teach me the fundamentals of writing *during* the process of writing. He provided me the freedom that I needed to be creative, but continually challenged me with his strict and constant editing. Perhaps I was a guinea-pig for his latest book, *Magic for Your Writing!*

I also need to thank the honest and bold guidance of my Literary Agent, Erica Spellman-Silverman of the Trident Media Group. After being kicked to the curb a few times, I finally understood that she was doing so for my own good. Eventually, her willingness to take my calls to voice her criticisms made me work harder and the story even better.

Enormous gratitude also goes to my professional editor, John Paine, who elevated the structure of the manuscript to an even higher commercial quality. His no-nonsense approach converted me from a writer to an author.

And finally, you would not be reading these words if it were not for the courage and vision of my publisher, Lida Quillen of Twilight Times Books. Many were enthralled with the contents of this story, but very few were eager to accept the challenge of publishing a novel that includes such controversial or delicate themes of abortion, rape, organ transplantation and human trafficking. Lida is another fellow entrepreneur who is willing to assess and manage risks in order to be "out in front of the curve."

Prologue

Women's Memorial Hospital, Human Genetics Research Laboratory, 1987

THE CONTENTS OF THE NON-DESCRIPT STENCILED BOX INSIDE THE LABORATORY door were neither hazardous nor controversial—except to lay persons, the religious and those with queasy stomachs. They weighed about the same from day to day, always emitting that strong, sterile, clinical odor known by lab personnel—aging, diluted blood mixed with alcohol.

This day's content was nearly double the norm, indicating unusual clinical activity the previous day. The technician groaned, for by the time he'd finished processing the batch he might be late for his nine o'clock Cytology class, way across campus. He lowered the lid and stood for a long moment, thinking. If he cut a few corners, maybe he could....

The thought was chopped short. Proceed with great care through a precise and methodical list of tasks while operating at breakneck speed? No way. He'd just have to give it his best shot. His budding reputation—even the job itself, and with it his rent—required concentration and diligence. Anything less was out!

He'd been hired because he'd presented himself as a dedicated and well-trained pre-med student, exactly the type needed for these often-tedious chores. Senior researchers had shown their satisfaction with free mentoring and cutting-edge scientific training, all of which would make a valuable addition to his virgin résumé. Even if other students made it to the MCAT exams, they wouldn't have anything like it. Twenty percent of his second-year classmates wouldn't survive the competitive curriculum at Pitt, with courses becoming more and more difficult. Another fifty percent would alter their career objectives prior to the entrance exams.

He'd survive—his grades predicted it—and his winner's attitude would survive as well. A position like this foretold financial success as well, unlike that part time short-order cook job at the Wooden Keg Bar and Grill, down on campus. Lab hours dovetailed nicely with classes, and the hospital was part of a larger medical center right on campus only halfway across town. Sadly, all that good fortune wouldn't help this morning. He'd just have to be late to class.

Processing the box contents, called "harvesting," was mostly completed within a bench-top fume hood that kept the work environment quasi-sterile. Swabbing everything down with distilled alcohol intensified the already-pervasive odors that would stay with him all day. It went wherever he did, lingering in his hair, on his skin and even in his urine.

The box could hold as many as fifty aborted fetuses, each wrapped in sterile gauze from the suction canister used in the abortion procedure. Each was placed inside a Ziploc bag, its ghostly contents hidden, the blood-stained covering providing an eerie background for the bag's outside label. Nothing showed there other than the abortion date and a serial number linking the aborted fetus back to the mother.

He'd managed to avoid the academic and personal arguments over what was moral and ethical about abortions. Far better to remain neutral, uncommitted as to pro-life or pro-choice. If he'd been more religious… but then his parents were agnostics. He and his brother had been dragged to Sunday School for a few brief years because his mother was convinced they needed to be baptized, her version of an insurance policy "in case there was actually a Heaven and a Hell." Quasi-religious? No, that wasn't right, either. Somewhere along the line he'd developed a level of spiritualism, his prayers more like an ongoing conversation with God, hiding there in the recesses of his mind.

Absent any religious or spiritual nature, these research materials… *his* materials… were providing real scientific value, not being discarded. His motivations were *scientific,* driven by a zest for knowledge and his interests in Life Sciences. Surely that counted for something.

The harvest box contained forty-two bags, a dozen above average. Each aborted fetus was logged by date and the last three digits of the serial number. Although they were to have an extended life from this day forward, he always prefaced the numbers with "*dd*", the "death date." It had been his trademark from the beginning. Others in the lab jokingly called him "Double D."

Final genetic data were correlated with a parallel project in the lab, one that maintained a link from fetus to mother. The unnamed project dealt with a rare defective pregnancy—a hydatidiform molar pregnancy. Oh, how he'd struggled with that word until he could say it without thinking his way through all the syllables! Mostly to assure himself that he grasped it all, he'd explained the whole phenomenon to his boss and mentor, a thoughtful senior research scientist from India who'd finished and defended her PhD thesis right there at the university. Soft spoken, she was demanding nevertheless when it came to accuracy. The "inspiring professor" within her would make sure he got it right.

As it turned out, none of the molar pregnancy characteristics appeared in the forty-plus samples. That saved some time. Otherwise the clinic would have been required to contact the patient, suggesting she undergo an amniocentesis in future pregnancies.

With the log completed, he piled the specimens in a back corner of the workbench. Stacks of sterile Petri dishes, properly sized, occupied the opposite corner. Each of the Ziploc bags was now emptied... *plop!*... into a Petri dish, recalling boyhood days when he'd bring home goldfish in a bag he'd upend into the aquarium tank. The "plop" sound was identical.

He then painstakingly peeled away the gauze with two pairs of forceps, always fascinated by what lay beneath—a small, intact fetus often the size of his thumb and sometimes nearly half the size of his palm. Even though he'd seen so many he could "guesstimate" their gestational age, the umbilical cord would divulge the true age later. Sex organs were not yet well defined, but one could see the fine outline of fingernails and even delicate hairs that would form eyelashes. It was truly amazing, but the following procedure was its antithesis. He had to push himself through it without stopping to think.

It was a mini-autopsy of sorts—an incision across the tiny, fragile chest to expose heart and lungs that were starting to form inside. Other organs were indistinguishable except to a better trained eye. The heart, lungs and kidneys were often the size of a fleshy-looking pea, easier to identify. He placed them into their own labeled Petri dish. There were two more tissues to collect, one a sample of the epithelial tissue, or skin, and the other the umbilical cord itself, miraculously programmed to live only about nine months before slowly dying in the culture medium. It was actually easy to calculate the approximate date of conception by noting the death date of the cord and the date of harvest.

The remaining material was incinerated.

The organs were gently broken down into their single cells by mechanical disruption—a mincing of the tissue—then mixed into a lytic enzyme solution that helped disintegrate connective bonds between cells. Cells were bathed in a culture medium containing necessary nutrients and antibiotics necessary for survival and growth. And grow they did! They'd be adhering to the bottom of the Petri dish by later that afternoon, when the depleted solution was replaced with fresh broth. A quick glance under the microscope would verify that the cells were dividing and happily growing. One cultured dish of heart cells would divide and grow, becoming eight to ten new dishes within a week… each growing until they had no more room to expand or else were so large they'd deplete the nutrients too quickly and turn the remaining broth nearly toxic. Senior technicians would then perform dozens of genetic studies with these cultured cell lines.

Most exciting was his personal discovery within the past six months. It seemed that a specific number of cells grown for several weeks could be manipulated and combined by gently centrifuging them together to form a pellet of tissue that could be suspended in large droplets of medium. Rather than growing flat on the inner surface of the Petri dish and being bathed by media washing over them, these "drop cultures" would hang in a suspension of nutrients, maintaining themselves in a three-dimensional shape like stalactites containing entombed living tissue, reaching down from the ceiling of a cave. The original suggestion came from his mentor, Dr. Rishi, but the lab work had been all his. It, too, would appear on his résumé when the time came, possibly in a medical journal article naming him as co-author.

In an associated phenomenon, not quite understood, these individual cells would *also* reorganize themselves to form features of the original organ. Heart cells would form a young fetal heart, lung cells would recreate the bud-like features of a developing lung, and kidney cells would organize into the complicated layers of tissues necessary to function as a normal kidney. Missing were the tiny conduits crucial for carrying nutrients to and removing toxins from cells deep within the growing organ, similar to the body's own blood vessels. In lay terms, the surface of the growing organ was being fed by nutrients in the surrounding medium, while the deep, internal cells slowly starved to death.

The puzzle's missing pieces bothered him for many months, until he'd mustered enough courage to try an experiment of his own. The opportunity was provided by an older fetus, probably from a misdiagnosed gestation period resulting in evacuation of the fetus in its second trimester. These were the most agonizing of all to dissect, because of the more developed features, but easier to handle because of organ size. It was the perfect opportunity to try something novel.

With a new scalpel, he gently removed the right hand of the fetus by making a clean cut through the forearm just below the elbow. He then took a long 22-gauge needle and cored out a central channel from the elbow side of the arm downward toward the fingertips. The needle emerged between the middle and ring finger, leaving a very distinct channel running from end to end once removed. He put the entire hand in the center of the dish and covered it with the nutrient-filled medium, then gently placed it in the humidified incubator that slowly rocked back and forth to ensure the tissues were properly "bathed."

Presumably nothing would be detectable for several days—the hand was significantly larger than the typical cell pellets—but a check of the Petri dish the following afternoon clearly showed the skin adhering to the dish surface. The fingernails looked clear and *healthy* and the tissue was firm to the touch. The tiny hand was growing! Three days later the epithelial skin cells on the surface had started sending silvery tendrils outward, like cobwebs extending from a skeleton. At first he hadn't noticed. It was only when he examined the specimen from another angle that he really saw the… the….

He sensed a doubling of his heart rate, blood draining from his face, the room spinning. A wild grab at the nearest bench saved him from falling, but did nothing for his psyche.

"My god," he mumbled to no one, "I've become Dr. Frankenstein!"

Chapter One

The Bronx, New York

PROFESSOR MARCUS LEVINE'S GRAD STUDENTS AND RESEARCH ASSOCIATES would soon hear that his research grant was about to evaporate, ending his long-term resident teaching program at Beth Israel Medical Center. There'd be genuine disappointment, or worse, but he couldn't have cared less. The grant and his prestigious faculty position would be pitifully tame compared to the exhilarating opportunities afforded by his secret development. All he'd need would be associates receptive to his "persuasive talents," plus adequate venture capital.

Most of the project had evolved deep in the basement of the Albert Einstein College of Medicine, thanks to privileges extended to Beth Israel faculty members. He'd accessed the facility at times when no one else was around, this visit typical. Who'd be up and about at four A.M. on a Sunday morning? Further, visits of this kind were unrecorded, as photo ID cards had long since replaced expensive human guards throughout the college buildings. A third swipe of his card through the well-worn magnetic card reader produced a welcoming *click* that preceded the acrid smell of primate sweat, feces and urine. The Primate Research Laboratory housed hundreds of primate species for various biomedical research projects ranging from AIDS to cancer, neurobiology, gene therapy and Assisted Reproductive Technologies, or ART.

There'd be no witness to the inaugural test of his latest invention's final embodiment, because no one knew about it. How absurdly easy it had been, concealing his ideas from students and hospital administration alike. He was, after all, *the* Dr. Marcus Levine whose credentials inspired awe. He brought prestige to the college.

Countless lectures, patents and published papers were responsible for triggering various interests and responses. Thanks to his scientific reputation, scarcely a week passed without invitations to speak as far away as San Diego, and once in Hawaii. Someone named David Thomas had left numerous phone messages all week. Calling from his residence in

Manhattan's posh Tudor City, Thomas wanted to discuss "mutual financial interests." Didn't they all? Everyone wanted to license one or more of the Levine patents, each with a different spin on how lucrative their "astounding new idea" would be for the patent owner as well as themselves. It would all seem so trivial once his brilliant, long-cherished strategy came to fruition.

The test utilized a uniquely different fluid mix; the extraction a modified pulsation technique with controls he alone had designed and constructed. His only assistant would be Sophie, a yellow baboon only eight years old. She'd have lived three times that age in her native central Africa, but most females of her species survived only fourteen to fifteen years in captivity. The last pregnant specimen in his particular research program, Sophie's long, yellow-brown fur made her look heavier than twenty-six pounds, even when considering the twelve-week-old fetus gestating in her womb.

Preliminary experiments on earlier primate specimens had run their course and the latest of his proprietary methods had yielded "promising results," as defined by his students. In truth, results had been incremental, nothing beyond an anomaly well within the margin of error—he'd seen to that—but student exuberance had mushroomed them into a "major improvement." Dozens of lab notebooks elaborated conclusions in nauseating detail. One female student wanted him to autograph her notebook page.

The *refined* version of the same extraction procedure, using his final prototype and the different fluid mix, would deliver what might be labeled a quantum leap in results. Most of a fully enclosed version of the prototype was already finished, waiting elsewhere for validation of selected parameters that Sophie would provide this very morning.

She'd arrived as a toddler, quickly winning over the hearts of all the lab technicians and animal keepers. Dainty, she was a meticulous groomer with a slightly up-turned corner of her lip suggesting a constant smile. She was judged infertile after repeated attempts, regardless of rich blood-hormone levels, but senior technician Lillian theorized that Sophie was simply unwilling to give herself to just *any* male baboon that came along.

Eventually, after what appeared to be a formal courtship, Sophie surprised everyone by letting her guard down and accepting Brutus, a top-breeding alpha male. Brutus had once mutilated another senior baboon for encroaching on *his* water dispenser. He'd since been segregated to an individual cage, but his aggressive personality seemed to *melt* in Sophie's presence.

Lillian wasn't the only one shedding a few tears when results came back positive. Celebrating, she'd given her tiny friend a small bangle bracelet that Sophie clutched tightly every minute of each day. She was clutching it now, alone in her cage at the far end of the lab, separated from others due to her pregnancy.

Coming close, Levine stared directly into her eyes, a technique he'd practiced on non-human primates for years. He'd always win the classic "stare-down," intimidating his animal opponent large or small, female or male. Sophie turned away within a minute, cowering in the corner of her cage while he whistled tunelessly, setting up the apparatus on a shiny, stainless-steel procedure table directly in front of her. His final prototype replaced the data-collection equipment of the past few months.

After plugging the eclectic arrangement into a standard wall outlet near Sophie's cage, he donned thick, elbow-length gloves, unlatched the cage door and in one swift motion grabbed her, neck and tail. She screamed as he forced her face down onto a stack of gauze pads soaked in formaldehyde. That, in turn, set off a chorus of howls and barks from alpha males in the adjacent room, a din that raised the hairs on the back of his neck. He'd have rapped on their cages with something hard any other time, deliberately riling up the largest males while serving notice that *he* was in command. Not today. He tightened his grip. When Sophie stopped struggling, he prepped the femoral vein in her right hind leg and inserted an IV needle with a rubber port through which he could continually inject a sedative. He wouldn't need much. A small speculum inserted into her vagina was quickly followed with his modified catheter system. A flip of the switch turned on the pump. With one hand lightly steadying her tiny, twitching body and the other on the catheter system, he watched the vacillating pressure approach its specified threshold. Then came the eventual *ssssurlop* that announced potential success. With one hand still on the catheter system, he held up the glass canister and focused on the contents, a grin spreading across his face.

"There you *are*, you little devil, free of your hiding place and out where I can see you. All intact, all in one piece. Perfect!" As he gently shook the canister, the small fetus twitched and gasped, filling its lungs with his special solution. "That's it, my sweetie, take it in … your first and final breath."

Placing the canister on the table between the open thighs of its mother, he filled a syringe with a lethal dose of pentobarbital and inserted the needle into the IV port. As the drug surged through Sophie's tiny body, her eyes dilated and her jaw fell open. The silver bangle bracelet dropped to the floor, bouncing away to lodge beneath one of the storage cabinets.

Levine pulled the power cord from the outlet and unfolded an industrial-strength trash bag. Holding Sophie by the tail, he dropped her in head first, followed by the bloody catheter system, IV tubing and empty syringes. Alcohol-soaked wipes, used to clean the table, were next, followed by his long gloves. Once the bag was taken to the trash-chute and shoved in, incineration was automatic. In twenty minutes there'd be nothing but fine ash.

That finished, he scooped up the glass canister, peering again at the tiny fetus. "Now, my little darling, time for you and Dr. Levine to make history. We're almost there." He carefully slipped his prize into a padded pouch in the corner of his well-worn duffle bag, unhooked his proprietary apparatus, locked it away and reassembled the original equipment. The spotless procedure table was returned to its earlier position. Yes, indeed, time to make history—and a fortune relating to some of those enticing offers… one in particular across town in Tudor City.

Strangely, this man from Tudor City knew all about the famous Dr. Marcus Levine and his accomplishments in the world of Human Genetic Engineering, though they'd never met. David Thomas was most complimentary during the first of several conversations, outlining a compelling proposition that was dizzying in its promise.

The treasure hunt began with affable Pete Lundgren, a partner in one of the Minneapolis venture capital firms, but only as the facilitator. Lundgren would be the key to securing the ultimate prize, one Roman Citrano. According to Lundgren, Citrano had been highly publicized as CEO of a device-oriented company that designed and commercialized an implantable widget to treat congenital heart defects in newborns. After struggling years of raising capital and completing exhausting clinical trials, the company successfully launched its products in the U.S. and throughout Europe. Unfortunately, the lead investor, a large private Wisconsin corporation, converted its debt to take majority control of his company. That corporation then demanded a level of profitability so large it jeopardized clinical support and the product's quality. Minority shareholders filed a class action suit against the greedy organization and its pompous executives.

The true "David vs. Goliath" battle played out in the courts and local media. After fruitless months of trying to mitigate the issues, Citrano finally joined the minority shareholders, sacrificing his own reputation and ego to fight for his beliefs, and was immediately fired from his founding CEO position. Permitted to address the jury during the court trial, he emotionally described how he compared the injustices of the takeover corporation to the molestation of one's own child!

The meeting with Lundgren ended with his offering to pitch the proposed venture to the now-infamous Roman Citrano, his long-time associate and sometimes rival.

Citrano was the right choice, David Thomas stressed. Unlike the classic venture capitalist who acted objectively and deliberately, he was known for physical, mental and emotional involvement with his ventures. Such a man would be quite easy to manipulate, once his innate enthusiasm had been nurtured. That Citrano *had* no children was immaterial.

Chapter Two

Minneapolis, Minnesota

INSTINCT!

The single word flashed into Roman Citrano's thoughts as he stared down from his 17th floor window. Instinct... and persistence. That described his whole career after all these years—especially when a healthy dose of audacity was thrown in.

His smile turned a bit grim. Maybe "lunacy" was closer.

His top academic honors in college didn't seem to count for much, nor did his oftentimes-heroic exploits on the Rugby field. Forget that remarkable "shoo-in acceptance" for medical school, or the prestigious good fortune of working in the Human Genetics Research Lab of Women's Memorial Hospital.

His instinctive—some called it rash—shift toward the business world made those assets worthless, yet in just a few years he'd nourished several startup companies into maturity with no more than a smattering of socio-economics for his "business training." How? Those who pointed to his inborn ability were just being kind. No, it was instinct, audacity and persistence! It had to be. The whole warped path seemed like being in a rowboat in the middle of Lake Superior during a storm. No... more like a canoe in the middle of the Atlantic in a hurricane! In comparison, one could tie a car's steering wheel in place and calmly drive from one end to the other of snow-covered Marquette Avenue, just below his window, without a single twist or turn.

The "road" leading from Pitt to his graduate days at UCLA, then on to the Founding Partner of Zorro Medical Ventures twisted and turned like the convoluted Mississippi River west of his office. There'd been other career paths without those pressures. He'd talked often and openly about changing directions, then confounded everyone including himself by flipping to the *dark side* and creating his own venture capital fund. He'd brought a solid med-tech background and proven track record to the party, but no formal business education or training beyond a strong instinct for the industry, developed from managing several start-up companies over the past two decades.

Still, even after all the due diligence and investigation involved with any venture, it often came down to personal instincts, a humbling experience since any real value in a new enterprise remained unknown until it was acquired or underwent an Initial Public Offering.

A canoe in the middle of the Atlantic, in a hurricane! That was it in a nutshell.

The sprightly clicking of women's heels became carpet-muffled footsteps behind him.

Sarah! When his door was open she always breezed right in without so much as a polite tap, not so much from being the only female in an otherwise male endeavor, but because she was naturally assertive... or was it pushy? A new junior associate, fresh from completing her MBA program at St. Thomas University, she'd decided one fine day that she might "consider" being a venture capitalist, as if it were that easy.

The footsteps stopped. "Roman, we need another review meeting to revise the offering document for the new Fund."

"We?"

"Your partners."

"We just *finished* revising it last Friday, Sarah."

"Apparently it needs something more. I rearranged your afternoon schedule."

"Wonderful."

Of all the tedious and dreaded tasks in the fundraising process, these never-ending reviews were the worst, all administrative and legal stuff required to "pitch investors" with the story. Putting the money to work was what he did best, but investor commitments were still pending. At any rate, she'd interrupted his stormy Atlantic canoe trip and now she could damn well wait if she expected him to turn away from his window just for her. Oh, she'd go about repositioning his prestigious awards gracing the mahogany bookshelves, pretend to blow the dust from their marble bases, inspect his two African violets and the cacti on the filing cabinet, then run through her virtual laundry list of things needing attention in his office, as if all that was her job. He'd replaced the awards with business and medical books, only to see the same awards right back in their accustomed places the following day. The books were neatly arranged between bookends on one of the file cabinets!

Sarah, whose world didn't include the "you're only as good as your last deal" adage, often boasted about his exploits to visitors and new clients. Attractive, outgoing and spontaneously flirtatious at times, she was quick on the comeback. Other times she'd be motherly, "properly dressing him" when he was compelled to don a tie for a more formal meeting or presentation. He'd never mastered a four-in-hand tie knot, using the fact as an excuse to wear a crisp, white open-collar shirt whether with a casual jacket or one of his most expensive tailored suits. It was his trademark, along with his dry comments from the podium such as, "Ties cause cerebral aneurysms!" When he *was* forced to wear a tie, Sarah relentlessly yanked it apart and tied it properly. Not particularly good for a male ego that had been badly bruised by divorce number two just prior to initiation of the Fund.

"Did you hear what I said, Roman, or were you somewhere off in la-la land?"

"South la-la. Warmer there. Where are Paul and Josh these days? Can't revise the already revised revisions without my two accomplished revision-specialist partners. Did they go along with your choice of time?"

"Haven't told them yet. I just passed Paul and I believe Josh is on his way in. We can make it a working lunch if you prefer. When it's over, you can take your customary afternoon nap."

"Great."

"Great which? Working lunch or afternoon nap?"

"Lunch."

"You got it. Toad-on-a-roll and iced lake water?"

"Sounds great! Horseradish on the toad, please." Without exception, she would always order him the same grilled chicken Panini sandwich from the vendor on the Skywalk below.

She was losing her starving-student physique and rounding out nicely, thanks to those upscale restaurants she could finally afford. Breasts and hips were widening a bit, and her ass had a firm, appealing shape. Though he was single, available and most likely more-than-willing, she couldn't know that he was already smitten by another incredible woman, a surprising relationship in view of his vow to take things slowly after the divorce.

Zorro was just now raising its second Fund, and the existing portfolio of company investments was doing well, but there'd been no liquidity events to yield any types of return for their investors. That made things more than difficult when trying to attract new investors for the next level, since investors expected returns within a reasonable period, preferably three years, and Zorro was already four years down the road with nothing at all to boast about. FDA approval on new technologies was slower than ever, capital projections were forever too low, markets were tight and the strategic acquirers seemed more selective and demanding. It all reflected on him more than partners Josh Dunham and Paul Morgan, who always fielded the easy questions while he shouldered the brunt of telling and selling the Zorro potential.

ᘓᘐ

While Paul slouched, both legs up at the far end of the office table, Josh kicked the meeting off by overstating the obvious, delivered in a monotone with palms up. "Our existing Limited Partners still want to see a new independent lead investor step up to initiate our second Fund terms. Sorry, Roman, I know you hate this."

"Look... we've been in front of all the potential leads. Am I missing something here?"

Josh sighed. "We have four prospects in due diligence right now, but no idea who might get there first... if at all. Perhaps we should consider a placement agent to identify some others."

Paul's feet came down. "That won't do it, guys. Damn, there's got to be a more efficient way. I'm making so many changes to the changes of my initial changes in the memorandum draft you can't even see the original—"

He stopped. Sarah had chosen that moment to stick her head just inside the office door. "Roman," she purred, "Pete Lundgren's on the line looking for you. Are you available?"

"Damn. Transfer him to the small conference room next to my office."

Excellent timing, Pete! With any luck, they'll move this discussion ahead without me.

Josh, a former investor and board member in one of those early, energy-draining start-up companies, established himself as a close personal and professional associate. Raised in a small Minnesota town, with the physique and demeanor of a Marine, he was extremely likeable, almost overly friendly and courteous, yet not at all hesitant about demanding the replacement of a wavering CEO. With solid grass-roots training and reliance on the fundamentals, plus years in the hi-tech sectors of the defense and healthcare industries, he was also a devoted Christian with high moral standards. Though his spiritualism was always evident, he never appeared "overly religious." He was extremely dedicated to his family and several non-profit groups of which he spoke little, preferring to keep his personal world private.

Paul was armed with an MBA from Wharton and training as an investment banker, with great depth of experience in healthcare. Using a no-nonsense approach in his diligence efforts, he dug in hardest on negotiating any deal, playing the antagonist, challenging others to convince him of the new opportunity's value proposition. Competitive in every aspect of life, he liked being the center of attention and could usually hold his own in any situation. With a Jamaican father, his dark color, thin build and short, tight haircut, people often compared him to Tiger Woods. He'd use that to his advantage with women *and* men.

They were the best partners he could wish for. Both pointed at Roman Citrano when the topic was balance for the team, since he'd spent years in the trenches creating new ventures, bringing hi-tech products to life. His instinctive investment skills provided quick reads on new technology feasibility, or achieving clinical validation, or even the real amounts of capital needed to succeed. Paul often said that when Roman Citrano liked a deal, it was hard to move him off position.

Pete Lundgren, a helpful and supportive mentor over the years, held that Roman was wasting his natural CEO talent by not running early stage companies. New technologies, good ideas, big markets and large amounts of working capital were *always* available, but good senior executives with start-up experience were not. Those with successful exits under their belts were extremely rare and hard to come by. And he'd been right.

"Hey Pete, how've ya been?"

"Great, Roman, just great. Say, how's the new fund coming along? Doing well, are we?"

There it was again—sarcasm. Always the same. "Nothing new to report, still trying to identify a—"

"Listen Roman," Pete interrupted, "got something interesting here. A clinical researcher contacted me last week. You should meet him. He's got a novel start-up company idea, but it's a little too early in the game for me and I'm not sure I could convince some of my partners on it anyway. This is more *your* type of deal."

"What's the space? A device play?"

"No, and that's the problem. It's more in the healthcare services area and I just don't know about the business model. It's also 'out there' a bit … somewhat controversial … but I thought of you right away."

"Appreciated—you've got me curious if nothing else."

The other end chuckled. "If the deal attracts too much controversy, you can hide behind that 'mask of Zorro' of yours."

"Spend a few bucks and rent the movie, Pete. You might actually come to understand why we picked the name for our Fund."

"You can't fool me. You've just got it on for Zeta-Jones."

Why even bother wasting your breath. The only thing that'll impress Pete is performance. The deal's probably something nobody sane would take on, but hey, it's something for Roman. Thanks, Pete.

"So who is this clinical researcher?"

"An MD/PhD out of New York… the Beth Israel Medical Center, associated with the Albert Einstein College of Medicine, former Professor of Medicine at Hopkins and a real prolific inventor. Dr. Marcus Levine. I've given him your contact information… you'll probably hear from him. He's a tenacious son-of-a-bitch."

"Can you send over a copy of the Executive Summary, or some brief overview?"

"I'll email you a PDF version. Let me know the outcome. He's a sharp guy, very convincing, and we've been trying to work with the folks at their Tech Transfer offices for years. Sorry, gotta run, meeting my son for lunch. Later!"

Lundgren had hung up, but not before getting his message through: "Here, Roman, old pal, I'm handing you an opportunity. It's challenging and a bit controversial, but hey, your name's all over it!"

Prick! You know damn well you have me intrigued.

ꙮ

Levine closed his phone, smiling. Not an hour since leaving Peter Lundgren's office, and already encouraging news. Lundgren had talked with Roman Citrano, as promised, and Citrano had clearly shown interest. It was all falling into place quicker than imagined. Best of all, Mr. Lundgren couldn't have guessed that Roman Citrano's interest wasn't all that important. Zorro Medical, after four tedious years trying to close its second Fund, was still without star power in the world of Venture Capital.

Now *that* was meaningful! They were ripe.

Levine smiled again, reopened his cell phone and punched in Citrano's number. Why wait?

Chapter Three

I'M ASSUMING MR. LUNDGREN INFORMED YOU I WOULD BE CALLING. HE THOUGHT we should get together... so when is good for you?"

Now there was a brash opening for you! *No general niceties? No dance?*

Levine had an odd, mixed Jewish/Bostonian accent evident from the first word, but with the unmistakable proper English enunciation of certain words. It was intriguing.

"Actually Mr. Lundgren didn't mention you would actually be calling, Mr.... ah, Dr. Levine. He merely suggested there might be a future time when we could take a look at your new venture. He didn't divulge any details surrounding your business proposal, as our conversation was very short."

"I understand what you are saying, but since we are speaking now, I do have several days open next week. How about you?"

Déjà vu. Levine had just painted himself as another cocky academic researcher believing the world should be beating a path to his front door, clamoring to exploit his invention while praising him for his gift to mankind. How many "Levines" had there been over the years, first-time entrepreneurs top-heavy in ego and light in substance?

"Dr. Levine, a face-to-face meeting usually follows some understanding of the kind of business you're proposing and, more importantly, what kind of proprietary technology you've developed."

"You see, this is always the problem," he barked back. "You financial types want things rolled up into a nice, neat package that doesn't take up much of your time. Well, this is going to take longer and it's *both* a proprietary technology and business model that addresses a large clinical unmet need! I was told that you and your firm were different and that *you* personally would have an appreciation for what I'm trying to do."

"Alright, Dr. Levine, I'm not sure why you believe I would be personally interested, but you've succeeded in piquing my curiosity. The person who told you we were different obviously failed to mention that we normally invest only in medical *devices,* not business models or healthcare services, but since I do have some availability, how about next Tuesday morning at ten? I believe I can see you then."

"Tuesday at ten is good for me, yes." With that, Levine simply hung up.

ᢂᢃ

Pete's caginess was understandable now. The Executive Summary was intriguing, if not somewhat shocking, but also a significant challenge. Successfully marketed, it could be a high-profile market leader with potential for significant returns as a listed company on the stock market. Follow through would take a very objective eye… and a great deal of fortitude.

At 9:45, he'd started a second run through the document when Sarah stuck her head inside the office door. Levine was there early, demanding to be seen!

"Tell him I'm in conference, Sarah. Offer him some coffee." *Pushy bastard! I ought to make him wait a half hour. Pete was right… a tenacious son-of-a-bitch.*

Levine's detailed *curriculum vitae* disclosed an Indian mother, highly educated in London and later teaching at the University in Delhi where she met her future Israeli husband. Marcus was the product of that union. His educational and professional credits were impressive. He'd graduated from Johns Hopkins with a dual doctorate in Human Genetic Engineering and Morphology at the age of twenty-one, quickly moving forward to obtain his medical degree at Harvard, followed by a residency program in surgical obstetrics at Beth Israel Medical Center, then back as a full tenured Professor at Hopkins for a couple of years. He also managed to maintain an associate professorship at the Albert Einstein College of Medicine, where he lectured on Anatomy and Physiology. One could well imagine his sense of urgency about things… he didn't seem to have much extra time on his hands.

Sarah ushered him in at twenty past ten, starting her usual introduction, but was rudely interrupted. Ignoring her, Levine strode forward, hand extended, more like a mongoose confronting a deadly cobra than anything else.

He was quite short, dark skinned and handsome, with a trust-inspiring face and poorly dyed jet-black hair. A home hair-coloring kit, perhaps? It was the old story of someone compensating for small stature with bravado and arrogance. His handshake was overly vigorous.

"Marcus Levine," he announced. "Good to meet you, Mr. Citrano." Taking the centermost visitor's chair, he nervously clutched a worn briefcase as if it contained the map to the Holy Grail. "We will not waste each other's time," he declared, "so I will be as brief and as concise as possible and you should do the same. I also have your word, Mr. Citrano, that this is all confidential and not to be disclosed to anyone outside of your firm without my written consent. Agreed?"

You're here looking for financial support and you start off by dictating your terms?

"Well, Dr. Levine, I prefer that you take whatever time may be needed to properly disclose your business opportunity. In the event we at Zorro are interested, *you* will need to grant us access to all of your materials and market intelligence sources so that we can verify your value proposition."

"Very well," Levine snapped back, fidgeting a bit on his chair. For all his bluster, he looked uncomfortable. "Let us forget the honoraria. To you, I am just Marcus. To me, you will be Roman. That is how I think it should be. Now... what I am to tell you might not be as exciting as some of your other deals, but I strongly believe it will address a very large market whose needs are currently unmet. My company is called EMBRYIA and I have already incorporated the business as a Delaware corporation with my personal funds. Unlike your other medical technology companies, we can be in the market in a matter of months—months, not years. We do *not* have to worry about FDA approvals and can easily solicit reimbursement from many government agencies or third party insurance companies. The market is huge and surprisingly underserved and all we need is capital to start and grow the business."

He paused and suddenly snapped open his briefcase, but took nothing out. More theatrics? Finally he cleared his throat.

"There are approximately forty-two million unwanted pregnancies throughout the world. Forty-three percent of all women will have at least *one* abortion before they reach the age of forty-five, and, although the mortality rate associated with abortion is ten times less than that of actually giving birth, major complications include severe bleeding that requires a secondary surgical intervention, torn uteruses, infection, scarring that results in infertility, incomplete abortions further increasing the risks of infection and even uterine cancer, perforation of the uterus and other internal organs and, although rare, even death. Complications occur primarily as a consequence of not having access to or knowledge of performing such delicate procedures."

"Wait, Dr. Levine, are you telling me, that—"

"We agreed to drop the doctor title. Please! Here in America, about fourteen percent of abortions performed are publicly funded," he continued, withdrawing a sheaf of papers which he subsequently ignored. "Sixteen states provide programs to pay all costs for underprivileged women who qualify. Fifty-two percent of all abortions occur before the 9th week of pregnancy, twenty-five percent between the 9th and 10th week, twelve percent between the 11th and 12th week and ten percent between the 13th and 20th. Those are the recorded cases. There are as many, if not more, unrecorded cases as you might guess.

"Although we believe we now live in a sophisticated, civilized world, Mr. Citrano… er… Roman, we still force hundreds of thousands of women to deal secretly with the termination of their pregnancies in seedy, backroom abortion clinics or even perform them on themselves, unsupervised and alone, with homemade equipment or something as barbaric as a coat-hanger." He paused again, glaring as if to imply he'd personally seen such atrocities. "EMBRYIA will provide such personalized, professional services in a controlled, sterile *mobile* environment."

There… the closing statement! The term "mobile environment" had been covered in the Summary, but there'd been no accompanying descriptions of possible designs, or discussion of the logistics required of such a business.

"You say mobile, Doctor… Marcus. Has this ever been attempted?"

"Exactly… a self-contained Mobile Abortion Unit, or MAU, that provides these discreet services to women all over the world in both urban and rural environments, where they otherwise wouldn't have access either for personal, social or political reasons. No more sneaking around in dark alleys, worrying about crossing picket lines, or clinic staff members worrying about death threats or vandalism of their clinics. We shall bring the therapy to the patient, in their neighborhood, their surroundings. This would be the first time ever attempted, and it's long overdue."

He seems to have done his homework, and he's well-rehearsed... or well coached! No arguing with his statistics, or the stigma surrounding abortion in general, or even his passion about a potential solution. Stumbling blocks? At least two. Yes, this may truly be a "market opportunity," but how will society react to abortion as an organized business? Equally bothersome is the lack of any real science or technical discovery tied into the concept.

"You have a question you are not asking," Marcus stated, staring down at one of his spreadsheets.

"Actually several questions. First, where do *you* add value as a medical and scientific scholar? Is it based in empathy for the women involved, or something you can claim as your own contribution in the professional sense? Why are you personally excited about—?"

"Why am I excited?" Levine's answer overlapped the question. He continued scanning his spreadsheet. "There is a novel technique that I would like to consider using in the extraction of the fetus."

He suddenly stood and went to one of the windows, hands deeply driven into his jacket pockets, and spoke to the window.

"It's a slightly modified technique that is more forgiving in the removal of the material. It takes a little longer, but it is far less damaging to the fetus... and the mother, of course."

"To the fetus? I can understand the importance of minimizing trauma for the mother, Marcus, but why does the fetus matter? Sure, ProLifers use images of macerated aborted fetuses as a tool to show the gruesomeness of this procedure, but do you honestly think that preserving the fetus intact will change people's perception?"

"No, of course not, as long as you extract all the fetal material, but I also have designed a special canister in order to inhibit cross-contamination with the maternal tissue. As to people's *perception* of this act, I'm neither a politician nor spiritual leader so I've no interest in so-called perceptions."

"Well, I suggest you give the ProLifers some serious consideration. Marketing and market adoption are key elements of success in any new venture, so people's perceptions should be your number one concern. I presume you've at least filed for patent protection and have obtained an expert opinion regarding patentability? You do have a working model?"

"Ahh… well, a disclosure has been drafted, yes, but such things cost money. Your questions say you are now interested, whereas before you were not." He turned, somber, hooking both thumbs into his belt. "However, if you are only interested in the extraction technique—"

"Let's just say I need to better understand why this presents a competitive advantage over conventional techniques. We must dig deeper into your Summary numbers and judge for ourselves whether your invention disclosure is patentable. We must also examine state regulatory and reimbursement issues. Have you started *that* assessment yet?"

"No, not each and every state… of course not!"

"Well, just give us what you have and we'll do some diligence of our own. Can you get us a copy of the draft patent application or put us in direct contact with your patent attorney?"

Levine's expression lightened a bit. "I will send you the draft application."

With that, he simply retrieved his briefcase, shook hands as firmly as before and walked out without another word. Possibly he'd never return, since nothing of substance had been discussed at length, certainly nothing about the exciting new extraction technique itself. In fact, the whole interview had taken eighteen minutes!

What was that on the chair? Levine had overlooked one of his… wait! He couldn't have missed anything like this. Two laminated sheets contained color photographs far too ghastly or even necessary to support any investment theses. Had he left them deliberately? *They… they….*

Turning quickly away from images already frozen in his memory, Roman Citrano fought a flood of raw emotion never before felt.

Chapter Four

Kolhapur, India

LUKE EVANS KNEW IT WAS TIME TO MOVE ON.

The problem wasn't India—which was just a disappointment—but that La Jolla had been too damned comfortable. The lab he'd joined as a technician in California had grown. He'd been a part of that growth, a source of pride in the same way a mother cherishes her child's advancement from kindergarten to the first grade. Glowing with its success, and while working for his PhD in Cellular Biology at the Scripps Institute, he'd been mentored by the best professors in the field. Another small but intangible bonus.

Add beautiful California shores to those small but intangible bonuses, and a plethora of blondes he'd rotated through his bed every weekend, and it was all a fantasy. Then Reality crashed the party and leveled the playing field. Industry competition grew and pay scale tightened and that meant a change in venue, like it or not. There weren't many opportunities for permanent jobs in his chosen field, but one held promise. Mumbai, India! The name conjured up images of Art Deco bars and restaurants, grand temples, endless bazaars, glistening skyscrapers and malls waiting to be explored. Modern Mumbai was hardly comparable to that of even twenty years earlier, certainly fifty. It was a booming metropolis. It was alive!

An assignment there sounded invigorating, exotic and definitely educational, particularly since his California living expenses and lifestyle wouldn't last long without substantial and continuous income. A bird in the hand?

Unfortunately, his new employment was in Kolhapur, described offhandedly by the recruiter as a Mumbai suburb. Suburb? It was halfway to Pune, south of Nowhere. Getting there took a day's sweltering train ride from Mumbai, miserably jammed together with families literally sitting on top of one another and in the aisles. No air conditioning! So much for his naïve plans for commuting on weekends to enjoy all those Mumbai visions and exotic adventures.

Kolhapur was a sprawling industrial area filled with chemical, plastic and steel plants and empty promises, or so it seemed. The city, known worldwide mostly for its Kolhapuri chappals—colorful leather sandals—was to replace La Jolla and those darkly tanned blondes? Reality didn't care.

A large, multinational biopharmaceutical company was rumored to be poised to acquire the small research company he'd be working for, but those empty words were uttered in California. Months of anticipation became years; whispers and mentions of any acquisition faded. His dreams of exercising valuable stock options and moving up the corporate ranks in a *real* biotech company faded with them.

Still, the facilities were constantly upgraded and modernized despite the constant undercurrent of financing difficulties. How were they pulling it off? Nobody talked about the commercial value of the company's work in his presence, nor had he met any of the owners or senior managers. Occasional visitors departed without being identified by so much as a name tag during their brief stays. Were they inspectors? Potential investors? There was no telling.

The technical demands of each new project were personally rewarding, however, along with the challenges of bedding the dark-haired, dark-skinned, black-eyed young technicians seemingly sprouting around him like mushrooms in the night. He'd done well in that department, with but a single strikeout in six "at bats." Unfortunately, the one he'd truly set his sights on—Kareem—confounded him with her shyness. She was from a wealthy Indian family who'd sent her off to Cambridge for her doctorate. Although not quite as curvy or sensual as his other conquests, she'd fueled his sexual fantasies ever since their first meeting.

She was an enigma, blushing easily, and yet she showed in all sorts of ways that she liked his cocky-American ways, hanging on his every word when he spoke about the vastness of his country and how *anything* was possible. The word "anything" was dripping with sexual overtones—he'd made sure of that—but she merely looked at him with big brown eyes, seeming to reach into his soul, but showing only curiosity. It was more than just a cultural thing. She was… different, unlike anyone he'd ever met.

Her "junior technician" status included responsibility for changing solutions in the holding chambers, monitoring temperatures and specific chemical parameters in the pre- and post-solutes. She was immensely overqualified for such tasks, but she, too, had been enticed by the pay scale and promises. Trained as a genetic engineer, she'd not yet published any significant research papers beyond her Master's thesis while at Cambridge, entitled *The Morphology of Inherited Metabolic Diseases.*

The recruiter from AMBRIA convinced her that the company would support her objective to defend her thesis and complete her degree. More empty promises. Her moratorium from academia indefinitely voided any process allowing her to defend her thesis and obtain her doctorate. If she'd been disappointed, it didn't show. She seemed comfortable in her position, happy to be employed, and no longer motivated to hang another diploma on her wall.

Alvarez Gerber, a Swiss technician who'd been in India a number of years, offered some sage advice. "She's playing with you, Luke. What she *wants* you to do is maneuver her into a compromising situation where she's forced to choose quickly between the constraints of her culture and her own lust."

"Oh, come on, Alvarez, are you—?"

"Believe me, they're all like that over here, some more, some less. They're all the hotter because they're so repressed as children. Back her into a private corner one day and have a go at her, just like you would with any of your American girls. Don't give her time to think. You'll see. If she doesn't push back, then she's hungry for more and then you make your move."

"I can't do that, not with her. No problem using that approach with others, just not with her."

He'd shrugged, grinning. "Well, Luke, I guess then you suffer, no?"

ꕥ

The current primary task was to design a portable, self-contained incubator that would sustain any of the different organs slated for special transplant procedures in children and young adults all over the world—and even that element of the business presented a greater mystery. How were the organs procured, and from whom? How were they marketed to those in need? What supporting organizations handled supply and demand? And why the apparent shroud of secrecy?

The current volume of activity was extremely low, serving only eight to ten patients each month. It didn't take a Wall Street genius or Wharton MBA to know a company couldn't sustain itself with such low revenues. And the argument that business would expand once they improved the quality of organs needing long-distance shipment? Nonsense! Where was the hue and cry for such improvements? Who defined quality? Surely he'd have heard that "just in time" surgical implantation worldwide was clamoring for better long-distance shipping methods just by keeping his ears open.

And what of that conference in Geneva, sponsored by the World Health Organization and the only such meeting he'd ever attended since joining the company? Its principal theme addressed global *shortages* of human materials—particularly organs—used for transplantation. Discussed was the growing phenomenon of "transplant tourism" caused by that shortage, along with quality, safety and efficacy related to transplantation procedures. Traceability and accountability of human materials crossing borders seemed to be a new major issue.

Patients traveled to a variety of countries where organs were more prevalent and accessible, albeit at a significant price. The primary concern of the W.H.O. was to ensure that commercial exploitation of organs did not jeopardize the health risks of recipient *and* donor. Regulation of donations from both living and deceased donors was designed to ensure safety and reduce organ trafficking. A specialized agency had been established to monitor such trafficking and initiate controls wherever it was detected. The same agency would administer the unified coding system adopted to track organs and tissues from origin to destination. The conference had been disturbing in that there seemed to be a disconnect of sorts when it came to his main project. Organ transportation wasn't the problem; *availability* was.

Even so, a rare company newsletter announced that an unnamed new group of private investors from both the U.S. and the Netherlands was planning to infuse a large amount of capital to support the redesign of a new biological incubator to expand the "production" of the lab. Expand production? That made even less sense. The bottleneck was in securing adequate donor organs. Why would any investor group be so cavalier with their money?

His own lab's final processing area typically lost half of everything it set out to preserve. Organs were attached to perfusion systems sitting in aquarium-sized containers, constantly flooded with a special solution containing a recipe of nutrients to sustain the starving tissues, but the majority weren't viable when the time came. Yet it was urgent to develop a more efficient *containment and transport system*. He'd been under enormous pressure, working overtime and on weekends. There had been no backlog of organs needing transport, yet meeting upon meeting stressed critical schedules and deadlines. Why the rush?

His normal workweek included collection of physiological data on ten of his samples. Most were human hearts between two and five years old. The chambers containing other organs such as lung, kidney and eyes were much more complicated. The heart was the simplest of organs to maintain.

He'd stopped dwelling on organ donors shortly after his arrival, forcing himself to think more about the recipients and how his work would impact *their* lives. It was a rewarding and fascinating assignment in that respect, but he needn't be in India to do such work. As for the incubator project, he'd been following orders, yes, but with a growing sense of discomfort.

Questions unanswered spawned more questions. Because of it, Kolhapur seemed more and more like a dead end on his personal career path, but he had some money put aside, plus a solid track record of employment with many novel achievements under his belt. He also had more freedom of choice. Time to move on, indeed!

At the end of the year it would be back to California ... and that revolving bedroom door.

Chapter Five

Minneapolis

THE PITCH TO HIS PARTNERS, ROMAN KNEW, WOULD TAKE SOME REAL SALESmanship, not just a few glib words. He saved the final changes to his presentation, then sat back.

The project, taking form quicker than anticipated, was looking pretty damn good. True, he might have overstepped a bit by engaging nearly all the junior associates to help with due diligence, but the effort had uncovered some intriguing information. This thing was so *different,* so compelling, that he had difficulty thinking of anything else. Marcus had been right in saying it wouldn't require a great deal of capital. They could be in the market in a matter of months, not years as with other early-stage medical technologies.

However, there was the specter of society using this venture as an excuse to re-open political and religious debates. He pushed away memories of his own unborn child floating in the toilet on that cruise ship many years ago. That had been a miscarriage, the last of three spontaneous miscarriages with wife number two. Just off the Baja California peninsula, the ship's doctor told them only to call him if there was excessive bleeding. She didn't have the courage, so naturally the supportive and understanding husband would be the one to flush the bloodied contents of the toilet out to sea. Who else?

They never spoke about having kids afterwards… never. Ironically, the event hardened her personality and seemed to soften his. She acted as though the events had never occurred and he often found himself staring at his desk calendar, calculating how old his baby sons or daughters would have been on that particular date. Six months later, they'd agreed to go their own ways as if the marriage certificate had never existed. The repeated loss of their unborn children left him with hidden scars that were much deeper than any caused by a failed marriage.

However, now it was not just business, but survival. Given the limited remaining capital of the first Fund and the delays in initiating the second one, a minimal-cost investment opportunity like this could add essential value to their portfolio. The Plan would fund twelve Mobile Abortion Units—MAUs—ten to be placed in various international sites and two in the United States. The U.S. cities hadn't been chosen. Mobile Abortion Units would be state-of-the-art, fully equipped rolling clinics with the proper equipment to handle any and every possible complication. Using the largest of recreation vehicles as a platform, modifications would provide three private suites, each supported by a nurse and technician team responsible for the patient from the time she stepped aboard until she'd recovered enough to leave.

Three suites, three medical support teams, three simultaneous abortions.

Each procedure, including recovery time, would run slightly less than ninety minutes. One MAU could theoretically complete eighteen abortions in a ten hour day, 108 procedures in a typical six-day work week and nearly 435 completions every month. A mere dozen MAUs could treat nearly 65,000 women every year, and that was just the beginning. At $600 per procedure, this would gross approximately $39 Million and be profitable in year one! Wall Street's reaction to a public offering would be explosive!

Then there was Levine's novel EMBRYIA extraction technique, deviating but slightly from conventional suction techniques except for its proprietary saline solution containing amino acids, proteins and growth factors proven to enhance the healing process. It thereby minimized any scarring or fibrosis of the uterus often associated with the so-called normal procedure. His system also used a micro-pulsed suction technique that *gently* extracted the fetus from its placental tomb and delivered it intact into a collection chamber. One hundred percent removal was thereby insured, providing a very clean and much safer overall procedure.

Conventional procedures used constant suction that *pulled* the fetus apart, vacuuming it out. Legitimate doctors finished the procedure with a loop-shaped knife, a curette, to scrape away any remaining fetal parts, or "products of conception." There was no telling what other devices might replace a curette when removal was done on someone's kitchen table or bathroom floor.

Levine's post-procedural program, as a result of Roman's encouragement, became increasingly important as a possible answer to the Plan's societal impact, perhaps the only one with any merit. The program evolved as a natural offshoot of the extraction technique involved, but Levine assumed credit for it. First it would argue that providing young women access to this sanitized and controlled alternative would be far better than seedy backdoor clinics or, worse, self-abortions. That part was a given. Complementing this "altruistic" solution, time would be spent with each patient to help educate her on various birth control methods.

The Plan included the offering of various forms of contraceptives, even the possibility of an IUD inserted free of charge. Normally an abortion patient waited several weeks or months before an IUD could be inserted, but the EMBRYIA procedure was so less traumatic that this would be an immediate option. Clinicians managing the MAUs would also be licensed to prescribe various birth control pills, patches and/or injections.

In summary, it truly addressed an unavoidable and unfortunate procedure that would be performed "one way or another," just one more step in helping manage over-population and growing famine throughout the world. As convincing as that argument seemed, selling the whole concept to Josh, Paul and the Fund's investors required the appropriate *pitch*, and that would not be easy.

Josh was the problem. You didn't use certain curse words in front of Josh Dunham out of respect for his personal outlook on life, not that he'd ever confront you on it. Josh was raising two wonderful teenage sons who'd sworn their celibacy both to their father and their Lord. How exactly did you pitch a deal like this to a guy like that?

The very thought made his stomach tighten.

"Well, Josh, we're going to back a new company that provides abortion services for women all over the world, helping them to terminate their unwanted pregnancies ... and in doing so we'll produce a phenomenal return to our investors and this partnership. Are you on board with this?"

The tightness faded. His two partners and literally everyone else needed to understand beyond any doubt that abortion was an unavoidable reality of global society, here to stay during their lifetimes. A safer, cleaner procedure, with more favorable outcomes—coupled with helping these unfortunate women avoid repeating the same mistake—was humanitarian!

Chapter Six

United Hospital, St. Paul, Minnesota

Andrea Robbins was part nurse, part social worker and part "hands-on healer." Her astonishing gift was acknowledged by the entire staff and by every parent whose child passed through her unit. Most in her profession couldn't tolerate more than two or three years of emotional torture in the Neonatal Intensive Care Unit, but she'd been able somehow to protect herself from the daily trauma of newborn babies suffering and dying before her eyes.

Other nurses were awed by her ability to bond with the small, frail children lying within incubators. She somehow made contact with them, often locking eyes with even the youngest as she slowly inserted a feeding tube down tiny nostrils or milked a blood sample from a small scalpel-prick in the infant's heel. Countless were the times when a crying child quieted while looking deeply into Nurse Andrea's bright blue eyes or reacting to her gentle smile. Her touch and soft approach had an equally healing effect on the hundreds of troubled parents she'd encountered throughout the years.

The only child of an upper class family, she lived a luxurious life, went to the best private schools and had her pick of any university. Her father was a "who's who" in the steel industry from the iron range of northern Minnesota; her mother the daughter of a world renowned surgeon whose father and grandfather before him were both pioneers in the surgical field. Accordingly, her natural affinity and appreciation for the medical profession was overshadowed only by her love of children. She'd thought herself blessed by her calling to be a Pediatric Nurse, never looking back, but now she was looking forward, moving on to a senior staff position at the Children's Hospital of Philadelphia, a dream come true.

The hospital had an exceptional reputation, with new, world-class facilities, but she'd miss her friends and the inter-workings of the charming community hospital that had become her home for over half a decade. The past several weeks had been difficult, but the farewell lunches, drinks after work and good-bye tears were behind her now and the moving van was scheduled for Monday morning.

It was her last hour on her final day, her last cruise around the unit, and one last stop to visit *Baby Doe*. Every so often the staff was handed a newborn with such a horrendous birth defect that survival chances were near zero. Oftentimes the malformation reasons were unknown, some possibly inherited or due to chromosomal changes, others resulting from specific environmental influences from the mother during her pregnancy, such as drugs or alcohol abuse, excessive tobacco or even poor nutrition. Many such infants would survive for days or even weeks with exacting care by the staff, but others were so grossly deformed they would last less than a day.

There, alone in the darkened corner of the unit, connected to a specially designed ventilator, was one of those unfortunates who were given less than twenty-four hours to survive: *Baby Doe*. She'd nicknamed him *Rambo*.

Rambo was born with anophthalmos—no eye sockets—and Grade III Microtia—the absence of any external ears—and such a severe cleft palate that the mouth and nasal passage were merged into one small almond-size opening, now fully obstructed with the ventilation tube. Despite Andrea's encouragement, the mother refused to even look at her poor child. She, like other parents in similar situations, simply waited for the inevitable, denying the need to start any sort of recovery process from her loss while attempting to deal with her own self-blame.

Andrea made the connection with Rambo during the very first moments of his arrival. Absent sight, sound and smell, his tactile senses seemed extra-keen. The slight touch of her finger upon the tiny palm of one hand caused his whole body to jerk, reach and tightly grab on to her. She'd grinned ear-to-ear in awe of his strength. Rambo justified his name. He was truly a fighter!

She'd spend extra time with him each day, her magical quality seeming to extend his existence hour by hour, day by day. His 24-hour sentence had expired three days back, yet his prognosis was no better. With her finger again entombed in his tight little grip, she bent over and kissed his tiny check, one small tear creating a wet spot on the side of his temple where his ear canal should have been. How long would he survive without her loving care? He was in God's hands… soon to face the inevitable.

Drying her eyes, she braced for a final farewell of a different sort. She'd fallen deeply in love with a man who had somehow snuck into her heart over the past six months, someone she'd known she needed to guard herself against, but irresistible nevertheless. Disappointed with herself for letting it go so far, she'd have to say good-bye, even if she'd soon be alone in a strange city without him. They both had their careers, and the timing just wasn't right.

ᵹᴐᴄᵹ

Roman wasn't surprised about the way his feelings for Andrea had grown. She was smart, loving, giving and very attractive. Beyond all that, she was extraordinary in all the other ways he could imagine. Despite her almost angelic appearance, she also had very few inhibitions, insecurities or fears. She'd approached him that first time during a healthcare conference, not the other way around, inviting him to her hotel room, controlling the flow of their lovemaking. But she had a turning point as well, one where she'd suddenly just melt into his arms and let him take over.

He was anxious to be there again.

He sat waiting for her at the bar in the St. Paul Grill, anxiously checking his watch every so often and swirling his glass of red wine. He had no real appetite for dinner, only for her. Anticipated heavy traffic from Minneapolis was in fact surprisingly light, so he'd arrived early, and waiting was *not* one of his strong suits.

The St. Paul Grill was a familiar place where he'd met several colleagues and CEOs over the past ten years. It had a manly ambiance, with high, mahogany ceilings and well-worn marble floor. He knew many of the bartenders and waiters, but avoided them, trying to blend into the gathering happy hour crowd. Not easy to do while wearing an open collar and indigo blue blazer, but the "casual professional style" had become his proud signature. In a room that was rapidly filling up with dark suits and ties, he blended about as well as a flamingo in a flock of starlings.

An involuntary quiver of excitement broke into his musings. She'd snuck up behind him and was suddenly pressing against his back, chin over his right shoulder to kiss his cheek.

"My god, you smell incredible." He whispered the words as his senses intensified. Heart pounding, he turned, wrapped his arms around her waist and pulled her between his open legs. Eyes wide and mouth open, she happily mingled his wine with her minty breath, seeking his tongue with a grip that threatened never to let go. Finally she broke the kiss, pressed even closer to him as they embraced.

He'd long since stopped wondering why he couldn't maintain a lasting relationship with a woman, but Andrea was truly different. Nevertheless, this one would end as well, but without blame on either side. She'd worn a clinging, short dress that amplified her curves and firm legs, thanks to years of running 10Ks and slaloms down the Colorado slopes. She knew his taste in women's dresses, and the name of her game was "Bet you can't keep it down." She'd already won round one.

He eased her away and shifted on the stool to give things a little more room below the belt, even as she glanced impishly at the smiling bartender and held up two fingers.

"*Two* more glasses of that delicious cab, please."

"So… how did everything go on the final day?"

"Sad, but let's not talk about it. I just want to enjoy the evening, so let's get out of here when our wines are gone."

ꕤ

"Your place or mine?"

The question sparked memories of their first meeting, where either choice had been a hotel room. They'd used it ever since as a prelude to play, and now it seemed appropriate as a closure, in a way.

She peered through the frosted car window, snapping her seat belt. "Roman, I have no blankets or sheets on my bed… they're all packed."

"I sorta guessed as much." The image of her bare mattress and a room full of packed boxes brought a chuckle. "Well, it so happens I've always wanted to take in a homeless person. You telling me you're homeless?"

She nodded, looking elfin.

"I know you know it, but we've never said it… I love you, Andrea."

"Honey, you've been in love with me for some time now." She made it a matter-of-fact statement, managing somehow not to smile. Teasing?

"And … isn't there something you want to say to *me*?"

"Ahh… how about thank you? That what you had in mind?"

"Oh, come on!"

"Just drive, baby. I'd rather show you than tell you."

Chapter Seven

Kolhapur

Luke Evans paused before entering the cafeteria for the company meeting. Packed as it was with lab employees, the smell reinforced his reasons for never eating lunches there. The aroma of native cooking spices such as garam masala, used in dishes he still couldn't pronounce correctly, was now blended with the sour essence of hundreds of bodies—worker bees from India and a dozen neighboring countries whose bathing rituals sometimes included only the hands and feet. Fortunately, the human brain took care of such offenses by dulling sensory response. A few added seconds to become reasonably desensitized, and he went inside.

The front seats were specifically for senior technicians and department heads. There... an empty chair right next to Kareem! On her other sides were Alvarez Gerber and a deeply pockmarked Indian tech, Dahana. Alvarez's advice on how to "make" Kareem still hadn't borne fruit. Worse, she was unintentionally playful at times, teasing without realizing what that did to his composure.

But backing her into a corner and "having a go at her assets" was out. He'd never do it. Unlike other girls, she was a delicate flower growing from a crevice in a rock.

She'd turned away, talking with someone in the row behind her.

"Mind if I join you, Kareem?"

She immediately blushed, pulling at her lab coat. "Of course, Luke. We were all saving this place for you. You've met Dahana?"

"Yes, absolutely, good to see you again, Dahana. Hello, Alvarez. What's this all about?"

Dahana showed a double row of perfect teeth. "Luke, have you ever heard of a Dr. Sihar Rishi while you were at the Scripps Institute? It's rumored that she just accepted a position here to run the lab."

"Oh, yes. One of my graduate courses used her textbook... ah... *The Genetic Morphology of Fetal Cells*, now among the foundation courses in Human Genetics. Unfortunately the U.S. further restricted experimental use of human fetal tissues right after I got my doctorate in cellular biology, so I was never exposed to her culturing techniques back then."

"You were probably too busy being *exposed* to those blond California girls on the beaches of La Jolla," Alvarez teased. He leaned forward. "Watch out for this guy, Kareem. I think he likes the challenge of the quiet types."

She smirked. "You think maybe I should go sit in the back, Alvarez?"

He shrugged. "You're safe here. Just don't let him sneak up on you."

"All right, you two, lay off or *I'm* moving back there." Luke made a point of rolling his eyes at the ceiling. "I'll have you know I spent all my time studying. I seldom *ever* saw the beach."

They both laughed.

"No, really! Besides, if I'd stayed there… well… there was no way I could have landed a senior position like this with a multi-national biotech company. The techniques we're using here are all so tightly regulated in the States that developments in countries like Singapore, India and Australia have now surpassed those in the U.S."

"Forget all that. Listen, Rishi is supposed to be here right now." Dahana continued, taking the earlier thread back up.

"I heard talk of a Nobel Prize for her earlier work at the University of Pittsburgh," Luke said. He was about to add something else, when suddenly there she was, the renowned Dr. Sihar Rishi he'd been reading about for years.

The room hushed immediately.

Dr. Rishi's brief opening remarks concluded with the announcement that their entire program was to be revamped, starting immediately! Minutes following those words, the sound of carts could be heard being wheeled down the hallway.

She explained that each carried large perfusion containers loaded with the delicate organs they'd been cultivating and caring for during the past several months. Where were they being taken? Why? No answers were forthcoming; it didn't seem to matter. The laboratory was to be revised *in its entirety* per direct orders of certain "Dutch investors" whose mixed team of Dutch and German technicians were supposedly well-trained in their fields. They'd arrive by week's end, completely retrofitting the lab with new, miniature, hi-tech incubators and large-scale, state-of-the-art organ culturing equipment.

As one of the few Americans on the staff, Luke felt intellectually inferior to the others for some reason, but he knew they respected his aggressiveness. The Indian and Asian technicians were better skilled and most likely better educated, but his outgoing Western mannerisms made him the self-appointed "group leader" even so. He finally raised a question about training on the new equipment and procedures.

Dr. Rishi answered without even looking up.

"You will all have new procedural manuals and we'll be scheduling daily training sessions all this week, starting tomorrow morning. Rather than maintaining organs from older donors, we will cultivate younger, more viable organs from fetal donors. They will initially be more delicate and challenging to work with, but more viable and easier to stimulate. We'll also be preparing a variety of new organs not available to us before now, engineering them in such a way as to make them more acceptable to a wider range of recipients, regardless of gender, race or tissue type."

She could well have been giving a keynote presentation at some symposium. Tightly bound jet-black hair, pulled back in a long, braided ponytail over a crisp white lab coat promoted an image of stern confidence, albeit a womanly one. Gone was all but a tidbit of Indian accent, thanks to all those years in the States.

Emboldened by Luke's question, Kareem raised a hand. When she wasn't acknowledged, she asked her question anyway. "And how are these tissues being provided to us... what is the source?"

Dr. Rishi finally paused, now looking about to see who'd asked such a question. Her jaw tightened when she saw Kareem's still-raised hand. "These are healthy, harvested organs from fetuses donated for the sake of human research. They are to be cared for and respected just as you have done for other donated organs."

Her gaze flicked momentarily to Luke, holding for an instant too long. Might she be seeking his support for some reason? Did she somehow know he'd had his eye on Kareem, or was it something else? Personal interrelationships would not have been among her thoughts on this, her very first day as the new director, and who'd have told her in the first place? Who'd have been interested? And on which cultural side, Indian or American?

ജ ഒ

Her new office would take a bit of getting used to, Sihar Rishi mused. Former research offices with their steam radiators and wood-paneled walls were much friendlier. She'd already arranged the only personal belongings permitted: framed family pictures, work-related certificates, degrees and awards.

The room itself was quite like all the other offices and workrooms, with white laminate walls, white marble flooring, white leather and chrome desk, two matching chairs in front of her desk and a frosted-glass office door that slid open on chrome rails.

She awaited two visitors—her first official meeting with other colleagues. One would be David Thomas, a middle-aged Englishman assigned as interim Chief Financial Officer. The other was Dr. Chin Liu, a masterful Operating Director with decades of experience in establishing large-scale biotech facilities. They'd both be looking to her to oversee all the technology aspects of the business, so it was important that they all functioned well as a team. However, she'd be reporting to Thomas, whom she'd not met. He'd intended to arrive the previous day, but had been delayed by bad weather.

She'd been told he was quite the handsome one. It was true! He beamed as he came through the office door with Chin right on his heels. "I'm David Thomas," he announced, extending his hand before she had a chance to offer her own. "Wonderful having you here, Dr. Rishi. I was actually quite doubtful that you'd accept when I learned they were trying to recruit you."

She noted the firmness in his handshake. "It's nice meeting you, sir. Yes, it's a dream come true to be back in India with access to such wonderful resources." A second man waited quietly in the background. "And *you* must be Dr. Liu."

Liu bowed slightly, coming forward. "A pleasure to meet you as well," he replied. "I look forward to the challenges that you will surely provide as we attempt to incorporate your cultivating and harvesting techniques." His English was precise and understandable, if a bit protracted, but he spoke as though needing to think about each word. He also had the nervous habit of stroking his beardless face, left side and then right.

Suddenly a third, heavy-set man appeared in the open doorway. Tightly bound in his three-piece suit, he was sweating profusely and appeared uneasy. Thomas acknowledged the man by way of introduction.

"Ah, Dr. Rishi, we're also honored today by one of our new investors, Dr. Benschöter, from Utrecht in the Netherlands. We respectfully refer to him as Dr. B. He expressed a desire to see the facility and meet you."

With that, the uncomfortable-looking man seemed to relax, but ignored her outstretched hand and made no attempt at eye contact. "Nice to meet with you, Dr. Rishi. Herr Thomas tells me some fascinating things about you. I am also so very much impressed with how he has organized things around here."

"Actually, so am I," she nodded. "As you know, this is my first day here, but I am told that—"

"Dr. B.," David interrupted, "has graciously offered to cover the additional costs of our new security department. He has great depth of experience in such matters. One of his best men will be assigned here to set things up and act as Head of Security."

"Security? Oh, yes, you mean industrial security, of course, but I'm surprised. Our field is an open one, is it not? There are relatively few secrets I know of, beyond individual expertise."

"Precisely—such as yours, Madam Rishi. However, some of the operational changes you and I and Dr. Liu will discuss could well be most valuable to competitors. There will be others who may join the venture from time to time, and *they* may have envious competitors. In fact, from now on we shall all be extremely conscious of *anyone* entering the AMBRIA buildings or being seen on the campus. We are already changing the lobby security system and elevator access."

She gave them all her warmest smile, then returned to her stern, confident manner. "Well gentlemen, I do have some questions leading to my own better understanding of how we should proceed. That is, if you don't mind, Dr. B?"

He bowed slightly, but still not one hint of a smile.

"I've read the history of this organization," she said, "and do appreciate the nature of the business in supplying various organs to V.I.P. recipients who are... how should I say this? ... willing to pay a premium price for high-quality organs, either for their clients or perhaps themselves. However, I'm already concerned about the enormous costs we're about to introduce with this new methodology. Overall costs will rise since we're starting with smaller, younger organs that need lengthy incubation before they can be of any functional benefit. I'm not a business woman, but I question whether the general market will bear a higher price for such a... product?"

David smiled even before she'd finished the question. "As you can imagine, Dr. Rishi, I've repeatedly run the numbers and fortunately do know the customer base quite well. Historically we have always been forced to wait until donors presented themselves, due to their, shall I say, untimely deaths. We started procuring these organs from various sources by simply outbidding any other buyer, and...."

His British accent made him interesting, even exciting—somewhat like a Shakespearian actor on stage, yet almost *too* charming. Compensating for some shortcoming, perhaps? But something he'd said set off her alarm bells. Outbidding any other buyer? She held up a hand, interrupting.

"My understanding is that organs are provided on an 'as needed basis' in accordance with an international or nationally regulated recipient list, *then* distributed according to the probability of acceptance based on tissue and blood type. Are you saying—?"

"Yes, you are certainly correct, but that is what is *visible* to the general public... especially in the U.S. and European markets. There is another commercial market driven by the private consumer... like anything else... based on supply and demand and Fair Market Value. There are hundreds of thousands of people living with failing organs—kidneys, lungs, hearts, eyes, and even livers—and I dare say many with failing, inferior brains." He paused, clearing his throat when his dry, British humor failed to take effect. "Only a fraction of these people are put on that recipient list you mention. They must then wait their turn as if standing in queue at the deli for a sandwich, until their number is called, so to speak. We offer an alternative for those willing and *able* to pay, just like the individual who wants to acquire a customized Maserati unavailable to the general public."

"I see… a Maserati. So in place of the Maserati, someone might substitute a young Philippine boy who is *unavailable* to the public, but not to the individual who wants to acquire him and is *willing to pay*? Is that the alternative solution you are getting at? Please don't tell me that I've somehow let myself be duped into some corrupt, dishonest operation thinking I'd be advancing my science? Is that what this is all about?"

"No, no, Madam, please don't get me wrong. These are organs that otherwise may not have been available or 'viable' without our intervention and your scientific expertise, of course. They would not have been on *any* recipient list without our existence. We are therefore providing what otherwise would not be there at all."

"Well… I see, but I don't actually wish to know any more right now. However, you need to realize that we are definitely going to incur a greater expense and I'm not sure your… *our*… clients will be willing to pay a higher price."

"That's the beauty of our business model, Dr. Rishi. It costs us approximately 5,000 Euros to purchase a donated fetus and another 8,000 Euros to cultivate each viable organ, today's prices and costs. Our average product sells for between 150.000 and 220.000 Euros… and we have a long waiting list of customers!" His smile was toothy.

"Well, that does change the picture, I must agree."

With that, Thomas turned to Dr. B. "If you have no questions for Dr. Rishi, I believe we're done here. I would like to show you around the AMBRIA campus before you head back." His arched eyebrow indicated a question that needed no answer.

They were gone in a flash, leaving only Dr. Liu.

Why are you discovering this just now, Sihar? They're describing a black market, no matter how they paint it! How could you have been so gullible after going through such an extensive interview process? Why didn't you investigate the business before you accepted? Now you've burned your bridges, and all because of the job description, location and salary. You can't possibly back out now, not until you have a better offer somewhere else.

They weren't talking about human organs in any moral sense, not at all. In fact, the example using a custom Maserati could easily be changed to rare artwork and the argument would still hold. Even if they incurred *three* times the normal cost, with the selling price of the organs *and* the increased volume becoming more apparent, this was a new multi-billion dollar industry. Who besides the ultimate customer would set any upper limit? It was all becoming even more viable now that they'd been able to control the growth and health of the organs biochemically, modifying their surface chemistry to eliminate any concerns of rejection by the host body.

Her meeting with Liu, lasting several hours, involved detailed discussions surrounding shipping and receiving, documentation requirements, personnel and equipment needs. He even covered many technical concerns she'd anticipated in dealing with the younger fetuses. However, he said nothing about the security issues.

Were they going to censor mail, E-mail or Internet access as well? Were armed guards going to be guarding the buildings and checking cars? Nowhere during her career had anyone been concerned about industrial espionage. Oh, yes, certainly there was concern about access to sterile or sensitive areas, but not to the extent David Thomas had implied.

What else had they not told her? After all, her involvement was purely *scientific*, not business. She was being paid to oversee a highly technical operation involving expertise and training only she could deliver. As long as she maintained a reasonable level of ignorance in the day-to-day business results, she might be able to live with herself. Well, perhaps "ignorance" wasn't the right word… she'd just leave that aspect for others to manage. It was simply too late for anything else.

ꕥ

Inspecting the newly refurbished labs some time later, she came upon a vaguely familiar young man working through a computer program. He looked up from his work.

"Hello, Dr. Rishi, I'm Luke Evans, one of your Genetic Engineers. It's such a pleasure to meet you."

"Oh, my pleasure as well, Dr. Evans. I recall reviewing your qualifications while examining the organization chart, and look forward to working with you." She smiled. "In the cafeteria meeting, wasn't it you who asked about the training? Your voice—"

"Yes, that was me. Actually, I'm surprised we're using young embryos in our program here. I thought we'd be working with fetal *organs*, nothing more." He motioned towards several newly arrived liquid nitrogen containers carrying what appeared to be frozen embryos, if the insignia on each container meant anything.

She nodded. "You're nearly correct. Our work will be with fetal derivatives. However, I can see how you might be confused. The name you are reading on the containers is that of the company supplying our fetuses and has nothing to do with *embryos*. EMBRYIA is simply the name of our supplier."

ᘓᘐ

Larger, liquid-nitrogen chambers holding an unprecedented number of frozen fetuses arrived later in the week. The long containment tubes had porous aluminum walls separating the fetuses within. Each tube was color coded according to fetus age, older fetuses to be given priority. It was a new and tedious process.

Luke wondered where all the fetus donors had come from? And why those changes in the front lobby, with elevators requiring access codes and magnetic badges? A computer had replaced the receptionist's station, turning the lobby's friendly atmosphere into something cold and sinister. None of it made any sense.

Chapter Eight

Minneapolis

Focus, man, focus! Lord knew he was trying while he went over the latest progress report from Marcus, but images of Andrea kept creeping into his mind. Those bright blue eyes and contrasting long dark hair cascading over bare breasts… there! Did it again! The solution was to add more work to his already busy schedule. Work was to become his therapy, details his medication.

Josh had rejected the deal, believing it morally wrong. He wouldn't even discuss it, and could have easily stonewalled everything by refusing to let the firm back the deal, but he simply abstained from voicing his support. Earlier, he'd literally bolted from a meeting. He'd pointed a trembling finger as if he were Moses himself, looking down from Mt. Sinai. "You will both have to live with your own conscience if you do this."

You didn't argue morality with Josh, or challenge him to compare the present deplorable practices to vastly improved ones. His commitments were an integral piece of his individual core. In his view, abortion affected more than just a woman's body and mind. It impacted her relationship with God.

In addition, *Paul's* attempts to be supportive were weak at best. Somewhat ambivalent over the abortion issue, he'd questioned the scalability of the business model, offering few tangible reasons for his numerous concerns, deferring to Roman's years of operating experience.

It boiled down to "going it alone," not even with other local venture capital firms joining in a co-investment. No one indicated interest. Once again he'd have to serve as chairman of the Board… and a very small Board it would be with just himself, Marcus Levine and a yet-to-be-named operations director. Marcus favored a senior operations director he'd worked with somewhere in the past, a Mr. David Goldberg, who'd be available soon.

A few rules were set down during the first "board" meeting with Marcus. First, they needed to execute the Plan quickly, given limited funding and no visibility to others who might join in the next round of financing. Next, prove out the business model in two key regions of the U.S. and within the ten foreign sites already selected and agreed upon, validating payments from relevant government agencies and/or private payers. Finally, *no* press releases or talking to the media! The project was to be kept as quiet as possible, for as long as possible. Anything less and distractions would rule the day.

Marcus, already growing weary of the process, didn't like being squeezed on the valuation and the amount of dilution he'd incurred. He resented anyone other than himself functioning as chairman, especially when there'd been no discussion. He made his sentiments known during the second meeting.

"Let me make it clear, Roman, that once we finally agree on these objectives and the operating budget, *I* will be in charge and responsible for executing the business. I'll assign Goldberg to organize the U.S. activities while I manage the foreign sites. Do we have an understanding?"

"Marcus, my ass is on the line here and we cannot afford to screw this up... so I'll be monitoring *every* aspect of this business, foreign and domestic, at all times."

"I don't—"

"I've already assumed ultimate responsibility for the venture, and we've covered my qualifications for managing this kind of deal on numerous occasions."

"Are you questioning *my* qualifications?"

"Not in regards to the medical or technical issues. Are you questioning mine where the business itself is involved?"

"No, of course not, but—"

"Then I believe we do have an understanding!" *Damn it... do all VCs go through this, or am I the only one stupid enough to start these companies without a full-blown experienced management team? Jesus!*

Times Square, Manhattan

Management! Ay, there was the rub. David Thomas mulled Shakespeare's famous phrase from *Hamlet* as he cast his British visitor's eye on the Ernst & Young building from half a block away. He'd done his own stint with E & Y at their London global headquarters, but it was always fun to check out the "lesser" locations wherever he went. He had no interest otherwise.

His brief meeting with "Q" in Tudor City had instilled a glow of satisfaction, anticipation and pride, albeit with some anxiety. Q needed someone who knew the course, who'd already operated in the trenches on both sides of the street. Formalities had their place, especially those acquired in up-scale London, but a well-developed "go for the jugular" attitude was more important. His prior involvement with a certain Sicilian organization had shown Q that side. Great financial knowledge, yes, but with an ability to handle many aspects of "business" at once, without emotion: management ability.

And now Q had given him all of Genesis! The Kolhapur operation would obviously need some personal supervision, but he'd still have time to whip the remaining four enterprises into productive operation. Finance was the key to control—that plus zero emotional involvement—and *control* was imperative at this point. As for the rewards… after the first ten million in the bank, who bothered counting?

Minneapolis

The first chunk of capital paid for the mobile units and special equipment Marcus had developed for the procedure. Everything was highest in quality, starting with modifications to vehicles made by a special division of Mercedes in Germany, who beat out proposals from all the other U.S. and Japanese manufacturers. The idea was to have the units look similar to mobile MRI scanners designed by companies like GE Medical, Phillips and Siemens Healthcare … slightly larger than a standard RV, but smaller than a large transport vehicle. That would project a medical image giving people some immediate comfort, plus credibility.

All would be painted with the blue and white EMBRYIA logo, but nothing more. Some might think them to be delivery trucks for a new yogurt, or maybe a special baby diaper cleaning service, but chosen communities would soon realize that they represented a different type of "cleaning service."

Two of the fully equipped Mobile Abortion Units, or MAUs, were destined for American cities, one an eastern suburb of Los Angeles and the other one of the seediest cities on the East Coast—Camden, New Jersey. Marcus wanted that smallish city, a surprise since Camden wasn't even on the list of possible sites. He claimed to know the city fairly well and there was no reason to argue. One seedy city was a good as another.

The personnel for each MAU included a licensed physician, one administrative person, a trained nurse and one or two technicians, the latter perhaps not of the highest quality, yet street-wise and willing to accept the substandard conditions they'd face.

Camden was the site of the inaugural test.

Chapter Nine

Marcus had decided to assist in the first thirty to forty procedures done in Camden before helping roll out MAU two in L.A. His new extraction equipment had only been tested in the laboratory using sheep and baboons, so there could well be post-procedure refinements resulting from patient and staff feedback. Although no official safety standards were involved, success would depend on how sensitive the new equipment was both to mother and aborted fetus. His attitude was nothing less than cavalier.

Years of research dictated that when blunt trauma was minimized during extraction, patient recovery time was dramatically reduced. Furthermore, the clinic's mobility would offer safe "solutions" to thousands of patients who would otherwise have extremely limited alternatives, sometimes none. There they were, Roman mused, the three most significant words describing the venture: mobility, safety and efficacy. They'd been constantly stressed in every pitch he'd delivered as chairman of the venture—and here they were coming to life. Yet the tension of anticipated social ramifications gnawed at him constantly. Sooner or later, the social thing was bound to surface. Marcus called ten minutes past noon to report that the pre-marketing program had worked better than expected. Their morning location was an abandoned store parking lot opposite an 1100-apartment housing project. They were shocked to see nearly forty people waiting. Fortunately, many appeared to be family members. Even more fortunate, there were no protestors. All efforts had been aimed at staying under the radar of the rabid right wingers for as long as possible, so this was good news indeed!

"Our administrative process and client screening turned out to be most tedious and annoying," Marcus continued. "We had to use the date of the woman's last period to determine the fetus age—a normal clinical practice—assuming she knew it. Many didn't, so we used the portable ultrasound system you proposed if we thought she looked too far advanced. Unfortunately we may use it more often than expected. You suggested we install it in just the first few MAUs, but we now think it should be in all units. We actually had a woman insisting she was only eight weeks pregnant, when ultrasound indicated she was well into her seventh month! We turned her away."

"Rightly so! So how has the day gone so far?"

"Surprisingly well, except for the administration process. We spent exactly four and a half hours in our first location before heading to the afternoon stop, with travel and lunch in between. Dr. Maibeck suggested we screen ten clients and prep seven to start. He was eager to get going so he could see how efficient our MAU would be. I went along with it because, as you said, everyone on the team should be properly motivated, but none of us were ready for the flow of clients or how to organize it.

"People immediately crowded the MAU front door, insisting they were there first," he continued, "and it was about to get ugly when Jean, the team's scrub tech, suggested a lottery. She'd taught junior high school in New York's Harlem before getting her technical degree, and had worked in various hospital emergency rooms, most recently right there in Camden, so she knew the environment. People immediately trusted the tone of her voice, and that averted disaster. It didn't take long before she had everyone picking numbers on scraps of paper from a Tupperware container. She then made a duplicate set and asked me to pull ten pieces and announce each number.

"I preferred to remain in the background, so I deferred that task to Raj Maibeck, but we were *all* surprised how well this lottery worked, especially me. Roman, we *must* come up with a legitimate way to control crowds, and some faster way to screen the clients. We need to make that a prioritized action item."

"We'll come up with something. What about your ePOD?" The acronym stood for Escalating Pressure Osmotic Device. The working end, inserted in the woman's vagina, looked fairly standard, but the collection chamber and staged suction apparatus, the ePOD, looked like something out of *E.T.*, the movie.

"I confess being truly anxious about that part of the procedure. The ePOD is actually—"

"Marcus, just give me the highlights. You showed the damn thing to me twice already, but you never got around to telling me how it works."

"Surely I… well… you inflate the balloon on the evacuation tube once it's inside the cervix of the uterus. This controls the internal pressure and allows us to better control extraction of the fetus. I'm oversimplifying, but that's the key. If you've ever done any SCUBA diving, it's the same idea. Your body controls internal pressure to overcome the water pressure outside—unless there is an unsealed opening. The ePOD balloon seals off the cervix, and the equipment controls the pressure specific to the size and volume of the uterus.

"Anyway, this one woman was already slightly sedated with an I.V. drip, but I noticed discomfort on her face so I asked her if she was feeling okay, and…" He stopped, suddenly laughing. Marcus Levine didn't laugh often. "Roman, you should have been there! 'Whaddya think?' she snaps back. 'Some skinny-ass Indian mutha-fucka has his hand up inside my box with you peeking over his damn shoulder like he was changing the oil in my fuckin' car? You better know what you're doing down thay, or you ain't leaving this parking lot with your balls.' I'm trying to say it the way she did. Of course, she was referring to Raj when she said skinny-ass Indian. Then I remembered this large black man standing outside, with a tattoo across his forehead, and I started to sweat. I mean, *really* sweat!

"But everything worked perfectly. Within minutes, Raj had the extraction tube properly located and the balloon inflated. I started the ePOD pump and we began monitoring her internal uterine pressure. I heard the familiar 'plop' sound as the fetus entered the containment chamber in the adjacent cabinet. The entire set-up is a closed system, so our gutter-mouthed patient couldn't *see* anything associated with the procedure. It was over within ten minutes. I would say it was more efficient than in any of our animal lab practice runs. There wasn't even much blood in the evacuation tube.

"I think Raj finally realized that the extracted fetus in the containment chamber was actually being collected in more than just your normal saline solution. The viscosity of the containment fluid suspends the fetus like one of those embryonic reptiles or rats he'd observed in his pre-med classes.

My method not only had gently preserved the wall of the woman's uterus, but also the body of the extracted fetus. Compare that to conventional procedures with their torn and twisted fetuses, often in multiple pieces, intertwined with surgical gauze that lined the evacuation chamber. I tell you, he was absolutely astounded even though we'd experienced similar results in our animal studies."

"So it went really well. You sound elated."

"There is no word for how good I feel right now. I knew that the fibrous consistency of the placenta in the human was not as dense as in the experimental animals, but I didn't realize how clean and fast the procedure would actually be, and that's why I called you this soon. I wanted to share this with you. Also, I think we can make the process even more efficient if we add a foot pedal to the pump to eliminate the need for one of the assistants. As we speak, we are moving to our second location. I will call you again tomorrow."

ꕤ

Marcus struggled to conceal his excitement from the team. Even with the delay in prioritizing and screening the patients, they'd completed procedures on ten patients within the four and a half hours allocated for the morning location, and the afternoon session was going even better.

While recovering, the women received free Midol tablets and a 3-pack of latex condoms, plus educational materials also handed out to those who'd accompanied the patients. Most of the written materials ended up strewn across the parking lot, looking like a rock concert "morning after," but patients often asked for more than the normal allocation of Midol and condoms. The remaining untreated hopefuls received what passed for EMBRYIA business cards, giving them priority in the following morning's scheduling process.

The afternoon sessions began with the lottery approach once more. Julie, the team's administrative assistant, had printed out large duplicate numbers on thick stock paper, then cut them into uniform pieces. The approach was the same, but it looked more professional. Raj had also become more proficient. They were actually able to complete twelve procedures, for the first day's total of twenty-two. The original plan suggested a possible eighteen daily procedures with MAUs containing three procedure suites, yet here they'd exceeded that number with only two suites. The first two MAUs were also stocked with enough equipment and evacuation chambers for thirty procedures—a lofty goal Roman had agreed to once units were rolling off the assembly line.

There was only one "event" that disrupted the procedural flow. A teenage girl epitomizing doubt, fear and uncertainty, panicked when receiving her anesthesia. She complained of heaviness in her chest, her labored breathing raising concerns of a potential heart attack, or perhaps a reaction to the anesthesia, but Raj made a quick diagnosis and actually increased the flow and concentration of her sedative, inducing an immediate calmness. Her symptoms disappeared. It was nothing more than a panic attack. With this one minor exception, the day finished without any complications. However, several women complained of discomfort, so it was agreed that the sedative would be increased for each patient and any related recovery time increase closely monitored.

The MAU was back in the garage by 6:30 that evening. In a rare moment of inspired leadership, Marcus assembled the team while wearing the first smile they'd ever seen him produce. He then characterized their efforts as *outstanding* and the results as *fabulous*, prudently offering overtime to anyone willing to assist with cleaning and restocking. Patrick and Julie volunteered. Raj opted out, as he'd had enough for one day. No surprise there. He cast a fleeting wave over his shoulder as he drove away.

Marcus smiled to himself. Perfect! Now he'd have the privacy while dealing with the evacuated fetuses. While Julie and Patrick were occupied, he loaded the twenty-two ice-cold miniature glass coffins into a cooler in the far corner of the garage, already prepared with an ice bath. Within fifteen minutes he had it loaded into the back of his SUV.

A quick glance in the rear view mirror, and he drove off into the darkness. No one saw him leave. By the same token, no one noticed the same SUV half an hour later as it backed into the loading dock of what had once been an Urgent Care clinic in Camden's north section, not that far from the MAU garage in Pennsauken. The outside signage had been removed, but most of the medical equipment and facilities remained intact after the clinic ceased to function, including two surgical suites, a walk-in freezer, the original track lighting systems, two recovery rooms, a front lobby and small waiting room, and, in the rear, the shipping and receiving area. Below all was a full basement formerly used for storage, but which also boasted two larger independent rooms with a functioning bathroom connecting between them. A third basement room was a kitchen and dinette combination where clinic staff members had taken their breaks.

Even with all its capabilities, the building was simply unsuitable for any kind of *private* medical practice due to its location and the urban decay of its surroundings. It had been on the market for nearly two years, without a single serious offer despite two price reductions and three different realty companies.

On the other hand, its recent new owner, an out-of-towner, was interested enough to buy the facility "on speculation" after *personally* checking and verifying the condition operation and calibration of every piece of medical and non-medical equipment. Assistance was offered, but refused. After the purchase, all but two of the ground floor windows were curtained, all locks were changed and arrangements made with ADT for security. The two basement rooms and bathroom were equipped with remotely controlled locks so that the bathroom might be entered from either side room while its duplicate and the hallway door remained locked. No keys were needed as a result, and control was managed from the break room.

Once those changes were in place, the owner rarely visited the building, although he might have come and gone daily without a soul noticing. Nobody was remotely interested; nobody cared. If he'd ever mentioned the facility or its location to certain business associates in Minneapolis, grave questions might have been raised about his reasons for favoring Camden over more significant urban areas for critical tests of a new medical concept.

So Marcus never mentioned it.

Chapter Ten

Istanbul, Turkey

Hasad Sahin slouched against the ancient brick forming a narrow alley between buildings, cradling his dilapidated cell phone against one ear while digging for another cigarette. The phone needed more duct tape over what was now greasy and tattered, but he didn't care. He'd soon have enough money for a better one.

Serkan, his superior was on the other end. "Hokay, Serkan. Look, I—"

A click left him talking to an open line. *Lanet olsun*! Hasad searched for the correct English word, settling on *idiot bastard*. So Serkan didn't like him talking English? Half of his new job involved being understood in English, even if he couldn't speak it clearly. At least people appreciated him trying.

Now with the organization for nearly two years, he was proud of his association with one of the many Kurdish clans whose heroin profits best supported his brother rebels in their ongoing struggle. The problem was that ever-increasing financial demands were forcing expansion beyond the drug markets to include dealings in pirated electronic and video equipment, counterfeit passports and identity papers and who knew what else?

He'd been assigned to a newer part of their organization responsible for expanding existing prostitution and slavery rings. The job was the easiest he'd ever gotten, thanks to his excellent counterfeit papers, but really crazy—an undercover driver for a new American company promoting mobile abortions. It was now up to *him* to establish ways of infiltrating and exploiting this new potential market.

He flipped up his jacket collar and left the artificial warmth of the alley mumbling. Serkan was stupid! They were all stupid. No way was this abortion thing going to be a good business until the politicos finished decentralizing the healthcare system. Until then, who'd pay for this service? They were treating him like a fucking idiot, and now he was babysitting knocked-up whores. Well, maybe they weren't *all* whores, but most surely had to be.

His phone vibrated. Serkan again. "Hokay, Hasad, thees time in Eeenglish... so you be hap-p-p-py. Dat wacky politico Napoleon, hokay? You brot'r send 'im to prison in Bayrampasa... hokay? *Hatiliyor...* uh... you r'member?"

"Yah, sure I r'member. Pays fortune to dress lak guard zo he can bang dat bitch—dat journalist what bribed da mayor. She a real piece, Serkan, vid—"

"Peece?"

"*Eşek parçasi,* hokay? A piece, Serkan! Vit good teeths and fake titties way out to here." He held his hand a foot ahead of his chest, chuckling at his brother's description. "Dey gag her, fix it so she don't see anyt'ing, and tie her down while he do his stuff. He real horny bull, my brot'r say. Almos' split her in two. A real koo-koo nut. So? What 'bout 'im?"

"Hokay... he hear 'bout deez drucks what drive aroun' full o' doped up hores. He vants in an'—"

"Serkan, dey ain't all hores. Tell him dat. An' dey ain't doped up, *kavramak?* Itz a medical ting you voodent understand. Some are... are *okay...* vimmen. Decent, *kavramak?* So don' even tink to fuckup my new... zhob here. I jus' got zhtarted." What bothered him most was that Serkan was probably on the other end of the phone making his jerkoff motion with his hand as he often did when he thought his subordinates were whining about something.

"Vell, not your choice, Hasad. He one o' our top payin' customer, and veere bringin' 'im in tonight. He pay more dan usual for someone klassier dan normal, *kavramak?* He don't vant vear no shipskin, eeder. You jus'icall me ven dairze a gud... *peece...* comin'in. Zomzing real güzel... knok off soks, hokay? He vill be qwick. I mak sure he don' leave anyting *pis...* messy."

"Hokay, Serkan, but no takin' hours to do his shit. He gotta be outta dere in tventy mints, no more. Deze people, dey go by da klok."

"Hokay, Hasad. Call me when y'gonna zet dis ting up, an' I do all d'rest. *Kavramak?*"

The line went dead. Hasad spit on the ground. Did he understand? Of course he did, and all too well. Serkan was right. Not his choice, even if it cost him his job. It could be done easily enough. There was time while the women were in the recovery area alone for sometimes twenty, thirty minutes at a time. Napoleon could be a visiting family member, vouched for by Hasad, the driver, who'd known the family for years. The "whitecoats" would accept that explanation.

Lanet olsun!

Chapter Eleven

East Los Angeles

RICO LEERED AT THE HAPLESS DRIVER HE'D JUST HANDCUFFED TO THE STEERING wheel. An oily rag hung from the man's stuffed mouth.

"You fuckin' think you gonna come here and pull this kinda shit on *our* turf, takin' money from *our* people… who the fuck you think you are?"

No answer was expected. It was all part of his own "crime-in" initiation to the 18th Street Gang, and he was damn lucky to have Popeye with him. Popeye was a cousin, but he was also a charter member of the Barrio Eighteenth STreet gang, proudly wearing the shark tattoo on his neck and the letters B-E-S-T across the knuckles of his left hand. Besides confirming the "young cadet's loyalty", he'd eventually choose a new righteous name to replace Rico, maybe something way cool.

Popeye patted the driver on the head and took out the 9mm tucked in the back of his jeans. His forearm bulged, same as his namesake, and a grin spread across his pockmarked face. "You ready, little man?"

Rico nodded. "Dis is all me… you know dat, Popeye… *all* me! Like I was born to do dis shit." He pushed through the MAU door with Popeye on his heels. None of these dumb-fucks were packin'—nothin' they could do. He was da man in charge.

"Don't fuckin' look at me… everyone back, back… back in there!" He pushed the closest technician with the end of his own gun, pointing to what looked like a bathroom in the back. It sure didn't look like no exit. Three dudes and a pair of skirts were working on the whores. He herded them all back, but it wasn't no bathroom neither, just a storeroom with sheets and pillows and medical crap. So what? Big enough to hold 'em for now. He slammed the door shut and spun around.

"And you bitches, don't any of you fuckin' MOVE. Didn't I tell you not to look at me?"

He headed back toward the driver, glaring at the three women in various states of their procedures, one still under anesthesia with her feet up in stirrups. Popeye had already pulled out a couple of canvas duffle bags stuffed up underneath his sweatshirt, zipping them open and nodding. Everything from here on would be part of the crime-in test. Popeye was back-up, only in case somethin' went wrong.

So far it had gone too smoothly, looked too easy. Gotta make it look harder, impress Popeye, maybe leave a little broken glass around. Whatever this crap was, it looked real expensive. Needles, yeah! Shiny stuff, bottles of clear juice, all kinda tools and shit. Hey, one o' them doctor things that listens to heartbeats and all that. Popeye was stuffing his own duffel bag up front, all kinds of drugs and cool lookin' shit. Okay, time to kick things up a bit!

"I told you not to look at me, *puta*!" he barked. One of the two women in the recovery area clutched her gown tightly about her and stared at the floor. The other was already staring into a corner. The third one, feet in the stirrups, was moaning, starting to come out of her twilight sleep, unaware of where she was or what was happening around her.

"So what we got here?" he sneered. "Some prima donna bitch couldn't get daddy to have her scraped on fuckin' Wilshire Boulevard… gotta come out here to the barrio to get it done?

"Cut it, Rico, we don't have time for this shit!"

"No, man… I told ya, I got dis… we ain't done here yet… look at her, she wants it bad, got her legs spread wide open for me… nice and dripping wet."

He yanked at the belt that barely held his pants from sliding off his hips. Popeye's deep, throaty laugh was a sign of encouragement, right? He approved? Well, he'd get his own turn at the bitch soon enough. Meanwhile, he could enjoy the show. Hey, they already had all the stuff there was to grab, so this was icing on the cake.

He grabbed her by both ankles and violently hauled her past the stirrups and onto the floor. Her head smacked hard as she landed. Then he twisted her face down, kicked off his pants and slipped one of the full duffle bags lengthwise between her ankles so she couldn't squeeze her legs together. She was moaning; she wanted it!

He grinned. "Oh, yeah, listen to dat, Popeye. She wants it bad." Pushing himself deep inside, he shoved her blonde head face first into the floor with his free hand. She made no sound until he suddenly pulled out and rammed himself deep into her rectum. The pain dragged her from her half-aware state and she flailed out, reeling around, trying to bite him.

"Damn *ramera blanca*!" He slammed her face back down hard and she was suddenly still, leaving him to switch repeatedly between her rectum and vagina until he reached orgasm. He pulled out and backed away, grinning and motioning Popeye to take what was left.

"*What?* I ain't goin' there after you, man... you *pig*... maybe I get some up here." His older cousin started unbuckling his jeans, lifting her head by her blood-stained hair so he could use her mouth, but her lips were splintered with broken fragments of teeth.

"*Jesucristo,* man, look what you did to her fuckin' face... you broke her nose and all her teeth! Let's get the fuck outta here."

As if suddenly realizing the brutality of their actions, Popeye gently placed her head back on the floor. He'd killed before, but only in the gang wars in the street... never a helpless woman.

They swept up the stuffed duffle bags and stepped from the MAU as if leaving a city bus. Popeye broke the tension, pulling them both back into *their* world. "After today, *mi amigo,* we call you *Puerco.* You are one *real* pig, and now you a member of the 18th Street Gang!" With that, he laughed and wrapped his large arm around Puerco's shoulders.

Puerco laughed, too. It had been a glorious day. Hell, it'd been great fun.

Chapter Twelve

Minneapolis

The European press seemed to accept the roll-out of this controversial business as a way of cleaning up "backroom and self-imposed abortions." Couldn't get a much stronger endorsement than that, Roman mused. Marcus knew what he was doing, no doubt about it, but he'd called several times the previous afternoon, never managing to connect and unwilling to leave a detailed message with Sarah.

His fourth attempt was successful. "Roman, we need an immediate Board Meeting to discuss a security incident. I tried reaching you several times, but now it may be too late. Read your email before you do anything else."

Why the tension? There! The referenced email, third down in the list. The subject line: URGENT — Confidential.

He fought back his queasiness as he re-read the message, heart racing. Talk about raining on a parade, someone had just *pissed* on theirs and burned down all the concession stands at the same time. There'd been a rape incident in Turkey *within* the mobile unit, and, as if synchronized by some malicious, organized gang, *another* similar incident a day later in Los Angeles. Unbelievable! "Sarah, get Marcus on the phone for me... right away!"

"I actually have him on hold. I overheard you checking your voicemail and waited for you to finish... here he is."

"Damn it, Marcus!"

"I see you've already read your mail."

"I wouldn't call email a formal notification... what the hell is happening?"

"What I failed to tell you the other day is that we've had more MAU staff turnover in these two regions than I would like to admit. I didn't think much of it—they were just... just support staff—but it appears we didn't perform the proper screening. I very recently learned that women in Turkey were receiving quite a bit more than the conventional dose of anesthesia for their procedures, more than we are using here in the U.S."

"You told me you were monitoring these cases firsthand."

"Roman, I can't be in two places at once. I only learned of this two days ago. The technicians were trained to use nitrous oxide—laughing gas—to induce drowsiness prior to numbing the cervix with a local anesthetic similar to lidocaine. Well, I thought we could turn more patients if the staff started using a stronger IV sedation to put the women into twilight sleep. This also had a secondary effect on short-term memory, actually leaving the women with no memory of the procedure. Thought that would be a nice touch, so—"

"Marcus, *none* of this was properly discussed. Why am I hearing it just now?"

"—so it didn't take long for some deviate transient employee to figure out that these women were left exposed and vulnerable for up to thirty minutes at a time... often lying unsupervised in a draped-off recovery area."

"Goddammit... if you weren't there, how do you know all this?"

"Turkish authorities arrested the driver. Turns out he was a member of some Turkish organized crime syndicate, and now he seems willing to cooperate, to help them infiltrate this organization. Sounds like he wants to get out, start a new life. I really don't see how that matters. Do you want to hear what happened, or not?"

"Okay, okay, keep going."

"The opportunity apparently came to this young fellow unexpectedly from another colleague of his. One of the women scheduled for abortion was actually a prostitute, working for the mob. She was brought to the MAU by her agent... no, not agent, what you might call a 'pimp'... who refused to leave her side. While in the recovery area he noticed how long the women were left there alone... sedated and unaware of their surroundings. It set things in motion. He convinced the driver to give him access to the unit the following night."

"Marcus, since when do we allow family members into the MAU?"

"He was not family, Roman. I was told by others that he was—"

"Her pimp? That makes him different somehow? Our Standard Operating Procedures clearly state that no one is allowed into the MAU with the woman concerned. No one! I seem to remember that *you* were the one who insisted on that rule."

"Roman, why don't *you* come out with us sometime and let me see *you* tell these people that they cannot accompany their daughter, wife or girlfriend? We hope to have better controls in place in the future, but it is literally impossible in these initial depressed areas we've chosen. Remember that *you* selected these sites. They don't trust strangers in their own backyards. I seem to remember that *you* were the one who predicted as much.

"Anyway, this man, or customer as they called him, didn't seem too particular who he got, long as she wasn't an everyday whore. He was just fulfilling another perverted fantasy which took him all of fifteen minutes before he was finished and gone. The problem was that the girl was no average whore. She was the daughter of a prominent local dentist whose *mother* made arrangements for the abortion. The mother was trying to avoid notifying her husband, the girl's father, you understand? That kind of thing happens, as you know. It turned out that one of our technicians, who has just resigned over this incident by the way, knew the family since childhood and felt compelled to tell the mother about this *violation*. She immediately notified the General Directorate of Security. This is a civilian police force in Turkey, with no political connections or personal greed. Therefore they would not consider any payoff by the mafia to cover-up the incident, so this has gone public."

"Marcus, how much of this has been written up by the authorities in a formal report?"

"By now… probably all of it. However they have not yet identified the rapist and refuse to provide the name of the driver. Because of his cooperation, he will not be implicated in the crime, *but* they have enough evidence to prove that a rape took place inside the MAU."

This can't be! "You're implying—"

"I'm telling you exactly what I learned, Roman. If you are standing up, you better sit back down, because there's more. The other incident… in L.A. was even worse, and this time we were able to get a copy of the actual police report. Two men held our driver at gunpoint, most likely with the initial goal of taking any drugs they could get their hands on.

Unfortunately, he was the only one armed and capable of protecting the unit and our employees. Someone also *thought* they saw a third man canvassing the area, a lookout, or so I was told. So they were well organized, as if they expected to be there for some time."

"And this time where were you? You advertised that you'd be in L.A. with this team, and now I'm going to hear a different story?"

"I had some personal business to attend to and was planning to arrive the next morning. Besides, I am not present at every procedure throughout every day even when I am in the area. Are you blaming this on me?"

"Of course not, but this should *also be* your personal business! I'm just reminding you of what you said. I'm afraid to ask, but keep going."

"Our driver was easily overpowered, cuffed to the steering wheel and gagged. The two men worked their way through the MAU, cleaning out everything they thought would be of any value. The driver saw them take away at least two large, canvas duffle bags. They forced the remaining staff to move into the linen storeroom in the back of the unit. Unfortunately, three patients were in various phases of their treatment. In particular, one young woman was coming out of her anesthesia and still had her feet up in the stirrups. She'd been…."

Marcus stopped in mid-sentence. Collecting his thoughts, or something else? A rushing sound in the background sounded like a handkerchief in use. Theatrics! What else? Marcus had never expressed any kind of emotion where women were concerned.

Then he continued. "She was vulnerable in her semi-conscious state. You've seen them, Roman. You know how helpless they can be. These animals… that's all they could be… their brains could not be normal. The other two women in recovery thought the younger hoodlum was proving something to his… to the other one. Neither one seemed too concerned about time. They had no fear. We were parked in *their* territory. The LAPD believe they were a part of a large gang that has a history of doing as they please. One of these bastards recently shot a police officer in the doorway of the courthouse as part of his initiation into the gang."

Sarah opened the office door and was waved off without so much as a glance.

"The young one pulled her to the floor like some butcher preparing an animal for slaughter," Marcus went on. "She was helpless. Then he raped, sodomized and beat her mercilessly. These bastards were on foot and simply seemed to saunter away, as if they did these things on a daily basis."

"The woman… did she survive?"

"Yes, but she's in a coma, in intensive care. I don't know her identity, or if her family is preparing to press charges."

"That may be the least of our worries. Where are you now? I want you here for a meeting with my partners and myself as soon as possible. You should prepare yourself for the worst."

Chapter Thirteen

Philadelphia

As Andrea admired the half-painted wall of her new apartment, her thoughts were all on Roman. Why hadn't he called lately? Had he already moved on to... other things? They'd only talked twice since she'd left the Twin Cities, and both times he seemed under a great deal of pressure, somewhat distant. Might he now be involved with Sarah? Perhaps, but Sarah hadn't sounded like a woman keeping a secret during the phone call to Zorro earlier that morning. Nothing said was overdone, no words carefully chosen. She'd been the same cheerful soul she always was, explaining that Roman had been running hard and his schedule had been anything but organized.

She'd met Sarah once during a holiday party a mere week after her first encounter with Roman—a wild, unexpected tryst that inflamed their attraction for one another. Sarah was cordial but overly curious, asking intimate questions and on more than one occasion was staring at them from across the room. Even so, there was no evidence that it was anything more than admiration, or perhaps infatuation.

Even if Roman *was* involved with her, he couldn't be blamed, not after their mutual attempt to avoid the traps of a total commitment that would most likely destroy their special relationship. They'd both "been there" before and the time wasn't right for either of them to make that mistake again. The unspoken rule was only that there *be* no rules.

She'd called his cell phone after hanging up with Sarah, leaving her new address and number, wondering how many times she should continue to attempt to reach him. What would be appropriate before appearing needy or worse, too deeply committed?

It had been nearly six weeks since their all-night session, and though she ached for *him*, she surprised herself by fantasizing about sexual encounters with other faceless men, all seeming to have the same talent and energy as her Roman. It had to be fluctuating hormones, she mused, as she pushed the roller back and forth in the paint tray. They'd been running rampant these past few days.

She'd finally found a free day to repaint her new Sixth Avenue apartment. It was a second floor unit in the historical section of South Philadelphia, an area she'd fallen in love with during her interviews. She'd quickly adapted to public transportation. Children's Hospital was only fifteen minutes away by bus.

The lead position in the Pediatric Intensive Care Unit, or PICU, was a dream come true and the staff made her feel as though she'd worked there for years. The emotional demands and clinical work were identical to those in St. Paul, but the institution's reputation for exceptional care brought children and their parents from all over the world. Sadly, there were now dozens of *Rambos* who required her devotion… and that special touch of hers. She hadn't had time to build any personal relationships with the other nurses, or the handful of sexy pediatric surgeons who showed her some "special attention." Alas, only one was single. Very tempting, but it was all too soon.

So… Roman had been running hard and disorganized? Sarah's suggestion of him being disheveled sounded odd, but he'd told her more than once about the sometimes-crazy schedules he kept. That new project he'd mentioned might be the reason, but once he got her message he'd probably call. She'd had her own share of concerns recently, not to mention the lateness of her period. Probably that was from the stress of her move and the new job. *Surely* she couldn't be pregnant—she'd been taking birth control pills since she was fifteen—but something didn't feel right. If another week passed without signs of her normal flow, she'd buy one of those home pregnancy tests.

Fighting a sudden flood of emotions, she allowed herself to consider the probabilities. Oh well, right now there were three more walls to go, plus all the trim. She pushed the thought from her mind and continued her painting, turning the music up even higher. It was a rare day off and she had much to do.

Chapter Fourteen

Minneapolis

CONSIDERING THE WAY RECENT MEETINGS HAD ALL STARTED THE SAME WAY—with heated words directed at *him*—there was no need for formalities, Marcus fumed, no need to knock. Something vitally important needed discussion, yes, but why did venture investors expect everything to click into place just because they had some money at risk? Damn their ignorant arrogance. All three Zorro partners needed to realize that *he* had every bit as much to lose as they did. Support and teamwork was needed here, not finger pointing.

Sure enough, it was an all-too-familiar scene. Paul sat on the far edge of Roman's desk arms folded, staring at the floor. Josh, standing at Roman's office window, headed for the door as if Hitler himself had just walked in. Clearly wanting out, he stared at the held-up hand with its palm forward. "Please stay, Josh. You need to hear what I have to say."

Roman preempted any response. "Marcus, this is totally out of control and we're thinking of pulling the plug. Suddenly we're way off Plan, which means we'll need to secure a follow-on investment just to reach positive cash flow, and with this kind of fucking press there is no WAY anyone would consider co-investing with us!" His voice had risen to a shout.

Paul leapt to his feet. "*Christ,* Roman, you're worried about cash flow when women are getting raped… in service vehicles *we're* providing? Do you have any fucking idea what this is going to do to our reputations while this plays out in the media *and* most likely the courts?"

Josh was no less vehement. "Paul's right, Roman, we've got to announce publicly that we're out of this deal and writing off the investment. I should've seen this coming. You get thirty days to clean up this mess, or I'll personally contact our Limited Partners and do it myself. If necessary, I'll take actions to dissolve this partnership… do you understand?" He charged out, deliberately brushing Marcus' shoulder enough to knock him off balance.

Silence followed.

"Now that you are all finished shouting, perhaps we can move ahead to my reasons for requesting this meeting?" Marcus said, sarcasm salting his words. "Roman, I need some time with you alone… please."

Paul shot to his feet. "Why, you arrogant sonofa—"

"Paul, *please!*" Roman's sharp look did more than his words. "It's a reasonable request, since this is my deal. My CEO has something he wants to pass by me first, okay? Any of us would ask for the same courtesy in his shoes."

Paul swiveled as if to lash out, stopped and twisted his mouth, then followed Josh's exit. This time Marcus wisely stepped aside.

"Close the door, Marcus. I'll give you your chance, but first I have a few—"

"Wait, there is something we need to discuss before you say *anything.*"

"Something to discuss? *Discuss?* You are out of your fucking mind, Marcus. Our discussions are over! Right now we're in free fall, and my only concern is damage control on the way down."

"No, you need to know this *before* you make any decisions. Look, it's terribly unfortunate that things went wrong in Turkey and L.A. We had some security measures in place, yes, but you and I never could have known that such awful things were possible. I take full responsibility for that part, and I'm confident we can manage through this. We're beefing up our security program, adding people. However, there's something else you need to know."

"*We? We're* beefing up our security program? You sound as though you represent some third party and are no longer working to fulfill your obligations to EMBRYIA. What does that make us here at Zorro, Marcus? Are we some sort of afterthought? Someone you supply with details only after two of the most damaging events we ever imagined have already happened? We needed to know whatever this 'something' was from the beginning, and you're going to tell us about it only now? Unbelievable! Fine, you have the floor. This time, don't leave anything out. You can start by explaining who 'we' is."

Marcus, finally closing the door, drew a long breath. What Roman was about to hear could only add to the living nightmare, but there was no other way. A set of disturbing new factors had entered the picture. Even so, it would be best to withhold some of the details for as long as possible. Among them, a name from Roman's past: Dr. Sihar Rishi. It seemed she not only knew *of* Roman Citrano, but had known him personally.

Nothing could complicate matters more than having her name enter the situation now!

ಐ೧

It took precisely six hours for the national news media to pick up the story from the L.A. local news channel. Although the vicious rape and robbery of an MAU in East L.A. was the lead-in story, the media had finally awakened to the entire concept of a Mobile Abortion Unit—at least from the "man in the street" perspective—and played it out for several days on both CNN and FOX News. It ignited renewed comments and debates from Pro-Choice and Pro-Life organizations. Ironically, there seemed to be a growing support for the concept as documentaries were quickly aired regarding back-room abortions and unwanted pregnancies on the upturn. Little attention was given to the ugly rape itself. It was almost as if such atrocities were to be expected in the east L.A. territory from time to time.

Even more surprising was the dearth of news about the incident in Turkey. The Turks immediately blamed crime syndicates, not the MAU program or its promoters. American media generally viewed such foreign news as only "back page worthy" anyway, yet there'd been no connection between the two events. This, even though the acronym MAU should have lit up a few bulbs.

Roman's breathing and pulse rates returned to normal four days later, helped by "business as usual" in spite of continued anxieties. Surprisingly, new investors were contacting him every few days. The only problem was Josh, who followed through immediately on his threats by contacting the Fund's limited partners. To his astonishment, only one withdrew support and filed a formal suit to terminate the investor's agreement. There would be an immediate settlement. The remaining *pro rata* investment, both in the Fund and in EMBRYIA, would be returned to the investor, a large, conservative family endowment fund. The capital would come from the unused portion of management fees supporting the partnership, fees suddenly more manageable with Josh's resignation coming only days later.

That had been a gut-wrenching day, but it had to happen to preserve any form of friendship that might be salvaged in their future. Josh was totally shocked and dumbfounded by the public's rapid acceptance of EMBRYIA. Controversy would always follow the venture, but he sensed something terrible and ungodly in store for Roman even as he said farewell. Josh was one of those loving, caring individuals who endeared everyone, but never was the type to *hug* another guy… until now. As he departed the office, Roman met him at the front door. Josh—surprisingly—gave him a bear-hug. "God loves you," he whispered, pushing his way out the door while fighting his tears.

It would be the end of the entire partnership, Roman knew. There'd be no Second Fund. He'd have to make the best of his portfolio companies and hope their returns would give him and Paul enough in proceeds to go out and re-start an alternative career. He was now more energized than ever to make EMBRYIA a huge success, but to do it he'd have to get to the bottom of a burgeoning problem—Marcus Levine.

Levine was spending but a fraction of his time and energy on EMBRYIA's operations now that early MAU trials were behind him. "I will call you," was his standard phrase at the end of any phone call. The phrase was open-ended, never specified as to date or time. He also traveled a great deal. The Turkey incident had occurred while Marcus was somewhere in India, supposedly visiting relatives. During the L.A. tragedy, he was consulting with a group in the Netherlands wanting to "buy some of his expertise as a consultant," thereafter back in India for a regional medical conference.

Notwithstanding the excuse of Levine's family ties, it might be time to see firsthand what he'd described as a "remotely related" operation somewhere close to Mumbai. It was a rather small undertaking funded by an unnamed group of investors headquartered in Utrecht, Holland, of all places. Was *that* the group wanting him as a consultant? And how small was small? Small could be one person, or hundreds.

Even though Levine could no longer be trusted as a truly dedicated business associate, he might be manageable if everything he uttered was viewed with doubt until verified. In this case, he'd never mentioned his personal involvement in another venture, nor hinted about dividing his time and efforts between EMBRYIA and anything else. The only thing he'd *ever* acknowledged was some company over there in India, specifically in Kolhapur, with the disturbing name AMBRIA. It dealt with organ preservation technology. *That* might be considered remotely related by someone with Levine's background, even if it had nothing to do with abortions.

The only sure-fire way to find out was to pay an unannounced visit to this AMBRIA concern. If Marcus was in no way connected to AMBRIA there could be other hints worth pursuing, but coincidences were not to be trusted any more than the man himself, not after the Turkey and L.A. incidents.

Roman had only been to India once before. It could be a quick three-day jaunt—but no sense rushing things this time.

He swung by Sarah's desk and, with a forced grin, jotted down his planned itinerary. Once in Kolhapur, he'd wing it on his own. She was on the phone to the travel agency before he reached his office.

Chapter Fifteen

Kolhapur

Luke didn't much care that there'd been little to no fanfare. The prestige of his promotion to Senior Project Leader was enough all by itself. He was to direct a new effort involving the incubation of younger fetuses to preserve as many organs possible through a longer gestation period.

The concept of fetal organ cultures was now well accepted and practiced, with much of the renowned work pioneered by the famous Dr. Rishi herself. Larger fetuses were quickly dissected for their organs and these organs sent to their own designated department. There, each was processed using a different protocol depending on organ type and size. The organs were cultivated in aquarium-sized chambers filled with the proper oxygenated, nutrient-filled solutions vital to the organ's survival *and* growth. This process included yet another proprietary solution developed years earlier by Rishi, along with the placement of fine semi-permeable micro-tubules—similar to those used in blood dialysis systems—to feed deeper layers of tissues.

Known as the Rishi Vascular Conduits, they were a key development she'd also been recognized for nearly a decade earlier. When cultivated organs grew to a larger mass, they were void of any sustainable vascularization, the complex network of arteries and veins that provided nutrients to cells lying deep in the center of the organs. During embryonic development these complex networks naturally developed, but in the explanted organ, man had to intervene and provide new intricate pathways, each containing a micro-structure similar to a screen door, allowing the good nutrients to be absorbed by surrounding cells and bad waste products to be carried away.

The organs appeared to be suspended in each tank by dozens of these fine spaghetti noodles connected externally to two small pumps leading to a collection of adjacent cylinders filled with fresh and "used" solutions. This fine network of tubing would eventually be replaced by the newly formed natural vessels and capillaries of the organ recipient.

It was a temporary circulatory system similar to that of the human body, except that blood was replaced with this "special sauce", the vessels were replicated by these unique polymeric tubules and the heart function replaced by two reciprocating pumps. One pump infused fresh nutrients and the other withdrew used, now toxic waste materials.

Nothing new there, but novel and fascinating nonetheless.

However, his newly assigned project focused on the pilot production of a system designed for the *smallest* of fetal organs—an unproven and challenging process. These delicate organs required a more precise balance of growth hormone supplements in their nutritional broth. They demanded extremely delicate handling and care during the insertion and exchange of the micro-tubules, now a fraction of the size required for larger organs. As a starting point, he'd read all of Dr. Rishi's published articles, plus new manuscripts presently under editorial review by the leading journals, and finally the new procedural manual she'd handed him only days earlier. Thereafter, the project was his to develop and, more importantly, he'd determine how best to scale up for significantly larger volumes. The current process required too much time and was too labor intensive.

Totally engrossed, he was vaguely aware of someone approaching. It happened several times a day, mostly curious technicians who found obscure reasons to wander by during their work breaks. Many were awestricken by the delicacy involved, but they all knew better than to interrupt his concentration. They'd watch for several minutes until their break was over, then silently disappear. This time it was Kareem—he'd know that flowery perfume anywhere—coming up behind him on little cat feet. Their bond was growing stronger, but even though she seemed more playful than ever, he still hadn't found the courage to make any advances. How anyone could be coy and teasing at the same time was beyond him, but she managed it.

"Simply amazing," she whispered, looking over his shoulder.

"I agree, but I'm not sure yet how we're going to ramp this up for mass production. Older organs can more readily adapt, as you know, but here everything has to be *exactly* right not only to keep these young fetal organs alive but to grow them to near adolescent sizes. Each one will require exceptional care and daily monitoring, and that will take a lot more techs than we have now. They'll really have to be well-trained and dedicated because even a single mistake will result in death of the organ."

He went on to describe his pilot systems for four different organs, six of each type. Twenty-four cylindrical, pint-sized glass chambers, aligned along the top of the dark granite workbench, were backlit with an appropriate wavelength of light, not only to heat their "bath water," but to stimulate cellular growth and aid in reorganization of specific surface antigens that would minimize rejection. She seemed fascinated with the intensity of the different colors of light and the crystal appearance of the chambers. Two dozen living organs the size of small walnuts, gently suspended in the center of their chambers, each representing hope for some faceless person in a far-off land? It was the stuff of fairy tales.

"You're excited," she observed. "I can see it in your eyes."

"Well, yes... it's hard not to be. I guess it's the challenge more than anyth—"

Suddenly she gasped, holding a hand to her mouth. "What is *that?*"

She stood frozen, pointing at an adjacent bench, one he'd been attending to minutes before she'd arrived. It supported a larger aquarium filled with a diluted bloody solution and an eggplant-shaped mass suspended in the middle. The darkness of the fluid made it difficult for anyone to see, let alone recognize beyond the fact that it was neither a fetus nor any of the other organs currently being cultured.

Damn it! How could I have forgotten to cover that? Now she'll be nothing but questions.

"It's just an experiment." He forced a grin as he threw an old, stained lab coat over the tank and closed the notebook beside it, all the while looking nonchalant. "It's just an independent research project—nothing too interesting at this point. Something longer-term I'm working on."

She smirked. "Do I hear a little subterfuge here? Luke, I've read *all* the new procedural manuals and there's *nothing* in them about any special research project. Dr. Liu hasn't mentioned it, and you report to him the same as I do. We're supposed to be in full-scale operations in another sixty days, so how can some new special research—"

"I hear what you're saying, but this is more of a special assignment Dr. Rishi gave me to try and solve… something to do with the eventual scalability of this whole program. I'm not to discuss it with anyone. That's why it's not in the procedural manuals."

She pouted. "That's not fair. I really miss doing fundamental research and would *love* to have something like this to break-up my tedious routine."

"Well, listen… I need to talk to someone about something else, and Kareem, there's no one I can trust as much as you."

"Luke, that's so sweet. You know you can trust me with anything!"

There… that impish little smile of hers! Alvarez might be right… she's playing with me.

For the first time he felt as though he was winning her over. It was more than just a cultural-thing. She had started to change his view about women and for the first time, he'd felt really *connected* to another person. He'd often joked with and even criticized his male friends when they referred to their girlfriends as *soul mates*, but now he understood exactly what they meant.

"How much time do you have before returning to your lab?"

She suddenly appeared suspicious, automatically clutching the top of her lab coat as if to pull the lapels tighter. "At least fifteen more minutes… why?"

"I want to show you something, but you must promise not to tell another soul! It would mean my job."

She took a step back, frowning, one eyebrow raised.

"No, no… it's not… oh my gosh, Kareem… it's about work, nothing personal!" Was she playing her little game? Her impish grin re-appeared almost too quickly.

"Is it about *that*?" She pointed a delicate finger at the murky aquarium.

"Yes, and much more. Come with me."

He pulled her down the journey of stairwells and corridors, her tiny hand in his, to the sterile-looking incoming inspection area. A series of small storage rooms, each with large, stainless steel doors and a keypad combination lock, was adjacent this brightly lit area. After entering the combination to Unit #107 and shoving the heavy door open just enough, he slipped into the dark, inner chamber, pulling her behind him. Motion detectors immediately switched the interior lights on, but nothing could change the pervasive odor. It nearly choked him as it always did—that mixed smell of blood, medical-grade distilled alcohol, and the special formalin-like preservative that had become a trade-secret of the company. He shot a quick glance to Kareem who again clutched the top of her lab coat, but this time to cover her nose and mouth until she acclimated herself. At a panel, he punched in another code and one of several stainless containers slid open. The sound reminded him of doors opening on the bridge of the Star Trek Enterprise.

Before them were nearly a dozen of the eggplant-shaped organs Kareem had seen suspended in his lab aquarium. These were different, however, being slightly larger and firmer-looking.

Grinning, he now imagined himself as Dr. Leonard "Bones" McCoy examining alien pods about to burst open and expose miniature, mind-controlling creatures. Within seconds the mental image morphed into conscious wonder at the vibrant human uteruses before him. Each had a funnel-like device inserted in the opening of the cervix so as to allow the surrounding solution to perfuse the inside of the uterus, bathing the endometrium and its precious cargo. His heart raced at the thought of what each uterus contained!

The grip of her tiny hand suddenly tightened.

"What... are they... human uteruses?"

"Yes, and according to Dr. Rishi, each contains three to four independent fetuses from various donors, each encapsulated in its own artificial amniotic sac. Could you ever imagine? I've read about her hypotheses, but heard they were years away from perfecting the delicate pseudo-umbilicus tethers allowing transfer of nutrients between uterus and fetus. Now here it is—all beautifully functioning in this artificial symbiotic environment."

She's still holding your hand, Luke, not even a hint that she wants to let go! Look at her eyes, so wide and bright. Maybe she really is your soul mate. And those little smiles... if only this was somewhere else, somewhere really private, not smelling so bad, you could....

Suddenly, Kareem's amazement shifted to bewilderment, then concern. "But, where... Luke, where did these *uteruses* come from? Who were the donors? Who's been engineering the process behind this?"

"What? Oh, sorry, I was thinking of... I'm... well, you raise an interesting point, but I'm sure there's a full team of researchers behind this. These uteruses were pre-treated with an agent to hyper-stimulate their production of naturally occurring hormones necessary to gestate the fetuses. They're the ultimate 'incubators', like delicate oysters holding many valuable, cultured pearls."

"Yes, but—who were the uterus *donors*? What was their motivation? Sure, some women need complete hysterectomies when disease enters the picture, but these appear totally healthy. Does that mean healthy women voluntarily allowed full hysterectomies just to support this? Why?—"

"My god, you're right. I've been so overwhelmed about being a part of this new project that I never really thought about...."

"Of course not. You're a male. If those were testicles floating in those chambers, would you have wondered about the donors?" This time her smile was truly teasing.

"Well, good point. Something doesn't make sense here. Let's go see if Dr. Rishi can provide some answers!"

"You are actually going to *ask* her? What if she doesn't have the answers?"

"Then we have even a bigger problem. Come on, we'll use the stairs. I don't trust those damn security cameras."

"Luke, please, I can't. What if she?—"

"Don't worry. I'll do the talking."

❧☙

He slowly opened the stairway door, checked nervously in both directions, then pulled her out with him. They were almost to Rishi's office when he stopped.

"Wait, Kareem. I've never really just barged in without an appointment before."

"But as a Senior Project Leader you have every right to go to her with a problem, right?"

"I suppose so, but—"

"But what?" The voice belonged to Dr. Rishi, her arms filled with log notebooks and her glasses at the tip of her nose. She'd apparently just left the elevator next to the stairwell. "She's right, Dr. Evans. What seems to be the problem?"

"Uh… can we talk in your office?"

Damn, did she see me holding Kareem's hand? What an ass I am!

She nodded, smiling engagingly over her shoulder. Behind a podium or in a lecture hall she appeared the opposite—menacing and omnipotent. Her office was immaculate except for the desk stacked high with log books and tablets. No personal or family pictures in sight, no trinkets, no potted plants. Two chairs were set tightly against each other and the side of the desk, seeming to ward off unexpected visitors. A form of protection?

She moved one of the piles enough to make room for the two new logbooks. "Please sit down. Now what are the two of you up to?" Another smile. "Dr. Evans?"

"It's… well, Dr. Rishi, I can appreciate the confidentiality of my special project but I need some assistance with the increased volume, and that of my other projects, and…."

"And so you think Ms. Dehiya here—"

Kareem leaned forward. "Please, Dr. Rishi, call me Kareem," she blurted, then blushed and bowed her head.

"Oookay…" Rishi glanced quickly at her, then back. "And you think Kareem is the appropriate technician for that job?"

"Well, yes, that's why she's here. I'm just not sure of the process to… ah—"

"Process?" She smiled. "It seems I misunderstood. Kareem's term was problem, not process. May I ask why you are choosing her over many others, Dr. Evans?"

"No, no, no… she's by far the most qualified and she's expressed an interest in helping me. I believe we'd work well together."

Rishi's quick glance at Kareem confirmed his suspicions about the hand-holding and his reference to barging into her office. The silence was more than uncomfortable.

"Very well, I will speak with Kareem's supervisor and see if we can carve out a portion of her time… assuming it doesn't interfere with her department's schedule."

"Thank you, Dr. Rishi. She'll be a great deal of help."

"But that wasn't *really* your reason for coming here," she added. "Was it?" This time her gaze was more intense, directed at him. "It's something else."

"Well… yes. I… ah, *we*, would really appreciate a better understanding of the *source* of the materials in my special—"

"Materials?"

"Yes, the special assignment. Unit 107."

"So it's *not* simply that you need an assistant to off-load some of your daily tasks, Dr. Evans. You intend to have Kareem work with you on *that* project. You have shown her the special containment room, of course. Now, I won't insult your intelligence by questioning why this suddenly has become an interest of yours, the source of these *materials*. Certainly you both recognize that these are fresh specimens that would most likely not survive transportation from distant countries. They are explanted from a privately subsidized clinic, in fact, managed by a separate group of surgeons and pathologists. It's located on a remote section of our campus."

She paused, looking away. "I've already asked many of the questions that you've probably formulated in your heads, but was told I should 'stick to my own knitting.' Then, as you both know, this whole facility was converted into what I would call a high-security camp, with a level of secrecy I never dreamt necessary in a medical field such as ours. We now have an armed guard on the campus, limited access to this building, and no access at all to that one, that clinic. They even removed the AMBRIA signs. No one is to know what goes on in here, unless they already know."

Kareem leaned forward. "Are you saying there is no way for us to visit this clinic, even though we might learn something from the extraction process that would even make them more viable hosts for our project?"

"*Our* project, is it? Well, let me make things a bit clearer. I asked about this particular clinic and its relationship to what we are discussing when I first arrived here. Naturally I wished to see and understand what they were doing, just as you two do now. My requests were denied by the new head of security, no reasons given. However, I've heard it's a horrendous place where uteruses are extracted from fresh bodies, women who have either donated their bodies to science, died homelessly, or died and were sold by impoverished family members. The same information source… I won't mention the name… said it's even supplemented by a government agency, most likely one skimming money off the sale of the bodies on that end of the supply chain and from the procurement of these precious organs from AMBRIA on our end."

She paused, then shifted to a whisper. "You're both highly educated professionals. Now listen to me, and listen carefully. There are aspects to our work that we are *not* to question, understand? For some reason known only to those who are funding this whole enterprise, we're to ignore certain areas. We have this security thing clouding everything we do. I must *also* say that I do not trust one man in particular here, the only one whose office has clear glass in the door and side wall facing the corridor. He had the original frosted glass removed the very week I arrived here."

Luke nodded. "Keeping an eye on things, including the traffic in the hallway."

"Right. He claimed to dislike frosted glass, but he watches *everything.* I think he has several informants here as well. So please… forget about the source of your materials. Forget the clinic. Remember that your work here is purely scientific. Your expertise is needed for a highly technical operation. Materials are supplied by others. Don't question, and above all, do *not* question Mr. Thomas, the man I mentioned. Avoid him if possible.

"But—"

"But nothing, Dr. Evans. I believe you both have work to do."

"Well maybe I need to reconsider if I *should* continue working here."

"Do as you please. I don't have time to counsel you in your career objectives. Now please excuse me."

Chapter Sixteen

Kolhapur

TWO DAYS OF TRAVEL AND FOUR TOTAL HOURS OF SLEEP FOR *THIS*? KOLHAPUR was Hell on earth, or at least one of Hell's bordering villages. The hand-held shower in his hotel room sprayed lukewarm water only long enough for him to soap up his hair. Then it turned cold and dribbled, forcing him to sluice himself down with a drinking glass. He should have known better than to ask for any room more than two floors up, but he'd wanted to look out across Kolhapur for reasons now unremembered. And he *could* have planned his arrival time at AMBRIA for later that day, not first thing. Getting out of bed mere minutes after finally falling asleep was pure agony, yet people were more receptive to surprises early in the day. After lunch? For some reason, afternoons were far less productive.

The address was in a less "seedy" section of the industrial spread, or so the taxi driver said. The four-story building, nearly the length of a football field, had no name on the exterior, just a number. No name in the unattended lobby, either. Every inch was covered in white tile and marble, accented with stainless-steel trimmings, abstract steel sculptures on both ends of the expansive, ivory-topped desk and a chrome digital clock next to stainless elevator doors. A computer screen with a flush-mounted keyboard occupied the middle of the desk. A quick glance at the menu showed only department headings, six in all, plus instructions on how visitors were to register.

The first department heading brought up a Chinese name: Liu. No first name or title. The department function was given as *Operations*. It was the next one, *Technology*, that sent his pulse racing. The name was Rishi! Again, no title, no first name. Of course, Rishi was a fairly common Indian name, but….

He clicked on *Security*. Name: Malovec.

Research. Name: Levine. Levine?

He quickly scanned instructions on registering, and after a few quick key strokes, a guest pass with his blurred photo crept out of a thin slot next to the screen. Then he noticed the tiny camera embedded in the computer frame. No chance of sneaking into a place set up this way. There! Another camera in one of the upper corners of the lobby. Whatever was going on inside was not meant to be seen by anyone unannounced.

The guest pass was no more than a name tag. No magnetic stripe, no barcode, just the picture and R. Citrano, the name he'd typed in. An American flag in one corner? How? From Citrano? That was Itali…oh, of course! He was already in their computer database, but why? He began to boil. They undoubtedly knew everything about him.

Within minutes Marcus stepped from the elevator, frowning. Bloodshot eyes told of overwork and late hours, contrasting greatly with his fresh, white lab coat. He was also unshaven, and had been for several days. The change was remarkable, sickening. He was a stranger! Was this how wives felt when they learned their husbands had been having affairs, living separate, secret lives and expending a great deal of deceitful energy? Or husbands, when it was the other way around? Roman's own first marriage was a prime example of *that*.

But this wasn't the time for reflection. Marcus waddled forward, head hanging like some child caught with his hand in the cookie jar. Gone was his usual arrogance; absent the swagger.

"Roman, I—"

"Finding you here is pure bullshit, Marcus! You've lied to me from the beginning, and what you're now doing is just short of fraud and extortion."

"No, I—"

"You're operating a separate business behind my back? My guess is that it's set up to benefit somehow from our EMBRYIA venture. Research… you're in charge of *research*? More bullshit! You're using the aborted fetuses in some way, aren't you? That's why you've been so focused on salvaging them intact and viable. That was never part of the business objectives you disclosed. We never discussed any such thing. In fact, you gave us every indication that you would be one hundred percent dedicated to the EMBRYIA operation. *You* would ensure its success. *You* would personally be responsible for every aspect of the operation. Instead, you've been here half the time."

Marcus took a defensive stance, continuing to stare at his feet.

"Look at me when I'm talking to you, you bastard!"

"It wasn't a lie, Roman," he countered, finally raising his head. "What you and I began with EMBRYIA is truly a quality service for hundreds of thousands of women throughout the world. It just happens to also provide a valuable by-product that will fuel another multi-billion dollar industry. Are you faulting me for being an entrepreneur... quite like yourself?"

"Don't you dare compare the two of us! You're seriously justifying your actions because you're an entrepreneur *just like me*? One more crack like that and you'll be swallowing your teeth, *Doctor* Levine. I might have been a fool to fund such a venture, but *I* don't operate behind anyone's back. I can't believe I was suckered into this. You were lying from the beginning. Was it legitimacy you needed? You apparently *had* the fucking funds the entire time. What are you calling this operation, anyway? What are you selling? When were you going to disclose any of this to me?"

Roman closed the distance between them, but Marcus had backed up an equal amount, chin shifted to one side. He was scowling, but then something changed. He stood a bit taller, glancing past his accuser as though someone was standing there.

A woman's voice confirmed it, a voice Roman remembered from the past. He'd heard it while working in the Human Genetics Research Lab at Women's Memorial Hospital. It belonged to one of the kindest, gentlest woman he'd ever met, a mentor with enormous patience who'd trained him in her unique tissue-culturing techniques. Their work together was so controversial back then that it seemed they'd shared some great secret over all these years.

The name on the computer screen *was* hers after all! What was *she* doing here? Why had he been so blind? Now the pieces were coming together. Those "valuable by-products" referenced obliquely by Marcus had been the basis of Sihar Rishi's renowned career. Now it made sense. His anger redoubled as she came forward. Graying hair and dark, deep bags beneath her eyes spoke of her true age, although her weight and size were as he remembered them.

"No, Roman… you were *selected*. I wholeheartedly endorsed you. We are actually quite proud of what we've developed here to this point."

"WHAT? Whaddya mean you *selected* me? For WHAT? Idiot of the Year?"

Roman fought down a wave of sudden nausea, finally finding his voice. "Sihar… excuse me, Dr. Rishi… what do you mean I was *selected*?" Her simple words provoked dozens of questions, but this particular word made him feel weak and manipulated.

"Exactly what the words say, that you were specifically selected, chosen just as I have been… as we *all* have been. Marcus is a *brilliant* clinical researcher and geneticist, not the naïve first-time entrepreneur you believe him to be. I know of no one else who can match his knowledge in obstetrics. I myself have only recently learned how he and our investors have orchestrated a number of very complex financing and business processes over the course of the last ten years."

"*Our* investors? Ten years? He told you that? How recently is 'recently'? That's what I mean by lies—"

Marcus stepped forward, interrupting. "Let me explain."

"NO! I want her to hear it from her. I want to hear all her justification for your actions, your lies, your deceit. Let's see just how far you've gone in this sickening excuse for…." He turned, facing her. "Just how long have you been involved in this charade, Sihar? I'd use Dr. Rishi, but formality doesn't apply here, does it? How long? Ten years?"

"I don't think that has anything to—"

"How long? Two words. Who did the choosing, and when? Surely you know… don't you? Marcus told you, of course, being the honest and forthright soul he claims to be."

Marcus just stood there. It was Rishi who closed the final distance. She'd entered the lobby through a door with no visible handle. "Roman, I don't think this is—"

"What huge secrets are you hiding? Who are you keeping out, people like me or… or the authorities? Is that it?"

"Roman, let's go to my office where we can continue in a quieter vein," she said. "There are some things I need to show you, but first please step back outside the building with me. Please?"

With that, she headed for the entrance door.

ᘓᘐ

"Roman, you will get the answers you came looking for, but everything said inside that lobby is recorded. Your observations about security are accurate, but neither I nor Marcus have any say in that. Now please… we'll go to my office, where we can talk sensibly and privately about your concerns. I would prefer that nothing further be said until we are all there. Agreed?"

Her quiet manner was enough. He nodded, but with teeth clenched. *They're recording conversations in the lobby? What have I stumbled into here?*

Chapter Seventeen

As Sihar Rishi led the way down a stark, white corridor, the odor of the facility became more and more familiar, yet he couldn't quite place it. The adrenaline of his confrontation and the craving for detailed answers had caused a sudden flooding of endorphins in his brain, intensifying everything: the smell, the starkness of the modern facility, even the strange level of humidity in the air. His thoughts jumped like those of a time traveler, from moment to moment throughout the history of this new venture, now trying to re-process what Marcus had said in his office when they'd last met. Perhaps it had been his state of shock at that moment, initiated by the two vicious rapes and all the emotion that had charged the air, but Marcus had never mentioned anything about being involved in another enterprise or some other established business. The man was a master at weasel-wording about *possible* related ventures, hinting of leverage into new fields using EMBRYIA's success when it happened. When it *happened!* EMBRYIA would have to achieve world-class stature first, of course. That's why it was so important to keep the venture alive.

Roman struggled with the thought of forgiving Levine for being so evasive. Why should he? Now the same man was being described as a brilliant clinical researcher and geneticist who'd orchestrated a number of very complex objectives over the course of the past ten years, *working with investors.* A lie by omission was no different than one by commission, and that lie promised to grow bigger yet.

In Dr. Rishi's office, she and Marcus circled around her big desk. Marcus stood off to one side, now looking almost defiant, while Rishi sat at her desk, composed and appearing serene. The changes in both were remarkable, contrasting with his own feelings of being a very small pawn in an apparent global scheme he never dreamt existed. Yet here it was, literally hidden in plain sight. A building without a name, housing what appeared to be a state-of-the-art biotech or medical facility and secured as though it held all the secrets of the universe.

Rishi opened the top drawer of her desk and pulled out three small glass vials, each containing an intact fetus. "These are preserved samples that have been generously provided by EMBRYIA," she said, lining them up in front of him. "Nine to sixteen weeks of age."

"Jesus Christ... *generously* provided? Marcus?" The words came spewing out as a sneer, but it didn't matter. "You expect me to believe that this greedy bastard *gave* them to you at no charge?

Her answer was delivered softly. "It is my understanding that Dr. Levine is handsomely compensated by the AMBRIA Corporation as well."

"AMBRIA?" He hurled the word back. "How in hell does AMBRIA fit into this picture?"

"Roman, I told you all about AMBRIA," Marcus stated. "I was very specific during many of our initial meetings."

"Bullshit! According to you, AMBRIA was a privately owned company with a similar sounding name, having something to do with organ preservation technology. You wouldn't have mentioned it even then if I hadn't told you it had come up in our trademark search when we were verifying the availability of *EMBRYIA* as our corporate name. We didn't want any name conflicts, and you helped convince our lawyers the name was different enough for us to ignore. Only then did you squint up at the ceiling and *vaguely* remember seeing the name in your travels. Other than that, you said you knew nothing about the company."

"Roman, I—"

"Shut up and listen for a change, Marcus. I found no corporate information on AMBRIA when I looked for it, nothing, so this is a private enterprise, *not* a corporation! From what I see right here, this multi-million dollar building and whatever is going on here *preceded* your first contact with Zorro Medical. So, I'm sitting in AMBRIA right now, is that right? There's no name on the building anywhere. No phone listings under AMBRIA. I managed to find the address by doing an on-line search for Medical Suppliers in one of several Indian business websites. I expected to find something closer to a tent when I got here. Somebody has gone to great lengths to keep this whole thing under wraps. The CIA couldn't have done a better job of it." *You must have chosen the name, too, you miserable bastard. Why didn't I see it?*

He searched Dr. Rishi's face, suddenly overwhelmed by memories of standing before her explaining the phenomenon called hydatidiform molar pregnancy. That had been decades ago, but he was intimidated even now by memories of her superiority as his mentor. Was his sudden nausea the result of agitation, or guilt? Either way, the sensations were horrible. She'd said nothing during his whole tirade, merely glancing from time to time at the vials on her desk.

He finally shook off the flood of recollections and broke his strangle hold on the chair arm, picking up the vial containing the largest fetus. At sixteen weeks it was nearly fully formed, with fingernails and fine hair covering its entire body. More coarse hairs were already formed on the brow and eyelashes. These "samples" were no longer clinically viable, as they were permanently preserved in a formaldehyde fixative.

The label said… it said…. He drew his breath in sharply as he read something all too familiar. In less than a handful of alphanumeric characters, it identified yet *another* of the originators in the unfolding nightmare. The serial number format was *dd*405xxx. That configuration was his! It was the one he'd originated working in Dr. Rishi's lab back in Pittsburgh. The abortion date was expressed by the "*dd*" part. *He* was the decadent originator; it was his scheme. Even at the age of twenty, he'd felt like a Frankenstein, turning uncorrupted human tissues into something sinister and dishonorable. Now he was an embarrassed and disgusted older monster. Sihar Rishi had continued using his labeling configuration all these years.

"Yes, Roman… it's the same," she said. "You may not have realized it at the time, but you were one of my best research associates. You pursued a career path that, ironically, took you down a different but parallel course that would eventually help me align my research interest with a commercial one we believe will now help thousands of people. It's fate!"

Marcus took up the thread. "The people behind all this identified the two of you years ago. You had the perfect background and set of skills to help us expedite our plan, Roman, but I knew that if I approached you in the normal manner I might have struck out. I enlisted your associate, Pete Lundgren, to help me open the door, so to speak. He'd been eager to find a way to work with the licensing department at my university and was glad to help, and—"

"I was fucking USED, that's what it boils down to!" The word was screamed at full volume. "I was manipulated and lied to. This whole damn operation, most likely corrupt, is being hidden from official sight. There's some kind of syndicate behind the whole thing, right, covering up this large an operation with some very seedy intent? You had no right to use me, and I don't care how you might justify it. You're both deceitful. How much did you pay Pete for his help? Don't tell me you gave him a fuckin' finder's fee!"

"Please, Roman," Dr. Rishi said, "we understand you're upset, but at least let's try to be civil. There's no need for such language. Marcus did what he thought was prudent to achieve our goals, something you of all people should appreciate. I'm sure you've played matchmaker and manipulator in your career more than once, but now you understand *why* we needed to keep EMBRYIA viable and growing. The business you funded for Marcus provides the raw materials we need to meet the demands of this extremely large market. EMBRYIA is a critical *and* legitimate supplier. In helping us create EMBRYIA, you've provided a rare resource that we need to make the whole thing work... namely young, properly preserved fetuses. You need to look at the bigger picture and realize the value of your contributions. You've provided an enormous level of credibility by backing EMBRYIA. You are right about the kind of backing AMBRIA has had from the beginning, but I assure you it is all legitimate."

Marcus continued as if they'd rehearsed their dissertation, "Although the financing of EMBYRIA was dwarfed by that of the investment behind AMBRIA, it was necessary to have the backing of a U.S. venture community. Otherwise this would have the appearance of dirty foreign money driving another black market, as you so wisely observed. The difference is that a black market operates in secrecy, whereas we are perfectly open about our offerings. We serve a need not addressed by any other legitimate system."

"Perfectly open? In a building with no name, that no one can find, with a security system rivaling Fort Knox, no phones listed, no official existence unless through some falsified front. How the hell can you convince yourself that this is legitimate? You don't even have the mothers' consents to use their unborn fetuses."

"Yes, we do," Marcus calmly answered. "The procedure forms we've been using have said as much from the beginning. Remember when you and I debated the use of the words 'discarded' versus 'destroyed' in referring to the extracted fetuses? I revised the language before going to print and indicated that the extracted materials would be dealt with *'appropriately'*. You read and approved it. Every treated woman or her prospective guardian signed the form. Is it not *appropriate* to use organs harvested from aborted fetuses to sustain life for others? If the fetuses are destroyed, is that not the same as turning our backs on those who may be dying without replacement organs?"

The questions were nothing short of crushing. Here was one of his lifelong mentors admitting she'd voluntarily joined what was obviously an underhanded enterprise. Beside her stood Marcus Levine, a man he'd constantly defended, not only to his partners but also to those he so desperately turned to for respect and professional admiration the local venture community.

A part of him wanted to know more, wanted to digest the sordid details, but something else inside told him to distance himself as far and as quickly as possible. The rapes of those innocent women in the MAUs and, from those days in Rishi's lab, the slow growth of fetal organs sucked from their uterus... now most likely being conducted in a grand scale in this Kolhapur building under a shroud of secrecy and deceit, just to make a return on an investment? No! Wrong! The first order of business was to get out of there and back home, back to where he could pull the plug himself before anything or anyone could stop him.

He felt the urge to lunge for the office door when Rishi suddenly stood and came around the desk to kneel beside him. She was the same warm and nurturing professor he'd once known, with the same gentle approach to difficult problems.

"I know what you're thinking and how you must feel," she said. "I went through the same mental anguish, but you need to understand that there aren't many alternatives for those suffering people who need these organs. You may feel this has the *appearance* of an illegitimate black-market source for human organs the world needs, but the company is making efforts to seek government support throughout Europe and the Asian continent. This will take time, but eventually we'll be recognized as an acceptable means of treating unmet clinical needs and promoting world health."

Unmet clinical needs? The words came through in flashing neon and the blare of trumpets. They were the very words Marcus had used to sway him at the onset. This was no different than sitting in a venture conference while someone at the podium pontificated on the same theme. There was nothing to say. The concept was no more than an ugly, foul, hollow mass painted clinically sterile white on the outside.

Rishi continued. "Recently I read a story from the ANSA National news agency out of Rome. It told of a wealthy young American businessman who had destroyed his body with overuse of steroids and human growth hormones for body-building. His internal organs grew faster than his chest cavity could accommodate and he eventually suffered from congestive heart failure. He became a candidate for a heart transplant and was put on a two-year waiting list, but he only had one year to survive. His condition became worse within months because of renal failure and other internal organ damage, so they were eventually forced to take him *off* the list. Six months later it was reported that he miraculously had a heart transplant in a hospital in Rome, from a twenty-eight year old donor. It was later discovered that he'd paid for a mafia-like 'hit' on this young donor after they identified him as a tissue-match from a simple biopsy he'd undergone months earlier. They had him *assassinated* for his heart! Roman, I've been told this now occurs on nearly a daily basis throughout many countries of the world. *This* is our competition; *this* is what we will shut down with our organs… a supply of stronger, more viable specimens from fetuses that would have otherwise been destroyed during normal abortion procedures. The marvelous extraction technique Marcus has brought to EMBRYIA along with my cultivation procedures will provide the world with an unlimited supply of organs."

"Unlimited?" His own voice sounded hoarse.

"There are over a million abortions each year in your country alone."

The reality was crushing. He had no immediate response... and the interim silence was deafening... then finally he found the courage to make his final demand, "Show me the operation you're running here."

She nodded, with a look as if she was winning him over. Marcus started towards her office door without a word. "Come," she urged. "Marcus and I will show you everything."

Numb with doubts, he allowed her to pull him from the safety of his chair.

Chapter Eighteen

IN THE SERVICE ELEVATOR JUST OUTSIDE HER OFFICE, HE STARED AT THE BUTTON labeled, "Gestation Lab," barely able to think before the doors opened at the floor below. The foyer was stainless steel, with a large panel of glass permitting full view of the lab beyond. It was immense, larger than any lab he'd seen before. He'd already judged the building to be about the length of a football field, over 100 yards long and half that in width, and this lab seemed to consume all but a few dozen feet.

Stainless steel benches squatted beneath six foot wide, vertical laminar flow-hoods with all-glass cabinets. Clean Bench was the term used. Stainless steel, glass and Formica were proven to be the best surfaces in the lab industry where sterility and cleanliness were concerned. Cross-contamination was practically impossible, if not non-existent. Each bench was eight feet long, as many as thirty benches end-to-end in four rows, more than a hundred in all, each equipped with state-of-the-art centrifuges, pipetting systems and a small water bath for heating reagents and solutions. Along the walls running the length of the room were stainless incubators with individual glass doors. Six to ten shelves in each held hundreds of large, double-layered drop-culture dishes, all rocking gently in unison so as to flush the surfaces of their precious contents.

Once in the changing room, he, Marcus and Rishi quickly slipped into surgical gowns and masks before passing through a series of glass doors that further controlled the laminar air flow in the room. He immediately approached the closest incubator, seeing further evidence of his early work in Rishi's lab, but the in-dwelling microtubules and connections made to infusion pumps were far more elegant and extremely hi-tech. He stood in awe as he read the headers of each large incubator section, printed in red on supermarket-type signs extending from the incubator wall. HEART, LUNG, KIDNEY, SPLEEN, and BRAIN were the categories down that side of the room. Were there even more on the opposite wall? He couldn't see.

"You can maintain and grow an entire spleen?" he asked. Cultivating spleen cells had been a challenge twenty years earlier, with no breakthroughs on the horizon.

Dr. Rishi's squinting eyes smiled above her mask. "And here I thought you'd be more interested in our brain cultures, but yes, it turns out that the spleen is extremely hyperactive when treated with the right hormones and growth factors. Although it doesn't readily repair itself in the body, we can do amazing things here in the lab."

"So *now* tell me about brains… you can't be serious."

She smiled again. "The brain has a wonderful means of reorganizing itself into its functional sub-compartments. Today we don't even comprehend growing brains large enough to perform transplants, at least not in my lifetime," she chuckled, "but we can cultivate fetal brains to the point where they differentiate into functional cells that can be implanted into adult brains to treat disorders including Parkinson's and Huntington's diseases and even Amyotrophic Lateral Sclerosis—Lou Gehrig's disease. This represents the interim step between fetal stem cells that haven't yet differentiated and adult stem cells that currently have limited diversity and viability. We take what we need from these cultivated brains and discard the rest."

She pointed at one of the drop-culture dishes. "For example, the basal ganglia of this brain can supply millions of cells that are producing high-level concentrations of dopamine, the neurotransmitter otherwise absent in Parkinson's patients. The cells are transplanted into patients where they eventually integrate with their surrounding environment to produce natural levels of dopamine, thereby 'curing' patients of that disease. That's right, I said *cure.*"

It sounded as though she was already polishing her lecture on this topic. Perhaps he'd been hasty. Going public with all this could truly be a game-changer. In spite of his anger and disappointment, excitement was beginning to stir within, but now he needed time to process the information. How would this affect EMBRYIA? How should that effort proceed? Ironically, without even knowing it, he'd become the sole gatekeeper to the EMBRYIA-AMBRIA enterprise, for whatever happened now to

EMBRYIA would affect this larger enterprise. Yet he had no idea whether any of it was *good*, in the true sense of meaning of the word.

It was uncharted territory, unfortunately, one that possibly included a mine field.

Philadelphia

Dr. Raj Maibeck drew a deep breath and replaced the phone. How could he have known that the "specialist from Children's Hospital" would turn out to be one of the hospital directors, a Marjorie Adams, or that Dr. Adams had just been contacted by a woman who'd claimed she'd left *his* MAU not two days ago after having an abortion? Further, that the unnamed woman had *additionally* undergone a hysterectomy, absent any consultation, diagnosis or medical history that would warrant such a drastic measure? Further yet, that all indications suggested the procedure could not *possibly* have been accomplished in a mobile unit, given the lack of surgical skills and facilities absolutely required, and even if those had been available, never within the time span of less than two hours, as the woman claimed? And if true, that those behind the mobile "clinics" had better have their house in order?

Dr. Adams had used the term 'victim' towards the end of her "professional courtesy" call, hinting strongly that the unfortunate woman was both emotionally and physically damaged and needed immediate post-op surgery to stem continued internal bleeding.

Fortunately, he'd had the presence of mind to disclaim any knowledge of the named "victim" or confirm Dr. Adams' statements in any way, but it came down to the very thing he'd said to Dr. Levine not four weeks earlier, when the new directive had been enacted. The taking of healthy uteruses was extremely risky, and surely criminal. However, significant increased compensation might offset the risks. At the time, he'd been thinking along the lines of a week's pay for each successful extraction. That Levine had tripled that amount and paid each bonus in cash made the risks seem far more tolerable.

There were measures to be followed in the event that anything went wrong, speaking in the medical sense. One of those measures involved contacting Marcus Levine without delay. Maibeck snatched the phone back up. Any action Levine might take would have to be immediate if disaster was to be averted, but that was Levine's problem.

Chapter Nineteen

Minneapolis

HE WAS IN HIS OWN BED FOR THE FIRST TIME IN FOUR DAYS, STILL DRESSED WITH shoes on along with the lights and his luggage dropped in front of the door. Was it day or night? Could he have slept the whole day away? Who cared?

The front door was unlocked. Incredible! He'd been so stupefied from exhaustion that he hadn't even pulled it shut all the way. First order of business—a hot shower. That would wake him up. Maybe it would make up for that cold, dribbling miserable excuse for one in Kolhapur.

Dripping wet, he stumbled directly from shower to kitchen in search of anything of value in the refrigerator. There was a lone Tupperware container of some fermenting, left-over Chinese food and an unopened bottle of Regusci Chardonnay—the only remaining bottle from the case he'd purchased during his last visit to Napa Valley. He'd try to find the energy to drive down to Caribou Coffee in the nearby strip mall for something more substantial. As he threw on some jeans and a sweatshirt, he noticed the flashing message light on his phone. Four messages in all....

"Hi, honey, we need to talk... please... please call me when you get in." It was Andrea, a voice he'd yearned to hear, but she didn't sound herself.

"Hey, it's me again... I need to speak to you urgently... any time... please call." Roman grabbed the portable phone as he waited for the next message.

"PLEASE, Roman... I need to speak with you. I need you." Now the hair on the back of his neck stood on end. She sounded so desperate!

The fourth message was simply a dial-tone that seemed to pierce Roman's ears as he strained to hear her next words, listening for any sign, any indication of what could have been so wrong. He hadn't taken the time to note when the messages were left on his machine as he dialed her number, so he was about to hang up when Andrea finally answered as if awakened from a deep sleep.

"Yesss?"

"Andrea, it's me, Roman... are you okay... I only just now received your messages."

"Oh, Roman," she gasped. "I've done a terrible thing. My period was late, very late and I, of all people didn't want to believe it... I let it go too long and then I panicked."

"Wait! You're pregnant?" He felt a rush of emotions and the burning desire to hold her. In less than an instant his heart seemed to swell within him and warm, powerful feelings swept through him like a floodgate had been opened. He pictured her being right in front of him, never more beautiful. Suddenly he just knew it, without doubt or hesitation... he loved her, and had for some time.

"LISTEN TO ME," she shouted. "Roman, you need to listen to me. I panicked and didn't want to use the hospital clinic, so I used one of your ungodly MAUs to *take care of it*."

It was all he could take, perhaps partially out of pure exhaustion, but the growing nightmare had now touched the one person he'd come to love the most. He fell to his knees, momentarily unable to respond, realizing at long last the mental turmoil women had to go through to make such a decision. He felt it now, in her words; heard it in her voice. All those women who'd been treated—no longer numbers in a business plan, no longer a statistic or data point in the revenue model. Their plight was now personal for the first time. He was embarrassed to be a *man*. He was embarrassed to say anything... he didn't know *what* to say.

"I drove across the river to Camden," she continued. "I know it wasn't the smartest or safest thing to do, but I called your office and pretended I was someone else and asked where the closest unit might be located. I intended to get back before dark, but it took forever... and... I think something went wrong."

He pictured her in the procedure room, his eyes closed, hoping the image would fade, but now he fought back the urge to cry out in frustration. For a long moment, he couldn't even breathe as the details and images of those rapes came flooding back.

"Andrea, I'm so sorry. I can't—"

"I couldn't reach you… this happened over a week ago. I thought I had a reaction to the sedatives, it took me a long time to recover… the bleeding was too severe… not normal… and the cramps were something like I've never experienced before."

"Honey, I'll be there on the next flight." He pulled himself to his feet.

"LISTEN TO ME!" she yelled again, catching him by surprise. "I finally had to see someone at the hospital where I work, someone I could trust… a Dr. Adams. She's a director there, the one responsible for my getting the job. She personally did a pelvic sonogram, an ultrasound, to see if maybe, just maybe, the procedure wasn't complete or something wasn't healing properly."

He wanted to tell her everything, all about the ePOD developed by Marcus, the terrible rapes, his trip to India, *how much she meant to him.*

"Andrea, the procedure, it's—"

"ROMAN…," she pleaded, sounding like someone about to drown, "they TOOK my uterus!"

Her shouted words completed the process that had begun more than a week earlier, an exhausting nightmare that began as horrible and moved to well beyond, something indescribable. The room swirled, his feet and legs went icy cold and he sagged once more onto his knees. It just couldn't be happening this way, not when so much had gone right. They'd taken her uterus? How? For what purpose? What the hell was happening?

Her sobbing shook him back to reality before the phone went dead. She hadn't hung up—it had simply gone dead. He tried to phone her right back, but the line didn't even ring. Fighting nausea, he threw a change of clothes and his shaving kit into a small travel bag and raced to the airport. He might be able to catch a flight that would get him to Philly without waiting half a day.

Thirty minutes later, his prayers were answered. There was a non-stop to Philly, and he'd be on it. Boarding pass in hand, he raced for the gate.

ꕥ

He'd made thousands of trips, flown millions of miles on dozens of airlines, but he'd never realized how inefficient the system was, how long it took to get through security, the mindless wasted time waiting to board the flight. It had all become so ordinary, so mundane. Now he simply wanted everyone out of his fucking way. No talking, no questions, no vapid smiles, magazines, earphones, drinks. No more delays. Nothing! Just get to Andrea as quickly as possible.

The actual flight was just under two and a half hours. Add the pre-flight garbage, boarding time delays and a long wait for a taxi once he got to Philly, and the total was double that. He only had an unfamiliar address in an unknown section of South Philly, and he'd never taken the time to visit her. They'd emailed each other just once since her move from St. Paul, but she wasn't a fan of texting or emails, saying they were too impersonal. He'd tried to lure her into phone sex once, shortly after they'd started dating, but that had bombed as well. Of course it might have been his calling her from a hotel room, half-drunk after a conference, but she was old fashioned and wouldn't have anything to do with it. Instead, she turned their conversation into a loving, caring discussion about how he should start taking better care of himself, drink less and sleep more.

Why hadn't he taken the time to visit her? How had it all come to this? Making things even worse, it was raining like hell and the taxi driver barely spoke English.

Chapter Twenty

Tudor City New York

SOMETHING BIG WAS BREWING WITH THE GENESIS PROJECT.

David Thomas swirled his cognac and maintained composure while Mr. Q outlined the promotion. The big man was obviously pleased, so it would be unwise to show undue pleasure. It was simply a promotion like any other, even though the new assignment meant untold millions of dollars added to the Cayman Islands bank account within the year.

He was now assigned total responsibility for the Kolhapur operation under the title of Chief Financial Officer of AMBRIA. The recent changes in MAU procedures, due to enhancements by Levine, were being implemented without problems in every country where the MAUs were operating. As the number of women lining up increased, fetal selectivity grew with them, lowering risks to the program while dramatically increasing volume.

It was then that Q asked about the situation at AMBRIA. "I have heard rumblings," was all he said.

"Yes, you have undoubtedly heard from our head of security, Malovec. I was preparing a report when I received your message to come here."

"You had trouble."

"Yes, with the man from EMBRYIA, Roman Citrano. We record anything said in the AMBRIA lobby, as you know, and Malovec delivered this to my desk right after Citrano's unannounced appearance there." Thomas leaned forward, holding out a flash drive. "Citrano had somehow traced AMBRIA to the Kolhapur address, although we all thought—and you confirmed it—that we had erased all direct references to the building. Anyone doing diligent searching for the name anywhere in India would have been led to a small building quite apart from our operation, where we have set up a reasonable but small manufacturing facility turning out components of incubation machines. Citrano circumvented all that and showed up two days ago. He was… I would say he was *dangerously* angry, threatening to close down EMBRYIA. We will be watching him closely."

"Absolutely. MAUs are now operating in eight countries, and although EMBRYIA has been most important to us, its importance is waning. Nothing can prevent us from expanding our own units as we see fit, especially in countries where I have considerable influence. Genesis is no longer dependent on American acceptance, or even on every procedure going smoothly, but Levine warned us that Citrano could cause us a good deal of trouble. He was apparently correct."

"Do you have a suggestion?"

"Brief Malovec and have him track Citrano closely. At this point in our program, I would say that Mr. Citrano is expendable. Wouldn't you agree?"

"Well...."

Q leaned forward, holding out the bottle of cognac. "David, as with all operations it's best to have alternative solutions in one's pocket. Might not it be best if something happened to Mr. Citrano before he had a chance to do us any harm?"

No answer was required.

Chapter Twenty-One

Philadelphia

ANDREA DIDN'T MUCH CARE THAT THE VOICE ON THE FRONT DOOR INTERCOM was unfamiliar—what mattered was what the woman said over the intercom. A Dr. Adams at Children's Hospital had sent her. There was a private clinic where they'd repair the bleeding, and that she please come down as quickly as possible.

The button to release the building's front door lock was just below the small loudspeaker in the apartment wall. She'd pushed it even before the woman's short message was finished, instructed her to come up, opened her apartment door and left it ajar, then turned toward her bedroom where she'd already begun filling a small travel case with things she'd need when checking into wherever Dr. Adams had arranged. A private clinic where they'd repair the bleeding? Marjorie Adams hadn't quite put it that way, but she *had* been concerned about the sensitive nature of what she called a crime. Perhaps there'd been a change. At least now someone was there to help, and not a moment too soon. Two fainting spells already, one in which she'd fallen and struck her head on the end table, knocking the lamp and vase off. A gash in her forehead testified to the impact.

And her vaginal bleeding was actually getting worse!

A tall form walked in mere seconds later. "I am Greta," she announced. "Take whatever you need, but keep the list short. We will have you fixed up right away. My god, is that your blood on the floor? You're hurt… your head!"

"Yes, it's… it's… I fell."

Suddenly Greta was no more than a dark blur and the room was spinning again. *Nothing to grab! Falling….*

ꕥ

Greta Huber put the alcohol swab into the Ziploc bag, along with the spent hypodermic. They'd be discarded later. The injection of scopolamine and morphine would last several hours before any kind of reality returned, although the "patient" would be able to make it to the car if supported.

As with anyone coming out of anesthesia, she'd remember nothing of her dream state later.

"Nurse Huber" then set about to finish filling the woman's travel case with what was already on the bed, plus whatever she thought would be needed, but the Robbins woman's purse was too big for the small carry-on case. No problem. There was a larger piece of luggage in the closet, big enough for a few more changes of clothes plus the purse, plus a couple pairs of shoes. The whole process took no more than ten minutes. By then, the patient was starting to come out of her fainting spell.

Fortunately the building had an elevator. Many did not.

Greta pulled the smaller woman to her feet, holding her. "You can hear me now? Gutt! You now go on a trip. I have your things packed. Lean on me and we now go to my car."

ꙮꙮ

Roman squinted through the cab's dirty front window from the back seat, frantically trying to read dwelling numbers between windshield wiper swipes. When the driver turned onto the brightly lit, well-maintained Sixth Avenue cobblestones of South Philadelphia's historical area, it suddenly *felt* right. It was typical of her style. He pictured her walking along the sidewalks with her hands full of groceries and freshly cut flowers from the market.

There it was on the left, number 407. He threw the driver what could have easily been twice the fare and ran up the single flight of stairs, two at a time, to the front door. He felt flushed as he recognized her name on the directory, as if done by her own hand. He pressed the button immediately under her name, over and over again without knowing if it even worked. *Come on, damn it!* A dozen presses later there'd been no answer.

Two names below hers was a plate reading Building Manager. He pressed that button hard and kept his finger on it until a tall, middle-aged black man emerged, unshaven and looking irritated. Suspenders hung on a skin-and-bones frame.

He peered down at the source of his irritation. "What the hell is your problem?"

"It's very important that I see one of your tenants. Unit 407," he pleaded. "I believe she might be in desperate need of some medical attention."

The other man looked down, fumbling with his keys. "Ms. Robbins? I know she hasn't been feeling well lately and I ain't seen her today. You a doctor or a relative or sumthin'?"

"Ahh, yes… I'm her brother. She left me an urgent message. I got here from Minneapolis as soon as I could, but she's not answering the buzzer. Something could be wrong."

Why'd you say you were her brother? What was wrong with being a close friend from Minneapolis, or even her boyfriend for that matter? She was carrying your baby for Chissakes!

The manager stared. There was nothing to do but stare back. "Follow me," he grumbled. After knocking twice and fumbling again with his ring of keys, he finally decided to open the door. Surprisingly, he stepped back and gestured, as if to say, "after you."

Lights were on in the bedroom and above the stove in the kitchen, but not in the small dining room or the room beyond. The manager was still standing in the doorway, as if it was inappropriate for him to enter without an invitation. "Ms. Robbins?" he called out. A tinge of anxiety colored his call.

My god! There—an overturned lamp! The bulb was broken, and beside it a shattered vase of flowers. What was that next to the vase? It might have been something from the vase itself, but instincts and a tightening stomach said otherwise. It was… yes, it was blood, thick and dark, there on the carpet. Fighting nausea, he delicately touched the edge of the large stain with a forefinger, immediately testing it with his thumb and realizing it was still sticky—no more than a few hours old. There was more of it extending up onto the edge of a nearby ottoman. This after—what?—two days since she'd… possibly three since….

He didn't quite make it to the small kitchen sink in time, throwing up what little was left in his stomach on the way. As he raised his head from rinsing his mouth, he heard the manager talking to someone. The man was on his cell phone describing what they'd seen. A '911' call? That would mean cops in a matter of minutes, and cops would mean hours of delay and questions, asking why he'd represented himself as her brother.

Get out of here, Roman! This is South Philly, not Minneapolis. It'll be homicide up front, until proven otherwise. Move your ass!

He pushed past the apartment manager without getting any resistance. The stairwell was safest. Two steps at a time. Out the door, into the street! Where are the damn taxis? You have to find one, but not likely on this residential street. That way? No. Wrong… has to be the other end, possibly near that restaurant. Cross traffic up there. Run!

Travel bag in one hand and cell phone in the other, he thumbed a call to the only person who might have some answers. Then, while waiting for Marcus Levine to answer, he ran like the wind, as if he were twenty years old again.

Andrea, where the hell are you?

Chapter Twenty-Two

Bihar Sharif, Northeast India

AMISHI MALIK AWOKE SHIVERING ON THE MOLDY, SOGGY, BUG-INFESTED PILE OF old blankets between her battered body and the cold concrete floor. Less than an arm's length away was her toilet, a funnel-shaped hole in the concrete, connected to the septic tank outside her cinder-walled "prison." She'd slept perhaps all of an hour in the past twelve, if it could even be called sleep.

The name Amishi meant *pure* in Hindi. Proudly given by her mother at birth, it became her curse when she was taken and sold as a young sex slave, providing a premium return to her new owner as her virginity—her *pureness*—was marketed to the highest bidder. She'd been an enticing fourteen year old then. Now she was of practically no value at all. Worn and battered, she'd be of interest only to the occasional transient trucker or local factory worker who couldn't afford the fresh, smooth-skinned, younger prostitutes.

Everyone in her prison-like compound had the same, miserable quarters. Exercise consisted of one fifteen-minute session outdoors, rain or shine, where she and others like her were "encouraged" to walk endlessly around a small courtyard. Food was a type of greasy stew, heavily spiced with curry and served once a day *provided* she cooperated in yielding her body to any of her pig master's whims. More than once she'd considered going without it altogether, so as to bring her suffering to an end, but her will to survive had always been stronger and there was plenty of the ishtoo even if it tasted awful.

New girls would come and go every so often, sometimes even a few young boys. Others simply stopped showing up in the common gathering area. Were they too battered to continue or even survive? Perhaps if strong-willed they had, but there came a time when faces and bodies could take no more punishment, or else became so disfigured no one would use them anymore. Then they simply disappeared.

She'd never understood the beatings, never done anything to make her masters angry, yet she, too, bore scars and marks. She'd lost three teeth and her nose had been broken twice. Other women—young girls, mostly—were worse off. They were simply sexual objects, to be used and abused until that day when they, too, would be of no further value.

And the sounds! The service rooms were open to the hallways with nothing more than metal grilles in place of the usual internal windows. Rooms for special clients all had real beds, washstands, decent toilets, even carpets on the floors. The guards despised screaming or crying out, all of which were quickly silenced by a sharp blow to the face or body.

Yet the cries and screams of children as young as twelve reverberated up and down the halls, punctuated by the grunts and moans of pigs forcing themselves on frail bodies. Without a pillow to muffle the sounds, there was no recourse but to listen and wonder, until it was her turn with the animals. Then she wondered no longer. Her pain was no less because she was an unwilling prostitute—a sex slave. Her dreams of being free no different than the dreams of others.

Before she was taken from her family, she'd been eager for life, an achiever who loved school and laughed with her friends. She'd owned a pet parrot and a small dog, both of which received adoring attention, and she devoured books, especially animal stories. When she was twelve, she'd graduated to romantic novels that were a little beyond her grasp at times, but not her reading ability. She'd had a secret lover, imaginary but very real in her private thoughts.

She even dreamt of starring in a school play, finishing her education and becoming a movie star. She would have been a beautiful woman by then, tall, with soulful brown eyes and long lashes. Admired and held in esteem. Others would be envious. But then her life had suddenly switched to a living hell and all those dreams lay shattered.

Her parents had no way of finding her. How could they? She didn't even know where her prison was, even if she could tell them she'd been stolen, kidnapped on her way home from school.

At first she'd cried out of fear, then for her pain, then for the loss of all that had been meaningful in her young life. Then the tears no longer came.

Her only non-sexual contact was with a toothless, elderly woman who looked after her, providing her a sponge bath after each of the *visitors* had finished with her. The woman was Romanian, or perhaps Hungarian—or possibly something Slavic like Bulgarian, with a heavy accent. After the first day, hopes of communicating had been abandoned. From that point on everything was non-verbal: a look, a movement of the head, a gesture. There had been only that one time after a particularly brutal and filthy sexual encounter with a group of men, her limp body soiled with pig excrement, urine and multiple ejaculations. She'd actually felt sympathy from this woman then, conveyed as an inability to make eye contact.

Her body became numb to most of the pain, uncaring, like feet that had become so calloused they could no longer feel sharp stones. There was only that constant burning that kept her from urinating for as long as possible. That searing pain began within the first few months of her captivity. Two years later, urination had become a part of her daily suffering.

How many men had there been, she wondered? Why was she even still alive? What happened to the women who'd been taken away? The questions were like seats on a merry-go-round, returning again and again, always sounding the same, always with the same answers.

Occasionally the expressionless old woman arrived with what appeared to be a fresh change of clothing rolled tightly in her arms. The shapeless, gray floor-length smocks were only changed when they became too filthy even for the guards to tolerate, when they got to stinking worse than the toilet hole. Replacements might be too long or short, or even torn, but none of her masters cared. She was always delivered to the pigs heavily perfumed, either naked or wearing something that would excite them, something they might tear off or soil in whatever way they wished. Then it would be back to her filthy smock again. Other than being constantly damp, even wet, from lying on her cold, soggy "bed", she'd managed to keep the current one fairly presentable.

On this particular day, the old woman brought more than a fresh smock. Stepping into the eight foot square cell right behind her was an odd-looking man, tall and lanky, wearing a long white coat. He looked for all the world like the stork in one of her childhood books, only this one held a syringe and a long piece of rubber tubing. Medication or narcotics—did it really matter? Struggle would have been senseless, but even though she remained docile, he acted as if she was some sort of vicious animal. With one quick movement he grabbed her forearm, locked her elbow and twisted her face down and fully at his mercy on the soggy bed, a position she'd been subjected to hundreds of times. After a swift wrap of the rubber around her tiny upper arm, he plunged the needle into her swollen vein, taking what appeared to be at least three small vials of her blood. She could sense the changing of one for another from her face-down position, even if she couldn't truly see. The tourniquet's release was made with a bony knee in the middle of her back, just as another needle pierced the side of her neck. No more than a whimper crossed her lips as she felt the tingling of her face, and then… nothing.

ജ്

The old woman straightened the limp body, pulling off the well-stained gown and replacing it with another, this one khaki-colored. It was more like plucking and prepping a freshly slaughtered turkey for dinner than any compassion. When she'd finished, two burly, middle-aged men rolled the drugged girl's body in a coarse burlap blanket and carried her to a lorry in the alley outside. She'd be given another injection at the mid-point of her twenty-eight hour journey to Kolhapur.

Chapter Twenty-Three

Minneapolis

THE RETURN FLIGHT FROM PHILLY WAS A BLUR, SPENT SITTING PROPPED UP against the window and half-staring out at his own reflection against the night sky. It was important to keep his eyes open—to close them would be to bring forth images of Andrea, her abortion and now her obvious disappearance—but he'd already pushed himself to the limits of exhaustion. Self-hatred flooded his mind, not only for his actual involvement in what had evolved over the past several months, but for lack of intuition and sensitivity as measured by the impact on people around him.

He'd left three voicemails for Marcus before they closed the door on his flight. On his fourth attempt, a recording announced that the cell phone mailbox was now "full", so he'd try reaching David Goldberg, the man Marcus hired to direct EMBRYIA operations, immediately after the initial funding. Goldberg was a faceless, quiet, middle-aged soul who always seemed to fade into the background. He'd given operational reports during board meetings, but was one of those hard-to-get-to-know types. What if Goldberg had been in on this from the beginning, even before Marcus had come looking for venture capital? What if he knew what was to happen, once EMBRYIA was up and running?

Would he even know who Andrea was?

ꕥ

Goldberg picked up on the first ring and agreed to supply all the procedural records from the MAU that serviced the Camden area, offering to have the appropriate materials delivered to the Zorro offices by the time Roman arrived in the morning. No, not good enough! Absolutely unacceptable! They had to be there that very night, regardless of the hour.

The terse demand was met with silence, then a nervous cough. "Yes, they'll be there."

That answer meant Goldberg was somewhere in the Twin Cities' area at that moment, but it made no difference. Those records had better be there even if the man had to crawl on all fours to deliver them! And there they were. A folder from Goldberg was sitting on the edge of the reception desk at 10 P.M. that night. He lunged for it, revived by a fresh surge of adrenaline. A handwritten Post-It note on the otherwise unmarked cover said 'Attention: Roman – Confidential.' Goldberg must have found the foyer unlocked and he'd just walked in.

Dashing for one of the two leather couches opposite the desk, he flipped the cover open. Inside were the Camden patient files for the past couple of months, several hundred in all. Each patient document had the required cover sheet to protect the contents, a requirement by HIPAA laws designed to maintain the privacy of the patient. They were serialized according to procedure dates, not alphabetical order—that would have been too rational. Even so, he quickly found the location of each patient's last name and starting flipping through them for those beginning with an "R". Each time he came upon one he began to tremble, and by the time he'd gone mostly through the folder he could hear his rasping heartbeat in both ears.

There it was: Robbins, Andrea.

It was all so unbelievable, the bizarre course of events that had brought him to this point. How in God's name could it have involved Andrea? She'd been forced to do this awful thing all on her own, with no one there for support, forced to terminate the life of *their* child—something so unique and precious to just the two of them. That life had been extinguished, like some candle blown out by the wind. It was gone, and so was Andrea.

The handwritten words were blurring before his eyes. He fought back tears, scanning the page for the date and time of the procedure. There! She'd been prepped at 7:14 P.M. and released from the recovery station at… at 9:10 P.M.! Two hours? Way too long. It was nearly twice the usual length. *How could this be?*

His attention shifted suddenly to quick footsteps in the hallway outside the foyer. Two seconds later, Marcus burst through the double doors. His expression was one of shock as the folder was waved in front of him, just out of reach, by the one man he most likely hoped he wouldn't meet.

"Might this be what you rushed here to retrieve before I had a chance to read it, Dr. Levine?"

"I... there are, there are... let me—"

"I knew Goldberg would notify you out of loyalty, but he never said you'd be here in town. You didn't return any of my messages, but here you are in person. Now, I want answers! What the hell's going on? She said that her uterus was taken from her, and—"

Marcus deliberately avoided the folder thrust at him, sitting on the edge of the coffee table instead. He tried to look up, but failed. Acting? It certainly looked like it. How could the man who wrote the MAU protocols and witnessed hundreds of procedures *not* know that others were going beyond his original intent—unless he'd been involved? Unless those changes were by *his* direction? He finally drew a deep breath and managed to make the briefest of eye contact.

"Roman, I only learned of this earlier today. We have been experimenting with another extraction technique." His voice cracked. "We've developed a method at AMBRIA to deal with all the younger fetuses that we were obtaining, a way to keep the fetuses intact so their organs could develop further in the natural state. You saw for yourself, it's much easier to harvest the organs of the larger fetuses—they are stronger and more viable—but we were failing at producing an appropriate environment for these smaller ones. We needed a more optimal, natural incubator."

"You fucking bastard! You and Rishi had the balls to waltz me through that gestation lab, the whole time assuring me that I was seeing *all there was to the operations,* and now you're saying there are other techniques, other procedures, human incubators? The two of you had a *need,* so you devised a method to steal women's uteruses? You make me sick! You're using healthy stolen uteruses as incubators. You did... you... you prick! You did it to... to *my* Andrea!"

"Roman, please. No one knew this woman had any connection to you. How could they? I didn't know until your phone calls. Prior to the abortion procedure we always perform a quick tissue analysis and she had a Class AA tissue type. The hormone level, blood type and antibody count identified in her tissue sample was of top quality—"

"God damn it, Marcus, don't you *dare* talk about her as if she was just some kind of fucking lab animal!" He was off the couch and inches from Levine's face. "Where is she? Something happened... someone TOOK HER FROM HER APARTMENT TODAY." He shouted the words at full volume, which did not diminish. "What the fuck is going on? Stop looking around the goddamn room, because there's no way out. And you can forget the fake trembling bit, because I'm not buying it either. Look at me, you sonofabitch!"

"You n-n-need to believe me, Roman... I really don't know. I don't. After getting the call from Goldberg, I came here for the files to get her address myself. Someone, somehow, made the connection between the two of you. I think it may have been that doctor at the university hospital who diagnosed her uterus extraction."

"Another fucking lie... unless you were in Philly! What's your connection with her doctor? How did you *know* that she went to see some doc at the university hospital? Do you think she went around telling everyone she was connected to me? DO YOU? And how in god's name could you remove a woman's uterus in such a short time in a mobile unit? Answer me that! ANSWER ME!"

He's lying. There's no way in hell a woman's uterus can be extracted in two hours, not even in a hospital if prep and recovery time weren't added in.

"We experimented with a modified vaginal hysterectomy procedure," Marcus sputtered. "In a healthy woman it is not that difficult to sever, cauterize and release the uterus to remove it through the vaginal canal. We perfected the procedure in India, developing the necessary disposable instruments to perform it quickly and efficiently in the MAU."

"Stop! Stop right there. You were experimenting with a new extraction technique... *experimenting*, Marcus. That was your word for it. Now you say you PERFECTED the procedure. That tells me you've been at this for months, maybe years. Nobody perfects something that delicate in a few weeks."

"Roman, don't judge me... you have no idea of the pressure these people can apply... it goes beyond threats... I had no choice but to assist them in perfecting these procedures. Many people have suffered in order to give life to thousands of others, yes, but—"

"You're fucking insane, that's what you are. You intended to eventually do this to women in the mobile units. You're lying about the rest of it. There's no external *pressure*. You didn't *assist* anyone. You perfected the procedures yourself, just as you did the rest of it. Look at you, cringing in the corner. I take one step toward you and you shrink down like the wharf rat you are."

Ironically, Marcus had pressed himself against Josh's locked office door. He had nowhere left to move, and no way out, but suddenly his gaze shot past his accuser. Before Roman could turn, strong fingers dug deep into his shoulders. The grip was one of desperation, or perhaps one driven by adrenaline. Either way, exhaustion ruled out any defensive move on his own part. He dropped to his knees, breaking the hold, then quickly twisted and looked up.

Goldberg! The mild-mannered man looked disheveled, as though he'd charged up the stairwell instead of using the elevator. How long had he been there?

"Please, Roman, this has to end," he said. "It was Dr. Maibeck who performed Ms. Robbin's abortion. He apparently did his residency with the female physician who diagnosed her at the hospital. Maibeck had been trying to recruit this same woman to join EMBRYIA. After the examination of Ms. Robbins, she naively conveyed to him that she suspected Ms. Robbins was going to inform the authorities. Maibeck then notified the new Head of Security, a man named Malovec, who became known to us after the rapes in L.A. This terrible man is being paid by AMBRIA, not us at EMBYRIA. I believe *he* went to see her, to convince her not to say anything."

"What do you mean you *believe* he went to see her? Did you talk to this guy? Did he tell anyone he was going to see her? How did he know where she lived? Why would she have let him into her apartment? The apartment manager didn't mention letting anyone like that in, so your story doesn't hold water. I want the truth, not bullshit." He got to his feet.

"And you might as well stop saying 'us at EMBRYIA'. There's no *us*. You and Marcus here are as fake as three-dollar bills, so I'm saying you both knew damn well what Maibeck was doing. He was following orders. This security guy was also following orders, *your* orders. How else could he have gotten the information?"

"He came here and demanded to see her files..." Goldberg continued, "her address... I'm sorry... at the time I had no idea why he was asking me about this woman. It wasn't until Dr. Maibeck called to warn me... He sounded scared."

"So he comes *here* to Minneapolis, gets the information, and moments later he's in her apartment in Philly? I've heard enough! Marcus—"

Levine had slumped down and was cowering on the floor, pressed hard against the same office door. He attempted to duck the angry hands grabbing for his throat, but was not fast enough.

"Where the hell did this prick take her?"

"They... AMBRIA... they have a private jet. He probably used it to get from here to Philly. I'm only guessing... I don't really know... but they'll most likely take her to Kolhapur from there."

ꕥ

Once the elevator doors closed behind Goldberg and Levine, the impact of their lies and disclosures slammed home. Damn them both! Damn everything! Had Andrea really been dragged off to India, or was Marcus just being Marcus? They both seemed to know that this brute being paid by AMBRIA had gone there specifically to confront her, and possibly even *silence* her. How does a head of security convince, unless with force? No doubt he'd taken her, and not without a struggle of some sort. The apartment manager had reported it, but such reports went to the bottom of the Missing Persons pile. The security goon now had at least a full day's head start. If Marcus had known where they'd take her, there must have been others, else why wouldn't he have played totally dumb? Who the hell *were* these AMBRIA people?

Reaching for the door, he noticed the dried blood in the crevices of his fingernails. Andrea's blood! The realization shocked him as he tried to push away the fears of what might be happening to her. How should he report her being… being… brutalized? Yes, that was the word, but what evidence could he give *anyone?* Her recorded messages? Had the Philadelphia police responded to the landlord's call? And what "evidence" would *he* submit, no matter who listened?

What of the physician at the university hospital? Would it be uterus thievery? The MAU records didn't show that, or even suggest it. They showed only a time lapse. Time, time, time! *Jesus Christ!* The only evidence was most likely on its way to India, and the only way it could be presented to anybody was to have Andrea do it in person. He had to follow her, find her. It was the only option open. He'd undoubtedly find her in some medical facility, assuming she wasn't….

Don't! Concentrate on what you need to do!

Clothing? One clean shirt left, maybe a couple of pairs of socks, and a pile of laundry already ignored for too long. That plus all the wrinkled stuff in his luggage, still unpacked, plus what he was wearing. No time for cleaners or laundries. No waiting for stores to open. Get something at the airport, or maybe in Mumbai. Shit! Four minutes past midnight, and the earliest flights out didn't leave for over six hours. No sleep possible. A shower, yes a shower….

ꙮ

Northwest flight No. 42 to Mumbai departed at 6:25 a.m., arriving the next day at 10:00 P.M., with two stops along the way. They'd be no time to pick up a rental car at that late hour and make the long drive to Kolhapur, so that meant another night at the Hotel Arma, near the Mumbai airport—more time wasted—and again, the attempt to sleep. With luck, he wouldn't get stuck sitting next to someone who wanted to tell his life story during the multiple flights required to get him there. He wasn't usually lucky when the trips weren't planned well in advance.

Once he began his search for Andrea, he needed to stay awake at all costs. The last time he'd used NoDoz pills was several years back, but there were still some in his top drawer. Two hundred milligrams of pure caffeine, and they were safe enough according to the label, as long as he limited himself to….

Damn! There'd be no limiting anything, not this trip. Someone would pay in spades for what had been done to Andrea, and this AMBRIA security goon topped the list.

ഌ

When Goldberg had driven away, Marcus sat in his own rental car and collected his thoughts. Goldberg couldn't be blamed for supplying the documentation as quickly as he did, given Roman's ire, but it would have been so much better if he'd delayed just one more hour. In his haste, he'd opened up Pandora's Box. The file he'd hand carried was all individual sheets, so the Robbins page could have been removed. Roman wouldn't have seen it, and that would have been the end of the crisis, but no. Goldberg was too accommodating and the damage was done.

Kolhapur was ten hours ahead, so David Thomas should be available. Even if he already knew all about the MAU fiasco, his orders were to alert him for *anything involving security*—and this mess certainly fit that definition. Malovec had no knowledge of Citrano's involvement, intellect, or rage, and now every sign pointed to Roman chasing after this woman. He'd now naturally assume she'd been taken to Kolhapur. That was how the man functioned, never using logic, driven by instinct, jumping without thinking ahead. The very aspects of his personality that made him so easy to maneuver also fueled a form of self-delusion. Even now he felt *he* was in control, that *he* would right the perceived wrong and possibly punish those responsible. Ignorant fool! Any ordinary man would have realized that EMBRYIA was but a pawn in a much larger game, and that certain forces well beyond his comprehension were at work.

At any rate, it was most likely he'd head right back to Kolhapur without a shred of solid evidence pointing him in that direction. He hadn't *seen* Malovec with the girl—no one had, of course, since Malovec was never involved—and Maibeck's post-procedure summary was no more than a checkmark on a form. *Nothing* had gone wrong in the MAU. It had been a "normal" abortion, like every other as far as the record was concerned. And that bit about Maibeck doing his residency with the female physician, someone he was trying to recruit, was a brilliant piece of disinformation from Goldberg.

The woman who'd phoned Maibeck was one of the directors, not an ordinary physician. However, there was little doubt that Dr. Marjorie Adams would indeed blow the whistle on what *she'd* see as illicit medical practice. She'd not be able to do that effectively if the Robbins woman was no longer within reach.

Greta Huber reported that she'd not been seen leaving the Robbins apartment. No one had taken notice when she'd backed her car up to the loading dock at the old Urgent Care building, but even if someone had, who'd have cared? The area was fast approaching the status of New York's upper Bronx, what with vacant buildings, rubble and rusted railroad tracks. That's why the Urgent Care owners had sold out and moved elsewhere.

In truth, the Robbins woman was no different than a dozen or so others whose uterus removals had not gone well, here or overseas. As with any new medical procedure, a few negative outcomes were to be expected along the way. The benefits outweighed the risks. In this case, the girl's uterus would survive even if she didn't, and one healthy uterus was literally worth more than the miserable, lonely life of its owner. The fact that this particular woman *happened* to be involved in some way with Citrano changed nothing. He'd get over it; they all did. Besides, she was probably no more than a sexual romp, a whore playing the field. One woman was no different from another when it came to indulging in physical pleasures.

However, David Thomas needed to know what had just transpired even if Roman *didn't* show up again at AMBRIA's front door, and he needed to know exactly what kind of problems Mr. Citrano might cause, given the man's explosive nature. With that thought, Marcus Levine opened his phone, albeit with trepidation.

Chapter Twenty-Four

Kolhapur

SHE CAME AWAKE GRADUALLY, DRIFTING IN AND OUT OF CONSCIOUSNESS AS IF waking from a dream that would not let go, but her first sensation was that of warmth and, strangely, being dry. Was that part of the dream? Typically she came awake shivering, gripping the moist rags they gave her for a bed, but she wasn't shivering. She returned to sleep, minutes later emerging a little further. Where was she? It wasn't her cell. It smelled better and was much brighter. What was this strange, new place? How long had she been unconscious?

Before she'd even looked about her, she wondered if she'd been sold to another whorehouse, a more legitimate one. Or... was it possible someone had come to save her, to snatch her away from that seedy whorehouse and its filth? Who could have even known about her? Who would have cared enough to...?

She glanced at her sleeve. It wasn't her old smock at all. This one was tan and it felt different, more like a cotton sheet than the burlap she'd worn for over two years. It was true! She'd been moved to someplace better, but where? Was she in some sort of hospital room? Could it really be over?

She was on a thin mattress—very thin in fact, but at least off the floor—with something springy under it. The room was larger, too, and she actually had a real toilet in the corner, and a little wash basin. She managed to sit up, conscious of her bruises and badly torn vagina, but feeling different in other ways. She must have slept for a long time. Her room had a door much like the previous one, with a small window in it. The door was locked, of course, but that was to be expected. There was also a single, barred window above her cot. She'd never had a window to the outside in her previous cell, her only light coming through the one in the door. This window was a lot bigger, yet totally obstructed by overgrown shrubs with broad leaves. At least it was a window. She caught tiny glimpses of light between the leaves.

She managed to stand on the far corner of her cot so she could see through the thick-paned smaller window of her new prison door. Across the corridor sat a large, fair-skinned guard at a desk on which was a black and white television. Behind him was a whiteboard with a long list of names, dates and some scribbled notes in a language she couldn't recognize. The letters and numbers were certainly those she knew, but not their combinations. Next to the board was a calendar, with days marked and crossed in red ink. As she squinted, the calendar became clearer. She'd been wrong in thinking it was two years—it was actually more than three!

How could that be? Why couldn't she remember much of what had happened? Were they giving her drugs all that time, so she wouldn't remember? For a time she'd been able to count the days, but not for long. Then she'd only been able to judge the time of year during her exercise sessions, but even that had become foggy. She'd had nothing to make scratches with, nothing to use to write, and certainly no paper.

Three years since she'd been abducted from her home! What of her family? Her father? Surely, given his powerful government position, they must have tried to find her, but a small voice deep inside provided unwanted answers. Even as a young girl she'd been made aware that governments were corrupt, filled with men who, were it not for expensive clothes and lofty titles, were no different than criminals. Even police often differed from the criminals they ruled only because of a uniform. Her father was definitely not one of these corrupt men, but he might well be surrounded by them. Perhaps she'd been a pawn in a business deal that had gone bad, or a costly penalty as a result of one of his unkept promises. How would anybody know?

She stepped back down, nearly falling when the cot tipped, and the sudden effort to right herself triggered an urge to pee. She reached down to hold herself, to relieve the pressure while she studied the new toilet, but felt something different. What was it? She slowly spread her legs and bent forward to see a small tube extending from her vagina... not from where she would relieve herself, not extending into her bladder, but into her vagina. Frowning, she pulled at it gently, but felt nothing. Angered and scared, she pulled harder only to feel it tug somewhere deeper inside. As if it were some foreign invader inside her body, she cried out in panic.

Wide-eyed, she started trembling violently, only to be startled by the guard's booming voice in her native language. "You should leave that alone… it will do no good, you pulling at it that way."

ꕥ

She was grateful that at least the violent rapes had subsided, but the weeks that followed were a bizarre nightmare. She'd often be bound and lightly sedated, then taken to a special room and stripped naked from the waist down. They'd connect syringes to the tube that continued to reside deep inside her. She wasn't sure if the young female nurses were injecting or removing contents from inside her, but the days that followed yielded severe cramps and nausea. And then there were the blood samples twice each day. She felt weak and hollow. At least the food was better. It helped her recover after each visit to the special room, but the discomfort and weakness never subsided.

All the rooms had numbers on the doors. Hers was room number 12, so that might mean that there were at least that many women like her, each in a different room. There could be more, of course, but she rarely heard screams or other sounds of agony. Many of the rooms were a distance away—there were just four that she passed each time she was taken from her cell or returned there—but room 12 was opposite that guard's desk, so she got to overhear plenty of conversations that took place at that spot.

Late one night a young nurse slipped silently into the cell to take her temperature. She'd pretended to be asleep, her usual practice, since there was no reason to resist. The next morning she was surprised to find a small notepad and pencil wedged between her cot and the wall. Had the nurse deliberately left it behind? Why would she have had it with her in the first place… surely not to write down something as simple as a temperature? Nurses all carried clipboards for things like that. It didn't matter. It was a welcomed gift, a treasure. She'd received nothing like it all during her ordeal.

So how was she to best use her new gift? The sharp pencil—did she have the courage or strength to kill one of the guards? Perhaps that one who occasionally raped her? She knew he chose her because she did not cry out as others did, but he was foul and careless, spitting on her when he was done. He deserved to die, and she knew just how she could do it, waiting for just the right opportunity to plunge the point deep into his throat, or maybe an eye. If she drove it deep enough.... No, the pencil would probably break in two. Better she use it on herself. Death would be a welcome relief, but then her captors would never be found and punished.

She thought for a long time, finally deciding she'd spend the next several weeks writing to her father, telling him of the terrible things that had happened, adding tales of the horrendous events that took place around her in this strange new place. She'd repeat the hideous stories heard from the nurses outside her cell, about something called *artificial insemination* of other women who were forced to undergo an abortion only to be re-impregnated again two to three months later.

She'd relay what she'd overheard them saying. All about their failed attempts to impregnate *her* due to the barrenness of her damaged womb. That was what the thing hanging from her body was all about. It was a way for them to reach inside her and do whatever it was they were doing to all the women. It made no sense at all.

There were no exercise sessions at this place, so no direct communication with the others was possible. She knew only what she overheard, but neither the staff nor guards sought to keep their conversations private. They often held discussions right outside her cell, at that same guard's desk across the corridor. The aborted fetuses were often defective and *they* were being blamed for the large quantities of drugs they'd been giving to the women to keep them sedated.

Guards would also often boast about raping the younger, more attractive women. They'd challenge each other to see who could produce a conception first, repeatedly raping their choice of victim until blood samples produced the desired results. Their only competition was the artificial method. Sometimes bets were paid off in money, right there at the desk. How could they boast about what they were doing, even boasting to the nurses, and how could the nurses join in the laughter? It was all too ghastly, a horrible nightmare made worse by the cavalier dismissal of anything approaching human feelings. *Human* feelings? They were worse than those animals that stole her virginity.

After four or five back-to-back abortions, the women would no longer be fertile and, just like her, experiments were then conducted to perfect a technique for the removal of their damaged uteruses. These women were eventually no longer seen or discussed. Perhaps they were killed, but some had fought off the effects of their sedation long enough to commit suicide. Others who were less-fortunate simply bled to death or were suffocated in their sleep once their hollow bodies were of no more use. Why had *she* been spared? Was it because that nurse had taken a liking to her? She'd never really seen the nurse's face, but was quite certain it was someone she'd not before had in her cell. Would the same nurse be someone she could talk to? Would she be able to send her father's letter out through someone like that? It didn't seem likely, but that didn't mean she shouldn't write it anyway. She'd be very careful, hiding it inside the thin pad that covered her cot.

She worked at the stitches with her broken fingernails until a few gave way, then opened enough of them so she could slip the pad inside the cover. It would be right there under her face as she slept. She could think about it all the time, but there'd be few times when she could actually write. The best time was right after they'd finished experiments on her and brought her back to her cell. They'd usually leave her alone for two or three days at a time, as they'd just done that very morning.

This reprieve was different. Deep in thought to distract from her discomfort, she was startled by the clicking of keys in her door, then the sounds of someone grunting as though lifting something heavy. Now what did they want with her? She pushed herself into the farthest corner, cringing at the thought that whatever they wanted, it could mean only something worse than usual.

The door only opened wide enough for someone to push another woman into her cell before it closed again. Unable to stand, she collapsed on the concrete floor and immediately curled up into a ball, looking like a wounded animal—frail, somewhat older and beaten badly—not moving or making any sound. For that matter, there was no sound from the corridor, either. Was the one who'd shoved her through the door still there on the other side, listening?

There had never been a fellow sufferer in her cell. Why had this one been so badly treated? Even in her own case, her broken nose had been the result of her own fighting and her bruises due to rough handling by the pigs, but this woman looked like she'd been deliberately abused. She seemed… broken. The urge to rush over and console her was fierce, but what if doing so was wrong? What if they beat her for doing it? Yet it was equally wrong *not* to reach out, to show compassion. No one had ever offered *her* the same tenderness, though she'd yearned for it since the first day.

Amishi pried herself from the sanctity of her corner and lay down beside the trembling body, wrapping herself around it. The woman stopped shaking and allowed herself to be held. "Are you alright?" Amishi whispered. She'd not spoken in months—the sound of her own voice was startling. The woman's large bright-blue western eyes filled with tears, but she didn't answer. Perhaps she couldn't. Her long, dark hair was snarled and tangled. Amishi tried to work some of the tangle away. "I can only imagine what you've been through," she consoled. "You're not alone."

ꟸ

The American-looking girl without a name, without a voice, died a few hours later, frozen in her fetal position. As the sun tried to bleach its way through the obstructed cell window, two guards entered the cell to remove the body, not even bothering to confirm that she was dead. Once again, Amishi shrank back into a corner, sitting with knees drawn up to her chest. They ignored her.

The older guard swore as he attempted to lift and straighten the stiffened legs. He drew back his hand, now covered with stale, thick blood that had oozed from the body. Some splattered his watch as he let go of her. The other guard snickered. "Why did you put her in here in the first place… should have put 'er directly in the freezer."

"She was still alive, asshole. Just throw me that pillow."

It was only then that the younger man acknowledged anyone else in the cell. He glanced at the darkened corner as he grabbed the small pillow from her cot. "Won't be long, honey," he smirked as he tossed the pillow to his colleague.

Once it had been stuffed between the dead woman's open thighs, they dragged her body into the corridor by her ankles. Then they pulled the tattered blanket from the cot and threw it onto the dark pool, using their boots to mop up the gelatinous mess. When they were done, they tossed the blanket back onto the cot and left without a word.

What did that guard mean when he said it wouldn't be long? There'd be no answer, of course. It was just another kind of torment, a way of increasing fear. The guards did things like that all the time. They were even crueler than the pigs.

Amishi sat there in the corner for what seemed like hours, afraid to move. The remaining smears of blood had not even dried before the older of the two guards was back, once again unlocking her door and coming in, this time with one of the nurses on his heels.

He was smiling!

ஐ

The vacating and cleaning of room 12 took all of ten minutes with nothing more than a tight rope and a wet mop. When it was finished, a new "guest" was carried in, unconscious, and dumped onto the cot. A fresh blanket was tossed over her still form and a new fresh pillow stuffed beneath her head. Unlike the previous tenant, she'd been pregnant now for several weeks. She was scheduled for the usual procedure the following morning.

The nurse who'd accompanied them stayed behind to adjust the pillow. As she did, a pencil fell from the thin mattress onto the floor. Curious, she discovered a tear along the mattress seam. The pencil must have been inside. Could it be the one she'd lost? If so, there'd be a pad in the room somewhere. She found it between the layers of mattress material. Five of the pages were filled with writing, both sides. She tore them off and stuffed them, crumpled, into her trash bag that was destined for the incinerator along with the prior tenants soiled garments.

With a final look around the room, she gathered her clipboard and slipped back into the corridor, locking the door. On her way past the guard's desk, she met the guard's smirk with one of her own. Room 12 was open for business once again.

Chapter Twenty-Five

The AMBRIA Lobby

NEARLY THREE DAYS HAD PASSED SINCE HE'D STOOD VOMITING IN ANDREA'S apartment. Since then he'd eaten very little, slept even less and consumed half a bottle of caffeine tablets. During the flight he'd managed only to down a small buttered roll, not even touching the artificial-looking piece of grilled tilapia on his plate. The "continental breakfast" at the Arma hotel might as well have been curried worms, passed up in favor of a double espresso. The nausea hadn't changed, but his nervous tension was even more intense as he once again approached the ivory desk and punched in Dr. Rishi's name on the keyboard. He'd have to start with her, even if she had no immediate answers.

Was this whole thing a wild goose chase? Was Andrea being cared for somewhere on a different continent? What if she'd been simply taken somewhere like... like Baltimore... and Marcus was lying through his teeth? She'd displayed so much fear and panic on the phone....

Unlike the previous visit, nobody appeared in the first few minutes. The elevator's lights showed it to be dormant at the fourth floor. There was a phone on the desk, but it didn't ring. There was nothing to indicate that the system was working, or that Dr. Rishi was even there. Was it possible they'd been warned he was coming? Had he been wise in giving his true name? That possibility had crossed his mind during the flight, but he'd dismissed it. How could they know? Marcus? Could he have... no, he'd have been guessing, unless....

Fighting exhaustion as the minutes ticked by, he stared out the lobby's corner window with images of Andrea flooding his mind. That last meeting in the St. Paul Grill, and her... *Stop it! Don't think. Better yet, consider something else...maybe so—*

His musings were interrupted when the elevator doors finally parted. A tall man with reddish-blonde hair stepped out. He'd be considered quite handsome by some women—probably a ladies' man ever since his late teens—but he wore a look of annoyance, or was it discomfort? He cleared his throat before approaching, then assumed a rather stern look, emphasized by piercing blue eyes. It was all quite theatrical, and a bit amateurish.

"Mr. Citrayno, is it? I'm Dr. Luke Evans," he announced. "Dr. Rishi is currently unavailable and she asked me to see if I could help you. Did you have an appointment?"

Appointment? She'd know damn well I didn't have an appointment, which means this is some kind of put-off they're using. He's an underling sent out to fend off snoopers, or perhaps delay an unwanted visitor. He sounds American. They're recruiting people from the U.S.?

"No! I didn't have time to make an appointment, but it's urgent that I see her. It's a serious emergency that only she can assist me with. When you say she's unavailable, what exactly do you mean? That she's here, but busy? Or she's not here? Or just that she's not seeing anyone without an appointment?"

The other's posture stiffened. "Excuse me, sir, but Dr. Rishi *is* extremely busy and I don't recognize the name Citrayno, so who exactly are you and what's the nature of this serious emergency?"

"My name is pronounced Ci-trah-no, not Citrayno, I'm from the U.S., and I'm an old colleague of Dr. Rishi."

Maybe that'll cut through this crap.

"I see. An old colleague. And the emergency?"

"Sorry, but I can only discuss that with Dr. Rishi. It may involve her, and if it does I'm sure she will want to know about it immediately."

He appeared to relax a bit. "Yes. Well, why don't you wait with me in our conference room until she's available? She'll respond to my message as soon as she's able. Can I get you a cup of coffee? You really seem like you can use one. I'm quite familiar with the ordeal of getting here once you land in Mumbai."

Easy, Roman, none of this is his doing. At least he expects Sihar to be available shortly and she's not away or being hidden. Maybe she's tied up in some meeting.

"That would be great, Dr.… Dr. Evans. I appreciate your kindness. I just arrived in Mumbai last night and didn't get a lot of sleep. You're American, right? Where ya from?"

It was forced conversation at best, fueled by his fourth coffee of the day plus a candy bar grabbed during a pit stop along the way.

ꙮ

The ironic similarities of their academic interests and the fact that both had undergone the "California experience" while completing their graduate studies was intriguing. For some reason Luke had opened up, foregoing his protective stance, explaining how Dr. Rishi had suddenly made an appearance at the company, how she'd become his *boss*, how she'd changed the program. He elaborated on his frustrations and disappointments with India. He even went into details about that first disgusting train ride from Mumbai and his dismay at not being able to experience Mumbai the way he'd planned.

He'd started down yet another tangent when the old "glance at the watch" trick shut down his diatribe, but still no Sihar Rishi and no answers about when she'd appear. It was time to bear down again.

"Listen, Luke, you asked who I was, but you didn't question my answer, so let me expand on it a bit. I was a research associate under Dr. Rishi when she was pioneering her culturing techniques. That was a few thousand years ago in Pennsylvania, shortly after she defended her PhD thesis. Our careers went in different directions, and as a venture capitalist I've recently funded an enterprise that provides the fetuses for this laboratory, at least *indirectly*. It wasn't set up that way, but that's it in a nutshell."

"Oh, then you must be with EMBRYIA, yes, I've seen your shipping containers in the receiving area. Are you here in that capacity?"

"No. Actually, I'm just the financing source behind EMBRYIA, but also a member of the board. I need to talk to Dr. Rishi about a different, very urgent matter."

He seems to be opening up. Should I risk it? Can't be too pushy here, or he may clam up. Besides, there may be a lot more to this operation than just this building, and he might not even be aware of the rest.

"Luke, I need to learn more about the use of extracted uteruses to incubate less mature fetuses. How much can you tell me?" He delivered the statement with intense eye contact. Evans didn't flinch, but he did look surprised, then abruptly defensive.

"I didn't realize anyone outside of a few of us here knew anything about that project. How do I know you're *really* with EMBRYIA? I need to speak to Dr. Rishi before I say anything more."

"Luke, I understand all that, and your reaction is appropriate, but I need your help. You say you're involved with the incubation side of things here, and you described how Dr. Rishi changed the program and all that. Well, something terribly wrong has happened and I need to understand the extent of this *project.* You simply *must* help me!"

There, he met my eyes again. I might have struck a chord.

"Surely at times you must wonder if you're pushing the fringes of human morality as well as corporate ethics. Trust me— I know… I'd had similar doubts when I was in your position. Do you really know what the hell is going on here? Are they telling you anything, or keeping you in the dark?"

Luke's expression went from stern to concern in a single breath, which he sucked in rather sharply. For a long moment he stared at his hands, then raised his gaze. The blue-eyed glare had turned somber.

"Let me show you something," he whispered as he pushed himself to his feet.

Chapter Twenty-Six

LUKE LED THE WAY, TAKING A SHORT FLIGHT OF STAIRS DOWN TO THE STORAGE rooms next to the incoming receiving area. Several of the doors had combination locks—another statement about the level of security. Then he stopped at the door labeled Unit #107, entering the combination as if he'd done it dozens of times every day. A firm tug and it slid back. Motion-sensing lights automatically clicked on as they entered. From that moment on, Dr. Luke Evans' body language and demeanor brought forth memories of another time, in another place, where one Roman Citrano had been a similar caregiver, devotedly maintaining and performing whatever was required to care for the precious cargo within the inner chambers. Even with all that prior experience, the smell and vibrant blood-hued colors were jarring, catching him off guard. He froze in his tracks, trying to refocus, to process the images, but the effect was no different than having a flash bulb go off in his face.

Luke didn't notice. He fixed his stare on the array of chambers in front of him as if he were looking at them for the first time. "We've been cultivating these uteruses and their fetuses for several weeks now. We refer to them as cocoons once the fetuses are inserted." He stepped back.

The glass chambers displayed hand-written index cards on the upper right hand corner, protected by a plastic sleeve. Would they in any way indicate that one of the chambers held the ghostly specimen belonging to Andrea? The first one showed no donor name, nothing that would show traceability. Of course not! Why would it? The uterus was no more than an incubating environment, not something destined for eventual human transplantation. The other cards were all the same format. His feelings were a mix of frustration and relief, then light-headedness. Luke had been watching him.

"Are you all right, Mr. Citrano?"

"A little… fatigued, I guess. I think maybe I should be sitting down. Can we talk somewhere, perhaps your office?"

"Let's go to my lab. We'll take the service elevator."

ꝏ

Their path took them past familiar yellow tape on the cement floor, often used to quarantine off a receiving area. In the far corner of this staging area sat a corrugated stainless-steel trunk, marked with a large white label. Large, dark blue letters riveted his attention and a second surge of dizziness unbalanced him. Bright spots flashed like a horde of fireflies, forcing him to squint as he read the label aloud: URGENT – FRESH SPECIMENS.

It had to contain Andrea's uterus… it must… it….

Fighting his way through the fluttering feeling in his head, he realized that Luke had dragged him the rest of the way to the elevator. Sitting slumped over, he couldn't break through to full consciousness, blacking out once more. It wasn't until his second awakening that he regained control of himself while sitting in what now turned out to be Luke's private lab. Someone was *helping* him drink a glass of cold water, someone young but with a motherly face. Luke was peering over her shoulder.

"You okay?" he asked. "You're a lot heavier than you look."

"I think so… uh, thanks." Roman waved the glass of water away, squinting up at the young woman. "Who might you be?"

She smiled. The motherly look was replaced by one much younger. Perhaps she was in her mid-twenties. "Luke and I work together. I was here in the lab when he carried you in. We don't get many visitors up here… my name is Kareem."

"I've never passed out like that before. It's embarrassing. I'm sorry… Kareem?"

"Actually, you're pale as a ghost. When was the last time you had anything to eat?"

He forced a smile, rubbing his eyes with his palms. "Probably two days ago. I slept most of the way on my flight here, got in late last night. Skipped breakfast this morning. I did grab a candy bar, though."

"And that sent you into a sugar slump, of course. I'll go find you something a little more substantial." She headed quickly out the door.

Thankful for privacy once more, he turned back to Luke. How much did the man know? How deeply was he entrenched in whatever was going on? Those chambers told a story of their own, and Luke was their caretaker. He was right in the middle of it.

"Luke, a woman very close to me was one of the... one of the... *donors* of the fetuses that were supplied from EMBRYIA. I... I don't know if you realize this, but these women are unaware that their aborted fetuses are being used in this manner. The fetuses were supposedly disposed of. Instead they have been shipped here."

Luke gasped. "Aborted? I had no idea! Nobody ever told us that. In fact, we were told the opposite, that they were all from miscarriages or natural deaths, and—"

"Think, Luke, think. What kind of organization would have access to hundreds upon hundreds of natural deaths? Do you really think there'd be some kind of fetal farm in Missouri, or maybe an international donation center set up like some Salvation Army thing? You've been lied to, and it's been deliberate. EMBYRIA performs abortions in mobile units... M-A-U is the short name... MAU. Have you ever heard that term? No? Well, unbeknownst to me, they've been secretly supplying your lab with preserved fetuses. No, let me correct that... *stolen* preserved fetuses... and most lately it appears that someone has also taken the liberty of extracting an unknown number of uteruses as well. I have reason to believe that my... my girlfriend's uterus may be sitting in that quarantined trunk we just saw in your receiving area. It was stolen from her during a routine abortion procedure!"

"My god! I never dreamt... that is I... that's not what we were told."

"Where did they say they were coming from? What exactly is the Company line? What did Dr. Rishi say about it? I want to understand the logic involved."

"Well, for openers we were constantly told that these fetuses came from multiple births, the results of various 'Assisted Reproductive Technologies' often simply referred to as 'ARTS.' I thought it was credible since infertility treatments sometimes produce multiple embryos, and once the physician is confident that one or more would survive to full term, he'd extract the remainder to make more room in the womb. This would increase the probability of survival for those remaining as well as improving the health conditions of the mother."

"He'd extract the remainder. That's what you're saying."

"Yes. Publications reveal that this 'multi-fetal reduction' has become more prevalent, but that the majority of the procedures were performed between the tenth and twelfth week. That part mystified me because we were getting both younger and much older fetuses. I asked, but never got an acceptable answer."

"No, you wouldn't under the circumstances, but weren't you at least curious when the answer seemed evasive?"

"I was pretty well swept up in the scientific end of things, but yes, I wondered all the more. There was no way to press the issue without jeopardizing my position here, but if what you say is true, then it all starts to make sense. I'm sure you wouldn't object to taking a look inside that container?"

"Let's go!" He shot to his feet, grasping the chair back until he was sure he could stay on his feet without help.

At that moment, Kareem returned with a can of Mr. Pibb, a garden salad and bag of chips on a small tray. She held the offering out with both hands. "Will this do?"

Roman took the can. "Thanks, but there's something more important right now."

Her quick glance at Luke was returned with a stony grimace. "Kareem, you'd better come with us," Luke said.

"What? Where are we going?"

Chapter Twenty-Seven

Camden

SHE CAME OUT OF HER DRUGGED SLEEP LITTLE BY LITTLE, SEEING A STRANGE CEILing and wondering why she couldn't hear anything. Then her hearing returned as if someone had flipped a switch, and with it the realization that someone was there with her, wherever "there" was.

"You are finally waking up?" a matronly voice asked. "Good. My name is Harriett. I'm one of your nurses, and I've just prepared a little for you to eat, here on this tray. Also, there are two pills in a cup, plus water. Take them first."

"Can I sit up?"

"Yes. Everything is fine. You are mending very well."

"Where am I?" Andrea asked.

"That is not important. When you are ready to leave, then you will be taken back to where you live." The overweight woman looked to be in her late forties, with steel-gray hair. Nurse or not, she didn't quite look the part, nor was there any cheer in her voice.

Pills? The very word rang alarm bells. One of the things any medical professional learned was to know *which* pills one was taking, or giving to someone, the dosages involved as well as the reasons. She stared into the small cup, and her alarm bells tripled in volume. They belonged to the morphine class, morphine sulphate, and the number on it, 200, was the dose in milligrams. She'd seen them multiple times, back in St. Paul. *Oramorph*! They wanted to keep her totally sedated… or kill her. Four hundred milligrams?

"What are these pills…? Hillary, is it?"

"Harriett. My name is Harriett. They are to help the healing. Have you any pain?"

"No. Why won't you tell me where I am? Is it a secret?" *They have nothing to do with healing!*

The location question was ignored.

"This door is to the bathroom," Harriett pointed. "I will unlock the door only when you need to go in there, so you push this button when you need it to be opened. For now, I will leave it unlocked, because there are two other doors, one to the outside hallway and another to a room like this one. No one is in that second room, so for now you can come and go as you wish, but the door to the hallway remains locked. That one is for staff only. Now here is a short menu so you can select from several meal types, and you have a TV here, and magazines. There is fresh air coming through the ceiling vent, and two lamps plus the overhead lights. Everything you need is here, but you must rest as much as possible. Do you have any questions?"

"How long have I been here?"

"Three days. Your doctor's name is Singh. He examined you earlier this morning, and will come back tomorrow. I leave now, and in two hours Nurse Greta will arrive and take over. Do you remember her?"

"Not very well. I think I fainted before I… before she… no, I don't remember her."

"You had hurt your head falling. Okay, if there are no questions, then I will leave you. Be sure to take both pills before you eat."

A moment later, the outside door clicked behind the nurse, then clicked again. Locked!

Something is very wrong here. I can't believe that Dr. Adams arranged this. There are no windows, doors all locked, and if I've really been here three days, then they've kept me drugged the whole time. If they talked to Marjorie Adams, then they already know I'm a threat to them, bleeding or not. So when am I no longer a threat? What would they do if…oh, no! They patched me up so I wouldn't blow the whistle, but the real reason was to lock me away. Couldn't do one without the other. I have to get out of here. Now!

Think, Andrea, think.

ꕥ

Harriett's departure was confirmed by the sound of a car being started close to the prison room wall. A check of the room's hallway door got nowhere. The lock was some kind of deadbolt hidden inside the wall. Next was the bathroom, but there were no answers there, either… except…

except the door to the hallway! It looked like the other two, but each of those opened out, into the two rooms. The hallway door opened in the other direction, *in*, and there… those *hinges!*

When she'd been a young girl, she'd lived in a house where a few of the inside doors had loose hinge pins that worked their way out from time to time, from no more than a fingernail's thickness to as much as an inch. They'd need to be tapped back into place every so often. *These* hinges were the same kind. One pin was up a full half inch, the other just a little, but enough so she could see a gap. She tried the upper one, twisting it. Yes, loose. The bottom one was also as loose, just not out as far.

She could be out of there in two minutes!

Her suitcase was alongside the bed, on a small table. In another five minutes she'd chosen a reasonable combination of clothes, but since there were no socks or stockings, she'd have to go barefoot in sandals. Her purse had been stripped of a few toiletry items like the nail file and clippers, but the remainder was untouched, including her wallet with four hundred dollars and all her credit cards.

It would be enough for the plan already forming in her mind, but first there were some things she needed to investigate. Harriett had said that the other nurse would be there in two hours. She could risk taking half an hour. A final check of her luggage, and she pulled out a light sweater. She might need that, at least until she could get to a department store.

She pulled the hinge pins with no trouble, then banged against the door with a hip. The hinges separated just as she knew they would, and the rest was easy. Information was next on the list. Walking up the flight of stairs brought a modicum of internal ache, but not pain. Further, she was dry below, no more blood and only an external pad. The information she hoped to find would probably be in a file cabinet. She found one, but it was locked and no key was in sight. Where would a key be kept? In a desk drawer?

There was no key in the reception room desk, but the top center drawer held what appeared to be a personnel folder that supplied the very data she wanted. Dr. Ram Singh was in fact a Dr. Marcus Levine—why was that name familiar?—and Harriett Crawford was formerly a medical assistant at a prison somewhere in New Jersey. Greta Huber was a citizen of Germany and had arrived in the U.S. from Amsterdam, in Holland. That was certainly odd. Neither nurse was important at this point. Levine seemed to be the key.

What was this? A letter written by Levine to someone in Clifton, New Jersey? Alicia Gregg? Six identical form letters were clipped together, all having to do with forwarding mail to an address. The space for the address was blank, to be filled in depending on where the mail was to be sent. Beneath the stack was an index card with the same address, plus a phone number.

The card went into her purse as she glanced at the digital clock on the desk, one that gave both time and date. She'd been there *five* days, not three! As for the building's location, that address was in the same folder—and the city was Camden. There was a huge, framed city map on the wall, with a street directory. Two minutes later she'd located the street in the north district, then figured which direction she should walk once outside. She'd need a cab, then a rental car. Rental car? There, a phone book on the desk. Four more minutes, and she had three of the popular rental agencies jotted down on a sticky-note. Twenty-five minutes spent. Time to leave.

She was slipping out through the loading area door when it came to her: Levine! Roman had mentioned a Levine once when he first described his excitement over what eventually became EMBRYIA. Yes, that was the name, Marcus Levine. And now he was Dr. Ram Singh? Levine/Singh was the one behind the MAUs. *He* was the one responsible for the theft of her uterus. Marjorie Adams had been so right in saying that whoever had performed such an atrocity was a criminal, but if the doctor in that MAU was following orders from someone superior to him? That superior was the bigger criminal. Somehow, the MAUs were being turned into something far removed from simple abortions, if there were such a thing. And Levine/Singh was very much a part of it.

She hadn't really checked the surgical rooms other than a glance. All the equipment was instantly recognizable, but only one had signs of recent activity. How about the shipping area? Could she afford the time it would take to check? Greta Huber could arrive at any moment, even though she wasn't due for more than an hour. If she did….

No, she had to check what she could, even if the danger was increasing by the second. Back through the door and into the building, but what was there to see in a shipping area? Records? Labels? No, nothing of that sort in sight, but what was this? In one corner, a stack of aluminum shipping containers occupied a large, wooden pallet. They were no ordinary boxes made of aluminum, but fully formed with fluted sides, heavy latches and a sealing ring. One was ajar. She pulled the twin halves further apart and peered inside.

ɛɔɞɜ

Thirty-five minutes from the moment she'd escaped her room, she left the building for the second time and headed east, barefooted in sandals with a sweater over one arm, carrying only her purse. Five blocks away she hailed a cab. On the way to the nearest car rental, a few more pieces fell into place in her rapidly developing plan. Roman could *never* have known about this. He'd have said something on that final call.

Oh, Roman, where are you?

Kolhapur

There was an obvious lack of security in the receiving area. One associate sat at a computer terminal in the far corner of the quarantine area. He looked up and continued with his work after receiving a nod from Luke, who was already entering his security I.D. into the combination lock of the container. Inside were four pliable, thick, semi-transparent plastic containers, slightly larger than a gallon of milk. Each contained fresh, nearly identical uteruses bathed in the same type of solution just seen in the storage rooms. Attached to each individual container was a series of two small hoses connected to an oxygen-rich air supply that created a low stream of bubbles, similar to an aerator in a fish aquarium. It was obvious that these uteruses had been previously treated and well-prepared for their long journey to AMBRIA. Who had such a training to do such a thing? Who'd instructed them? What procedures were being used?

The container wasn't something typically used for transplants; it had been designed for a specific purpose. Who'd done this? Where? How much of it was done under Levine's direction? Marcus implied something much more sinister behind the whole operation, someone was putting pressure on *him*, and that same someone or something was definitely behind AMBRIA. Now a shipping container *specifically* designed for shipping human organs long distances?

Luke pulled up one of the laminated documents tethered to each container. He slid it around so they could both read it, but a quick scan showed no donor information. In fact, there were no names at all, nothing to show who'd done the extractions, not a clue as to the team leader. Not until the final line.

It read 'Harvest Location: Camden, NJ, USA'. Harvest? Of all the sick!...

Gripping the container for support, he reached for the remaining three laminated pages. They *all* read the same: Camden, NJ, USA. One of these *had* to be from Andrea! Hands trembling, he stared at the cursed words, unable to accept them. *Harvest?* Another memory flashed from the past.

Luke was clearly stunned by the same word. He met Kareem's stare with mouth agape, shaking his head from side to side. "Wait a minute, this doesn't make sense. Harvest location? I've never seen those words on *anything* arriving here." He turned, "But, Dr. Rishi did recently mention a clinic here on the—"

"Roman!" It was Dr. Rishi's voice, directly behind them. "I thought you'd left days ago!"

She'd appeared without a sound. How could she have known to come to the receiving dock? The associate who'd been there had vanished, so he must have alerted her, but her tone was brittle, almost accusing. Why? The change was remarkable, almost sickening as the words on those cards.

"I came back to get the *other half* of that story you and Marcus conveniently forgot to tell me, Sihar, the half *you* could have told me before, but didn't. What the hell is going on here? Uteruses being taken from women... *stolen* from them? There's a full-scale operation going on here, a barbaric and illegal operation that's been set up in total secrecy, and I'm here to put an end to it. Someone... a personal friend of mine has been involved, her uterus is probably sitting right here in front of me… and now she's missing. There's every indication she was taken forcibly from her Philadelphia apartment, while still bleeding internally two days after her uterus was taken, and I was told she was brought here, to Kolhapur. I'm here to find her, so if you know where she is, tell me now. I hope to hell she's getting proper care, because if she isn't—hands off my arm, Sihar! I'm not your lab assistant anymore."

She softened her clutch, then let go. "I have only learned about this a couple of months ago and, like many of us here, I did not ask the appropriate questions regarding the source of our materials. There are many facilities on this campus, including an old clinic that has been here for over fifty years. I've only recently learned that they've used it to house the women donors in the original uterine extraction program. She may have been taken there."

"Donors? The original uterine extraction *program*? *PROGRAM*? Show me… NOW."

"Roman, you don't understand. This is bigger than *all* of us. They have political protection, more financing than you could ever imagine, and now high-level security that would intimidate any organized crime syndicate. If she *is* there, they'll never let her or you leave the facility. You *must* believe me."

"Is that a threat? Are you threatening *me*?"

"What I'm *trying* to tell you is that we… all of us… look, Roman, there are other ways to deal with this. Let me look into it. I'll ask about your personal friend, and—"

"No! There will be no 'looking into it,' Sihar, because you just finished describing the very crime syndicate you compared them to, whoever they are. I have no choice, and no time… she is very important to me. She was carrying our child… *was*… and now both our unborn fetus and her uterus are *specimens* here in your lab. I'm going to the authorities with every rotten thing that's going on here, and she is all the evidence I need to somehow stop this madness. Now let's go!"

"But—"

"Move! Take me there!"

Chapter Twenty-Eight

It took nearly twenty minutes in Rishi's poorly maintained Range Rover to reach what appeared to be the distant border of the property; this after numerous twists, turns and admitted errors on her part. Finally she slowed, approaching an old, dilapidated building nestled deeply in lush, densely overgrown woods. It looked more like an old, abandoned schoolhouse than a medical clinic, except for the few cars parked in front.

She pulled in, barely stopping before Roman was out and striding toward the monstrous wooden front door supporting a sign in bright red letters: AUTHORIZED PERSONNEL ONLY! The very nature of the oversized capital letters and even larger exclamation point indicated something more ominous than a simple warning to unauthorized personnel who might wander by.

Luke surged past him, hurdled the single porch step and yanked at the handle with both hands. Nothing! He braced his feet and redoubled his effort. It didn't budge. Was he trying to clear the way for some reason? Preparing to notify someone of their arrival? Or perhaps just exhibiting his own anger for not knowing all the truths about his place of employment? There was a real sense of urgency about the act, but it wasn't *his* woman who was missing. He'd professed to ignorance about the place, other than its existence. Rishi had apparently mentioned it to him quite recently.

A few seconds later he embarrassingly discovered that the door swung inward, not toward him. He shoved it open, wisely stepping aside for the even angrier man on his heels.

What the hell? The entryway gave the impression of a time-portal: lush overgrown forest and weather beaten façade of the building on one side; modern, stark-white interior of a clinic on the other. Everything inside had been totally refurbished in the same décor as the lobby and labs in the main building. There stood the familiar ivory-colored reception desk with its automated system, but in place of an elevator were two large doors with mirrored panels, not the usual frosted glass. Otherwise, they'd be identical to the swinging doors to an operating room. A sliver of light shone between them—no locks or deadbolts!

Kareem had lagged behind, but now she headed directly for the double doors with arm outstretched. At that instant, both doors burst open, one smashing into her hand. Her scream masked the sound of the doors smacking against their adjacent walls as she stumbled back. Luke was close enough to catch her as the doorway filled with the cause of her pain—a massive man, dressed all in black, a snarling pit bull defending his territory. He wore heavy boots and a brown shoulder holster holding a well-worn pistol. He'd also been running, or so it seemed, as his broad chest was heaving with each breath and he was sweating profusely.

There'd been only three people who could have warned him of their visit—Luke, Kareem… and Rishi. Had all those twists and turns of hers been deliberate? She confessed to making wrong turns twice, but were they wrong or deliberate? Buying time for this guard dog to make it to his post, perhaps?

Guard dog! Goldberg's description of the AMBRIA security guard fit this man perfectly. It had to be him. *He* was the one who'd taken Andrea! The sudden realization released a surge of fury.

"YOU BASTARD!" Roman screamed, lunging at the massive figure without thinking, hitting his target just above the belt with a firm right shoulder. His strength proved worthy. The Czech was caught off balance, crashing backwards into the now-closed doors. One of the mirrors broke and glass shattered everywhere while revealing its interior, a sterile-looking operating room, fully stocked with state-of-the-art equipment.

Roman lunged after his quarry, but slipped on the glass before he'd taken a single step. He broke the fall with both hands, but wasn't fast enough to evade the heavy black boot that came crashing down on his upper back. Something snapped inside his torso; he could hear it. But before he could react he was picked up by the back of his collar and thrown back out into the lobby, where he landed on his stomach, sliding on more of the broken glass with arms extended, vaguely aware that someone was running out the open front door.

It was Rishi!

The snapping sound must have been a rib, possibly multiple ribs, because his legs still worked. Rolling over, he clutched his chest and managed to sit up. The Czech stood a mere four feet away, glaring but making no sound.

"*You* know why I'm here, you sonofabitch. Where is she?"

"Sir, if you are talking of the American girl, the doctors said something about a complication when she was brought here." His voice was surprisingly considerate. "She was already not doing well when she arrived."

"What doctors? God dammit, this is no ordinary hospital or clinic. Is she here? Is this where you took her? If not—"

"I followed orders, sir. She is gone." He said it so matter-of-factly, his words still so vague that their meaning was lost.

"Gone where? WHERE DID YOU TAKE HER?" Wincing, Roman scrambled to gather his legs beneath him, shouting the words.

"She's with God, sir… she is dead." There was no emotion. The guard might as well have been reading from a script.

The anguished scream started deep from within, driven by pain far more severe than any damaged rib. It never made its way to the surface. Taking its place was the shock of hearing what his own psyche had rejected during the past two days. He was trapped in a ghastly nightmare without any means of waking up. Andrea was gone, gone as surely as if she'd been deliberately murdered. Was the murder weapon a scalpel, wielded illegally in a back-alley setting by an amateur who worked for little to nothing? No! It was his *own* doing, his *own* project. *He* was the abomination that had destroyed the very one he'd cared for so much. Others were involved, yes, but it couldn't have happened without Zorro, without *him*.

Roman started shaking violently. Nothing mattered anymore. If only he could reach that holster, he'd turn the gun on himself. One leap and he might be able to surprise the guard enough to grab it, then point it straight at his own abdomen. He'd suffer that pain on his way to death, just as Andrea had.

Kareem's sobs brought him back to some level of sanity as the guard stepped back with arms folded across his chest, alert to any move. There'd be no snatching of the gun, no heroics or suicidal moves. They had to get out of there, but not before learning where her body had been taken. He pulled himself up far enough to look the animal squarely in the face.

"Did you bring her here to die? Was that what they wanted?" Someone was standing at his elbow; it was Luke.

"Sir, there was no one who wanted to help her. She was left to die with her secret. Her body was put with the rest of them."

"The rest of… the *rest* of them? There were more?"

"Many of the early experiments did not work. We were not told what they were trying to do, but we brought unwanted prostitutes from many cities, from Mumbai to Bihar Sharif, here to this clinic. We did as we were told… and were paid well to do."

"Where are they? Where are the bodies?" He grabbed the guard's black shirt collar, aware that he might well be killed with a single blow. It mattered little. "For God's sake, man, if you're human at all, show us!"

The beast glared down and swept away the hands pulling at him, but said nothing. His attention had shifted to Luke, who chose that moment to ease past him and into the surgical suites beyond. He was back in moments with materials for a temporary splint to secure Kareem's badly broken wrist. It had swollen to nearly twice its original size.

The man in black simply waited until Luke finished applying the makeshift splint. He then broke his stance and moved towards the front door, finally turning, without expression. "Follow me," was all he said. There was something different about him, an aura of confusion. Was it because he was making a decision on his own?

He was already out the door.

Chapter Twenty-Nine

Despite Luke's support, the searing rib pain was spreading fast. Perhaps the fracture was more than just a crack, but there'd be no tape or sling, not until this was over. Triggered by pain and shock, endorphins were flooding his body, adding to the adrenaline that had driven him since leaving Rishi's vehicle. He was still shaking, but not from fear. He pushed through the pain, moving for the same door. They all did. Kareem was on Luke's other side, gingerly holding her splinted wrist.

Shortly they were on a narrow, wooded path surrounded by lush foliage. Although the ground was reasonably level, he was wheezing heavily. That could only mean the fracture was compound, possibly piercing a lung, but he shoved that concern into the recesses of his mind. More pressing was the question of *why* the same heartless brute involved in Andrea's kidnapping and death was now suddenly willing to cooperate, whereas Rishi was nowhere to be seen. Where had she gone, back to her Range Rover? Had she driven off and left them there?

They walked deeper into the brush for at least fifteen minutes before coming upon a small broken-down shed. Was *that* where they'd put the bodies… it couldn't be… and yet, the animal hadn't said how *many* bodies.

"There," the Czech grunted, but he was pointing beyond the shed at was what looked like a large, freshly tilled garden. He stared back at them. Roman, clutching his rib cage, was compelled to ask the very question whose answer he feared most.

"What are you showing us?"

"They are all buried there, in one grave. She was one of the very last ones." He pointed at a massive mound.

Flooded with fresh grief, he ran past the guard, searching even then for verification of some sort, falling to his knees, driving his fingers deep into the fresh soil. The searing pain in his ribcage further fueled his desperation, making him feel more lost, more alone, adding to his guilt. *It doesn't make sense. It's not happening. No! Not Andrea!*

Someone lightly touched his shoulder. It was Luke. "We need to go now… we need to bring others to help us."

He was right—there was nothing any of them could do—but she couldn't just be left this way, not yet. He crumpled, falling forward on his face into the dirt and curling up on his knees into a fetal position. For a long moment, tears soaked his face as he clamped his teeth together, blocking out any sound while he fought to turn it around in his head, to get a fresh grip. Grief wasn't what Andrea needed, not any more. Grief was his alone. She needed justice. This all had to come to an end. It was his duty to stop it, stop everything, stop the MAUs, stop EMBRYIA, even stop AMBRIA if he could. Surely the bastards couldn't have *that* much political clout. He could damage them, at least, expose their far-reaching crimes.

He tried collecting himself, tried getting up, then felt Luke's strong hands helping him. Kareem stood waiting while he regained his composure and again crossed his arms, pressing with one palm against the broken rib. Other than sobbing, she'd made no sound since the door had smashed into her hand. Now she showed silent compassion. He drew on her stoic strength.

As they headed back to the clinic, he realized the Czech was no longer with them. He'd disappeared, yes, but seemingly not back the way they'd come. Neither Luke nor Kareem had seen him leave. He was still out there in the woods somewhere—watching them.

Chapter Thirty

Rishi jammed on the brakes, skidding to a stop in a totally foreign part of the AMBRIA campus. She couldn't remember how she'd gotten there, or how to get back to the clinic, and now she was shaking too hard to drive. She covered her face with both hands, trying to think.

It had been fairly easy to lie to herself at the beginning, back when she'd rationalized the black market aspect of the operation. She'd side-stepped her own conscience by separating her scientific world from AMBRIA's business world. By knowingly turning a blind eye, she'd benefited from AMBRIA.

And then there was David Thomas, AMBRIA's man from the very start. Oh, how he'd masterfully twisted things. He controlled all records and all expenses. He monitored all communications, whether electronic or mail. She'd not been involved in any of the actual business dealings, nor had much been divulged to her from others in the organization. He'd seen to that. She'd been told only what he wanted her to hear, or what he thought she needed to know: AMBRIA was working legitimately with governments everywhere, striving to meet worldwide demands for transplantable organs; problems were being smoothed out day by day; she was not to focus on the company itself, or its dealings, only on her portion of the day to day operations.

All lies.

Marcus Levine was yet another she could blame, a slithering, two-tongued snake even though he was brilliant in his own right. She'd listened to his "versions" of the facts, suspicious of his motives from the beginning, yet too willing to let him go unchallenged. Yes, he'd been chosen—or so he claimed—just as she had, as Roman had, but Marcus *always* had a reasonable explanation for *everything*, or at least a plausible excuse.

She'd suppressed the nagging suspicion that he might in fact be calling the shots for the syndicate as far as the Kolhapur operations were concerned. He definitely made all the EMBRYIA-related decisions, but he was the *victim* whenever it suited his purposes, confiding all sorts of things to gain her confidence. Later he'd change his tune. Thanks to him, she'd found some of David's lies almost believable, but still she'd known that AMBRIA was in fact concealing the Kolhapur operation as much as possible, that those so-called governments were being fed all sorts of propaganda about the sources of organs, about donors.

Records were being falsified, but she'd done nothing to pursue the fact. She didn't want to know details, for without knowledge she had no choice but to continue in the usual way. Without proof, who could expect her to do anything else? Why had she been so willing to be led like a docile sheep? There had been a time, early in her career, when she'd been a fearless advocate for truth. No longer. Her wall of integrity had eroded now to rubble.

She'd never trusted David Thomas, but she'd ignored her innate common sense and washed her own mind of its doubts in order to work with him and his associates. Financial types, she'd rationalized, always seemed disingenuous. She was, after all, realizing a personal dream through her work. If the AMBRIA management appeared to function more like the Nazis of Hitler's time, she was no worse off than the scientists and researchers of those days. *They'd* despised their masters, but they'd survived. She'd survive, as they had. In surviving, she'd become the very thing she despised. Her fears had grown stronger, but still she'd ignored them. After all, she was Dr. Sihar Rishi. Her reputation was insulation enough. She could claim plausible deniability and point at those who'd deliberately kept the truth from her, who'd fed her lies.

Innocence was no longer possible. She'd found it possible to convince others that she'd accepted their assurances about fetus sources, but at the cost of more personal guilt. Any high-schooler would have been able to conclude that the numbers didn't add up. Aside from those specimens from EMBRYIA, the rest were supposedly from "similar" sources, never identified. The number of MAUs was known and the survival rate of fetuses was a solid number, no longer an estimate, but the influx of fetuses arriving at the lab was twenty percent higher than those numbers supported. Were there MAUs operating in another venue, controlled by less savory factors? Had she questioned the discrepancy even slightly? No!

The uterus "whitewash" was worse. By the time she'd been fed the typical cover story on uterus origins and donors, she'd already compromised her integrity beyond repair. Her head was capable only of moving up and down, not side to side. Yes. I agree. I accept. You are right. The end justifies the means. You just provide the materials. I will perform the miracles you demand.

She'd no longer cared. Now she couldn't even leave AMBRIA for a position somewhere else, for if this travesty on human dignity were to be exposed, she'd be exposed with it. It was too late to escape. She'd known it was all a lie, that by continuing to maintain her silence she was at worst an accessory to murder. Sleeping pills had helped her sleepless nights, but she could do nothing but play AMBRIA's game during her waking hours. She'd become their watchdog, jealously guarding the horrible secrets she'd helped bring about.

Roman's sudden arrival was the turning point. When he'd returned to the States, just days ago, she'd breathed a sigh of relief, but now his return and stunning revelation had triggered all sorts of alarm bells. He couldn't be allowed inside the clinic. She'd alerted security, never expecting them to send Malovec, but then she had no idea who AMBRIA maintained for security there in Kolhapur. As far as she knew, Malovec was still in the States.

And now?

She had to re-assemble whatever character and conviction she had left. She rallied her forgotten courage and would finally attempt to do the right thing. She'd first return to the clinic to face whatever awaited her there. She dried her eyes and restarted the engine. She couldn't have made more than a few wrong turns. If she backtracked....

Chapter Thirty-One

Camden

THE CAR WAS A FOUR-YEAR-OLD FORD WITH SIXTY THOUSAND MILES ON IT. A comfortably nondescript grey, it had four new tires. The dealer came down $1500 when she offered cash, but it wasn't until later that she discovered the dome light wouldn't come on. Probably just a bulb.

She'd sold her former car after accepting the Philly job, since garaging a car in any big city such as Philadelphia would be too expensive. St. Paul was a little different, because her apartment there had its own parking, but compared to renting a car for the overall plan she was hatching, buying a used one seemed more reasonable. It was also *much* safer. Cash was untraceable, unlike credit cards, and there was no way of knowing what kind of people she might be up against. Who were they? What were their resources? How had Roman come to be involved in the first place? He was a venture capitalist, yes, but what had drawn this Levine person to Zorro Medical? Certainly not the company name.

Her questions all pointed to a single answer: power.

A simple phone call to her bank in St. Paul, and the money transfer was completed within an hour. She waited out the time in the diner across the street, eating what might have been her first real meal in five or six days. By three that afternoon, she was cleared to drive away on temporary "plates," but first she'd locate a motel somewhere, then the nearest shopping mall. The grey Ford with the broken bulb could wait until the following morning, after she'd returned the rental car.

As for her apartment, it might be watched. She couldn't risk going back there, not until this was over. From this point on she was a fugitive. Her life was in danger.

During her time in the diner, she mulled over the letter in the folder. She'd scanned the single page, but it all had to do with forwarding mail to "the Minneapolis address." Alicia Gregg seemed to be an associate, not a client, rather like an attorney paid to forward mail. Levine had addressed her as Alicia, not Mrs. Gregg or even Ms. Gregg, but whatever was to be forwarded wasn't described. Did that indicate some sort of established pattern? Was she holding mail for Levine, or something else, or both? What was their relationship?

Clifton was not much more than an hour north on the Jersey Turnpike, and Alicia Gregg had answers.

Kolhapur

Rishi was waiting in the Range Rover when they got back. Her expression was a mixture of shock and fear. Roman fought down his emotions, deciding to hear what she had to say, but before he could speak his mind she preempted him.

"I should not have run out. I panicked, and I'm sorry. I'm terribly sorry about your loss, Roman. I can only imagine how you must feel. However, please hear me out before you damn me. I had no intention of putting you all in harm's way, no idea of the violence you and Kareem came to suffer. I'm especially shocked by that awful man. He's the worst I've ever imagined in any human being. I can tell you now that his name is Malovec and that he was formerly a Czech assassin—that's right, someone our Dutch investors found under a rock in some swamp. He was never introduced to me… I found out by keeping my ears open and my mouth shut. It has become unhealthy to ask the wrong types of questions since he was put in charge of security.

"While you three have been gone, I've been trying to come to grips with what we all now know, the very things I've suspected for some time. As I said before we came here, I did not ask the appropriate questions about anything. Roman, please believe me that, although I've been highly suspicious for many months now, I did not have the details necessary to take any action against them. I have certain avenues open to me, but without evidence I can do nothing. You just can't imagine how powerful these people are. Nevertheless, I'm guilty of looking the other way on many things, and I admit it. Luke and Kareem, you have both been spared my torture, for you are closer to the specific tasks of your daily work whereas I'm dealing with the corporate, political side of AMBRIA directly.

"Roman, I can no longer look the other way. When we get back to the main building, I want you all to give me roughly half an hour inside. I must gather some… materials. Then we shall reconvene *outside* of the building, perhaps here in the car, and discuss what we should do. I warn you again that we are dealing with a monster that could squash us all like bugs. Our main concern should be our own safety, but if we are to do anything to stop these horrible atrocities, risks must be taken."

There was silence from the back seat. She twisted around, looking back. Luke had his arm around Kareem, whose eyes were closed.

"Kareem, you need to pull any records associated with the latest specimens. And Luke, please assemble proof that all fetuses were received from EMBRYIA. All, not some." She didn't wait for their responses. "Take the *original* documents, no time for copies. You must bring them with you when you leave for the States with Roman, which must happen as quickly as possible. Roman, they may be looking for you at the Mumbai Airport, so I would suggest driving to Goa and flying from there to Delhi, and then from Delhi to perhaps France or Britain. Are you in great pain?"

"He broke at least one of my ribs. I'm managing so far."

"There is a hospital in Goa. They will assess the damage. Tell them you and Kareem were in a car accident, anything but the truth to avoid further questions and delays. When you get to the States, seek government protection. Once you have it, you should use the documents, but not before. Be very careful and move as quickly as you can."

"What about you?"

"There is something I must do, now that I know the truth. Do not worry about me. Think only of yourself, Roman… you, Luke and Kareem. Do you have money?"

"Not enough for three people. My credit card is pretty well at its limit."

She reached into the glove box and held out an envelope. "Don't use credit cards at all, any of you. This contains 500,000 Rupees in large bills. I began carrying it for emergencies many months ago. Take it. Pay cash for your tickets and anything else."

Roman hesitated. "I don't understand. You seem to be saying AMBRIA is—"

"I'm simply repeating what I said earlier. Your lady friend was brought here, and they know that. She apparently died while here, which they also know, and then you returned here just a few days after leaving for the States. They won't *let* you leave now, not on your terms, only on theirs, and now that Luke and Kareem are involved, all of you are in terrible danger. If you think otherwise, remember who they sent to stop you at the clinic, a former assassin. You've confirmed my suspicions about a burial site, something I'm quite sure he was *not* supposed to show you. That may have been his last act of compassion before he exterminates all of you. It's time to get the evidence we need." She started the engine. "If there is to be trouble, they will confront me right there in the lobby."

ℵ

Once she'd left the SUV, she changed her mind about the front lobby, letting herself in at the back door and taking the stairs in lieu of the elevator. It was out of her hands now; she'd no longer have to deal with any of it. She was a clinical researcher, a biologist trained to solve genetic and physiological problems, not a business manager paid to deal with such monstrous activities. It was all going to be exposed, sooner or later, and who better than Roman for the messenger? He could handle it. He'd already shown he had the right stuff as a person, but with incriminating evidence in hand, who could tell what damage he might be able to do to them?

Her own career was over. With disclosure, she'd now lose the respect of her colleagues, and—more importantly—that of her family. Standing in her office, she gazed at the long series of framed diplomas, awards and certificates, now meaningless.

AMBRIA would never release her. They'd make her their scapegoat.

She closed her office door and secured it, then opened a locked cabinet on the far side of her office and removed one of three cylinders about the size of small hand-held fire extinguisher. Sitting behind her desk she stared at the three vials containing the fetuses shown to Roman during his first visit. There was something so elegant, so pure and precious about the delicate geometric folds in their embryonic state. What others may have viewed as scary and grotesque, she found comforting and peaceful. She continued to caress the smooth surface of their glass coffins and once again scanned the wall of certificates. On the corner of her desk stood her official notice that she was to be the 2009 recipient of the Nobel Prize for Physiology and Medicine. She would be the 193rd laureate of this majestic award. It would be the ultimate embarrassment to have such an honor bestowed only to have it redacted later in front of all her peers.

She'd never felt so alone, so ashamed.

She placed the cold canister between her knees and slid her chair back just far enough so she could place her head on the edge of her desk, looking down on the white and red label that read, "100% Formalin Gas – Toxic." Without bothering to wipe the tears now falling from her chin, she opened the valve with two quick turns and folded her arms in front of her, laying her forehead gently on her forearms. She closed her swollen eyes as she deeply inhaled the familiar smell of the formaldehyde. Within seconds the thick gas had burned the lining of her nose, then the entire volume of her lungs.

As the pain sensors deep in her brain started processing the destruction of her vital organs, her body convulsed and she was pathologically dead before her body hit the floor.

Chapter Thirty-Two

ROMAN STARED AT HIS WATCH. "SHE WANTED US TO GIVE HER THIRTY MINUTES. Was that before we all came back here, or just a head start before we followed her?" He took a careful breath and reached for the door handle of the Range Rover.

Luke shook his head. "I… I don't know. I think she meant before we all came back here. Maybe we should all go in now? Something must be wrong, because she headed around to the back entrance. I thought she was going through the lobby."

Roman nodded, wincing with just the slightest of movement. "Do you suppose she's trying to avoid something, or someone? How can they confront her in the lobby if she uses the back entrance? What's back there?"

"Just the loading dock and those labs where we were, and the service elevator. We all use it because employee parking is at that far end of the building. Maybe she changed her mind. She said she had to get some materials, and her office is on the top floor. She'll use the stairs."

"Service elevator?"

"Yes. Maybe she thinks someone will be watching the elevator up front. They could be waiting behind the front stairway exit door, although they'd have to listen through it because it doesn't have any window. I think Kareem and I should go in the back way, too. We all should. You can take the service elevator to the top floor. Dr. Rishi's office is around the corner to your left."

"I remembered that, but don't remember any door in the lobby."

"It doesn't have a knob or handle on the lobby side."

"Okay, yeah. That's what she used a few days ago. Well, the longer we sit here, the less likely we are to get out of here in one piece, according to her. Let's move."

He paid for the effort in fresh pain. While Luke and Kareem were carrying out their assignments, he'd head for Rishi's office, just in case. Everything she'd said might be true, but there might also be things unsaid. *They* could apply to anyone, not just a former assassin. *They* were powerful, but how and where were they powerful? Here in Kolhapur? Were they her bosses? He glanced again at his watch. Already past 6 P.M. There was a good chance the senior staff was already gone, whoever they were. And if they were still there?

The service elevator was set up with wood bumper rails and padded movers' blankets on the walls. It was used mostly between the first and second floors to move equipment between the labs, but it went to the top floor. Luke explained that his small personal lab and office were up there, so Kareem would go up first, using the stairs while Roman was to wait several minutes before taking the elevator. Stairs were out of the question, even if they were much safer. Meanwhile, the information Luke needed to get would be in the shipping department files.

Once they were all back together, Roman's rental car would be their next goal—assuming no one was watching or guarding it. No one mentioned Rishi. She'd either be there, or not.

ꕥ

Even though Luke did most of his work in the labs, his status as lab manager afforded him a smallish office on the top floor, with a desk and single lab bench, including sink and various amenities—more like a doctor's examining room than office. It was actually at the other end of the building, but he still preferred using the service elevator. He kept his lab notebooks on a shelf, Kareem knew. Older ones were organized in black "notebook jackets," while more recent ones were stacked horizontally between bookends. She headed for those first, thankful she hadn't encountered any of her colleagues. Her splinted wrist would have been hard to explain. As for pain, her training in yoga had taught her that, with proper concentration and breathing, it could be spread all over her body, thereby diluting itself. The human brain could be fooled at times.

All the offices, except for one, had glass fronts, but the panes were frosted. She'd paused for several long moments, listening, but could hear nothing. There was just one office with the lights on, the one with the clear glass! It belonged to that creepy financial man, David Thomas. Luke didn't like him one bit, calling him Janus in private and showing her a picture of the mythical two-faced Roman god of beginnings and endings and other things. She suddenly froze. Roman god... *Roman* from the United

States? Was there some esoteric connection there, something fateful? Her wrist began to throb mercilessly with that possibility. No matter, since she had no choice but to continue.

She slipped by several offices on little cat feet, stopping once more to listen. Why was that office lit up? Was that disturbing Mr.Thomas in there? Then she heard it—a few spoken words, almost whispered, then silence once again. Talking to someone on the phone? That's what it sounded like, except that—*there!* Yes, it had to be him, and he was definitely on the phone.

She crept forward inch by inch until she could see just a sliver of his form behind the desk. He had his back to the window wall that formed his office, talking toward the interior wall with a voice so low she could barely hear it, close as she was. Could she slide by without being seen?

He didn't seem to move… oh, he was looking down at something he was holding. Now! In four quick steps she was past the clear glass and safe, at least for the moment. As long as he didn't step out into the hall before she got to Luke's office, she'd be okay.

At Luke's office she stopped halfway to the shelf. Some of the recent lab books were missing! There was a gap between the bookend and remaining books, some of which had slumped down. Then she spotted a small pile on Luke's desk. He'd been organizing them. An already-filled jacket occupied one corner of the desk, and half a dozen individual lab books were spread out awaiting front-cover labels, along with a stack of papers that looked like summary sheets. They were, going back many months.

Relieved, she started gathering the books, pausing when she caught the title of one in particular: *Cocoon Viability.* So how long had Luke been really working on this special project? Given the volume of his lab books, he'd kept it from her for a long time. Why wouldn't he discuss it with her, often saying only that it was highly confidential, something he was asked to do on his own. Even though her wrist was throbbing and the Czech was out there lurking about somewhere, even though she'd promised to meet up with Luke and Roman in short order, she couldn't resist scanning through the first several pages. Luke's style of note-taking made it easy to put the pieces together quickly. It was all there: the essence of his special project, the need for more uteruses, the intensity of what was happening behind all the closed and locked doors throughout the facilities.

He'd *known* something was fishy! He hadn't told her, but then he didn't share everything about his projects. Here he was more than suggesting, he was declaring what he knew and suspected. Wasn't that dangerous? If someone read these books, wouldn't they immediately do something? Luke could get himself in real trouble. She was suddenly afraid for herself as well as for him.

They all had to get out of India, and these lab books were her responsibility, those and the loose papers. They were precisely what Dr. Rishi wanted, a history of fetuses processed to date, with data covering everything including origins. It was all there, but she'd only have one good hand and the books were slippery. She could manage half a dozen, no more, plus the stack of papers. She slipped those inside the Cocoon Viability notebook.

Goa was no more than two hours away by car. She could manage her pain that long, knowing the hospital there would take her in immediately. She'd have something to ease the pain, once they set her bones and made the cast. Dr. Rishi was right about going south instead of north to Mumbai. The Goa airport was too small for international air travel, but not so small they couldn't get to Delhi. Anyone trying to intercept them would naturally assume they'd use Mumbai and would watch the airport there.

She stacked the notebooks, placing *Cocoon Viability* on top, then left with everything cradled in the crook of her good arm, careful to listen before stepping back into the long corridor.

That office was still lit up! This time she listened at least half a minute before deciding no one was talking on the phone. If she took the main elevator down one floor—no, that wouldn't work. There was no other option but to pass that office a second time, but then she had every reason to be in the building at this time of day. Hadn't she sometimes worked quite late in the lab?

She was almost to the lighted office when the door was flung open and David Thomas stepped into the aisle, blocking her path. He had an odd look on his face.

"Can I help you?" he said.

Chapter Thirty-Three

STARTLED, SHE FORCED A SMILE NEVERTHELESS, STRUGGLING TO MAINTAIN HER full-nelson grip on the bundle of papers and lab notebooks. "No, but thank you anyway. I just had some things I promised I'd do for Luke… Dr. Evans… coordinating his lab notes. I often help him this way. We work together."

"You seem nervous about something. Are you sure I can't help in any way?" He took another step, blocking her completely. When she twisted slightly, the slippery lab books began to slide and the two top books fell, spilling the loose papers all over the floor. *Cocoon Viability* landed open, pages down and labeled cover facing up.

Thomas bent down as if to recover them, but made no move to pick up anything. He stood again, immediately grabbing her bad arm and pulling her into his office. Everything she was holding tumbled to the floor, papers fluttering in every direction.

"Why… why are you doing this?" she cried.

"Who gave these to you?"

"I'm… it's… they're Dr. Evans' notebooks. I usually help him during the day, but I haven't had the time, so I decided I could do them at home."

"You have no authority to be handling this material, my dear. This is very delicate and proprietary work." He released his hold. "Do you have any idea of their contents?" His voice had turned from harsh and brittle to velvety. "I'm sorry, but I do not know your name." His British accent sounding distinctly more pronounced than ever.

"I'm Kareem," she replied, wondering why he wasn't inquiring about her wrist. He'd looked at it several times. Are you aware of what the company is doing to women for the sake of expanding the business?"

"Of course, my dear, I'm the Chief Financial Officer here. It's my job to not only know details, but to ensure that this organization is run efficiently and profitably." His smile was insidious. "But I've *also* been informed that there has been a breach in security and that our mission here may have been compromised. That is why I thought it prudent to question you in the hallway. Might you know anything about that?" He seemed to be gloating. Had he even heard what she said?

"Sir, I mean do you *really* know what has happened... that women have lost their lives during experiments to remove and maintain their uteruses? My god, there is a mass grave not far from here. I don't suppose they tell you things like that." Her words had come tumbling out, uncontrolled. Hearing them made it seem surreal, as in some terrifying nightmare.

His smile became a leer. He circled her like a hawk sizing up its prey. "You need to realize that those poor miserable women were of no value to society, none. They were drug-addicted, homeless prostitutes who, only because of our efforts, have now actually contributed something of value from their pathetic lives. We *gave* them some worth... some purpose. What we have learned from them has given us the ability to cultivate an exponential number of fetuses, hundreds of thousands of potential organs that otherwise would have been lost. What AMBRIA has done for mankind will be a landmark in the history of healthcare. We will offer survivability, new life, new hope and even cures for many diseases that would have otherwise taken generations to develop." His face appeared cool and calculated as he continued. "It is people like *you* who are our biggest problem. Your misguided sense of values has no place in organizations like ours, for you fail to see the importance of our mission. You and others like you lack vision. You are obstacles, all of you."

He went to his door and closed it hard, then faced her. "So tell me, young lady, just *who* do you expect to inform about these activities and what exactly do you intend to do about it? Hmmm?"

Her heart was pounding. She moved further into his office, backing up until she was behind his desk. How could she have mistaken him for someone who cared about human life, about right and wrong? He was just another of those sociopathic corporate executives who'd let nothing stand between them and success. He suspected *her* of being someone who could jeopardize his divine mission.

A quick glance at his desk showed him to be in the process of cleaning out his own files. Yes, there was the file drawer, open. On the floor was a large carry-on bag half full of documents, and there on his desk an open briefcase. Money! Euros and dollars, each banded into thick stacks. A pair of passports lay there. He was running! She was in real danger now, with no means of escape.

Suddenly he was at her side, his face contorted, reaching for her broken wrist and snapping it back with such force as to break Luke's temporary splint. Radius and ulna were misaligned for the second time, but now the fragmented ends broke through her skin, severing blood vessels. Blood spewed from an artery, splattering all over the white marble floor. A wave of intense pain coursed through her body, but her scream was cut short by a strong hand across her mouth. In a flash, she was pinned on his desk with his bloodied hand spread across her face, smashing her head down hard. He momentarily removed his hand, but then it was back. She felt metal against her cheek. No! Desperate, she clawed at it with her good hand, but he was quicker.

She felt the blow to her side, just below her upraised arm. He'd stabbed her with whatever he was clutching, then stabbed her again. By the time pain registered, his hand was back across her mouth again, stifling any sound she might make. It no longer held the metal object. It had happened so quickly she couldn't even react. A letter opener! That's what the metal thing was. As she realized the terrible truth, her eyes were already losing focus. Everything was a blur. She was falling.

From her crumpled position on the floor, she watched him go to the water cooler, where he washed his hands and shook them dry. Then the room darkened. She was aware of him stepping over her, of the sounds of zippers being zipped, of the briefcase being snapped shut. A scuffle of papers, and then everything was quiet.

She knew where he'd stabbed her. A letter opener was usually five or six inches long. The distance to her heart was less. She fought to fill her lungs one more time, but there was no response. Other than the sensation of being very cold, she felt nothing.

Janus… the god of beginnings and endings. Luke had been right.

Chapter Thirty-Four

ROMAN STOOD NEXT TO THE SERVICE ELEVATOR FOR NEARLY TEN MINUTES, deter-mining the threshold of how high he could lift his ribcage allowing himself to breath. It entailed expanding his chest, then using his abdomen to pull down the diaphragm. He just needed a little practice, now that his broken rib or ribs had inflamed his whole left side. After that, he had to learn to walk while breathing the same way. It wasn't going to be easy, but he could tough this thing out.

When he finally did take the elevator, he arrived at the top floor thinking more about his posture and breathing than anything else. He stepped gingerly out, careful not to bend his torso the slightest bit. His only other visit to Rishi's office had begun with the front elevator, not the one in back. For a long moment, he was disoriented, knowing only that her office was at the rear of the building. Then he remembered Luke saying to turn left. The subtle body twist made him wince, but there it was, just around the corner, and barely in time, too. He could hear a man's voice from the opposite direction, faint but definite.

The light in Rishi's office was on, but her glass office panes were frosted, preventing him from seeing anything at all. She was probably still in there, but for safety's sake he'd best not join her until he understood what that distant voice might mean. There shouldn't have been anyone in these offices at this hour. There was an alcove at the end of the hall in that direction. He made his way to it, holding his side, then stepped into the shadows, out of sight. Yes—footsteps, growing louder. They stopped—right at the elevator by the sound of it! Oh, no… the elevator was probably still there, tipping off anyone that someone had just used it. If there was anyone still working on this floor, other than Rishi….

Think, Roman! Kareem used the elevator when she was on her way to Luke's lab, yet it was back there at the loading dock when you were ready to use it. That means it automatically returns to the main floor every time, so relax. If those were a man's footsteps, he's waiting for it to come up. Yes, that's the hydraulic pump you're hearing.

The wait was less than a minute. He heard the doors open, close, then nothing at all aside from a metallic sigh from the elevator's main piston. He exhaled carefully. A minute or so later and he'd have encountered whoever it was, but now there was silence. Perhaps it was safe?

He returned to Rishi's office door, doubtful about knocking. What might she think if she was in the middle of something? It would be better to simply stick his head inside and whisper her name. If she wondered why he was there, he'd ask her to identify two or three of the major AMBRIA officers responsible for the Kolhapur operation. The names were listed with many others in the front lobby, but not their titles or functions. Even if she chose to stay behind—which she'd hinted she was going to do—he'd need those names.

The door was unlocked, just as he'd hoped, but his first careful breath changed everything in a heartbeat. Formaldehyde gas! It was diluted, to be sure, but already his eyes and nose felt irritated. He covered his nose with his shirtsleeve and inched forward, suspecting she was dead even before he saw her body on the floor. Her eyes were staring outward. Blood oozed from her nose and parted lips. Her fall must have knocked the sample fetus vials onto the floor, but only the largest was broken. It had held the 16-week fetus, which now was lying only inches from her face, positioned as though it was looking directly back at her.

The Czech! He must have been inside the building, jumping her as she unlocked her door. Maybe he'd been wearing a gas mask and had knocked her out with a single, fatal whiff. Nothing else in the office was touched, nothing strewn about. It was time to exit. No sleeve material could stop further damage to his mucous membranes.

He backed out, closing the door as noiselessly as possible as he steeled himself for what might await him down the hall. That male voice could have been the assassin, and Luke's lab was at the other end of the building, near the front. That would mean that Kareem….

A spasm of fresh pain forced him to pause long enough to resume his abdominal breathing. Then, carefully, he returned to the elevator and from there followed the hallway around a bend. There was no one in sight and everything was quiet, but as he made his way to the far end he passed an open office door with the name David Thomas on it. Inside lay the

Czech's second victim—Kareem—slumped like a rag doll in the middle of the floor with what appeared to be a dagger protruding from her ribcage, almost where his own rib had been broken. No, not a dagger... something with an acrylic handle.

He took one step into the gruesome chamber. The handle was emblazoned with the gleaming AMBRIA emblem. A letter opener? Why would the Czech have used such a weapon? Or... was the murderer David Thomas? That made more sense. Thomas would have had a letter opener on his desk. Yes, it *had* to be Thomas, whatever his function within AMBRIA might be. A glance at items around the office said he was the operation's finance guy. He'd most likely stopped Kareem as she tried to pass. Perhaps she'd already snagged the records she was after, and he'd seen what she was carrying.

Conjecture, yes, but surely she'd not be dismissed as a lone operator, someone he needed to dispatch so brutally. Her presence in the building on this particular floor could mean that he'd gone looking for others. Rishi? No, he wouldn't have used gas to end her life—probably didn't even have access to it. The Czech might well have access to all locked supplies, but what about Luke's safety? Which of the two murderers would go looking for him?

Assuming Luke had found what he was looking for, he'd have gone out the back door and around the building. He'd be somewhere outside, waiting. Perhaps David Thomas was at the back landing right now, watching to see if anyone else used the service elevator. Maybe there were others at the front entrance, waiting inside the lobby elevator or even behind that exit door Luke had described. There was no other course but to use the front stairs and deal with whatever was at the bottom.

This time he'd be dealing with his own ungodly death.

He glided his way to the front of the building, nearly crying out when he pushed the crash bar on the stairway exit door. In the process of trying to maintain silence, he'd forgotten to keep his torso stiff! The new jolt to his senses made stairs seem like a nightmare in the offing, but he had to use them. Maybe if he went down sideways, one step at a time, right leg down and left leg trailing. Yes, that seemed to work.

Breathe with the abdomen, keep the torso stiff, maintain your balance, ease the right leg down. That's it. Now regain your balance, and left leg down. Great! Only forty or fifty more steps to go. What will you do if there's really someone down there? What will you say?

There really was no way out—he'd just have to wing it. He'd made it to the first landing without losing focus or making noise. Time to listen. He checked his watch. Two minutes gone, and still no sounds. The story was the same at the next landing, and the next, but then he thought he heard someone clearing his throat. It was the slightest of sounds, but enough to double his heart rate. No use—if there'd been someone this side of that lobby exit door, it was all over. He was a mere two dozen steps from the bottom.

Then he heard the noise again, but it was more like the building creaking, a sound he'd never have heard if not for the total silence otherwise.

Breathe with the abdomen, keep the torso stiff, maintain….

Finally he was staring at the last remaining door. Another crash bar! Could he be as noiseless with this one as the one at the top floor? This time he focused more on balance, backing up against the bar. A small click—and he felt it give. Only if the elevator doors were open could a sound like that be heard.

He stepped carefully through the door, relieved to see the elevator doors were shut. Half a dozen steps now separated him from the entry door. He clenched his jaw and eased the exit door shut, not allowing it to latch. Then he turned, feeling the warm sun on his face. He was still alive.

ജ്യ

Luke heaved a sigh of concern. Roman and Kareem should both have been back twenty minutes ago, but in Roman's case the delay was understandable. The man was moving slower than a sleepy turtle, appearing to be in deep pain with every step. He'd come out the front entrance unchallenged, which was a good sign since he'd been on the top floor. That was the dangerous floor, but his success in negotiating it meant that Kareem had probably been just as lucky.

Roman was nearly back to the rental car, but still no Kareem. Why hadn't she used the front stairs too? His office wasn't more than fifty feet from the stairway.

"Where's Kareem?" he asked, speaking low when Roman was close enough. "She should have been here even before I was."

Roman stopped. His voice conveyed a mixture of sadness and panic. "Luke… I… she's not coming with us." He paused. "She's dead, Luke. So is Rishi. I think the Czech killed Rishi, but I can only guess about Kareem. She was in David Thomas's office… I think he caught her and killed her."

"No! Oh, no, not my Kareem! Jesus, no! I *knew* that bastard was—"

"She probably had your documents with her, Luke. They weren't there with her. I'm sorry. I didn't know she was… anyone you… but I can tell she was. It seems we've both lost someone—"

"Precious. She was precious, Roman." He blinked back sudden tears. "Oh, why is this all happening? This morning… before you came… we were happy. Well… more than happy, we had something more than just our jobs here. Now everything is gone."

"We have to leave… *now* Luke, right now! We need to get to the American Embassy in Mumbai. Somebody has to know what's going on here, what happened."

"I thought we were going to Goa. Rishi said—"

"There's no embassy there. We both need protection, and we have to know who we're talking to. Here, you drive." He handed over the car keys. "I can hold on if I move slowly enough and am really careful."

"But it's nearly a whole day's drive, Roman. Besides, we probably won't even get out of here. What if they're just waiting for us out where this complex meets the main road?"

"We take that chance, which is no different if we were heading for Goa. Kareem gave her life trying to get us those documents. Rishi's dead because they suspected she was turning against them. Remember, *she* was the one who took us to the clinic. Our only chance now, without the records Kareem was to bring out, is to raise the alarm as soon as we can. We have to report these murders and those in the… in the burial ground. The U.S. Embassy will shelter us. At least *they* aren't corrupt. AMBRIA doesn't own them."

Chapter Thirty-Five

Clifton, New Jersey

Alicia Gregg's address called out a road that ran along the Passaic River. That area looked complicated on her new map, Andrea considered, but the Garden State Parkway exit seemed to take her close enough. On the way there, she'd decided the only course that would work was the unvarnished truth. Someone fitting the name Alicia Gregg would hopefully answer the door.

When a middle-aged woman appeared, looking distinctly Indian both in features and skin color, her own surprise must have shown. The dark-skinned woman noticed.

"I am Alicia Gregg, and who are you?" she said. It was a strange but welcome opening.

Don't reveal your last name. "My name is Andrea, and I'm desperately hoping that you can help me. It appears that we both know a Dr. Marcus Levine, or should I say Dr. Ram Singh. I'm guessing that you know him through some sort of associate relationship. I'm also guessing that I'm one of his victims."

"Victims?"

"Yes. You do know about the MAUs, do you not? The mobile abortion clinics that Dr. Levine is involved with?"

The darker woman's expression immediately turned defensive. "Abortion clinics? No, I know nothing about any abortion—"

"Listen to me, Alicia. I needed to terminate a pregnancy that should never have happened, and decided to use this new service. My... my lover, the father of the... of... he was part of the organization that financed the mobile clinics. Because of him, I felt that my decision was safe. These clinics are supposedly helping to put an end to back room abortions, and horrible things done in alleys and bathrooms, but instead of just doing my abortion, they completely removed my uterus and left me bleeding terribly. The bleeding got worse and worse. Do you know what losing your uterus means? Can you… do you have children? Have you ever been pregnant?"

"No. I don't understand you. Why would they take out your uterus?"

"I don't know, but what they did has ruined my life. In fact, I nearly died."

"Did you go to a hospital? To an emergency room?"

"Yes. I actually called someone high up at Children's Hospital, where I work. I'm a registered nurse, Alicia. The person I spoke with said the removal of my uterus was a criminal act. She was within an hour or two of arranging corrective surgery for me, when someone working for Dr. Levine came to my apartment, a woman. She was taking me to a place where they would stop the bleeding. I naturally thought she was connected to my counselor at the hospital. I must have fainted a few seconds after she arrived… I was very weak from loss of blood. When I woke up, it was five days later.

"They can't *perform* a uterus removal in less than an hour, Alicia, and certainly not in that type of mobile facility. The whole thing was crazy. I was just one of many women, and all they knew about me were a few physical details and whatever my blood sample told them. Most of the women using these MAUs are from impoverished areas, ghettos, you know what I mean. Someone in that organization is *violating* us all, for whatever reason they have. Now I can never *have* the children I wanted, once the timing was right."

Alicia's defensive expression softened, then turned sad. "I cannot believe that Marcus is aware of this thing."

"He's aware of it now. It was he who repaired my inside damage and stopped the bleeding, not over five days ago. He is using the name Singh, Dr. Ram Singh."

Alicia sighed, slowly shaking her head. "This is most difficult to accept. How did my name enter this picture?"

"They had me locked in a basement room in a building near Camden, and kept me heavily sedated all that time. I managed to break out of the room when they left me alone for a couple of hours, but before I ran away

I discovered a letter Dr. Levine wrote to you, something about forwarding mail. I copied down your address. They didn't know that I was an RN, but just before I escaped I was instructed to take two pills… actually capsules. Do you know what morphine is?"

"It's for… pain?"

"Among other things, yes. I was told to take what amounted to a guaranteed lethal dose, 400 milligrams, yet I was not having any pain and the bleeding had stopped several days earlier, so there was absolutely no reason I should have been taking anything. Even if there'd been some reason, the appropriate dose would have been ten or twenty milligrams. When I recognized the pills and their dosage for what they were, I knew. My nurses thought I'd follow instructions, you see. Later, they'd claim I was instructed to take just one of the capsules, or something like that. They wanted me to *die*, Alicia. Their superiors figured I'd blow the whistle on their criminal practice, so they wanted to silence me forever. Stopping my bleeding was just a convenient cover story, a way to keep me locked away until they figured out how to eliminate me altogether.

"Now I fear for my life. There may have been other women who have been mutilated, perhaps left to die. Who knows how long this has been going on? Can you tell me… *will* you tell me what you know about all this? Please?"

The woman from India did not answer for what seemed like an eternity. Finally, she looked away, then down at the small porch. When she once again lifted her gaze, the sadness had been replaced by something else.

"Please come inside… Andrea."

India

The long, monotonous drive back to Mumbai might have been minimally tolerable if only the damn rented car's front seat worked. It didn't. It wouldn't recline, adding to the pain that had Roman shaking most of the way. Further, he and Luke had fled the AMBRIA parking area without so much as a thought to what one short stop at Luke's apartment might afford them for the trip. Luke had prescription pain killers there, leftovers from a torn ligament episode but enough for the Mumbai trip and even a couple of days thereafter. Survival dictated there be no stops anywhere along the way. The Tata Indica compact car was one of the few available at the rental agency, that or a dilapidated Mercedes for three times the price. Who'd have known it would come to this—a return trip spent in agony?

Luke said little for the first few hours, but he did manage to mumble a few questions about Kareem. Why had she been found in David Thomas's office, when she could well have gone down the front stairwell? If she'd been surprised during her search for the information in Luke's office, why wouldn't the murder have happened there? Thomas wouldn't have dragged her back to his own office, would he? There wouldn't be blood all over his desk and floor and his letter opener wouldn't have been the murder weapon, would it? The questions were rhetorical. There'd never be an answer now.

Between bouts of pain, his own questions consumed him. Where was he to look for the truth, and why would he even want it? Was his desire to know driven by courage or fear? He'd never given in to fear, not this kind anyway, but it wasn't fear for his own safety. It was a bigger fear, one for the very world he'd come to know, with all its faults and shortcomings. India was the world's largest democracy, with decent laws and excellent discipline. If an operation like AMBRIA could methodically murder people to achieve its monetary goals, if someone like this Czech assassin could be legitimized so he could go on killing anyone in AMBRIA's way, where was the safety? How many Andreas had there already been?

There was no doubting that AMBRIA had every bit of the clout Rishi said they had. They were apparently beyond reproach, meaning he'd have to be doubly careful. The embassy authorities might even be tainted, or at least some of their personnel. And if he knew he could trust whomever he reached, what would he report? How would he make his own personal case? He no longer had any partners, no co-investors, and no support. EMBRYIA was *de facto* belly up, the American side of it, even if the operation continued elsewhere. MAUs in the States would be decommissioned now, their staffs disbursed, perhaps even their existing records destroyed by others like the Czech, by AMBRIA security. That part might already be underway.

The revolving list of questions intensified his pain rather than dulling it. There was simply no way to sit without his teeth chattering, no position that gave relief.

Luke finally broke the heavy silence once more after their first pit stop.

"I can't believe any of this is happening," he said. "I don't have my passport, don't have my clothes, no contact lens solution. Even if Rishi handed you money, how the hell can I even leave the country? And why the embassy, Roman? What are we going to tell them? That someone is chasing us? Are we going to tell them about Kareem... your girlfriend... and Dr. Rishi? Do you think I'll be implicated in what happened back there? After all, I kept all the records that Kareem was after. I was in charge of the new *in vivo* experimentation. Won't they say that I knew all the time what was going on?"

Questions without answers. Perhaps they both should have gone to Goa as suggested, but there'd been no assurance they'd not be followed when he checked in at the hospital there. This way was better.

There was a city map in the glove box. He had Luke take it out and try to locate the U.S. Embassy among all the government buildings. Amid the rustle of map unfolding and fumbling, he closed his eyes and once more tried deep breathing to help the pain. It didn't work. The rest stop had ADVIL and aspirin for sale. He'd asked Luke to buy the ADVIL and then tripled the recommended dose, washing it down with plenty of water, but it wouldn't go to work for another hour, if at all. Food was out of the question, not even another candy bar.

A listing of all the government buildings ran down one edge of the map. None of them had the title "embassy", but one said U.S. Consulate General. Its tiny black square looked to be near the ocean, on a small peninsula in the western part of the city. The map was sprinkled with dozens of tiny blocks showing such buildings, but the only recognizable streets were the biggest ones. It was like looking for tiny Bower Street on a map of New York City that showed only the avenues and major cross streets. They'd have to ask when they got there.

ꕤ

It was nearly daybreak when Luke worked his way into that part of the city. During his time in India, he'd only become familiar with the airport and one or two districts, but Mumbai was huge. He got lost twice just getting somewhere meaningful. Several people gave him directions, the most precise and useful ones coming from a beggar who held out his cup for a reward as he polished the car's already clean window with a dirty rag. He was either starting his day early, or had been up all night as they had.

They reached the embassy at dawn, noting the near total absence of lights inside. Most of the staff was understandably at home, but someone *had* to be there on duty. Embassies never slept.

The ADVIL had dulled the pain enough to reduce shifting about, but he now paid the price as stiffness translated into anguish—again. Roman was able to walk unassisted only if he hooked his thumb into his belt on the bad side. Why hadn't they looked for some sort of wrap for his chest back there at the rest stop? The suggestion should have been his, not Luke's, but at least they'd made it. Things would go better now.

A night guard escorted them into the sanctity of the massive building, where they were greeted by a process officer who asked for proof of their U. S. citizenship. After presenting his own passport and vouching for Luke, Roman quickly explained that it was an emergency—that an American woman had been kidnapped in the U.S., brought to India and murdered in Kolhapur. The officer, who was writing something at the time, stopped abruptly with the word "murdered," not even bothering to inquire further about Luke's passport.

Luke tried to add how they'd both fled the scene in fear of their own lives, and that there were actually several murders, but the man wasn't listening. He immediately ushered them to the senior consular officer on night duty, a fat, elderly man with a handlebar mustache and pot belly. The man had been slouching at his huge, mahogany desk playing solitaire on his computer. Roman caught a glimpse of the screen just before it flashed to the benign "desktop" display.

"These people want to report a murder," the process officer announced. Other than a pair of raised eyebrows, the fat man looked almost bored. He swung about, tapping the fingers of both hands together, eyeing Roman and waiting.

"Sir, my name is Roman Citrano, this is Dr. Luke Evans and we want to report the kidnapping of a U.S. citizen which resulted in… resulted in…."

Why did the back of his throat suddenly feel like sandpaper? His mouth was parched and his words cold and rehearsed, more like a bullfrog croaking than anything else. Nothing was coming out right. All the rehearsing on the way had been for nothing. He could barely think, let alone organize his thoughts. When he tried to breathe, his lungs burned. Unable to continue, he groped in his pocket and produced one of the vials that he had taken from Rishi's office, the 12-week-old fetus. He reached forward, nearly losing his balance, and placed it on the desk. Perhaps the old gent would help provide some questions to get things started.

Meanwhile Luke took up the slack. "It was a lot more than just kidnapping. There are … we want you to know that—" He stopped, watching the man's reaction to the vial. Both elbows had been put down on the desk blotter, and the man was leaning forward. He hitched his chair closer and squinted at the vial, spreading both hands palms down.

"What the hell is *that*? And what does it have to do with a kidnapping?" He had a strong New England accent, almost a "down Maine" drawl. He stared at the process officer. "Did I hear you say *murder*?"

Roman swallowed, willing his dry mouth to loosen enough to talk. Even so, he had to force the words. He held up a finger to stop Luke's reply before it began, then pointed at the vial.

"*This* is why a woman in Philadelphia was physically violated, then kidnapped and brought here to India where she was deliberately left to die. She was murdered… to cover up an atrocity that includes the slaughter and death of many other unknown women, all buried in a mass grave down in Kolhapur."

"Plus two *other* murders that just happened!" Luke blurted out.

Other than the fat man's mustache twitching, he'd shown nothing in the way of shock or concern, not even of unusual interest. Luke's outburst had all the qualities of someone screaming without the scream, but nothing seemed to have registered, not one word, as if the man had been addressed in a totally foreign language! He stared at the fetus as though it was a high school "frog in a jar." Was he that dense? Did the words kidnapping and slaughtered and mass grave mean anything at all? Or was he simply itching to get back to his solitaire?

Finally he leaned back in his chair again, still staring at the specimen as he jabbed an index finger at two visitor chairs. "Please, both of you sit down and start from the beginning."

Roman eyed the chairs, then shook his head. "Sir, part of my story is that I was attacked and at least one of my ribs has been broken for nearly twelve hours now. I need to remain standing, at least for now."

The story came out as requested, beginning with Marcus Levine's phone call and thereafter to the creation of EMBRYIA, the rollout of the MAU units, the terrible rapes, Andrea's pleading calls, and the scene in her apartment in Philadelphia. His voice was a little better by then, his throat less parched. Luke was hearing most of it for the first time. His stare spoke volumes, and he hadn't even heard details about Dr. Rishi or Kareem yet. When Kareem's murder scene was described, the stare became a mask of agony.

"...and I have no idea how many women are in that grave," Roman concluded. "My impression is that it was added to over time... the freshest portion most likely containing... Ms. Robbins' body."

There, it was out, not all of it, but enough for someone else to take over.

The consular officer reached toward the vial with a trembling hand, but stopped just short of touching it. Then he reached for the phone. "I know it's late there, but get me the U.S. Embassy in Washington", he barked, "and after I'm through, place a call to the FBI offices in New Delhi. Yes, I know it's early *there*. Just do it."

Roman sighed. It was the confirmation he sought, the one he hoped for. He'd no longer need to carry the burden alone. He twisted a bit, trying to force a smile in Luke's direction, but a deep-rooted cough found him unprepared. He'd unwittingly turned his torso, rather than his full body, and immediately tasted salt and iron. His own blood! Then one of his eyes seemed to be looking up at the ceiling—not both, just one. Everything whirled, but only for the time it took him to collapse.

Chapter Thirty-Six

Kolhapur

David Thomas drove as far as the new building's parking lot, a distance of some three miles, then sat there in the dark, thinking. Emergency plans had been created to handle situations exactly like this one. Chin Liu's management of the new building project had been masterful in itself, in that there was already enough capacity to handle all of AMBRIA's existing cultures. None of the labs had yet been populated with their products, but the equipment was all there, thoroughly tested and ready. Crews had been selected and trained. Many others would be transferred from AMBRIA once a transition was required. At present, they knew nothing of the new building. Liu's quiet absences at AMBRIA were attributed to the man's oriental nature, one of remaining silent unless something of importance was to be said. Liu was simply one of those individuals who could manage fifteen things at a time while being able to come and go as a ghost.

Now that AMBRIA had been compromised, things had quickly come to a head. Recent discussions with Q in New York strongly suggested that "staff reduction" should begin anyway, patterned after the extremely successful South African elimination program he'd arranged in their first enterprise together, prior to his appointment to the U.N. There'd been four key players involved that time, and, like falling dominoes, one killed off the next until only one remained. Malovec had finished *him* off, a simple matter once the others were removed. It was time to repeat that little game of dominoes. In spite of immense expenses over the past two years, Genesis had already turned a profit of twelve million, and there was no end in sight.

Marcus Levine was no longer needed, nor was Rishi. Of the two, she'd been the most worrisome in Q's view. And then there was this Roman Citrano. He'd been necessary for starting up the MAU program, of course—his talent and drive were quite valuable—but now that the

MAUs of EMBRYIA were no longer exclusively supplying all the necessary products, Citrano was a liability, therefore expendable. Profit was *not* totally tied into abortions. It only provided an enhanced inventory. Transplantable organs were the key, and now there were enough MAUs and alternative sources to provide all the basics.

Rishi must have taken her own life—he'd checked her office on the way out, unlocking the office door she'd thought that only she controlled—and had quickly backed away. That odor... it had to be formaldehyde. The Indian girl had been stopped, fortunately before she could do any damage with those lab books. That left Dr. Evans, who'd escaped with Citrano to report everything to anyone who'd listen. There was very little time to make a clean sweep of the AMBRIA facilities, but emergency plans anticipated such problems. Fortunately, *they'd* been in readiness more than half a year.

He thumbed the first of many phone numbers he'd need to call in the next half hour or so, the first belonging to Dr. Chin Liu. First on the agenda was the evacuation of AMBRIA, which would fall to Liu. His teams were practiced and ready. Then a call to Malovec to check on anything involving the clinic. Rishi might have taken Citrano there. She'd been seen driving away from the main building with him, Evans and the girl in her SUV. If necessary, the clinic would also be evacuated and swept.

And then there was Marcus Levine himself. Who better to act as the final domino than someone who'd spent his whole professional life killing animals, mostly primates, in pursuit of fame and fortune? He'd need some incentive, of course, but the rest would be easy, especially if he were supplied with the appropriate "tools." A few other incentives, played against his immense ego, would guarantee complicity. In fact, Levine had already surmised that he owed his most recent successes to a huge global syndicate. Presented with an invitation to *join* that elite organization, Levine could be counted on to follow nearly any directive.

"Staff reduction" could begin once all the rest was in motion. Levine would receive a phone call he could not ignore. After that, a call to one of the FBI's finest—in New Delhi.

As for the clinic's burial ground, a few gardening tools strewn about should do the trick. The shed over there was filled with appropriate items to be used for just such a purpose.

Cleveland, Ohio

The gray Ford felt almost comfortable by the time she reached the city outskirts and pulled into a small motel. By then she'd absorbed everything Alicia Gregg had given her, not only information handwritten on a sheet of paper, but everything said. Alicia was Marcus Levine's half-sister! Her mother had been widowed before the age of twenty, remarrying when Alicia had been five years old. When her British husband Alan Gregg had been killed in Afghanistan, she'd chosen to move to the U.S. rather than live in England, but not because of her conceited brother. Marcus had little use or respect for her, unless he needed something. She tolerated him more because of her proper upbringing than for any sibling affection.

Levine's most recent "need" amounted to using her as a mail-forwarding tool, not even bothering to compensate her for the sometimes-significant costs involved. She got no thanks, not even acknowledgement. After all, *he* was the famous one, with a string of letters after his name, and she was just another woman, a utility. She was to feel honored.

By the time the folded paper of details passed between hands, her description of Marcus Levine more closely resembled a snake than any doctor. "Do not trust him, Andrea, no matter what. He manipulates everyone and everything to suit whatever he's after, lies upon more lies. In his world, women are actually less important than the animals he destroys with his research." She went on to explain that Marcus became Dr. Ram Singh, or businessman Ram Singh, or Professor Ram Singh whenever he wanted to conceal his true identity, wearing what was typically a light blue turban and emphasizing his Indian heritage. He knew nothing about tying turbans, Alicia scoffed. His were all pre-tied and stitched.

He could also add heavy inflection to his everyday English until it was nearly impossible to understand. The ruse got him places; it got him respect. She was quite certain that he often traveled using a faked passport and papers. His professional qualities? Oh, well, *those* were accurate enough. He was unquestionably a genius, remembering that a very thin line separated genius from insanity.

And yet Roman had apparently trusted him! Was Roman aware of his mistake by now? Was he even safe?

Although the picture was so much clearer, so was her fear—for herself, and now for Roman. She was no longer safe by any stretch of the imagination. Her world, so certain since the move to Philadelphia, had become a shambles in mere moments. They'd already tried to kill her; they'd try again. They might even try to kill Roman.

She needed something she'd never considered—a gun!

ꟸ

Once in her motel room, she phoned Marge Adams, who was horrified to hear what had happened. Dr. Ram Singh and the two nurses were unknowns. However, Dr. Adams had already placed Andrea on administrative leave at the hospital after hearing about the bleeding, so the job was preserved. However, *she* could be in real danger as well. In her calling and speaking to Dr. Raj Maibeck, she'd unintentionally cast her own role as an antagonist, and those behind the bigger picture could well be out of reach of any local protection there in Philly. Understandably, she'd sounded upset.

The second call was to Uncle Chuck Robbins, whose army background was the antithesis of her parents' vocations and careers. Officially he was Lt. Colonel Charles Robbins (Ret). Unofficially, he was just Chuck; the "uncle" part had been dropped long ago. A lifelong bachelor, he'd been involved in the Federal Firearms program since leaving the army, and knew the system backwards and forwards.

After the obligatory niceties and chit-chat, she got around to her reason for calling.

"Chuck, if I ask you for advice and direction on something I absolutely must get, promise you won't go ballistic? This is between you and me. I don't want my parents to worry, okay?

"Agreed, little darlin', but this sounds serious. Whaddya need from your favorite uncle?"

"A handgun. I want something I can legally carry for personal protection."

"*What?* What kind of protection? Who's out to hurt you?"

"Let's just say I'm being stalked by someone or maybe a group. I don't know who they are, what they look like, or where they'll find me, but they're international, and if they do find me I may end up dead like these things you hear about on the news. I need something that can stop anyone at all. Trust me on this."

"Whoa! Slow down. First of all, I can't see you with a gun, Andie. It's not you. What's behind this stalking, as you call it? Who'd stalk someone like you in the first place? You haven't been doing any of that stuff on the Internet, have you? Facebook, and all that? You didn't go fishing and end up with some weirdo on your hook, did you?"

"Nothing of the sort. Look, if I promise to tell you as soon as I feel I'm safe, will that be good enough for now?"

"Guess it'll have to be, long as you're not going out killing someone. Is this connected to your new hospital job there in Philly?"

"No. Actually I'm on my way back to St. Paul right now. I'm driving. It's not safe for me to use any other method. Flying is out."

"Do you know anything at all about guns?"

"I stopped in a gun store today and was told that women were mostly picking Glocks these days. I think the man said Glock 26 was a good one. Was he right?"

"Well, darlin', it's light, small, holds ten rounds and makes a wonderful paperweight. Look, you want to *stop* someone, a single 9-millimeter round won't do it. You pretty well have to shoot him three or four times just to slow him down. Far as I'm concerned, I'd want a '45 like the one I used to have. One shot anywhere with a '45 does it. He's down! In your case, with a smaller hand, I'd say a Taurus Millennium, '40 caliber. Almost the same knockdown power. Buy one new, not used, and fill it with Hornady 180 grain jacketed hollow point bullets. Go to a gun store around here."

"So I ask for a… what? A Dorus?"

"Taurus, like the bull. Then add Millennium. Forty caliber. They'll know what you want before you finish telling them. Have him break it down for you and show you what's involved. And once you have it, go buy yourself a *real* gun safety course and learn what you have to know. Shoot the sucker until its second nature, and learn to shoot in the dark. Are you *sure* you want to do this?"

"These people have already tried to eliminate me once, Chuck, and they almost did. It's very complicated, and scary."

"Tell the cops! That's what they're for."

"What do I tell them? I don't know who it is, or how many, or where they are, or… it's something big like… like the Mafia, but—"

"Okay, so scratch the cops. They'll think you're loco."

"I'm a fugitive. I can't go anywhere I'm known, or use credit cards, or even my cell phone. I can't even go back to my apartment in Philadelphia. They know where I live."

"But you can still use your head. Always could. You're going to carry this weapon here in Minnesota? Then call me as soon as the papers are completed, and I'll watch for our part of it here in the office. You'll need a CCW, a license to carry a concealed weapon. Leave the state and you're on your own with the gendarmes. Stay out of Wisconsin and Illinois if you have the firearm with you. The dealer will explain all that and give you a map, I hope. Better yet, come on up to my place. I know the sheriff who'll do your background check, so that the process will take all of five minutes instead of a month. Then you'll have to go to a mandatory gun safety class, sit through that and get a certificate, which you take to any FFL gun store or pawnshop. But that safety class isn't enough. I'll connect you with a *real* place where they'll teach you everything. So… you don't have any idea who these stalkers are?"

"I'm working on it."

"Well, *keep* workin' on it. You have to know your enemy if you're going to stay one step ahead of him, and be goddamned careful. Get a couple of those prepaid cell phones, and keep your personal cell phone turned off. Take the battery out. Wrap the rest of it with three or four layers of aluminum foil."

"Thanks, Chuck. I'll do just that. That takes some of the pressure off. When I get to St. Paul, I'll find a motel and call you again."

"Don't use motels, Andrea! I've still got that place on Lake Minnetonka you can use. It has a landline phone. Remember how to get there?"

"Are you serious?"

"You're my favorite niece, darlin'."

"I'm your *only* niece, Chuck."

"Just one thing... there's a big raccoon comes to the patio door every so often, name's Bandit. Raised in captivity and was let go. He's really tame, but a nuisance sometimes. Hand him an ear of corn from the big box on the porch and he'll go away happy. *Don't* let him inside or he'll want to crawl up and go to sleep next to you. He snores."

ꟸ

She found a 24-hour drug store less than a mile from the motel and was there at six the next morning. The drug store was in a shopping mall that had a Wal-Mart, so she spent twenty minutes there after leaving the drug store. When she returned to the motel, she had a bagful of purchases from the first stop, two throwaway prepaid cell phones and a box of aluminum foil from Wal-Mart, plus breakfast from McDonald's in its own bag. Later still, the woman who'd registered the previous night as a long-haired brunette checked out of her room as a tousle-headed blonde wearing sunglasses and chewing bubble gum. She'd already removed the battery from her own cell phone and, for good measure, wrapped the phone in six layers of foil.

Her first stop in Minneapolis would be Union Bank and Trust. She did all her banking there, but rarely in person. She was nothing more than an account number to anyone there. She'd be safe in withdrawing whatever she'd need in cash.

On her way to the car and a long day of driving, she blew a bubble, just for practice.

Chapter Thirty-Seven

Camden

THE ROBBINS SITUATION NEEDED IMMEDIATE CORRECTION, MARCUS CONCLUDED. It was bad enough spiriting the Robbins woman away from her Philadelphia apartment, although that part had been necessary in light of what Raj Maibeck had reported. Keeping her heavily sedated was correct as well, because disposal of her body, absent a large incinerator, was impossible to arrange overnight. Stopping her internal bleeding was also a wise move, since any unforeseen inquiry would find that all appropriate medical steps had been taken to improve her condition. Such an inquiry was remote, yet there *was* the call from Dr. Adams to consider. In any situation where unknowns might crop up, it was prudent to anticipate as many as possible.

As it had turned out, a fisherman in the coastal town of Ocean City, New Jersey, was quite willing to dump a large, heavily weighted aluminum shipping container into the ocean thirty miles out, for fifty grand in cash. The container, designed to be airtight, would be "ventilated" and so would sink. Sanitation would therefore have taken place not more than twelve hours after Robbins escaped, but that fact was no longer relevant.

Every effort had to be made now to find out exactly *who* Robbins was, where she would run, her family, her friends, her resources. She would not have escaped unless she'd already concluded that she was in danger, yet neither Greta nor Harriett had given her any reason for such an assumption. Further, she could not have identified the two pills unless she was intimately familiar with the field of medicine. Had that been the case, she'd never have used the MAU in the first place.

Why had she called a *director* of the Children's Hospital instead of seeking the nearest emergency room? What was her connection with Dr. Adams?

New Delhi, India

FBI Special Agent Norman Bassard swore under his breath, then rolled over and reached for his cell phone. Who'd be calling at this hour? The night crew couldn't handle things until he was back on duty? He wrenched himself into a sitting position, acknowledged his junior associate, and listened. The message was simple enough—it was a phone number he was to call immediately, an emergency associated with someone named Donahue, in the U.S. Supposedly it was personal.

He jotted down the number. It wasn't personal at all, and it wasn't in the United States even if the phone number began with the numbers 001. The clock on his nightstand said it was 4:38 A.M. When the terse message was completed, he dug out a second phone—one rarely used—called a memorized number, repeated the code he was to use, then listened for a second time. By the time the man with the distinct British accent finished his message, Bassard knew he had but one decision to make, and quickly, but he'd already made it nearly two years back. Two million bucks was worth three times that amount in the right countries, particularly those with clear, blue waters and white sugar beaches. The man making the offer knew well what that kind of money could mean to someone in the Bureau, especially someone far from home base.

All he had to do was get himself to Mumbai on the next flight, check in at the U.S. embassy and take over from the OIO boys. He could achieve the objectives he'd just been given, and stay clean as long as he stayed reasonably within FBI guidelines. Satisfaction with his handling of the matter would be demonstrated in *very* short order thereafter, by way of a sealed envelope delivered to a previously chosen drop.

As for that country with the white sand beaches, Bassard had already been supplied a portfolio of such spots pending retirement some time in the future. His caller had reminded him that he'd be able to choose any one of them, maybe even a few.

None of the dream spots were in India.

His folder of airline schedules was across the room, in a small secretary desk. There'd most likely be a flight or two to Mumbai somewhere around six, and his quick-trip overnight bag was packed and ready. He could be at the airport in less than half an hour. As for the girl he'd been entertaining, she'd find a note with her money when she finally woke up. He'd never gotten around to asking her last name. It didn't matter.

Breach Candy Hospital, Mumbai

Luke stood helplessly by while an emergency incision was made in the space between Roman's third and fourth rib. A drainage tube was driven into the chest cavity surrounding the right lung and nearly a half liter of blood removed. Then an airway was shoved down Roman's trachea to re-expand both lungs. The other lung was undamaged, but the pleural space was compromised, resulting in a pneumothorax, an air pocket that was actually causing most of Roman's pain.

All this immediate treatment was done on a gurney, right there in the hallway. At first there was a single medic with one assistant, then two more and finally a cluster as equipment was rushed up, carried or wheeled.

Inside an Emergency Room, another trocar and catheter was advanced deeper into the pleural cavity to release the air pressure, and Roman's breathing immediately started to ease. The medical team could well have been working on concrete pavement at some highway accident scene, or inside an EMS vehicle. Everything was *ad lib.* They'd started preparing for another move to Radiology, where an X-ray would help assess the damage to his ribs, when the fat consular officer with the handlebar mustache appeared on the scene, flanked by a uniformed embassy security guard.

"It appears that we must arrest Mr. Roman Citrano as soon as the hospital releases him," he announced. "He will be returned to the embassy, where we shall read him his rights. There he will stay until he is returned to the United States."

Luke snapped back a retort before anyone on the hospital staff had a chance to respond. "Are you people out of your *minds?* He ain't going anywhere. *He's* the wronged party here, not someone you should be arresting."

"Dr. Evans, please! The FBI in New Delhi has suggested—quite strongly, I must say— that Mr. Citrano could very well be part of a major syndicate behind the illegal activities of the very AMBRIA Corporation Mr. Citrano named in my office. New Delhi has been investigating various aspects of these or similar events with regard to the syndicate, which they did not name, at least not to me, and the patterns are similar. Until that is proven one way or the other, our decision is to detain him at this time. When Mr. Citrano is well enough to travel, he will be returned to the States, hopefully to assist in the investigation. That will be his choice."

Luke glared back. "That's absurd. Don't you understand *any* of what we… what he told you back in your office?"

"What I understand is irrelevant. You will also come with us, back to the embassy for questioning. Although you are *currently* not implicated, that can change depending on new information we expect to receive at any moment. Your cooperation is greatly appreciated."

"Information you receive from where? My god, who are you listening to? You're all wrong. There are two companies with similar names. Mr. Citrano is connected with EMBRYIA, not AMBRIA. EMBRYIA is a legitimate company in America. Actually, I—"

The security man stepped forward. "That's quite enough, Mr. Evans. If you are not willing to cooperate, we would have no other choice but to arrest you as well, as an accessory by your own words just now." He began unhooking a set of handcuffs from his belt.

"Me? *Me?* Look… sir… one of the murders we just reported was a girl I cared about a great deal. Mr. Citrano lost someone he cared about as well, someone from the States. She was kidnapped and brought here, to Kolhapur. She may have been killed, just as the other women were. These are *murders* we're talking about, can't you understand that? You just said that AMBRIA's activities are illegal. We're telling you it's far more than that. They are *deliberately* murdering people, slaughtering women to get their organs." The security guard looked as though he'd yawn at any moment, while the fat man simply stared. "Can I at least ask *where* you got your erroneous information about Mr. Citrano?" Luke continued. "Is that too much to ask?"

"We have no reason to doubt our own FBI, Dr. Evans," the consular official replied. They have reason to suspect that your statements to me are no more than fabrications you and Citrano have cooked up to cover your own illicit activities. I strongly suggest you withhold further comments until you are asked. Is that clear?"

The gurney was already being wheeled from the room. Luke reached back as if to control its departure, feeling alone and vulnerable. What could he do but cooperate? The FBI? How could they have gotten their information so quickly? The hospital wasn't more than a mile from the embassy, so even counting the time it had taken to ease Roman into the rental car again, no more than a half hour—forty minutes at most—had gone by since the consular guy made that phone call. How would the FBI in New Delhi have known who to call, especially at this early hour? How could they have verified their input in such a short time? All in forty minutes, including the usual times spent just making the phone calls?

It was a numbing ride back to the consulate, where he was asked once again to start from the beginning. This time it was his story, not Roman's. He began with his own recruitment and its misrepresentations, told of his surprise when the AMBRIA "investors" came in and changed everything around, described his work for Dr. Rishi and her sometimes-evasive answers to questions, then finished his story with the sudden arrival of more fetuses than seemed possible—and then uteruses. He'd been assured that it was all quite in order, that the materials had all come about from untimely deaths of the donors. Roman's arrival shed a different light on everything, casting doubt. Someone dear to him had been horribly violated back in the States, losing not only her uterus but eventually her life.

The Czech security guard was included in the account.

The only part left out was his own version of his imagined relationship with Kareem. She and Dr. Rishi had both been killed—murdered—as they prepared to flee the organization for fear of their lives. He and Roman had no choice but to chance what turned out to be a six-hour drive to the embassy, in spite of Roman's pain and the danger of traveling with the damage already discovered. That time didn't include an extra hour spent correcting mistakes once inside the city, or asking directions.

ꕤ

Luke was forced to repeat the entire story twice after two quasi-FBI types finally showed up. They were actually from the Office of International Operations, or OIO, a fledgling FBI-spawned effort designed to support and expand international partnerships in the fight against global crime and terror. One of them kept referring to what looked like a protocol document, whispering to his partner. It appeared they were running through this kind of assignment for the first time. Trainees? Great, just great.

After verbalizing his story he was then asked to write down *exactly* what he had said, using two different forms, one for the U.S. Consulate, the other for the Federal investigators, who were now awaiting a senior field officer from New Delhi. The same information appeared on each form, but in different orders and priorities. Apparently the modest space allowed for comments was meant to limit his word count, since there were no blank sheets supplied for attachments to either form. He was then told that he'd be traveling *under guard* back to the AMBRIA building in Kolhapur first thing the following morning. For the rest of that day and throughout the night, he'd stay in small guest quarters right there at the consulate.

Nothing was mentioned about his own legal representation or rights as a U.S. citizen. Those were apparently only available inside the continental U.S. or the embassy building itself, and even then after much bureaucratic red tape. Ironically, if he'd been wronged by any foreign government, the very consulate that now served as his jail would have been instrumental in freeing him. Well, he could forget that little irony, since he hadn't been arrested. So could Roman, whose arrest was imminent. Nothing was mentioned about *him,* either. They were both suspects, and it was increasingly evident that somebody within AMBRIA had been the source of the FBI's information. Sure, go to the very organization branded as operating illegally to ask questions requiring truthful answers. No wonder the FBI acronym was defined as Fucked-Up Bumbling Idiots.

Chapter Thirty-Eight

Camden

MARCUS KNEW HE'D HAVE TO CONTACT DAVID THOMAS WITHOUT DELAY, BUT his alibi had to be airtight. He'd need to rehearse everything before he dialed for Thomas had a skillful way of entrapping him with his need to appoint blame.

Above all, none of the unfortunate incident was his fault. Maibeck could not have known the Robbins woman was anyone more important than any other pregnant whore showing up at the MAU. He looked only for the right blood hormone levels, freedom from any apparent disease and the client's desire to keep her abortion a secret at all costs. Robbins fit all those criteria.

There was always a risk of residual bleeding when doing laparoscopic surgery. The Robbins woman was atypical, no doubt hysterical, which made matters far worse. She'd gone to an equally excitable *woman* high up in the Children's Hospital administration… the reason beyond anyone's guess… and that woman had no trouble *on her own* contacting Dr. Maibeck. The MAU operations were not exactly hidden from the general public.

And then Robbins had escaped due to someone else's ineptitude. The Urgent Care location had been professionally inspected by a certified security agency. *They* had declared the basement rooms secure when the remote lock system was installed. It was *their* idiot who failed to see the obvious, that the bathroom door hinges had removable pins. All three doors to the bathroom had the same hinges. It was only the one opening to the hallway that made any real difference. If not for that, the Robbins woman might have been "sanitized" without a trace.

He took a deep breath before initiating the call.

ഇ൬

"It would seem, Dr. Levine, that you have lost control of things," the unctuous voice purred.

David Thomas had just summarized what *he* knew about the Robbins abortion and uterine problems, and he was not far from the truth. How had he learned all that, almost as it had happened? Where was he getting his information?

"Marcus, Marcus, Marcus," Thomas oozed, "these things happen. We all *know* that, and we also know that such an unfortunate occurrence is temporary. However, I may be able to help you a bit. The Children's Hospital director, a Dr. Adams, was instrumental in hiring Andrea Robbins to work in the Neonatal Intensive Care Unit. It seems Robbins had developed an impressive reputation in St. Paul, Minnesota, where she did identical work. She's a registered nurse. Of course, you *knew* that and we know that you'll execute the appropriate damage control.

"Now, on to another topic altogether. We… that is, my associates and I… would like you to consider a major step upward in your career. How shall I say this… a step onto the world stage along with the rest of us? Of those involved with EMBRYIA and AMBRIA, we all feel *you* are the singular most important asset to our organization. The others can be replaced, do you agree? No one can replace you."

"Mr. Thomas, I—"

"David, please. And let us forego any false modesty. You have earned this advancement."

"All right, David. Since we are now talking about a change in my status, am I correct in assuming I will have a much larger role in everything medical? And that my demonstrated talents will be accepted by others in your organization? That has not been the case so far."

"You are correct, Marcus. There *have* been those who doubted you, doubted your value, but no longer. Those who have been no more than necessary to your progress and ours will… shall I say… fall by the wayside while you will soar like the eagles. Incidentally, our organization is not only worldwide in its scope but is connected to a great, humanitarian need. The business end of what we are doing is properly estimated in the hundreds of billions of American dollars. I believe the amount could be ten to twenty times what you might have guessed. What do you say to sharing that with us? Well, no need to answer, but before we can totally disclose who we are and who all the important players might be, there are things you must first do for us."

"Of course. Nothing is for nothing."

"There is a time when staff reduction is absolutely necessary, something I believe you already know. You alone are in a position to know everyone with knowledge of our most sensitive secrets regarding both EMBRYIA and AMBRIA. I am referring to the top echelon only, not those who have worked for either organization as bit players. Those operating the MAUs, for example, know only what they needed to know in order to perform their jobs, am I right?"

"Yes."

"They cannot hurt us, whereas several others know all there is to know. You know who these others are, of course."

"Of course. I have kept their number to a minimum."

"Yes, you have done well in that regard, but they are now a definite threat to our operation. They know too much. We want you to reduce that threat to zero. How you do it is up to you, but a doctor of your standing should have little trouble deciding on the method to be used. Do I make myself clear?"

"You want me to—"

"Zero, Marcus. There is only one definition for zero. *Then* we will introduce you to our top management, and with that will come a substantial bonus. You truly have done well so far. I have personally put my own reputation on the line in speaking for you in this. Have you any questions?"

Kolhapur

The morning sun was just surfacing above the tree line when the gray, Edsel-like government vehicle pulled into one of the AMBRIA building's visitor parking spaces. After a day filled with anguish, uncertainty and isolation, Luke's night at the embassy had produced little to no sleep. He slept instead during the drive back to Kolhapur, which for some ungodly reasons began at 4:00 a.m., wedged between two OIO types. Neither was one of the pair who'd questioned him the day before. They apparently all worked in shifts, like some factory. When the whistle blew at shift's end, an agent grabbed his lunch pail and headed for the exit. Done for the day!

Normally a five-hour drive in the best of conditions, it had taken a mere four at speeds exceeding 130 kilometers per hour, aided at times by the car's concealed flashing blue lights whenever needed. But something about the AMBRIA building was different. There should have been cars in the parking area at all times. There'd been shifts working around the clock to maintain the cultivating organs ever since he'd worked there. Everything had to run like a Swiss watch.

One of the two agents motioned toward the building entrance. Was he to get out and lead them inside? Of course! Now he understood. He was their key to the facility, since there were no cars evident. No one else would be there. As a senior employee with access authorization and security codes to nearly all the labs and many offices, he'd get them anywhere they needed to go without needing a warrant or even leaving a record of the visit! Did that mean they'd already sent everybody away? Was it just to give them enough time for a once-through without anyone observing? Even with the ghastly events happening as they had, *someone* should have been there to monitor the incubators. Nearly two days had passed since the… since he'd lost Kareem. If the incubators weren't tended, they….

He stopped himself in mid-thought. At this point who cared? "They" could do whatever they wanted. His concern was no more than a remnant now, a vestige of responsibility left after years of diligence. He'd already quit, already walked out, already run. His psyche simply hadn't caught up with the rest of him.

When the same agent prodded him into moving, he pointed out that the front entrance served only the elevator—there was no door between the lobby and main floor—that they'd best use the rear entrance for access to all floors. That seemed to make sense, so they moved the car to that end, and all three agents got out. The tallest of the three seemed to be their leader. At least he looked old enough to be in the most senior position.

After punching the numbers on the keyboard at the back door, Luke swung it open and immediately spun to his left, disengaging the alarm system. The head agent pushed past him and through the double doors, heading directly for the service elevator where he waited until everyone was inside. In his hand was the detailed facility map all employees received during their orientation. Who'd given it to him? Had someone delivered it in Mumbai? Was it possible they had access to such information simply by picking up a phone and calling somewhere? It made no sense. Why would it have been available anywhere other than right there at the building?

The agent pushed the top floor button. The offices? They wanted to check those first? They'd include Dr. Rishi's office… and the one belonging to David Thomas. Roman said he'd seen Kareem's body in Thomas's…. Luke swallowed hard, forcing back the devastating thought. His mouth was suddenly so dry he couldn't swallow. Then the elevator doors opened, and the lead agent turned left—toward Rishi's office. Luke tried to linger behind the remaining two, but he was being pushed in the small of his back by one of them.

Ahead, the leader had already opened Rishi's door and was surveying the interior. Everything inside was in disarray, including one of the broken fetus specimens shattered on the floor, but there was no sign of Dr. Rishi's body. That much could be seen from the hallway. The leader went inside and stood behind her desk, staring at his cohorts still in the hallway.

"Nobody in here," he growled, looking quite like a bloodhound, "and no evidence of any murder. Definitely looks like someone's rifled her files, just as we were… let's check the others."

What was it he'd almost said? Just as we were told? He led the way a second time, sliding one door after another open until he got to the one marked David Thomas. That door was already wide open, but inside everything was in place. According to Roman, that had been where he'd discovered Kareem's body. According to Roman? Everything was according to Roman, or so it seemed.

"We need to go to my lab," he said to the trio, pointing toward the far end of the hall. "My records are all there… or at least they were."

The lead agent looked surprised. He'd already started back toward the service elevator. "We do that *after* the gestation lab," he replied. "That's something I've got to see for myself. So far, your story is full of holes, Dr. Evans, big ones. I hope for your sake the rest is a little closer to the truth."

But they were obviously too late. The doors to the gowning room and the secondary interior doors to the labs were wide open and everything was quiet. No audible hum of the laminar flow system, no subtle sounds of multiple rockers within the glass incubators, nothing but eerie silence. Everything was gone: specimens, records and documents, even the employees. The technicians shared common workbenches at each end of the cavernous room, but even those were neat as a pin, white surfaces all but totally cleared of the usual bustle.

One of the agents stepped on a hazardous waste can pedal, raising the top. There was nothing inside, just a fresh plastic liner. Likewise with the ordinary trash container next to it, not even a gum wrapper evident. Another of the group turned one of the faucets at a lab sink, but no water came out of the high, curved spout. The water had been turned off!

It was incredible, surreal. He and Roman had spun away from the building at roughly 8 P.M. The following day and night were spent in the clutches of the OIO in Mumbai, up to what must have been eight this morning, their arrival time in front of the building. Thirty-six hours, no more! There must have been a whole army of people descending on the building to have moved so much so quickly, and even then, where had they taken it all? No sense in doubting Roman any further. The "janitors" had cleaned up the bodies, too.

Bodies! "The buried bodies," he exclaimed. "They surely didn't have enough time to remove *them*."

The lead agent shook his head. "Evans, right now you and your wounded buddy better hope they didn't. What we've already seen here is exactly what we were told we'd see."

"What do you mean, 'what you were told?' Who could have told you? Who knew?"

"That's our business. Now where's this burial place?"

Within minutes, their small caravan was back on the campus road. The scene at the refurbished clinic was a repeat of the one they'd just left—doors wide open, no cars, no personnel. Nobody stopped him when he took off by foot through the wooded path, but they were right on his heels. As he burst into the opening beyond the tree-lined path, he was both saddened and relieved to see that the grave site was untouched. He glanced up at the lead agent, then tossed his head at the freshly turned soil. "They're all buried here. It's the mass grave that we told you about."

One of the other two agents was already on his radio, calling for a forensic team and proper equipment for excavating the grave site. Where was he calling? Mumbai? Did the OIO have such teams and equipment strategically located all over India, or...?

Or what? The only other explanation was so far-fetched, it was inconceivable. Had the whole episode with the Czech security guard been orchestrated? Were there actually bodies there or had it all been a huge lie, one the guard had been instructed to tell?

If so, who'd given those instructions, and why?

Chapter Thirty-Nine

South Bend, Indiana

THE THOUGHT CAME TO HER AS SHE WAS FILLING THE FORD'S FUEL TANK. SHE'D paid cash for the motel in Cleveland. The clerk had asked for a credit card, but she'd explained that all her credit cards had been stolen and would her driver's license do? The same ploy wouldn't be safe to use once she got to Minnesota, because her license had one of those computer chips in it. If the state authorities could track her location, then why couldn't someone else? Maybe they could, maybe they couldn't, but she still had the box of aluminum foil.

There—six wraps on that, too!

The image of dark-skinned Levine wearing a turban and speaking with that thick accent Alicia had described loomed large in her mind as she drove on. With so much going on the world of politics and social unrest, who'd question such a person as long as he appeared to be who he said he was? He'd move about unchallenged, except perhaps for airports, and if he had faked papers and passport…?

The image wasn't comforting at all. On the plus side, such a man would be easy to spot.

Mumbai

Special Agent Bassard read the OIO report while ambling along the ocean shoreline not that far from the embassy. The call from Kolhapur requesting a forensic team and excavating equipment had fortunately come in on his standard phone while he'd been alone. Nothing official would come of it. There'd be no excavating equipment sent to the AMBRIA site as requested, no experts. Further, the OIO boys were "not convinced" that anything they'd seen at the site had matched the wild stories provided in the written reports. Dr. Evans had been noticeably excitable, nearly frantic in his accusations and repeatedly saying there was no way anyone could have removed all the evidence he claimed existed.

The OIO team had already been reassigned to other casework, and the AMBRIA developments reported to the man with the London accent. However, it seemed his *assignment* had been expanded to include a little proxy "wet work," if agent Bassard could manage it—for an extra million. The Czech assassin would be his to control, a highly intelligent man with proficient and highly aggressive skills and years of equal field experience.

"There'll be little chance to eradicate Roman Citrano while en route to the U.S.," the voice purred, "but once he arrives, your chances will improve."

FBI Agent Bassard's influence would hold considerable sway, since he'd have been in Citrano's close company the whole time. A word or two to the right people would serve to free the man on his own recognizance, or at least with a modest bail amount. Citrano wasn't a high-profile criminal, after all. He was simply someone holding too much sensitive information, in a position to do irreparable harm if allowed to disclose it. The domestic FBI never moved quickly, so Malovec would have time enough to achieve his "surgery." He could be trusted to choose the time and place for it. Agent Bassard would then be free to return to New Delhi, where he would collect his just compensation.

Norman Bassard couldn't help noticing a touch of humor in the words. He wasn't expected to answer, so he didn't.

ജ൯

Luke knew only that his fellow sufferer, discharged from the hospital, had been taken to the consulate, arrested there and interrogated repeatedly by authorities—consular agents, the New Delhi FBI, its junior offshoot OIO, and the national police of India. Otherwise, Roman was allowed no visitors, nor had any asked to see him. Could it be that no one in the U.S. even knew where he was or what had happened?

Luke's situation was better. He had quarters inside the consular compound and was allowed travel within Mumbai city limits no earlier than eight in the morning on any day, after telling them where he was going and why. Curfew was 8 P.M. They took their time re-issuing his passport, making it clear that they'd "hold onto it" until his return to the States, so he was free only if "free" was redefined.

Roman was nearly unrecognizable when they were finally reunited. The once-robust individual was slumped in a straight chair, staring out of one of the embassy library windows, looking almost bony from loss of weight. Shoulders once broad were now thin and rounded. The salt-and-pepper hair, so striking when they'd first met, was disheveled and appeared much grayer. A tall, Indian security guard stood nearby. Why was he armed? They thought their captive would try to escape?

Roman remained seated, hands trembling uncontrollably. "I heard you were still here," he said, his voice a monotone. "Other than that, nothing… just questions, day after day. They pretended not to hear me ask about you, so I thought they'd locked you up somewhere. Did they tell you anything?"

"Only where you were. We're both supposed to be kingpins in AMBRIA, as stupid as that sounds, but I think it's only a test to see if one of us breaks with a different story. Did they say when we can return to the States?"

"Not really. I'll probably travel in handcuffs like some low-life criminal, and yet they're careful to avoid charging me with anything at all. It's all for my benefit, they say. They read me my rights, all that stuff, before any questions, but the questions tell some of the story. Seems they're investigating EMBRYIA to see if *we* violated export laws by not abiding by U.S. Customs requirements for shipping biological materials. Can you believe that? Until just a couple of weeks back, I thought the aborted fetuses were being properly destroyed. The original papers for EMBRYIA were drawn up that way, and they're on file in the States. Later Marcus Levine admitted he'd made a 'small' change in the wording—something like two or three words. I don't know, maybe I even signed it without realizing he'd done that."

"Wouldn't you have noticed something like that?"

"Luke, you read the same words dozens and dozens of times and you can miss tiny changes. Your brain skips right over them. I had our lawyers reading and re-reading the thing, but the same applies to them. If I didn't sign on to it that way, then the documents were altered later and signatures or initials were forged. I never had time to find out, even after I'd been told of the wording change. The FBI guys either haven't looked at the EMBRYIA corporate paperwork, or they have and decided to use me as a scapegoat anyway. They could at least round up Marcus Levine and turn the screws on him. He was the one shipping you the fetuses behind my back. He and his cronies ran the EMBRYIA operation. I was just the money end of things, the guy who made it all happen. That's what venture capital is all about. Now they tell me I'll get five to ten years, minimum, and that's just the Feds. There are some local statutes EMBRYIA supposedly violated in Minnesota. Probably enacted long ago to govern the sale and trade of horse or cattle semen used for breeding purposes. I hope you're making out better than I am."

"I haven't been charged with anything... yet... but they still insist that I knew all about the fetus origins. They don't believe for one minute that I was kept in the dark, and now that Dr. Rishi's gone...."

The statement needed no completion.

"Luke... did they find Kareem when they took you back to Kolhapur?"

"No, everything was gone... everything and everyone. Even the wastebaskets had been emptied. They still haven't found her or Dr. Rishi."

"And the others?" Roman whispered.

"I showed them the burial site and heard them calling someone for excavation equipment and all that, but I don't think they really believed me. I was whisked right back here. They told me *nothing* all the way back, even though they were in touch with someone by phone two or three times. Roman, the damned burial plot looked like someone's garden when we arrived. Someone had just gone over it with a tiller, and there were gardening tools lying around, just like any other garden. That mound was either leveled or the parts around it raised. It was barely noticeable."

Roman finally stood, facing him. "So they didn't find a thing. No bodies, no blood? You're not holding out on me because of my feelings, are you?"

"*Your* feelings? Holy shit, what about *my* feelings?

"Goddamn it, Luke, they're telling me nothing here, either! *Nothing!* Whatever you've heard, share it. I need to know, do you understand? I'll take my own chances on its being right or wrong."

"In other words, you think I'm lying. You think I know everything, that they found everything we figured they'd find, that nobody showed up there to work in the labs the next day, that they all magically stayed home, that—"

Roman sagged, waving off the retort and gripping the back of the chair he'd been sitting in. "Enough! Sorry… I don't know what to believe anymore. Maybe I do deserve to spend time in prison for all the pain I've brought to others. Maybe I deserve to face ridicule and prosecution. I can't help thinking this is my entire fault, that if I'd just been more careful, she'd have been alive. Now, thanks to me, she's dead. I've lost her forever."

"You don't actually *know* she's dead, just that you were told she was. And *you* told me Kareem was dead, so I don't know the truth about her, either. You're wallowing in your own self-pity. Well, wallow all you want, but don't you *dare* think that you're the only one who lost someone in all of this. I want nothing more to do with it, Roman, nothing. My world was fine until *you* showed up. As far as I'm concerned, none of it would ever have happened if you'd just stayed back there playing your game of Monopoly."

They were strangers once again. Luke stormed out of the room and never looked back.

Minnetonka, Minnesota

Uncle Chuck's cabin on the lake was far out on a peninsula. Sure enough, Bandit the raccoon came calling as soon as dusk turned to darkness, drawn by the light spilling through French doors onto the patio. Andrea had an ear of corn ready, but was preoccupied when Bandit began pawing at the door a few minutes later.

Bandit finally had given up as she sat on the musky bed rereading Alicia Gregg's handwritten sheet of information. Alicia's verbal descriptions of her half-brother left little to the imagination. Marcus Levine was a despicable rat whose only ambition, other than stroking his own ego, was to make a fortune that would set him apart from ordinary men. Alicia had known about EMBRYIA almost from the beginning, and she'd also known about his purchase of that Urgent Care building in New Jersey because she forwarded certain categories of mail there. He maintained two addresses in Minneapolis, one his personal apartment, the other an office he shared with his long-time associate David Goldberg. Both addresses were listed on the sheet. He also had an address in New York City.

Alicia supposed that *someone* was paying the bills for all these places, but knew better than to ask.

The sheet's most puzzling entry, she'd said, was a New York City mailing address that Marcus had recently added, a Tudor City apartment building. The addressee was just D.T., with the apartment number and then the building's postal address itself. Marcus would say nothing more about it, most unusual for him. Any other time he would trumpet an important, new contact in the same manner that anyone else would display a trophy.

The fact might not have been so alarming by itself, but its date suddenly set off a virtual carillon of alarm bells. It was just a few days before Marcus Levine's first meeting with Roman at Zorro Medical. Roman had actually referred to that very meeting with him when he'd called Andrea to set up their last evening together. She had circled the day he'd called her on her calendar.

And here was Levine adding a new, fresh address to his list just two weeks before he became a prominent player in Roman's business world? What connection might there be between D.T. and what later became EMBRYIA? She was almost ready to turn off the lamp and go to bed when the awful thought struck her: what if Roman *had* known about the uterus atrocities? What if he'd been a willing partner in crime? Wouldn't that explain why she'd had to call him and leave messages three times before he answered at all? She'd already wondered more than once why he hadn't called her earlier, not even to ask about her apartment in Philadelphia, her new job, whether she was all right. And then, even with three messages….

Might it not suggest that he already *knew* about… her… going to the MAU? Wouldn't that make him as devious and crooked as Marcus Levine?

It was the wrong thing to think of just before turning in for the night. When she finally heard birds singing in the pre-dawn light, she hadn't slept one wink.

Chapter Forty

Chhatrapati Shivaji International Airport, Mumbai

ROMAN STARED AT THE MAN WHO'D BE HIS ESCORT DURING THE FLIGHT BACK TO the States. It was Bassard, the New Delhi FBI agent who'd questioned him twice and who'd literally dictated procedures from that first day in the consulate! The name was fitting enough, just one letter wrong. He was stone-faced, huge by any standards although not overly tall, and used *way* too much musk. What was the almighty FBI thinking, that somehow a man recovering from a broken rib would overpower any lesser man and escape *en route*? Or was it that the New Delhi chief needed a change of scenery?

They sat shoulder-to-shoulder the entire trip without saying one word. Not only were the seats in coach, but the term shoulder-to-shoulder might well have been shoulder-*against*-shoulder.

Coach class! He hadn't flown a transatlantic flight in coach class since scrambling to start his first company. He'd achieved Diamond Elite status with his frequent flyer miles, guaranteeing an automatic upgrade on every flight, but it didn't matter. He actually welcomed the anonymity of sitting in the bowels of the aircraft with other *peasants*, a term he'd often used while teasing Sarah when she booked his flights.

Eyes closed, he felt the numbness of extreme cold. It was said that freezing to death was preferable to burning simply because at some point the victim felt no pain, no sensations. Yet nothing addressed the victim's mental state, and it was that mental state he struggled with now. It was guilt, topped with apathy. Perhaps emotional exhaustion was to blame, but he no longer cared about his own well-being, no longer felt vengeful against Marcus or angry at Luke. He had no burning desire to seek out and punish those responsible for his *selection* as a pawn in what had turned out to be an elegant, deceitful game he didn't know was being played. Games were played in every facet of business, provided it was large enough. Pawns, yes, always—but knights and rooks and queens as well. Kings? They fell only after the game had been played to its completion.

People were the variables in all sorts of businesses, the tires on which all else rolled. Be it Ferrari or Yugo, when tires went flat, nothing else mattered. He'd lived by that axiom for as long as he'd been in the venture capital arena, knowing that even the best of promising business enterprises could go down the tubes in a flash if the wrong moves were made by those entrusted to make correct ones.

Maybe he really was tired. Maybe it wasn't only emotional exhaustion, but true physical breakdown, the collapse of his adrenal system, loss of stamina. No more "fight or flight."

The eventual landing jolted him back to partial reality. No sooner had the wheels touched down than Bassard slapped on a pair of handcuffs. What idiocy required such treatment after weeks of cooperation and convalescence? The mute, expressionless robot was probably a direct descendent of J. Edgar Hoover, chosen and promoted for his skill in sitting indefinitely without communicating anything of value. He certainly looked and acted the part.

Then again, perhaps an assignment to New Delhi wasn't a promotion.

St. Paul, Minnesota

The accelerated processing through Customs was designed specifically for dignitaries, diplomats and criminals, the latter being photographed full face and profile. At least Roman wasn't required to hold a placard with a number on it. Outside the airport they were greeted by two black town cars with three large, pale-faced men standing between them. Their apparently casual discussion suddenly turned uneasy as Bassard pushed Roman forward.

The smallest of the trio stepped forward from the pack. "Special Agent Bassard," he bellowed, "the Federal prosecutor has decided to allow the State to prosecute their case in first order, given the amount of evidence still being collected for the Federal case. He's to be turned over to the State."

It was a scene right out of the Three Stooges. Bassard looked for confirmation from the tallest of the three, the only one wearing dark, wraparound sunglasses.

"Yes, it's out of our hands… let's see what they can do with him first."

In one deliberate, military-like move, Bassard swung around him and unlocked the agonizing handcuffs. Without so much as a word or glance, he and the tall one entered the first vehicle and pulled away. The door to the remaining vehicle was held open by the small bellower.

"What, no restraints or leg irons? No fear of me overtaking you two and making a getaway?"

"Just get in the car, Mr. Citrano, you've already wasted enough of our time today."

ᘓᘐ

The flight had touched down at 10:40 a.m. An hour later Roman stood before a grumpy-looking Minnesota magistrate whose early lunch period was suddenly "on hold." No formal processing, no consultation with counsel, not even an explanation by some brown-shoed administrative clerk! A walnut nameplate identified magistrate Thomas Donalty, but the eight or so others in the room weren't identified by name or function. Some left; others took their place. A few were curiosity seekers on lunch break. One could have been a reporter, since he was taking notes. There was no court stenographer.

Donalty had a thick file before him, well-worn by the looks of it. Did that mean considerable time spent reviewing the materials, or was it simply a reused folder? After several minutes of page turning forward and back, he peered over half glasses and asked for proof of identification of the man in custody. The bellower handed over Roman's worn passport, stepping back. Later, Roman would learn that the short guy with the loud mouth was a Minnesota Duty Officer accompanied by two State Detectives. None of the three were FBI.

Donalty quickly scanned the photo, glanced once at the prisoner, then added it to the file.

"Mr. Citrano, the Attorney General has prepared three felony charges in regards to your activities associated with the—," he peered through his glasses, "—the EM-BERRIA Corporation, and federal charges are still pending. Therefore this is merely a preliminary hearing. As indicated by the Miranda rights of which you were already informed, you have the right to retain counsel, and if you're so inclined, a public defender could be assigned to your case. Bail has been set at $50,000 in recognition of your cooperation to date. You will be confined to the Ramsey County Jail until bail is met, or a formal hearing date set. At the time of your post-indictment arraignment, you'll be asked to enter a plea for each of the charges."

Donalty then stood, sweeping up the file and his walnut nameplate, and exited the emptying courtroom.

That was it? No charges, not even a clue? This was all to satisfy some statute, not to serve justice. It didn't make sense. EMBRYIA was a Delaware corporation. The MAUs operated in New Jersey and California. Where did Minnesota come in, unless… Marcus? By some chance had he been funneling his fetus shipments through one of the Minneapolis international freight forwarding companies? The containers were refrigerated. They didn't need to come to Minneapolis to be air-freighted anywhere in the world, but the operation could all be handled from the small office Levine shared with Goldberg "right down the street." That had to be it. There were ways of disguising shipping point records, and those containers had no more than the EMBRYIA logo on them, plus all the shipment forms slapped on the outsides. They'd never be opened, not even by Customs in India.

As if choreographed, the bailiff came forward, handcuffed his "new prisoner" and escorted him to a holding cell. No hint of when any assigned attorney might appear, not a clue as to when he'd be allowed his "one phone call."

Roman's temporary peace lasted less than an hour before he was shoved into a large transport vehicle like any other damn criminal! Twenty minutes later he was processed in the Ramsey County Jail and placed in a cell with fifteen other "criminals," four of them total drunks. Not even four hours on U.S. soil and every indication was that he'd already been convicted. Three felonies, not including others possible on the federal side?

Mug shots at the airport, yet? Which system was in force here, justice or injustice?

Charges against those in the tank with him ranged from rape and assault with a deadly weapon to first-time DUI's, based on what he managed to overhear, and of course there were the four drunks, one dressed in formal clothes. He loudly volunteered the details of his "heinous crime" to anyone who'd listen. He'd punched out someone eyeing his date's ass at a party!

The other three were sleeping it off in various poses on the floor.

The so-called justice system clanked into motion once the holding cell reached sixteen occupants, triggering the arrival of several guards. Prisoners were then escorted three at a time to another cell, visible from the first one, where they were issued something similar to a two-piece pair of doctors' scrubs, two pairs of briefs and brown plastic sandals. Pocket contents had been confiscated earlier. Roman was treated differently. He still had to give up his personal clothing, but now he could finally make that phone call. One of the guards grunted something about the process to make bail, and pointed at a small desk with a standard phone on it. No paper or pens, no phone book. He was supposed to carry around phone numbers in his head? Or was he to ask for a phone book? This couldn't be happening anywhere in the U.S. It had to be North Korea, or some other police state.

He sat staring at the thing, wondering who to call even if he had the numbers memorized. Should it be a bail agent—someone who could do it on his behalf? His partners had abandoned him, his brother lived over in northern Wisconsin—they hadn't spoken for nearly a year. The attorney who'd helped draft their Fund documents? Surely his legal firm could handle such a mundane request as bail. He remembered the phone number and started to dial, but was interrupted by another guard who was literally standing at his shoulder.

"Citer-rano, Roman… you've made bail", he barked, reading from a clipboard to all those within earshot.

Roman stopped dialing. "What? That's me. Who supplied bail? I haven't even called anyone yet!"

The guard shrugged. "Your fairy godfather?" He beckoned with a thumb. "Follow me."

In another room where fingerprinting and photographing were in process, he signed three documents without even reading them and was shown the door to the visitors' waiting area. As he pushed through the door, his "fairy godfather" came forward.

"My gawd, you look awful!" she said.

Chapter Forty-One

"Sarah! How did you know? Who told you I was here?"

"Oh, the FBI paid me visit number three just yesterday, and the press did their part with repeated and conflicting stories about EMBRYIA and you. I knew you were due back here today because I asked the FBI guy what would happen, and when. He was quite accommodating, even if he was a total nerd. I think he was a trainee. Anyway, he said you'd be brought here."

"They all seem to be trainees. Can you imagine spending half a day in a plane with a guy who didn't speak one word the whole time?" Roman tried not to gawk. Stress had obviously taken its toll. Sarah was no longer her perky self, in her trademark swishy skirts and heels. In their place were jeans with a pull-over sweater, hair pulled back in a ponytail and no visible make-up.

"Did they indict you?" she asked. "Is that the right term?"

"It was kind of an arraignment hearing without any charges being read. Felonies that weren't described and undefined federal charges on the way. Justice at its finest."

She led him out into the parking lot, where she unloaded. "Everyone's gone and Paul packed up his stuff only a week ago and Josh never returned after your meeting with Marcus, who is missing and no one can locate him, and the FBI has a tap on our phone thinking he's going to try and reach you." She continued babbling non-stop all the way to her car.

"Thank you," he finally managed to say. "Thanks for being there, Sarah, and for getting me out. Is there anything left at the office?"

"If there is, it's probably tied up legally. I wasn't sure how long I *should* stay," she went on. "I haven't been paid since you left… without telling me where the hell you were going, by the way!" She flared her eyes. "I just kept coming in every day. The cops and FBI showed up one day and took all records relating to the EMBRYIA investment, including your board minutes and *all* your notebooks. The things they were saying about you were *terrible*… they're not true… are they?"

"No... none of it, but some awful things have happened. Things we can't undo."

"Roman, there's something else," she said, snapping her seatbelt. "There've been threats... threats against you on your office phone, and some ugly letters, mostly from some radical ProLife organization. Oh... and some guy with a British accent wanting to know if Marcus was here."

That had to be David Thomas, the CFO he'd met briefly during his first visit to AMBRIA. As soon as the name came to mind, he remembered the sign on the office door where he'd found Kareem's body: David Thomas, Chief Financial Officer! Thomas was looking for Levine, which meant that Dr. Levine had come up missing. What else *could* it mean? Marcus was last in the Zorro offices, cowering in the corner while he spun his lies. Were those lies his swan song? Did he decide to lay low while the AMBRIA atrocities were uncovered, waiting to see what came of them, then emerging once again like some snake slithering out of hiding beneath a rock?

Or was he running? Who'd be after him? Who'd want to know where he was, when a simple phone call would?... Ah, but what if he wasn't answering his phone these days? What if he *knew* he was no longer needed at AMBRIA? He'd perfected the final phase of their operation, so there was nothing else they needed from him. Now he was a liability. He could even become a target. The same reasoning might be applied to anyone involved with EMBRYIA.

If Kareem had been killed by Thomas and her body left in his office, then Thomas had nothing to fear because he *was* AMBRIA. He'd declared himself king, which meant he was highly placed in the cartel.

"This British guy... I think I know who it is, but best I don't mention his name. You have enough to cope with, but when did he call?"

"Yesterday. I haven't mentioned any of this to anyone. I played dumb with the FBI and local cops. I had no idea where you were and hadn't heard from you in weeks, which was the truth."

"Well, the FBI knew where I was the whole time, starting with a hospital in Mumbai and later when I was recovering in their convalescent ward under armed guard. I'll tell you about it later. They were probably tapping those phone calls from this British guy as well. Where are we going?"

"Back to the office?"

"Wake me up when we get there."

"When did you last sleep?"

"I have no idea."

Chapter Forty-Two

THAT TOO-FAMILIAR DEPRESSED FEELING HAD SETTLED ON HIM LIKE WET SOD—the same feeling he always got when returning to his empty apartment after a long business trip, but worse. Worse than the time he'd returned from his European office while struggling to build one of his first start-up companies, only to find that his wife had left him, taking all the furnishings of value, everything she'd ever given him, even the refrigerator contents. She'd left a jar of dill pickles on the kitchen table. That was her version of the stiff third finger.

He'd slumped to the kitchen floor, crushed and abandoned, overwhelmed with despair, not knowing or even caring how to move forward. Defeated and alone, he'd managed nevertheless, one day at a time.

This time the feeling was laden with depression of a different kind. He had no direction or ambition, no projects to take his mind off his personal tragedy. As he pushed through the Zorro entry door, he knew a void would greet him. The entire support staff had followed the Minneapolis Tribune stories. All seven had resigned. Sarah had stayed.

"Paul hung around the longest," she said, sensing his disappointment. "He took a CEO position at a start-up orthopedic company here in the Cities, one we'd considered investing in. Josh never returned at all after your last meeting here, between all of you and Marcus. He took his laptop, but he never came back, not even for the family pictures in his office."

"No good can possibly come from this deal." Josh's prophetic words echoed as he visualized Marcus, cowering against Josh's locked door.

His own inner office suggested he'd missed the marauders by mere minutes. Every desk drawer was yanked out, the file cabinets were all open—some drawers all the way—and papers were scattered everywhere. Folders covered the floor.

He spun around. "What's this, Sarah?"

"I… I thought it was best if I just left it as I found it… so you could identify what they took. Shall I straighten it all up?" She knelt, scooping up a folder.

"No." He squatted and grabbed both wrists, looking deep into her eyes. "It's over, Sarah. There's no Fund and no partnership. Terrible things will be brought out in court, things you need to know before you hear the ugly rumors and stories that might develop."

She started crying. Had she already heard them? He pulled her close, holding her as he'd wanted to hold Andrea. He wanted to tell her everything would be okay—as he wanted someone to tell *him*—but all he could do now was try to save himself.

"We have some remaining management fees in the Fund that I can pay you from," he finally said. "I need your help in preparing my defense and to… unwind the Fund and notify our investors. There's much to do… can you stay?"

"Roman, you have no idea… do you? No idea of how I feel about you… I'm here for you, for as long as you want me."

She tilted her head back and closed her eyes. He knew what she expected, what her words and actions meant, but his mind was elsewhere, staring past her without seeing.

"Can you get me Tom Martinez on the phone," he said, pulling himself to his feet. "You'll find his contact information under the law firm of Dorsal & Whilley. I've used them multiple times for my other start-up companies and they were the firm that my *former* partners and I used to set up the legal structure of the Fund."

She sighed, disappointed. "Yes, of course." Wiping away her tears, she scrambled to her feet, nearly slipping on the papers and open folders. He reached, steadying her.

"Tom can guide us through dissolution of the Fund and I'm sure he can recommend a good defense attorney… God knows I'm gonna need one." His depression was finally evolving into pure anger. Numb, he pulled the materials together on his desk and slammed the desk drawers shut, trying not to reflect on the fact that dissolving the Fund would probably cost a fraction of what it cost to set it up.

Damn it! By the time the lawyers are done, there may not be anything at all. He shoved the bottom file drawer shut with a foot. It bounced back out.

All right, get a grip! Think! What are your next steps, and the ones after those? Get back in control. The mental organization process would be his escape from the gut-wrenching horrors of the past six months. He'd win this fight, and then he'd rebound, build another partnership, do what he did best. Most of all he'd go after Marcus Levine! If ever he found him, there'd be nothing more than a shell, an H.S.O. The term "human shaped object" was something he'd used in jest back in his rugby days when pumping himself up before a game. It implied his intention to completely eviscerate the opposing player, brain and all.

But first he had to gain control.

His office phone buzzed less than ten minutes later. It was Sarah—she had another line on hold. The Press, or was it another threatening call? "I have Martinez on the line," she announced, sounding annoyed.

"Roman, Tom Martinez here. I've been wondering when you'd finally find the time to call me."

"Tom… I *just* got back to the office minutes ago. I'm sure you've heard what's happened here. Not much time to discuss the details, but we need to notify our Limited Partners, potentially dissolve the Partnership and return any remaining funds back to our investors."

"Breathe easy, Roman. I've had several meetings with Paul and Josh in your unexplained absence… the documents are finalized and simply need your signature. There were sufficient funds remaining to pay the legal costs, and after deducting what we've estimated, you'll only have about a hundred thousand remaining in your account. Josh has also taken actions to assume the lease agreement on your office space, which only needs your consent. Apparently he's already set up a consulting company with another firm and recently signed a deal to manage the investments for the new Mayo Clinic Technology Incubator down in Rochester. That guy doesn't waste any time!"

Those bastards! They wrote me off without waiting. All our years together, and it comes down to a big, fat zero? They didn't even reach out to me, never even tried. Well, at least I won't have to deal with shutting down this mess. Partnerships were supposed to be more than that. Dumas had it right in The Three Musketeers: all for one, one for all. That's how they had defined themselves when they first agreed to form the partnership. That's what they promised each other. All bullshit!

"Well… what can I say, Tom," he finally replied, pulling himself together. "Saves me a helluva lot of trouble. Should I come over there and finalize the documents?"

"Sure. Anytime tomorrow morning would be fine."

"While I have you… as I'm sure you've heard… I'm in need of your best defense attorney there at your practice. Who would you recommend?"

"Ron LaForge would be willing to handle it. He's the best in the firm and he has experience in international law as well. Sounds like you might need that from all the rumors we've heard. Should I have him give you a call?"

Willing to handle it? What's that supposed to mean, that they drew straws and this LaForge got the short one? "Yes, please do so… give him both the office and my cell number. I'll see ya in the morning."

He'd known Martinez for nearly twenty years. Though they'd never really socialized together, they'd always had a pretty tight and intimate working relationship, but apparently that was no longer a sure thing. Tom's voice had a cold edge to it. The Press had worked their poison, as they always did. Stories and rumors had replaced truth. It was what they did best—smearing—and it would get worse.

Martinez had La Forge's name "front and center," offering it before the question was totally out, yet no charges had been read. What rumors had been heard, and how might La Forge have learned of the specific charges? Three undefined felonies were mentioned, yes, but no formal charges and no pleas. It was simply an informal "prelim" hearing, not an arraignment, so how could La Forge or anyone else say they were "willing" to take on the defense? And how far could a hundred thousand go? Ten times that amount might not be enough when the Feds were done loading up *their* ridiculous charges. Hell, it could be twenty or thirty times that much.

As Roman finished with Martinez, Sarah half-ran into the office with something looking like a greasy lunch bag in hand. She was shaking.

"This… this was just left at our outer door," she gasped. She held it out, and three drops of reddish fluid splattered on his desk. A closer look at the "grease" on the brown paper bag showed it to be diluted blood. Inside was an all-too-familiar folded piece of gauze, soaked with serous-thin blood. He turned the bag upside down, dumping its contents on his already compromised desk. Sarah's hand went to her mouth as he pushed back the edge of the cheese-cloth with a pencil, disclosing a twelve-week-old unpreserved fetus, already bluish in color, with letters written across its small arched back. He turned it gently, disclosing a single word in ink: MURDERER.

After what he'd seen in the AMBRIA labs, this no longer moved him at all, but he had to notify the police officially in the event something were to come of this… this threat. Or was it closer to a definitive statement? A declaration would well *become* a threat. It was just a matter of time.

Sarah went to call the police, sobbing as she gave the address over the phone. Moments later, more composed, she returned with a Tupperware container holding remnants of her lunch. She tapped out the remaining contents into the wastebasket, set the now-empty container on the very edge of the desk, turned quickly away and left the office without a word.

ꟸꟷ

The two Minneapolis Police officers took a short statement from Sarah and had him repeat nearly the same. He had to explain that the lump of fleshy material was actually a human fetus. After a few brief moments of disgust, they photographed it and indicated that it would be "properly discarded" back at the station. The junior man put on a pair of throw-away gloves, then "borrowed" a sheet of paper from the yellow, lined pad on the desk and used it to push the fetus and gauze into a black plastic zip-top bag. The crumpled, bloody paper was left on the desktop. The officer's job was to collect evidence, not perform janitorial duties!

The senior officer finished his notes on a worn notepad that barely covered the palm of his ham-like hand, using a stubby wood pencil with a point last sharpened a year or two earlier.

"If you want any sort of formal protection, you'll have to come down to the station with us and speak to our captain," he said. "We'll also forward our report to a specific investigator in another department that handles such matters. You should expect a follow-up visit from them."

Expect a follow-up visit? Now there was an understatement if there ever was one! Cops wouldn't be cops if they weren't badgering someone every minute.

Roman's cell phone rang at that moment. It was a local number, perhaps the sender of his little "welcome home" gift? Both officers stood fast, waiting for him to answer, but the calling number was suddenly too familiar. He quickly nodded an "okay," shook both officers' hands, then punched the "talk" button while heading back into his office.

"This is Ron LaForge, with Dorsal & Whilley," the caller announced. "It appears we need to talk."

"Yes… indeed, we do. I'm—" A tiny beep interrupted him. Damn! His cell phone battery was about to die. "I'm meeting with Martinez tomorrow morning—" *Beep!* "Ron, is it? Ron, my cell battery's just about out. Can you call me back—" *Beep!*

He gave his office number, apologized, then hung up. Of all the stupid… he hadn't had a chance to charge the thing since… well, since Kolhapur. Sarah had a phone adapter. Might as well start charging while he waited.

But Sarah wasn't there. Her purse was gone; she'd fled. He was alone—again—abandoned, with that same depressed feeling. How long would it take him to shake it this time?

Chapter Forty-Three

Minneapolis

ANDREA'S BACKGROUND CHECK FOR THE CCW TOOK LESS THAN ONE DAY, BUT by the time all the bureaucratic red tape was added on, the time stretched to four more days. She used the time to visit three gun stores and two important addresses, one that Alicia had listed as Levine's private apartment and the other the office he shared with a man named David Goldberg. Neither of those addresses showed any activity even though she'd watched each one for several hours, sitting in her car several doors away.

Then she swung by Roman's place, more out of curiosity than any hope of finding him. He'd either be at Zorro, which was downtown on Marquette Avenue, or traveling god-knows-where for business. Sure enough, there was no car in his driveway.

Her basic plan was simple enough: find answers. With all that had already happened, there'd be no returning to her job in Philadelphia wearing a *status quo* mask, if indeed she even had a job. Dr. Adams' administrative leave might not hold forever. Her quest was saturated with danger in light of what had happened to her in that basement prison. Who exactly should she fear? How many were there? Who knew about her? And finally, was Roman really a part of it all?

Only when the answers were satisfactory, when she felt safe again, could she even think about her career. She'd described herself correctly to her uncle. She was a fugitive, but, as he'd so wisely said, she could use her head and always had. One fact stood out above all others: her true identity was known to her enemies, whereas she knew little about them. It was not the best of situations.

At the gun stores, she'd found that her uncle had been right. A Taurus Millennium fit her hand really well, could be carried comfortably in her purse and seemed simple enough. Although none of the stores carried all the versions there were, the salesmen she talked to nodded approvingly when she stipulated a model 140BP. She got even more nods when she mentioned the Hornady 180 grain jacketed hollow point bullets.

"Someone certainly knows her guns", the final store owner remarked. "We don't get many real savvy gals in here." His prices were a bit higher than the others, but she knew she'd go back there once her paperwork was ready. She'd already signed up for the full-treatment gun safety course. If ever she was confronted by her enemies, perhaps to be abducted again, or worse, she'd be ready. There was no such thing as "it can't happen to me."

Her stakeout of the two Levine addresses finally paid off on the fifth day. She'd parked the gray Ford within sight of the Levine apartment duplex, knowing already that he had the right hand side. Shortly after she settled into her watch, two black cars arrived together and parked almost directly in front of the door. Each of the cars disgorged two men, and all four gathered at the door. Three seemed to be watching the fourth man do something, and in seconds they were inside!

Were *they* members of whatever group was behind the EMBRYIA atrocities? Did that mean that Marcus Levine had been there all along, just as she'd suspected? Did he let them in? It appeared that the group of men had opened the front door, not someone inside, but there was no safe way to find out. All she could do was wait until they came back out, maybe to see a fifth man with them. That would be Levine, if it happened.

The original four came out almost an hour later, carrying several shopping bags with handles, but there was no fifth person. They drove away almost immediately. What did all *that* mean?

She decided to move to the other address, but when she reached it the same two black cars were there ahead of her. Both cars were empty; the same four men were already inside. They reappeared some time later with more shopping bags, then drove away. Once again, no one came to the entrance with them.

What on earth was going on? Who were they? What did they have to do with Marcus Levine? Andrea fought down a flash of anger. According to Alicia, both addresses were visited only when her rat brother was in town, or possibly his sidekick, this Goldberg person. She usually received notice when Marcus was heading for Minneapolis, because he'd want his mail forwarded there if the visit was to be more than a couple of days, and he hadn't contacted Alicia with any such announcement.

Yet here was some kind of activity involving a quartet of serious-looking men who'd gone inside both places empty handed, and come out carrying bags. Who might have been inside? Might it be a man wearing a turban? If so, he didn't plan on being there very long, or he'd have informed his sister.

Minneapolis

The Citrano fighting spirit returned within four days of setting foot on U.S. soil, but his actual arraignment took half a month. Sixth Amendment guarantees were ignored, thanks to his signature on one of the three forms he'd executed without reading. His right to a speedy trial was waived for "good cause," and the pace of preparations for trial was at best lethargic. He was free on bail, so what was the big rush? After more delay, the judge assigned to the case set a tentative hearing date, which was shoved back three times for reasons unknown.

As it turned out, two of the three felonies as defined by Minnesota were in the White Collar category, with one of the three also involving aiding and abetting. LaForge opted *not* to press for a faster legal pace since there were still missing links. If things moved too quickly, the necessary outside attorneys and academics would drain precious funds. LaForge emphasized that this was an "all or nothing" battle. Conviction on any of the charges would lend credence to the slowly building but more far-reaching federal case, a case evidenced by repeated questions and clarifications directed at LaForge by the FBI. It was badgering, pure and simple. The FBI *had* all the existing records, plus all the legal records filed with the State of Minnesota, and the locals were assumed to hold the same. It had been the FBI who trashed Zorro Medical's offices and removed all the files.

They constantly questioned Roman's relationship with Dr. Sihar Rishi, beginning way back in his early college days, trying in every way possible to implicate him in the AMBRIA operation through that relationship. There was no way to know what documentation they held, but his name might have appeared in dozens of ways without his knowledge. After all, *he* was the money and the brains behind EMBRYIA. Federal indictments, still being prepared, could come at any time, LaForge said.

Sarah remained in the picture, but eventually detached herself to take an administrative position with the University of Minnesota, not far from their old offices. She'd been identified as a potential witness in any litigation and had already given a deposition. When she started receiving death threats, she moved in with her parents, admitting that she was terrified.

There weren't too many other witnesses. EMBRYIA was no different than other corporations in terms of services, expertise, materials and procurements. Even the MAUs were straightforward, not much different than custom "land yachts" for the affluent among the world's sightseers. They looked pretty much the same to any bystander, and contained standard medical equipment and supplies when fully furbished.

Depositions were taken of several former EMRYIA employees in LA and Camden, but with the exception of Dr. Raj Maibeck, none were truly relevant or harmful. Maibeck provided all the gory details of the abortions, the special extraction techniques and his personal suspicions of Marcus Levine, but told a convincing story supporting his claim that he had nothing to do with the preservation and shipping of the fetal remains.

In Maibeck's view, disposition of the remains fell to others directed by none other than Marcus Levine, and in fact had started with Levine in the Camden MAU operation. For as long as Levine had monitored Camden, he'd always been the one who collected remains and removed them, or else arranged for others to take on the task prior to his moving to the LA operation. Various unidentified individuals in white coveralls would arrive at day's end, following orders from Levine and using "appropriate transport equipment." They were the last to leave the MAU, always emptying and servicing the usual trash and waste containers in the process. Who ever questioned cleanup crews?

Chapter Forty-Four

The FBI not only found Levine's small downtown apartment and took everything thought important, but found the even smaller office shared with David Goldberg as well. Any evidence implicating Marcus was impounded, recorded messages on the telephone answering machines were copied and erased, and every bit of trash removed. Both sites were now secured.

LaForge assumed Marcus Levine was dead. AMBRIA's henchmen would certainly know more about Levine than anyone else, he stated, so the likelihood of them rubbing him out in any of dozens of ways was high. Roman didn't share that view. Levine was an inveterate liar, unpredictable, quick-thinking and street wise. If anyone could disappear without a trace, it would be Levine. The only personal information he'd revealed were listed in his *curriculum vitae*—a list of credentials restricted to his profession. He'd once mentioned that both his parents were dead, but the rest of his life was a total mystery.

Marcus would have seen the disaster brewing in the Kolhapur situation after Andrea's perceived threat to blow the whistle. Until then he'd led a double life, offering all sorts of answers and excuses for anything going on in Kolhapur while treating AMBRIA as though he was indeed in control of his own destiny. The master juggler had no doubt planned his disappearing act long before Andrea was flown out of Philly, and could now be in some remote country, never to be found. He might as well be dead, but he could also reappear if the assumptions were wrong. If so, he'd have an airtight alibi for things that "he had no way of knowing." He'd also screw things up royally as far as the legal process was concerned, depending on when and how he reappeared.

Those fears were doubled with Luke's phone call. Considering his explosive departure in the Mumbai consulate, the call came as both a shock and surprise. Luke wasn't only apologetic for his earlier outburst, but actually friendly. He'd done a bit of sleuthing just to get Roman's cell phone number, and he was also in the States himself—as a potential witness! The New Delhi FBI, in their infinite wisdom, had finally connected Dr. Luke

Evans to one Roman Citrano, presently under indictment for something or other in the U.S.! Those in India who'd made the remarkable discovery couldn't tell him what the Citrano indictment was all about, because they didn't know. They only knew the names Citrano and AMBRIA. The head man in their office, name of Bassard, was presently in the U.S. on that same case, and *he* was the one who'd made the connection. Luke was then flown to Minneapolis, where he'd voluntarily reported to those who were preparing for the federal trial. He was concerned about Levine.

"I suspect that this guy might have already set up another facility like the one at AMBRIA," he explained, "most likely in a nearby town. That would allow them to move all the specimens quickly, without loss. He's probably running the place for them. I've been told that the original buildings are now empty, but there are dozens of small towns in that region with hundreds of industrial buildings that could house a parallel operation. Anyway, you're not my enemy, Roman. I shouldn't have blown up the way I did, and I'm sorry, and right now if I had Marcus Levine within reach, he wouldn't last a minute! I called one of the lab techs from Mumbai—the only one I had a number for—and she screamed one word as soon as I said my name: *Hatyaara*! It's Hindi for murderer. Then she hung up. I think *he* was the one who told everyone that I was the murderer, that Rishi and… and Kareem…."

"Are you free now, Luke? Out on bail, like me?"

"I'm not charged with anything—yet—but I *am* cooperating. Hell, I want to. I have no job and, unless this thing gets straightened out, no career. I want to see whoever's responsible strung up, and I realize now that's not you. I realize lots of things now."

"So are you free to travel? I'm not permitted to leave the States without notifying the court, but I say we should join forces and find Levine if he's still alive. I think he is. The Feds ransacked his apartment here in Minneapolis, and they got to Goldberg's office, too. Goldberg was Levine's operations guy and I think he handled those shipments out of the U.S. to Kolhapur. Where are you now?"

"Right here… in St. Paul."

ഇഓ

Bassard punched in the phone number he'd already memorized, one with a 212 area code, then started recording. Several moments later, the answering end picked up and several words were spoken with a British accent. He answered with the code word.

"Hello, my friend," Thomas said. "I see you have set things into motion quite nicely. Our 'mechanic' has been in touch with me, and assures me that the quarry is now being tracked at every opportunity. He gave you high marks. You have done well."

"Thanks. I try. You were right—he's very intelligent. When do I get my—"

"Your payment? We've wired it to a bank account we set up for you, in the Cayman Islands. The amount will not raise eyebrows there, whereas you would be hard pressed to place it safely elsewhere. However, I will personally send you a retainer— shall we say a quarter million?—in bearer bonds, to an address you'll supply me. I presume you will leave the FBI once you are financially... comfortable?"

"Cayman Islands?"

"Yes, a haven for funds that have no owners by name, only by number. I have an account there, as do so many in our business. Swiss accounts are no longer desirable. Too... perilous thanks to new Swiss tax laws. You should begin thinking on a larger scale anyway. A man with several million dollars needs somewhere to put it besides his mattress."

"I'm not set up at this end to receive anything safely. Is there a way that a package can be handed to me elsewhere, away from Minneapolis? I can easily come to New York."

"The reason for your concern?"

"The Minneapolis FBI knows where I'm staying, but I don't know them or their habits. They're being altogether too hospitable."

"I understand. You want to avoid being drawn into their activities during your stay in the city."

"Correct. They think I know far more about all this than I do. I can't afford to have any official mail, or even a courier, show up here or it will reinforce those beliefs. I have reason to be extremely cautious even when in New Delhi, where I *do* know my people."

"Good thinking. Can you arrange to be in New York, say... six days from now? Grant's tomb, overlooking the Hudson River, is a convenient meeting place. Let us make the time early... seven thirty. I will bring cash."

"I see no problem with that."

"Excellent. Also, we can talk about another assignment for you if you are interested. You have completed the present one to my satisfaction."

"How much?"

"Interesting that you should jump without knowing what the assignment will be." There was a soft chuckle on the far end. "Shall we make it another two? I should think that would make your future quite secure, don't you agree?"

"For that much, it must be wet work. Am I correct?"

"Yes. We'd like you to handle this one yourself."

"The target?"

"Marcus Levine. We know where he is, what he is doing and the name he is using. Are you prepared to jot down a few details?"

ꕥ

LaForge's courtroom skills were immediately evident. The prosecution had been overly smug in its belief that the accused man was indeed guilty, even though most prosecutors took that approach automatically. Seeing that, LaForge changed his opening strategy to educate the jury in the basics of venture capital and entrepreneurship. Things took an even better turn with Dr. Lucas Evans' testimony the following day. Evans corroborated many statements taken from Roman's earlier depositions, augmenting LaForge's picture of an entrepreneur who'd decided—with misgivings—to pursue an unpopular and risky venture with the aim of improving the state of women's healthcare in general, this even though abortion was a politically explosive topic. Without coaching, Luke brought several depositions into sharp focus with his description of Roman's passion for the project. It wasn't at all about money, Luke offered, but rather about a solution of one of society's ills. Roman was proud to have the talent and knowledge to achieve specific goals and make the prospects attractive to would-be investors.

The jury's reaction to this fresh, all-American looking young man was extremely positive. It wasn't until Luke was cross-examined and mentioned Roman's caustic comment about the fetuses coming from a "fetal farm in Missouri" that LaForge jumped to his feet to object. Even that was more about "good theatre" than any real necessity. LaForge made his point that the remark was a sarcastic response to a mindless question, nothing more.

Later that night, LaForge called with even more good news.

"Roman, we found Goldberg... in Argentina... but only after tracking him first to relatives in New Orleans. Apparently he flew the coop to the Big Easy just days after you took up residence in that Mumbai consulate. That's when the Feds looted his office here in the Cities, but there's something odd. He must have removed the EMBRYIA stuff *before* the raid, because the Feds didn't go after him then, and haven't even now. Was he even in the picture when you set up EMBRYIA?"

"No. Marcus was the acting president, chief operating officer and secretary at the onset. I served as the interim-CFO and treasurer, but Marcus and Goldberg went way back in some collegiate way, never well explained. Marcus wanted Goldberg as his man Friday."

"Which means the original corporate documents didn't assign anything to Goldberg in the way of responsibility," LaForge concluded, "but the Feds later stumbled across his name and went after his records... interesting. He didn't head for New Orleans because of the Feds raiding his office—he was gone well before that—but he was in New Orleans only a couple of months before scramming down to Buenos Aires. He might have been running from AMBRIA to save his own neck, not running from the Feds. Anyway, we know where he is at this moment and he's *our* witness if we play things right. I'm wondering if we could loan him to our Fed friends later, along with whatever records he has with him, in return for some leniency in their case against you, as yet undefined. Goldberg may be good for our side in lots of ways."

"He eventually became the *de facto* Chief Operating Officer, Ron, privy to every damn thing that EMBRYIA did and everything Marcus was doing outside of EMBRYIA, so if he has all the records it can only help us. If you can get him on the stand, the stuff in his head could *really* help us. So how do we get him?"

"Won't be easy, but if he was running from AMBRIA we might be able to arrange some witness protection through the locals or even the Feds themselves. Otherwise, he could end up being dead meat right along with Marcus, for all the same reasons. We can send a man down there to persuade him. I'll send the bloodhound I use from time to time."

"Why would Goldberg come back here? If he's running, that is?"

"If *we* can find him, so can someone else. He'll understand that in spades. This is important enough for us to ask for a trial recess, maybe a week or two."

"You don't sound too excited about this, Ron. Is there something else you haven't told me?"

"No, there's… okay, yes, I guess there is. But it's not about Goldberg; it's something personal, something that was bound to happen sooner or later. Something you should know." LaForge's tone was noticeably more somber. "I arrived home to find my wife with a house full of police officers. Someone had killed…" His voice nearly broke. "…someone had killed our dog. He was a Westin Terrier that I bought her on our tenth wedding anniversary. Similar to the fetus that was delivered to your office, they'd shaved the one side of his small body and left me a message, 'DEFEND and DIE.' My wife is taking this pretty hard. I'll be driving her over to Madison to stay with her mother this weekend. I'm also accepting the full-time security the police commissioner offered us both until this thing is over. I just hope Goldberg makes it to the stand. We haven't any airtight way of keeping his transit back here quiet, if he comes, and of course the media will be onto this like flies on horseshit as soon as we produce him."

What was there to say? The long pause had reflected an unspoken understanding that had grown between him and Ron LaForge. He'd kept many of his own daily threats quiet and to himself, but Ron had repeatedly predicted there'd be threats, knew they were happening without being told, knew they were relentless. It made little difference to the threat-makers that important evidence was coming out of this case, evidence showing that Roman and EMBRYIA were just small pawns in a huge, global black-market that had been unknown until now.

The press, in particular, interchanged EMBRYIA with AMBRIA, constantly casting EMBRYIA as the master perpetrator responsible for the black market sales of fetus-derived organs, continually mentioning Roman Citrano in connection with *illegal* abortion mills spreading world-wide. He was hung in effigy twice within a stone's throw of the courthouse. He was filth, and filth was grist for the media mill!

Nobody reported that MAU abortions were subsidized by several organizations in both New Jersey and California, wherein public funds were paid to the same degree that any "legitimate abortions" were covered. The media were after sensationalism, failing miserably when truth became the issue. Truth never sold anything, nor did it contribute to ratings or circulation.

LaForge got his recess. The prosecution considered Goldberg's discovery extremely beneficial to their side and were immediately cooperative. A two-week hiatus was declared.

No sooner had arrangements for Goldberg's return been put into motion than LaForge and his team uncovered the financing scheme behind AMBRIA. It appeared to stem from a collaborative cartel involving a Dutch organized crime syndicate and an existing Israeli organ procurement business that had been illegally buying and selling human organs all over the world *prior to* the creation of AMBRIA. This cartel was also involved in other well-investigated activities out of Singapore and Tangier, including the marketing of white-slaves and child prostitutes. Although this information diminished any notion that Roman was simply "illegally exporting biological materials," they still needed evidence that he was deliberately misled, that the aborted fetuses were *not* destroyed, but in fact were shipped to India to supply an underground organ market.

If only they could produce Marcus Levine now! When LaForge expressed the thought for the third time in as many minutes, Roman decided to follow an instinct. "Ron, how much time do we have before the Federal case?"

"I would guess five to six weeks, maybe more. They'll give us plenty of advance notice. Why?"

"Because Luke and I think we might be able to figure out where Levine is hiding if we can come up with a couple of clues. Can we get permission to go through his apartment and that office he used with Goldberg?"

LaForge shook his head. "You won't find anything. They went through that stuff with a vacuum cleaner and took away anything connected with the medical field, leaving only a few personal belongings in the apartment. I doubt they left as much as a wooden pencil in the other office. I still think you're chasing a ghost."

"Maybe so. Can we get permission anyway?"

"Probably. What do you think you'll find?"

"Something in whatever is still there. Ever read Sir Arthur Conan Doyle?"

"Who?"

"He wrote the Sherlock Holmes stories."

"Oh, *that* Sir Arthur Conan Doyle! Sure, but don't let me hear that they've brought you guys in for breaking and entering."

Chapter Forty-Five

EVEN BEFORE GOLDBERG WAS READY TO FLY BACK TO MINNEAPOLIS, HE WAS duly recognized as a defense witness and was set up for protection by the State of Minnesota. The prosecution had apparently set its eyes on a more significant target, not described as of yet. That official explanation bothered LaForge. It *could* mean they'd been able to find Levine and wanted to be sure, or that the Feds had found him and passed along the information. It could also turn out to be a bogus tip of some sort, someone with an axe to grind. The ProLifers were watching the trial closely, and they were known to screw things up when their purposes were served by doing so. They were already enjoying the biased media coverage of the trial because the bias was in their favor. The local TV station was owned by a ProLifer!

The prosecution's other reason was practical. Goldberg could hardly be expected to testify that Roman Citrano had duped the Levine-Goldberg duo into believing the fetuses were being destroyed. Goldberg controlled the flow of expenses; he kept the records; he knew everything about the EMBRYIA operation, and of course he knew where the fetuses were being shipped and the methods used to ship them. He also knew about things like the AMBRIA corporate jet and the brutal security guard who'd been a former assassin. Oh, yes, he knew *that* fact in ways the jury would appreciate without one word being spoken!

His testimony would no doubt begin to define an intricate, interlocking world-wide operation which, like the iceberg, was ninety percent hidden. His words *might* set the stage for a larger federal case, LaForge explained, but in the interim the prosecution's case against Roman would not be helped if Goldberg was their witness. It would be better for them if he belonged to the defense, so that *they* could cross-examine. Therein was the reason for their generosity.

ꕥ

The office shared by Goldberg and Levine turned out to be a fair approximation of an explosion in a pillow factory. Nothing had been left unscathed, of course, but files had been jimmied open, drawers dumped and even wastebaskets upended. It was all left that way. After twenty minutes of careful searching, Luke and Roman headed for the Levine apartment empty handed. They were bound to hit pay dirt there, Roman said, but not with any conviction.

The apartment *was* a bit tidier than the office, probably because there was only one small wood desk the FBI could destroy. Sure enough, two of the drawers were shattered. The kitchen had never been equipped, other than with a coffee pot, some cups and cheap silverware. The bedroom was next. There, a single chest of drawers had been eviscerated—every drawer yanked out and left upturned in the middle of the floor or on the bed. Behind the gutted bureau lay a shattered photo frame, with glass shards spread about, and in the bedroom closet, a dinner jacket was hung haphazardly on a wire hanger next to two sweaters and a pair of pants. Bedroom slippers had been tossed into a corner.

"I expected more," Roman sighed, flipping the bathroom's mirrored medicine chest shut. There was nothing in that, either. "I even *dreamt* about finding something here. Should have listened to LaForge. He was indulging me, but he'd already been here. He knew."

Luke was on his knees, scooping up the shattered photo frame. "What about Levine's private life?"

"Haven't a clue. He never referred to it."

"This is a woman's picture. She looks fairly dark, most likely Indian. Did he ever mention a girlfriend?"

"Never. You say it's a picture. You mean a photo?"

"Yes, a professional one. Here." He'd carefully picked away the remaining glass and slipped the frame's backing out of its slots. "Nothing on the back… no inscription."

Roman took a look. "Well, he never mentioned any women unless they were the objects of his research. This was taken in Totowa, see? Totowa Studios 057203." He pointed to the stamp in the lower corner. "The only Totowa I know is in New Jersey."

"So who's the woman?"

"Good question. Certainly not his mother. That could mean a possible girlfriend, or maybe a relative."

"Sister, maybe? Did he have brothers and sisters?"

"Luke, he never *once* mentioned family. When we checked references on him before starting EMBRYIA, we found out who his parents were, but we never… I wonder… this could be a lead. If this Totowa Studio is still there, and if the Totowa is the one I remember, the number refers to their files. They'd have a record on this. That could give us a lead of sorts."

"Do we check it out?" Luke asked. "My attorney says I can move around as long as I keep him posted."

"Same here, and we have more than a week before the trial resumes. This woman might actually be living in that area. If we can find her, she might shed some light on Marcus."

"Unless he's dead, or living in Lower Tasmania in a grass shack."

"But it's the only thing we have, and we can drive there in a day. I'm so sick of flying I think I'll shed my feathers! We'll just take this with us. They saw it and left it, so it's ours."

ꕥ

Even though the four men in those black cars had offered no clues as to anyone who might have been inside either address, continued surveillance seemed reasonable, Andrea reasoned. Early morning and later afternoon were both good times. Noontime was also good, since people did go out for lunch, or they might have lunch delivered. She could watch for that. Any kind of activity might lead her to Levine. Once she'd zeroed in on him? The answer to that question still eluded her, but she *could* choose that time to ask Chuck for help. He might know how best to go after the bastard.

Levine's apartment produced nothing the next morning, and the mid-day stint was no better, so she shifted to the shared office, arriving there at half past two. A gray Ford looking much like the one she was driving was parked almost directly across from the entrance. She pulled into a space two cars behind it and shut off the engine. Something to read would have helped pass the time, but then she might miss the very thing she'd come for. Someone could leave the building, hop in a car and drive away, and she'd have missed the whole thing.

She sat, alone with her thoughts… and doubts. The more she reasoned that Roman had been as much as victim as she'd been, that he'd been duped by these strangers, the more often black thoughts snuck in when her guard was down.

"NO!"

She'd literally shouted the word half a dozen times in the past four hours, as if volume alone could chase the thoughts away, but the "imp of doubt" kept hammering away. Roman couldn't be in on it; he just couldn't be!

But what if he was?

ꕥ

They were returning to Roman's car when Luke gasped, grabbing Roman's arm and pointing at a dark grey Ford across the street. The car was pulling out into traffic.

"Roman, look quick… over there! That car pulling away. Did you see the driver?"

"No. Who was it?"

"Malovec. I'm sure of it."

"Shit! What would he be doing—"

"Two guesses. Three, if you count Levine. Remember what Rishi said about Malovec being an assassin."

"Yeah. So you think he's here looking for Levine? No? Why not?"

Luke was shaking his head, staring straight ahead. "What are the chances he'd be across the street on the same day, and at exactly the same time, that we're here, and why? He's not looking for Marcus Levine. In fact, he may already have found Levine and finished him. *We're* next on his list."

ꕥ

It was him! Roman!

Startled, Andrea nearly screamed. He was with another, younger man, and they'd both come out through the office entrance. The younger man was pointing at the gray car in front of hers, which was already pulling away. She immediately scrunched down, hiding and confused, before remembering that she looked so different he'd never recognize her from a distance.

Why was she hiding? Why not leap from her car and run to him? She was shaking. When she finally raised her head above the dashboard, both men were walking away from her. They were getting into... into Roman's car! It was half a dozen doors further away; she'd never spotted it.

She had to follow them, see where they were going. Quick! Head spinning, she started the car, pulling out immediately. So Roman was right there in Minneapolis, not in India, not far away! He could easily have called her after she'd left the first message... unless he'd just returned from some overseas trip... but he always checked his voicemail. Didn't he?

A traffic light put an end to any pursuit. It was a long light, and she'd been three cars back of the one that had stopped for it. Roman's car was already out of sight when the light finally changed. There was no way to track him unless she saw the car parked in his driveway or hung around the building of the Zorro offices on Marquette. She couldn't show her face anywhere in that area, even if she did look completely different. She couldn't call the Zorro office without knowing which side Roman was on.

Nevertheless, she drove past the office building on the off chance that she might spot his car. No such luck. The building had inside parking, and she wouldn't brave that!

On the way back to Chuck's cabin, she decided it might be a good idea to pick up a couple of local newspapers. A newsstand yielded the Star Tribune and St. Paul Pioneer Press. On impulse, she also bought an issue of the Twin Cities Daily Planet, mostly because it had a headline with the words, "Baby Killers." Later, she nearly threw it away without reading it—more agonizing baby thoughts she didn't need—but decided there might be something in it. It was more of a gossip rag than the other two.

It had been a puzzling, gut-wrenching day that raised more questions than it answered. Foremost among them was her own reason for returning to Minnesota in the first place. What exactly had she expected to accomplish? What did she expect Roman to do if she suddenly appeared... and was *she* emotionally ready for whatever that might be?

She stopped the car twice on the way to the cabin, pulling off the road until the tears had stopped enough for her to see.

Back in the cabin, she tackled the newspapers, starting with Baby Killers. It was sick! ProLife attitudes wouldn't be so terrible if these people weren't always jumping off the deep end of everything. Hatred lodged between every word. Her quick scan abruptly screeched to a halt when she spotted the name Zorro. Of course! Anything having to do with abortion automatically included Zorro and the MAUs, but in the very next sentence Roman Citrano was depicted as a murderer! Oh, it was cleverly worded so the usual "alleged" tag was implied, but in fact it was a sickening indictment by the article's author.

The bashing continued with lies about the cleanliness and efficacy of the MAUs, about incompetent staff recruited from the ranks of unfit doctors and Candy Stripers masquerading as nurses. Then she spotted the line that changed everything. *"Citrano and his associates are finally being brought to justice right here in St. Paul."* What? The article went further, mentioning a trial in process. What trial?

She grabbed the Star Tribune, rapidly scanning the front page. There, on page two! Citrano, arrested by the FBI in India and returned to the states for various felonies yet to be determined, was free on bail while State of Minnesota prosecutors prepared their indictments, etc., etc. As far as the media were concerned, Roman Citrano and Zorro Medical were responsible for "uncounted" vicious rapes in "roving carriages of carnage," unreported abortions and illegal international shipments of human fetuses.

Suddenly angry, she flung the newspaper at the cold fireplace. Lies! They had to be talking about someone else, not her Roman, not the man she loved. The MAU had been spotlessly clean, and the staff professional. She would testify to that! Her mistreatment wasn't due to either of those factors, but to something else, something sinister. Roman could never have… he….

Her sobs were interrupted by Bandit's warbling at the patio door. She decided to let him come in. He immediately set about checking everything, purring in that musical way. When the ear of corn was gone, he neatly tucked the cob into a corner and crawled up onto her bed. In minutes he was snoring.

It was only then that she realized there was a message waiting on Chuck's phone. Her gun license was ready, her CCW. She could pick it up at Chuck's office, then go buy her weapon. Her *real* training course had already been arranged and paid for. She could literally go from the gun store to the Mack Daniels Firing Range and begin her training immediately.

ꟚꟚ

Malovec's appearance in that car outside Levine's office had changed everything. Gone was any nonchalance about safety or freedom, because the Czech could be anywhere in the city. LaForge, informed about the sighting within minutes, immediately contacted the Feds to see if witness protection might be supplied to his client. Then he suggested that Luke pursue the same, with his attorney acting as a facilitator. Both efforts would take several days, but, unless Malovec was found and corralled quickly, the next best move would be to "go into hiding" and disappear underground—underground, in this case, being Totowa, New Jersey.

LaForge was intrigued by the photo, more because it was the only piece of evidence in that apartment. How was it missed? No other picture frames, no snapshots, no memorabilia of any type mentioned in the compilation supplied him by the FBI, so why did Marcus Levine have this one unsigned photo? Why was the woman in the picture special, and how? Answers might bring them all one step closer to finding Levine, and a quick end to what could be a lengthy legal wrangle.

Unfortunately, Luke's attorney was worried about Malovec and put the brakes on any further sleuthing work. Further, he strongly suggested that Roman rent a car for use in the area, leaving his own in the driveway, unused. It would be too easy for someone like Malovec to zone in on Roman's red Beemer.

As for going into hiding, both men should completely alter their daily routines and consider "hotel hopping" until the Czech was captured.

Chapter Forty-Six

Minneapolis

MALOVEK FELT MORE AT EASE JAMMING THE MICROWAVE SENSOR IN THE BMW's alarm system than he did drugging and tying up young women for long journeys to Kolhapur. The next step was tricky, a leap of faith in assuming the jamming mechanism did its job. He quickly picked the lock on the passenger door, held his breath, and jerked it open. No alarm sounded. Just as a precaution, he clicked open the glove box and used the edge of a credit card to pop out the center onboard computer and disengaged the factory alarm plug. That done, Malovec allowed himself to breathe once again. In one seamless movement, he ran his thick thumb underneath the seam of the central console, releasing the entire panel from the clips that secured it to the frame. The simple snipping of the cigarette lighter wires allowed him to splice in the detonation wires of the C4 explosives that he then molded to the underside of the console. Gently snapping the panel back in place, he checked his watch. Approximately three minutes? Yes, he was getting a little rusty. The watch also told him that he'd be on time for his next important meeting.

ꟷ

Bassard watched his "contact" select a spot on the curving seawall along the river, where the huge Czech sat down and opened a book. He wasn't reading, just faking the act, but he played his role well. They'd used this location for two earlier meetings, mostly because two people could converse without seeming to do so, one standing at the railing and watching the river flow by, the other sitting mere feet away.

"They have both disappeared," Malovec reported, "but they will reappear when the trial is set to begin again. I believe they are being hidden or else are hiding on their own."

"Not good, my friend. The younger man named Evans is not that important, but Citrano is. How do you propose to take him out if he reappears at the last moment?"

"I was trained in explosives, sir. His BMW is parked in the driveway of his house. No one else uses the car, so he will evaporate along with it when he next prepares to drive. The explosive charge has already been installed."

"I see. You were supplied with the device, or did you make it?"

"It was supplied to me, sir."

"He left it unlocked?"

"No, sir. I unlocked it after defeating the alarm system." Anyone else might have smiled at making such a statement, but Malovec's expression remained stony, his voice emotionless.

"Do you have a backup plan in case he decides not to use the car and instead uses a taxi to go to the courthouse?"

"No sir. He has not established any patterns of movement I can use, although I have purchased a good rifle that I will zero-in shortly. American handgun restrictions do not serve us, I'm afraid. Also, you yourself told me the time and place would be mine to choose, but you did not stress any time factor. You implied that the local trial would drag, and that it was the federal one that would be important. Are you now changing that?"

"Not really, but zero-in the weapon and prepare a backup plan anyway. I want to review it at our next meeting."

ꕥ

When Malovec was out of sight along the river walk, Norman Bassard reflected on what he'd already learned about the assassin. Extraordinary intelligence, yes, but coupled with an almost canine obedience. The vision of a well-trained attack dog came to mind, a German Shepherd that would attack whomever his trainer was pointing to when the right command was given.

If the "attack dog" was right, Luke and Roman were changing their patterns, going underground. Why? Had they seen Malovec, by chance, recognized him and doped out his intentions? Or was their disappearance from the scene connected in some way to Marcus Levine? Were they even in the city any longer?

Also, David Thomas' sudden willingness to have a face-to-face meeting suggested he was finally ready to disclose his own identity, or assumed it was already known. Thomas couldn't possibly know when that might have happened, but he'd be dangerous if he now suspected it.

Either way, the game was getting riskier. It would pay to be extremely cautious when approaching Grant's tomb. Thomas hadn't said where he'd be in the park, only that he'd be carrying a black attaché case. There were all sorts of approaches and walkways, and of course there was the mausoleum itself. He could remain unseen, watching from dozens of places for someone to show up at the correct time. And if the meeting time were to pass without any contact, what then? The whole thing could be a test of some sort. Finally, David Thomas might not appear in person at all. He might send an intermediary.

The Mack Daniels Firing Range

In her very first day, Andrea fired two hundred fifty rounds from her new handgun, broke the gun down half a dozen times for cleaning and inspection, then studied for what would be a very tough written and pictorial exam. Daniels was a former Marine NCO and knew his stuff. There were few others there at the range that day, so most of his instruction time was spent with her.

By the time she left, she was equally capable with either hand, though not yet close to being "on target." Mack's version of the term meant placing a shot within a circle the diameter of a baseball! She'd get there, he assured her, but it would probably take several more days.

Angered by what she saw as media bias and downright distortion, she went at the course with a vengeance. Alicia Gregg's words became a driving force: "Do not trust him, Andrea, no matter what. In his world, women are actually less important than the animals he destroys with his research."

Might not women be "animals," where Dr. Marcus Levine was concerned?

ꕥ

Roman's BMW was blown up during the night, with someone in it. A police forensic team was already investigating the dead person's identity, but there was little doubt someone was attempting to rig some kind of bomb and made a mistake doing it. Of course, the media was all over the story, and Roman Citrano was back in the spotlight. Safety dictated that he and Dr. Luke Evans be housed in some protective way until the unholy mess was finished. Without the FBI's protection in place, there was no better scheme than moving them to a motel in the suburbs. They were smart enough to handle the rest by themselves.

The cartel's obvious power was not to be downplayed, now that Goldberg had arrived from Argentina. *He* was already being kept safe… in jail… at his own request.

Chapter Forty-Seven

Minneapolis

Norman Bassard was no stranger to deceit. For one, the financial sweeten-ers and initial payoff arranged back in New Delhi through anonymous contacts and voices on the telephone were either too high or too low, depending on one's viewpoint. Too high if the cartel thought it was dealing with the typical disgruntled FBI agent slaving away at bus driver's wages in a foreign setting while the rest of his world coasted to financial comfort in numerous but illegitimate ways in the good old USA. Too low if that same agent were to be lured away from a life of dedication to high moral standards, comfort be damned, to one of corruption. They'd been willing to pay two million for the handling of the AMBRIA mess—their mess—and another million just to "manage" Malovec. Way too much! It came with a "buyer beware" sign attached.

And now Mr. Thomas wanted Agent Bassard to do a little personal "wet work" by taking out Marcus Levine, the mastermind of their golden egg setup, for another two million bucks.

Above all, Bassard hadn't seen any of the original two million and was even now required to step into a clearing in the middle of that proverbial forest and wait for someone to appear with... what? A black attaché case filled with greenbacks, or an ambush? There could be arrows coming through the forest trees in place of that "someone."

It might pay to arrive well before 7:30 A.M. in such a case and set up his own observation, knowing the other party or parties might appear early as well if they intended to set up any kind of ambush. There were all sorts of possibilities.

His flight into Newark was just under an hour away. He was on his way to the airport when his cell phone rang. A quick check told him the call was coming from the Minneapolis FBI office. It was Agent Sinclair, the man in charge of the whole affair.

"We were just called by LaForge, the Citrano lawyer, "Sinclair announced. "Seems his client's car was blown up last night, along with whoever was trying to plant a bomb in it. The local police are trying to piece it together and learn who the dead guy was. LaForge also said that Citrano and this Dr. Evans came up with an address and M.O. for Marcus Levine."

"Let me guess. The address is in Queens. The M.O. puts him in the Einstein Center way up north in the Bronx certain days of the week, like all nights Saturday or Sunday?"

"Yeah. Yeah, that's right, but how in hell did you *know?* LaForge swore he hadn't told anyone else."

"Little bird told me. Now listen... this changes everything. We have to move like lightning. I'm on my way over. Assemble whoever's been working the case on your end and get 'em in a room together. I'll be there in half an hour. Wouldn't hurt to contact New York City FBI, either. Get the S.A.I.C. to stand by. I believe his name is Corey."

He closed the channel without waiting for a reply, swung the car around and headed back to the hotel. Once there, he checked in at the main desk and took possession of the thick folder that had been kept in the hotel safe, then returned to the car and headed for the FBI field office, 111 Washington Avenue South.

Funny how quickly a single incident could kill one plan and launch another, he mused. *Sorta like Pearl Harbor.*

Clifton

It was well past eleven P.M. when a well-known knock brought Alicia Gregg to her front door. Marcus? The knock was one he'd used often—a single rap, then three in a row, followed by two—but he usually called first. Yet who else would use that particular knock?

She opened the door just a crack, enough to see the familiar outline which this time wore a turban and a dark sweater, then opened the door further.

"Marcus?"

ꓽ

Ram Singh pushed the door open far enough to slip through, then closed it quickly behind him. He dropped the Luger-style tranquilizer gun into his black, leather doctor's bag, then withdrew forceps and approached Alicia's still form. The dart was lodged in her abdomen, where he'd aimed it. Kneeling, he carefully removed it and dropped it into a plastic bottle. Etorphine, otherwise known as M99, was lethal within a few minutes. At least a thousand times more potent than morphine, and used only on very large animals, it would be detectable only with an autopsy, which was extremely doubtful as Alicia Gregg lived alone. She had no known living relatives in the U.S. and her genealogical records were all overseas. By the time anyone discovered the body, it could well be in advanced stages of putrefaction.

He removed his turban, replacing it with a Phillies baseball cap. Then he went into the small study where she kept all her records. Those having to do with his addresses and correspondence occupied a single folder, which joined the turban in his black bag. He then plucked off the hanging file label and dropped the empty jacket in with several others, all empty as well. Fortunately, there were no photos of him anywhere in the building, but he checked nevertheless.

Returning to the front room, he stepped over the female carcass, never looking back. He checked the street outside for several minutes, then slipped away into the night. Nobody had seen him arrive; no one saw him leave.

FBI, Suite 1100

They were waiting when Bassard arrived, four agents including John Sinclair, who'd been the agent in charge of the project from the beginning. After introductions to those he hadn't met before, Bassard placed the folder on the conference table and remained standing. Everyone else sat.

"What you're all about to see and be involved in is my one-man sting involving this EMBRYIA-AMBRIA mess. It goes back about two years, and yes, Washington has known about it for most of that time. This folder contains information on EMBRYIA, AMBRIA and the cartel behind both of them, plus complete accounting on the original bribe money they used to sway me, a quarter million to be exact. I put it into Treasury Notes, and there's more now so that we can all have one helluva party when this is over. I'll let home office decide where to put the original amount. Maybe they'll use it to upgrade my New Delhi office, but I'm not gonna hold my breath.

"Put this folder together with what you all know, and we'll be a lot closer to the truth about this mess, but first we have a little cleaning up to do, and it has to be quick." He removed the top sheet and passed it around.

"First name on the list is Damek Malovec, who you may remember was mentioned a few days ago in the courtroom. Not hard to spot, about six feet five and two-fiftyish, all muscle and *lots* of smarts. He was assigned to me… that is, I was to act as his mentor and director, and his assignment was to take out our man Roman Citrano. I had this guy on a tight leash, believe me. The blown up car you just heard about is his piece of work. Somebody else the forensic guys will I.D. for us must have had the same ambition, sat in the car, and *boom!* It wasn't Malovec, thankfully, since he's going to be one of the lead singing canaries, the way I see it. We have enough on him to make an arrest, but be real careful. That address is where he's staying. That's his cell phone number, and he'll be looking for the password. This guy is *extremely* dangerous, people! Do not underestimate him."

"Next sheet… Marcus Levine, the slimebag who was central to this whole thing. We'll ask New York's team to pick him up. That's his present address, but he also hangs out in the Einstein Center. I'll help you there."

"Next sheet, David Thomas. He's the master conductor behind the AMBRIA thing, ran it and a few other operations, although he's not the top dog. There's someone else above him, someone well concealed. If we get Thomas, we may get the top guy, too. I was to meet Thomas in New York tomorrow, receive two hundred fifty grand of seed money against three million bucks I was promised for my services, then learn how I was to evaporate the good doctor Levine, for another two million. Five and one quarter million bucks in all. These guys are playing with *big* dice! How many of you here think I'd have made it to my next birthday alive, based on what you've just heard? Hmmm?

"Back to Thomas. There's his background, all the stuff I could dig up on him. He made one little mistake about three months after he first approached me in India, just dropping a name, you know how it is. From that, I doped out who he was and what school he'd gone to. It was the Imperial College of Business, in London. They publish the whereabouts of their alumni, and he'd headed for India after a stint with Ernst and Young. Bingo! Any questions so far?"

Each of the four was reading. Sinclair shook his head. "There's more? Who's the top dog?"

"Don't know. Like I said, we may get that from Thomas, but even that is problematical. He's supposed to meet me tomorrow morning in New York, the marker a black attaché case with what we'll call my "allowance" in it… two hundred fifty grand… but lots of "ifs" about this meet. First, I don't know what he looks like. Second, he may not show. Third, he could send someone else. Finally, New York's not his haunt. He only uses it as his U.S. base. It might mean the top dog is there, maybe not. But we *can* feed our people what we know and see if they can nab him."

One of the four agents at the table let out a soft whistle. "Why do some guys get all the fun?"

ꙮ

Andrea read the headline story twice, both times through a mist of tears. There was no way of knowing if the body in Roman's car was Roman, or someone else. She hastily bought two other papers, but the story was the same: a car belonging to Roman Citrano was blown up in his driveway with someone inside, a man. Police could not identify the remains without a DNA analysis! Citrano was a key player in the ongoing trial at the state courthouse in St. Paul. Anyone with information should contact the….

She drew a long breath, holding her head with both hands as the emotions she'd suppressed came rushing forth. It couldn't be that he was… dead. This wasn't happening. None of it was real! Her world a sudden shambles, she took out one of the prepaid cell phones and called her uncle at his office. Although he'd called her twice at the cabin, he'd agreed to her wish to work out her problems alone. That was all about to change.

Rather than drive to his downtown office, she opted for a McDonald's parking lot where he'd pick her up for a long lunch together. When he swung by the gray Ford where she stood waiting, he slowed but didn't stop. Instead he circled the parked cars, drove around the backside and out the exit, then finally turned back in for a second pass. This time he stopped, window down, studying her. She decided to lift her sunglasses.

"Andie? Holy shit, honey, I never recognized you! Get in."

ꟾ

Chuck closed his cell phone and winked. "Forensics came back with a blood type, Andie, and it wasn't him. Probably someone connected to the Pro-Life movement. So your guy, Roman, is still alive, okay? Know what I'd do, since you fooled me all to hell there in the McDonald's lot? I'd go sit in on that trial. If Roman's there, he'll never recognize you with those shades and you as a blonde. Take it from me, no amount of time in bed prepares a guy for a complete changeover in his woman unless he's been warned. Besides, he'll be a little preoccupied with his neck in the noose, wouldn't you say?"

ꟾ

Malovec submitted without resistance. Clearly he'd be a hostile witness, unwilling to cooperate in any way, but at least he was behind bars—as a foreign national. The arrest was reported to LaForge, the prosecution's team and, of course, the presiding judge, but it was mutually agreed that the alleged assassin *not* be brought into the proceedings until there was some reason. First he needed to admit to something, since everything so far had been based on hearsay, circumstance and accusations. Luke and Roman could testify that he'd broken Kareem's arm and Roman's ribs with his brute strength and viciousness, but there were no elements of proof that he was even there at AMBRIA. Roman's car had yielded zero clues about the bomb planter identity, so the only evidence that Malovec might in some way be involved in any of it was his passport and international driver's license. Nothing connected him to the cartel—yet. That could change with Goldberg's testimony.

As for Roman's BMW, suspicions pointed to someone angry at Roman for his involvement in what the media was painting as a form of murder.

It could well be a ProLifer lying there in the city morgue, *another* finger pointed at Roman as though he'd blown up his own car just to "do in" one of his accusers. The columnist, Suzy Strickland, was particularly vehement in her accusations, crossing the line that separated allegations from outright libel.

Meanwhile, CSI experts insisted that the car must have been left unlocked in the first place, that the intrusion alarm must already have been inoperative *and* that the ignition system had been compromised previously and left exposed. Otherwise there was no way anyone could do what Malovec claimed to have done, especially in the dark. He'd have needed to remove the whole dashboard.

Chapter Forty-Eight

THE COURT GALLERY WAS PACKED! WEARING HER STYLISH SUNGLASSES, ANDREA chose a spot farthest from the rail, on the very outside, as latecomers filed in. One group of women came in together. They sat in the same back row, but on the other side of the aisle. The rest of the gallery was a hodgepodge of ones and twos, but if any were from the local media, they were either using voice recorders or paper and pencil to cover the proceedings.

Finally Roman entered through the side doors, accompanied by someone she assumed was his lawyer. They were followed by the prosecution and, in short order, the judge. She quieted her hammering heart, gritting her teeth so hard she was sure she'd cracked them.

Roman's lawyer, addressed as Mr. LaForge, opened by announcing someone named Goldberg, who was then escorted into the court room. Emaciated and totally bald, the man's sunken eyes resembled something from Halloween. It wasn't until he ascended the witness stand that the most severe change became evident. He had no fingers! They'd been cut off—both hands—leaving only his thumbs, but even those had been broken and twisted. They stuck out grotesquely, as if he were forever "hitching a ride." Several in the jury gasped.

LaForge focused on the obvious, trying to set the tone for the jury. "Mr. Goldberg, before we begin, please state your full name and the title that you held with EMBRYIA… *and* explain how you lost the fingers on both of your hands."

Goldberg seemed to shiver, staring straight ahead. "My name is David Ethan Goldberg and I was formerly the chief operating officer of the EMBYRIA Corporation. And these…" He held up both hands, now facing the jury. Strangely, he smiled. "…these are the workings of the head of security, hired by AMBRIA to protect their interests in EMBRYIA."

"Okay, Mr. Goldberg, we'll come back to who was hired by whom, to do what, but please continue to explain what led to this… this mutilation." LaForge beamed as if leading a child, although he'd not interfaced with Goldberg prior to the moment. There'd been no rehearsals.

"I received a visit after Mr. Citrano traveled to Kolhapur," Goldberg stated. "He apparently had an encounter with him and—"

"Excuse me, Mr. Goldberg," interrupted LaForge. "Who are you referring to as 'him'?"

"Yes, sorry, by "him" I mean a Czechoslovakian by the name of Damek Malovec, Head of Security, *not* to be confused with the famous Czech composer, Malovec." He smiled weakly a second time, again in the direction of the jury, but all eyes were still on the mangled hands.

"Please, Mr. Goldberg, please continue."

"Um, yes. Apparently Mr. Citrano had an encounter with Malovec, who somehow blamed me for providing him… that is, Mr. Citrano… with too much information. All I really did was provide Mr. Citrano with a reason, a purpose, to revisit Kolhapur. As punishment Malovec tracked me down and slowly cut off each of the fingers on my *right* hand with scissors." He held only his right hand up to the jury. "He swore he would return and do the other hand if I spoke to anyone again about AMBRIA. It was then that I went to live with some relatives in Louisiana." Goldberg then lifted his left hand and looked directly at LaForge. "Apparently he believed I had then talked to someone in preparation for this case. He found me in New Orleans… how, I do not know… and carried out his threat."

"Did he name the person he thought you had talked to?"

"No."

"Did he cut off your left hand fingers before or after I contacted you?"

"Before. Nobody had talked to me about anything, not you, not anyone. I could not convince him otherwise."

"And after that you fled to Argentina?"

"Yes, but I knew he could find me there eventually unless I found some way out of the country without leaving any trace."

"Where did this finger-cutting individual have his confrontation with Mr. Citrano?"

"I really don't know. I suppose in Kolhapur."

"You'd never met Mr. Malovec prior to losing your fingers, yet you knew he was hired as the Head of Security for EMBRYIA. How did you know that? Did you ever see anything concrete that would confirm that? Did others see him, know him and know about him being here in this country?"

"We… that is, Dr. Levine and I… were told that Malovec had been assigned to EMBRYIA, yes."

"Told by whom?"

"By… well, I was told by Marcus… by Dr. Levine. I didn't hear it from anyone else. I don't know where he heard it. I assume Malovec is dead. There is no way they would allow him to be detained and brought here to testify. They'd kill him."

"Who is 'they'?"

"AMBRIA. He worked for them as well."

"So AMBRIA was *also* his employer? Did someone at AMBRIA tell you that?"

"No. I assumed it from things Marcus said."

"Would it surprise you to learn that we have Mr. Malovec in custody at this moment, right here in Minneapolis? He's very much alive."

Goldberg trembled, hearing the words.

ꕥ

The revelation that Malovec had been captured seemed to open the floodgates as far as testimony was concerned. Goldberg backed up his deposition, describing his relationship with Marcus Levine and the early days of a new venture, EMBRYIA. Goldberg spoke of how he and partner Levine were running out of financing for their independent research, and how certain unknown "Dutch friends" had pressured the National Institute of Health to deny them additional grants. In this way they were forced to accept lucrative, new offers from the "Dutch uncle."

Their shady new masters then specifically targeted Roman and Zorro Medical not only to provide capital for the procurement of fetuses, but to legitimize a business that would yield the volume necessary to support their world markets. Everything was researched and scripted out to the most intricate detail… even the relationship between Peter Lundgren and Roman Citrano. They postulated that Roman would be more willing to consider the deal if it was recommended by his valued mentor and past business associate. The past connection between Roman and Dr. Rishi further validated that the right players were at the table, but Citrano was *not* to be made aware of anything amiss for fear that he would reject the proposal.

Goldberg's hatred for the cartel and everyone associated with it was increasingly evident. He assumed that everyone involved in any way with AMBRIA was either dead or soon would be. As with any organized crime syndicate, they didn't like loose-ends. He openly spoke about the death of Dr. Rishi, but could offer nothing about others. He was physically upset when he mentioned that his dear friend, Marcus, would most likely never be found.

He went on to describe the convoluted shipping procedures used to transport fetuses overseas to Kolhapur, the only final destination as it turned out, albeit with a port of entry where the cargo was redirected. The international freight forwarding agency was right there in Minneapolis, whereas the fully prepared shipping containers were delivered to the two U.S. locations where the MAUs operated—Camden/Philadelphia on the east coast and greater Los Angeles on the other side of the country. Other than the permanent EMBRYIA logo and country of origin on the container exteriors, nothing indicated the container contents. The paperwork concealed everything, Goldberg explained, stating for the record that the original instructions had undoubtedly come from the cartel along with clandestine codes to be used on labels and such. While he was familiar with some of the process, his only true involvement was initiation of each shipment and the subsequent record keeping.

Then Goldberg shifted to the sudden "unforeseen need" to harvest uteruses, knowing only that it was supposed to extend the viability of younger aborted fetuses. The new Dutch masters and their cronies chose to include Raj Maibeck, M.D. in their clandestine activities because of his experience in MAU procedures and his lengthy involvement in the abortion business. They secretly introduced him to the senior people at AMBRIA, challenging him to develop a solution to their expressed needs. It was *his* idea to vaginally harvest the uteruses from women who were undergoing abortions so as to match uterus with fetus. If then the fetus was reintroduced to its original uterus, hormones and nutrients necessary to support life would continue to be produced. Introducing "foreign" fetuses of an identical blood and similar tissue types was also proving to be successful. However, criteria for the "when and where" of taking uteruses was still being developed.

Quite a few of the early vaginal uterus extractions came with complications, Goldberg volunteered, ranging from bothersome to extremely serious. He was quite certain that more than a handful of women had died, but not on U.S. soil. They'd been flown out of the country, most likely to India where they'd never be found. In every case, the women had approached the mobile units secretly, without any support from family or friends, fulfilling one of the criteria proposed by Dr. Levine before a uterus extraction was considered. These women simply disappeared if they developed complications.

As to the identity of the "senior people at AMBRIA," Goldberg produced no names other than Dr. Sihar Rishi. He characterized the whole thing as ghoulish thievery of the worst kind, akin to grave robbery, but of course he had no recourse but to play along, fearing for his life if he didn't.

It was at this point when FBI agent Norman Bassard came into the courtroom and managed to get LaForge's attention by moving to the defense side of the gallery, as far forward as he could get and stay behind the rail. He simply stood there, staring at LaForge, until the lawyer glanced that way and took the cue.

LaForge suddenly rose. "Your Honor, I would prefer to take a short recess here and continue Mr. Goldberg's testimony immediately afterwards in regards to my client's lack of involvement and/or any knowledge my client may have had regarding these activities," he said, sweeping his hand in the direction of the defense table, "this being the heart of the matter of this case."

The judge, a bespectacled man in his 60's, nodded before the request was finished. "Yes, indeed... I agree. If the prosecution has no objection, this court is hereby adjourned for recess until 1:30 this afternoon."

As everyone rose for the judge's exit, LaForge immediately approached Bassard, and the two men talked for several minutes. Finally LaForge returned and sat at the defense table. He let out a long breath as Bassard headed for the prosecution table.

"New developments, Roman. What do you want first, the good or the bad?"

"Just tell me, Ron."

"Okay. The New York feds went after this David Thomas character yesterday at the time and place where Agent Bassard was to meet the guy and collect his down payment, which we now know was all part of the sting Bassard was orchestrating over the past two years or so. The New York team got there real early as a precaution, but nobody showed. Bassard had already warned that a 'no-show' was one of the possibilities even if *he'd* been there instead of the New York boys, so it's very possible Bassard saved his own life by not showing up. There was a good chance they might have chosen to erase him. They knew what *he* looked like, but he didn't know them."

"Shit! How soon did you say I'll get protection here? Yesterday?"

"We're working on it. See ya later."

"Ron…."

"What?"

"Someone should be worried about this Raj Maibeck, don't you think?"

ꟷ

As the proceedings unfolded, Andrea rediscovered breathing. It was all so strange, hearing for the first time what Roman had been through. The pieces of her own puzzle were coming together—everything, her violation, the lies, Alicia's warnings, even her own instincts. Her hands were no longer moist with anticipation and her anger could finally be directed at something substantial.

When the gallery had all but cleared, she couldn't will herself to leave with the others. Roman was still sitting there, alone. It took everything she had not to go to him.

Chapter Forty-Nine

ROMAN TWISTED ABOUT IN HIS CHAIR. THE COURTROOM WAS NEARLY EMPTY except for a group of women huddled in the extreme back row of seats. They seemed bewildered by the sudden change in direction of the proceedings. On the other side of the gallery, a short-haired blonde woman wearing sunglasses sat quietly in the back row. He'd not noticed her earlier. Probably a reporter. She looked the part.

Meanwhile, the grey-haired, black bailiff sat alone, sipping coffee from the well-worn cap of his thermos and reading the Tribune sports section.

So much had happened since that infamous day when Marcus had barged past Sarah, hand extended, to pitch his new venture. What signals might have been missed in that meeting, signals that could have helped expose the scheme behind the façade, helped Roman to foresee Levine's true intentions? He'd had misgivings, yes, but all for the wrong reasons. He'd been so focused on the technical side of it, patents and all, that he'd bought into the snake oil salesman like some wide-eyed novice, not the hardened entrepreneur he truly was. He'd been stupid, stupid and blind, thinking only of his personal triumph once the scheme proved out and delivered. And yet he'd already begun serving the sentence for his crimes, irrespective of the Minnesota courts.

His career was dead in the water, he'd lost Andrea, lost his own self-respect, contributed to other deaths, taken one side of the ProLife/ProChoice moral issue even if he'd convinced himself otherwise. He had no family, no real friends, no admiring peers. His life had gone from triumph to madness in the course of a mere few months.

He folded his arms on the defense table and rested his head on them. Eyes closed, he saw all the faces of those who had been damaged by his need to provide a *return on an investment*: Andrea, Sihar Rishi, Kareem, all those faceless bodies purported to be in the Kolhapur burial ground. And those rapes! That L.A. police report—so graphically brutal.

"Sir, excuse me," said the bailiff, standing in front of him with coffee cup in hand, "you ain't alawd to sleep in here."

"Oh, I'm sorry… I'm not sleeping… just deep in thought. None of this has been easy for me."

"I understand, suh, what I'd jes' hurd in dis courtroom I ain't never hurd befo. I know ya heart must be hurtin', but God, He still loves ya."

"What… what did you just say?"

"God, He… He still loves ya."

"An old, dear friend once said that to me at the beginning of all of this, but I didn't realize the importance of his words until just now… thank you. Thank you very much."

The old man nodded and shuffled back to his chair.

Allowed to sleep or not, Roman mused, there was no harm in sitting with one's eyes closed. That wasn't exactly sleeping, as much as demonstrating an art form long ago perfected on countless, boring flights. The trick was to stay upright and still doze.

The upright part worked just fine, but in what seemed like mere seconds others were starting to reconvene in the courtroom. He'd dozed after all. More than that, he'd been totally out for more than half an hour, waking in the same position he'd held at the start. Had it not been for a flurry of activity from the corner of the room, he might have been embarrassed by having LaForge wake him up or, worse, by hearing the spectators return from what would now be a long lunch break.

The commotion came from that small cluster of women who'd not left when the room cleared. Whatever had occurred while he was coming awake had all four now glaring in his direction, each with her own brand of vitriol. One stood out due to a grotesque "port wine" birthmark that wrapped underneath her eyes and down the right side of her face and exposed neck. Not the result of any burn, it was the clinical condition *naevus flammeus,* a vascular birthmark he recognized as a result of yet another business plan he'd once reviewed, another proposal to treat an "unmet clinical need." Her appearance was rendered all the more bizarre by hair she'd dyed a flaming red. If anyone could claim a reason to be perpetually angry at the injustices of life, it would be someone like her.

She'd purposely locked eyes with him, while her comrades faltered, looking down or away. No doubt they were all ProLifers, along with at least half a dozen others of various descriptions, taking in his trial as a means of fueling whatever fires they stoked within. The gallery was large enough to hold three dozen in the pew-like benches, half one side, half the other. LaForge had warned him to expect such displays of angry emotion, and just to turn away. That seemed like good advice in this case. The birthmark woman was like any angry bear in the woods—you never looked such an animal directly in the eyes.

ꕥ

LaForge spent the whole lunch period with the prosecution team. When the trial reconvened, he immediately rose, announcing that he and the prosecution team had come to an agreement regarding disposition of the case, and requesting permission to approach the bench. After several minutes of a hushed conversation, both attorneys returned to their appropriate positions while the judge scowled toward the defense table. He was noticeably uncomfortable, clearing his throat twice before addressing the court.

"Given new information by both the state prosecutor and defense counsel, and in light of this morning's testimony, I must unfortunately adjourn for another recess of approximately twenty to thirty minutes while I review some precedent case materials in my chambers. I will then return to a make a statement regarding the status of this hearing. My apologies to the members of the jury."

"What did you tell him?" Roman whispered as soon as LaForge was free to listen.

"That Goldberg's testimony so far suggested that without an appearance by Levine there could be no substantial charges against you, and that the prosecution agreed with me that there are presently no other living witnesses who were uniquely involved with the formation and operation of the EMBRYIA enterprise. No Levine, no case. They can't convict you on anything Goldberg has said, and in fact his testimony has vindicated you."

"What about the Raj Maibeck connection?"

"Tangential at best. Maibeck performed the abortions. Much later he was inducted into the cartel, according to Goldberg. Doesn't involve you at all, because you couldn't be expected to see that possibility, and the judge viewed it that way as well. Prosecution agrees that you're no longer critical to their game plan, but requires you to testify as to the venture capital aspects of the EMBRYIA creation, augmenting my own opening remarks for an altogether different jury when the State of Minnesota pairs up with the Feds later. Goldberg will move to the prosecution's side at that time."

"He better be guarded around the clock, Ron, by at least a tank battalion and several platoons of Marines. I could use a platoon or two myself, until the cartel's disassembled."

Chapter Fifty

ROMAN CITRANO, PLEASE RISE," THE JUDGE DIRECTED. "THE STATE ATTORNEY'S office has officially requested that all charges be dropped against you in return for your full cooperation in the forthcoming federal investigation and trials, so you are therefore *acquitted* of all offenses identified in docket number 36-701, entitled the *State of Minnesota vs. Roman A. Citrano.* In reviewing additional state and federal statutes, which I will cite in my final written summary, I also hereby direct the discontinuation of all EMBRYIA business activities, the immediate liquidation of all the assets of the EMBRYIA Corporation, dissolution of the corporate entity and distribution of any remaining monetary proceeds, following proper allocations in accordance to any material claims, liabilities, or debt settlement as determined by an assigned Trustee, shall be distributed on a pro rata basis to all the shareholders.

He removed his reading glasses and slowly scanned the courtroom, ending his sweep with LaForge, the other two attorneys and the jury. Then he cleared his throat several more times.

"I thank the members of the jury for taking the time to participate in fulfilling the duties of citizenship," he boomed, "thereby ensuring that justice is served in my courtroom. Before I dismiss you, however, I would like to address the defendant.

"Mr. Citrano, although our justice process has been well served, understand that your acquittal is merely procedural, not something you've earned. You and those like you should realize that this state *and* this great country of ours will *never* allow such capitalistic activities to prevail over the Godliness of conception, birth and the right to life. Your goal of turning a profit was an inhumane and downright reckless disregard for all humanity, no matter *how* you justify it. I'm not interested in hearing anything you might say for yourself. Members of the jury, you are now dismissed… case adjourned."

With that, he grabbed his wooden hammer and struck the gavel as if he were driving in a railroad spike. It was finally over.

ꙮ

When Goldberg got to the part about uterus removals, it was all she could do to keep from gasping. *That* must have been what Roman was told when she'd come up missing. He'd been on his way to her in Philadelphia, trying to reach her, but she'd been spirited away from her apartment before he could get there. Surely he'd seen her blood on the carpet… she'd not had the time or energy to clean it up… and that broken lamp. And if what Goldberg had just said was true, Roman might have believed she'd been dragged off to India, to die there. Which would mean he'd truly thought she was dead! Well, wouldn't it? She'd fit the MAU standards perfectly, according to Goldberg… single, alone, no boyfriend, no friend of any kind, no family members. She'd never had to state her profession or background, or identify those same family members. No "next of kin" should anything go wrong. Nothing that anyone could use to track her, aside from her name. The practice guaranteed her privacy, so she'd been told.

They'd sampled her blood, a normal procedure, taken her age and the time of her last period, then the usual pro-op steps involving blood pressure and a quick exam of all her primary responses. Not one word about what *they* were about to do, only about what *she* should expect following her abortion. They'd assured her that she'd walk out of the MAU in well under two hours, free of her pregnancy and the wiser for the experience. To that end, she'd be handed excellent information about safe sex along with some condoms and a modicum of pain-relieving medication, "in case she needed it."

Roman seemed as surprised as anyone else in the room with Goldberg's words. She'd watched his reactions, seen him shaking his head in what looked like dismay. At one point he'd leaned forward, holding his head in both hands with elbows on the table. Was he thinking about her at that point? It changed everything, including her inexplicable reluctance to present herself to him. Her sudden appearance would shock him, but how could that be avoided? Certainly he had to be alone when she made herself known, not surrounded by people of all sorts, but how could such a thing happen?

Her quandary doubled not many minutes later when all charges against Roman Citrano were suddenly dropped! No sooner had the judge left the bench than several in the gallery were already heading for the exit. Others were stirring, looking confused. She couldn't stay seated now, couldn't risk him seeing her, recognizing her. That group of women was filing out of the back row on the opposite side.

She followed them out.

ꙮ

The judge's comments didn't register until a smiling LaForge turned to shake his hand. Even then, Roman felt numb as he turned to see stunned spectators, all strangers, quietly shuffling toward the large double doors. Some stared at him, others appeared upset; one woman was in tears. That angry group of ProLifers had stormed out already, so these might be family members of those treated in the MAUs. Some might even be patients.

Only when the gallery was empty did he hear the word he'd expected: *murderer.* It came from the gaunt red-head with the birthmark covering half her face, pressed up against the corridor's marble wall with hands folded as if in prayer. Definitely a ProLifer. The acquittal had no bearing on *their* collective opinion of him. Realizing it, he looked away but briefly, and moments later she was gone.

The prosecuting attorney and LaForge filed out ahead of him, shoulder-to-shoulder as if to form a shield. He'd been warned that the verbal abuse might be severe, but none was forthcoming. The judge's harsh words had been abusive enough.

He was nearly through the sea of strangers and well into the central hallway when Sarah popped into view, as confident and pretty as ever. She threaded her way past those still lingering about, planted a kiss on his cheek and immediately started adjusting his tie. She'd been hurrying and was somewhat out of breath.

"Here I thought I'd surprise you by taking the afternoon off and slipping into the courtroom unannounced, and I find you walking out. I just heard the news. They dropped all the charges? I can't believe it!"

"Believe it. After the prosecution heard Goldberg's testimony, they realized that there was no case against me unless Levine suddenly appeared and refuted everything Goldberg said. That was so unlikely—nobody knows where Levine is—that any further attempts to convict me on any of the charges would have been a waste of taxpayer dollars. Ron says the prosecution was more interested in damage control. I'm to cooperate in any federal cases upcoming. The rest is procedural."

"Well, I'm delighted it's over," she said. "Maybe now you can move forward with your life. As for me, the threats have stopped and I've finally found the courage to return to graduate school to finish my Doctorate in Economics, at St. Thomas University."

"That's great, Sarah, but better talk to me before considering venture capital." His forced smile felt wrong.

"I'm not surprised you'd say that, Roman, but you're damning yourself and venture capitalism for all the wrong reasons. How many times did you tell me that risks were more a function of people than markets or technology, and *that* even when all the prospects were positive? In the end, you said, people were the biggest challenge. Wanna know something? You were so right. This whole mess boiled down to conniving individuals, like Marcus Levine. I never trusted him from the very first words he said to me on the phone that first day, and from what I've been able to learn from your trial, I was right. He was crooked from the start."

"I don't want to talk about him anymore."

"Okay, but he's proof positive of those things you said. Look, forget the bad stuff. I've got very important news for you. I've met several impressive people through the university, with access to capital, looking for someone exactly like you to set up a new partnership."

"If it's venture capital, I'm not interested. Besides, I have no personal funds left. Without contributing equity, I'd be no more than a consultant."

"Which means you *would* consider it if you did have capital to invest. They know that, and they said there are alternative ways a partnership could be structured. They've been following the trial, Roman. They've talked with me at length about Zorro and what we did, what *you* did there and even before that, and they're impressed. It would be a fresh start for you, not medical, nothing to do with medical devices, hospitals, clinics or even patients. I do know enough about venture capitalism now to know in my heart that you'd be interested. Their focus is the renewable and bio-energy markets, and they need someone fairly bold with lots of technical savvy. Your past diverse experiences in biotechnology, fund management and operating skills should easily apply to other non-medical ventures. This could be a clean slate for you. A way to put all this agony and nastiness behind you, and you'd be back doing what you do best." She smiled. "Look, can we have dinner tonight? I have many more good things to tell you, but not here."

"That would be real treat, Sarah. I haven't relaxed once in the past year. I'll call you when I get home, but I'm told there'll be some sort of protection arrangement from now on, requiring me to check with them every time I go out. That may change now that this guy Malovec is locked up, but Ron said the prosecution is insisting upon it. The Feds, too."

She shrugged. "Okay, call me later when you know. Here's my *unlisted* phone number. I see that Mr. LaForge is waiting, so I'll let you go. Take care, Roman."

He leaned forward and kissed her cheek, making her blush before she floated down the courtroom stairs like a schoolgirl who had just been asked out to the senior prom. Maybe those "impressive people" of hers did deserve some consideration. He needed something creative, to shake off the horrors of EMBRYIA and his profound disappointment in people. Distraction, even if it was in a different discipline. Hell, it'd be better than teaching, and she was right about his involvement with other venues. He'd championed three successful ventures outside the medical industry, each requiring unique technical developments. One actually *was* an energy industry spin-off. That company was booming, and had been for over four years.

Thank God for Sarah. He drew a long breath, considering how drastically things could change in a few moments. No sooner had he heard that all charges had been dropped than here, suddenly, someone he'd learned to trust more than he realized was talking of a potential fresh start. Better still, she actually had him considering such a thing.

Sarah'd turned at the bottom of the steps, waving. He cupped his hands. "Want to make it Stella's Fish Café? Say about six?"

"Yes! I'll meet you there," she shouted back, showing him a "thumbs up" before dashing away. She didn't see him grinning while he undid his tie.

She'd been boasting about Stella's for years. Once there, she'd insist on her favorite booth on the second floor, next to the window overlooking the Minneapolis skyline. They could watch the sunset as she delivered the rest of her good news.

He failed to notice the short-haired blonde woman wearing sunglasses, standing less than a dozen feet from him. She'd suddenly turned away, looking in the direction of the other woman at the bottom of the courthouse steps, a woman showing exuberance at the prospects of a dinner date at Stella's Fish Café at six that evening. She'd watched that same woman kissing him, heard him call her name, seen his reaction. Perhaps she needn't have worried about shocking him, or even approaching him. She'd come looking for answers, to the place she called home, and found one she hadn't quite expected. Perhaps it was the only one she'd really needed anyway. Others seemed far less important now.

Slowly, she drifted away with the crowd.

ஐ

This witness protection thing wasn't exactly going to be a bed of roses. LaForge was indeed waiting for him.

"Listen, Roman," he said, "we're to meet with the Feds tomorrow morning at their offices on Washington Avenue. Do you know the building?"

"The Federal Building on Hennepin Avenue, right?"

"That's it. Meet me in the lobby about nine. They'll have several possibilities to consider, but it could take a couple weeks before you have any real protection. They weren't ready for this sudden acquittal and dismissal of your case. I could be wrong, but you just have to be careful. Don't follow any set patterns and all that. Watch your back and don't advertise your plans to anyone, like you just did there with that little lady. Now everyone within earshot knows where you'll be in a few hours. Too late to change that now, but keep a low profile until tomorrow morning and get some rest. You've had a big day."

With that, LaForge turned toward his fellow counselor, the prosecutor, mentioning something about a long-overdue drink.

ஐ

No! Her heart would not accept the loss. Andrea was almost back to the cabin when the impact of her courthouse discovery smashed through the protective shield she'd erected in her mind, even before she'd reached her car. She couldn't just give up and walk away. Of *course* Roman would find Sarah attractive, but then he was convinced that there was no longer an Andrea Robbins. He needed to know he was wrong, that the woman he'd loved wasn't dead. He needed to understand what *she'd* been through, hear how she still felt about him. She'd survived; she'd kept him in her vision, her soul refusing to accept her deepest doubts. He needed to know everything. Only then could she accept whatever awaited her.

She spun the car around and headed back. Stella's Fish Café... he'd meet Sarah there. That meant they would both drive separate cars, arrive at different times, park in different places in the restaurant's big lot. She knew the place; she'd been there several times. If she could just confront him when he was alone... but then, he hated being early, so Sarah would undoubtedly get there first. It was a wild gamble, but other chances might present themselves if it didn't work.

She got there just after five, when the lot was fairly empty, but it would fill up fast. Stella's was a popular place. She chose a spot in the farthest corner, reasoning that any remaining spaces would be way over there as the dinner hour approached. Bolstered by the triumph of her change in appearance, she could leave her car windows open, even stand outside while she waited. He hadn't recognized her in the full light of the courthouse hall. And now, in what would soon be twilight? Then she remembered that his car had been blown up. She wouldn't know what he was driving, and that meant she'd definitely have to be outside her own car, standing so she could see over car tops. She had a dark blue head scarf with her. She'd wear that, just in case he remembered her blonde hair from the courthouse.

He arrived at two minutes to six, parking just five cars away from hers, but once he was out, he ran... toward the restaurant! He and Sarah would probably be in there at least two hours. Meanwhile she could go inside and use the ladies room, once she was sure they were both inside and seated.

Cautiously, she headed for the entrance.

ꙮ

Being alone with Sarah brought back a flood of memories. Roman had not expected the evening to rival that final night with Andrea at the St. Paul Grill—nothing could compare to that—but he hadn't even had a woman's *company* since then. Here was one he not only knew, but knew well. He was comfortable with Sarah, relaxed. Instinctively reaching across the table to meet her outstretched hand, he was surprised by the intensity of that tingling sensation when his fingers met the silkiness of her skin. Even so, he needed to take things one step at a time for his own sake. It was a fresh start, and their dinner topics of her new opportunities, exciting new frontiers and other refreshing topics made him feel re-energized. Yes, he'd survive, start anew, rebuild….

She'd insisted on separate cars so she could return to the St. Thomas library after dinner. A major dinner topic was her doctoral paper on *Myths of the Venture Capital Thesis.* It was smart to listen for once, letting her pursue her line of thought without his intervention. After all, he'd had no formal academic business training, therefore had no right to argue what she was paying handsomely to learn. He simply listened, savoring his glass of red wine while the bullshit flowed from her sweet lips.

Then, finally, she shifted to his preferred topic.

"I'm really keyed up about you meeting the founders of this new fund. They're all former investment bankers and really need someone of your caliber to join them. You should have heard them when they learned that I worked with you at Zorro Ventures. Roman *this,* and Roman *that,* it's all I heard for weeks!"

"Really? No 'Roman-the-baby-killer'?"

"You said that, I didn't. You never knew what you were getting into, not really."

"And you did?"

"Roman, let's not go there, okay? We all have our deep-rooted opinions and beliefs, and what's done is done. I stuck by you, end of story. Seriously, why on earth would you insist on defining yourself just by your last deal? They respect your entire career and, despite the abominable outcome with EMBRYIA, they praised your fortitude and business acumen for building such a challenging business in one of the most controversial markets. What was it one of them said? Oh yeah, the only thing bigger than your reputation was your tolerance for risk. They admire you!"

"Well, that makes them very intelligent, well-informed young men. They must be looking to add some grey hair to the partnership."

"Two are greyer than you are. They also wondered if you'd be interested in speaking at the upcoming Midwest Venture Conference and afterwards have dinner with the whole team."

"Interesting. You wouldn't be trying to work your way onto this team as well, would you? Hmmm?"

She smirked. "Would that be such a terrible thing? With your endorsement, there just might be a Venture Partner position in this for me as well. Wouldn't it be great to work together again, babe?"

"Babe? Did you just call me 'Babe?'"

"Oh, come on, Roman, lighten up! You used to like my attention and all that ego stroking you pretended to ignore. Maybe you just haven't been stroked enough lately." The sudden color in her cheeks had him laughing aloud.

"Okay, Sarah, you win, and you're right. It does feel good to finally have a little recognition out of all this... and... and I'd be delighted and honored to meet this new team."

"Purrrr-fect! I'll set it up. Now *you* have to tell *me* about your interview with that venture magazine."

"How'd you hear about that? I just got the call from the reporter late last night. When I agreed to it, I wasn't even sure if I'd be doing it from a jail cell or not."

It was her turn to laugh. "How do you think they got your cell phone number? They tracked me down through Martinez, at Dorsal & Whilley. So what did they want? Was it good or bad, my giving them your number?"

"It's one of those business rag-sheets, *Venture World*. They want to do a story on *me* as a successful operating entrepreneur-turned-venture capitalist? You don't suppose my indictment, alleged felony charges, implosion of the partnership, funding of technology that resulted in rapes, stolen organs and human trafficking impacted their impression of my skill-sets in some way, do you? I may not have any say in their workup… haven't seen their contract yet."

"Hey, enough with the self-flagellation bit already. You've earned a reputation for starting and building companies that others don't have the balls to even consider. You've taught me to identify risks and how to manage through them. No one could have foreseen the underlying deceit and greed of others beyond your control. The whole topic was toxic from the beginning. Damn it, Roman, Martinez even told me about the Red Cross wanting to acquire the MAUs to convert them to mobile clinics that would address women's *health* in third world countries. Good things will continue to come from this—you'll see!"

"Yes, he emailed me about the MAUs, and I did feel good, but that was before this afternoon's development. Now that the cloud over my head is gone, well… I'm sure they'll be put to good use. I'll call Martinez tomorrow. I also owe a call to a guy down in Atlanta who wants to acquire the rights to the ePOD system—wants to consider using it in other laparoscopic surgical procedures. You know, it's great thinking about technology and helping people again!"

"That cloud you had over your head is going to reveal its silver lining."

"You're absolutely right, good things *will* continue to come… maybe even my faithful friend Sarah, if she plays her cards right." Wearing his best mischievous smile, he lifted his wine glass. "Drink to that?"

She took all of three seconds before blushing and throwing her napkin at him. "Now that's the Roman I know and love… touché!"

Chapter Fifty-One

THE SKYLINE STILL SHOWED DEEP RED AGAINST THE WESTERN SKY AS THEY LEFT Stella's, and Minneapolis had turned on her lights, adding sparkle. It was one of those rare warm spring evenings when coats were left in cars.

He'd arrived ahead of Sarah by a mere minute. Patrons usually ended up walking several blocks after finding open meters on the streets, but he'd fortunately found a spot in the adjacent parking lot, even if it was way out in the far corner. Sarah had been even luckier, arriving as another car pulled away, directly across from the restaurant's front door.

Roman took her hand to the driver's side, where she spun around and pulled him close. Her passion spoke for them both. As her lips met his, she slightly opened her mouth, welcoming his tongue… oh, how long had it been? Suddenly dizzy, heart racing, he pressed his body against hers, letting his swollen groin speak his thoughts. She broke the kiss, playfully pushing him away with a teasing smile.

"Well, big boy, if you're alright with it, I'll stop by after I'm done at the library. You can help me put a *climactic* end to my paper, the final *touches*. With your *input*, it should be awesome!"

"My gawd, Sarah that would be great. You've been there for me over the years and it's about time I delve *deeper* into understanding *your* needs. I've been so selfish."

She threw her head back and laughed. Yes, she'd turned into a beautiful woman who'd adored and supported him for years. This was a new beginning for them both, time to put the past where it belonged. When she'd headed off to the library, he turned toward the parking lot, astonished at how quickly two hours had passed. Did libraries stay open this late? Ah, but she'd said the St. Thomas library, not the public one.

Not quite 8 P.M. and the lot was nearly vacant. Apparently Stella's patrons knew enough to arrive early, except that in so many of them doing that to "escape the crowds" they created their own crowds. Others arriving late enough actually had an easier time parking. Renewed by the ending of the trial, the anticipation of Sarah's next kiss and a possible new fund with new partners in a refreshing new industry, Roman drew a long, satisfied breath. How difficult it was, in the midst of chaos and disillusionment, to remember that a few bright rays of sunshine could cast away all gloom.

Damn… his overcoat! It was back in the restaurant, his car keys in the pocket. Sarah had been so engaging that he'd completely forgotten he'd checked his coat. She'd worn that seductive, tight-fitting turtleneck sweater and kept her jacket with her at the table, otherwise he'd have….

"You mother-fucker!"

ꕥ

There! Roman's coming out with her; they're crossing the street. Sarah must have parked there, right across from the entrance! Now don't watch them. You know what he'll do; he's done it with you. Go back to the car. He'll have to walk right past you, and you can confront him then. His mind will be on her, not on others in the parking lot.

She decided to stand behind the adjacent car, an SUV, intending to step out at the final moment. He was already threading his way between the cars when she saw someone wearing dark clothes converge on him, walking quickly. There wasn't much light, but….

She froze.

Is that Levine? What's he holding? Is it… oh, my god! That's a gun… silencer on it… a goddamn CAN! Mack told you about silencers and the people who use them, so do something. Don't just stand here. Whoever that guy is, he came to murder Roman and you have a deterrent right in your purse. Use it!

ꕥ

The angry voice behind him was high-pitched, raspy, stopping him in his tracks. There was a snapping sound a split second before excruciating pain seared through every muscle in his body. Even as he twisted toward the restaurant, knees crumbling and body contorted, he saw the pavement rushing up at him; heard his own head smacking on the hard surface. Then everything went black.

ꕥ

Oh, my god! He's down. He's been shot. Oh, no! It has to be Levine. You have to stop him. You know how. His right shoulder, up high. Try to spin him. No time for anything else. Get behind him. Remember your night training and aim a little higher. Make it count. Don't let him shoot a second time.

Run!

ℰ⊃ᑕ♃

Emily Coe tossed the Taser aside and flicked open the switchblade. The bastard had been so preoccupied that she'd easily gotten within a car's length. Even better, the only light spilled out from the restaurant and nobody else was in sight anywhere. He'd be coming out of shock in seconds… might even scream. No time to waste. She kicked the Taser electrodes aside and knelt on him, grinding her knee into his groin. Good! He'd groaned; he was recovering. He'd hear her words, feel her vengeance. He'd see her face, her hair, and know who'd killed him.

Her dark hood fell free with a shake of her head. *Look at me, you fucking maggot!* Yes! He was staring up, seeing her, focusing. She brought the knife up so he could see that, too. He wasn't moving yet. A few more seconds before the pain was gone, before he began to struggle. Too bad it wouldn't last longer—much, much longer.

ℰ⊃ᑕ♃

There! Between those two cars. He's down on Roman. Get him! Stop him! What's that flash? A knife? Oh, no! Dear God, no! Stop him! Stop him!

Six cars to go; a dozen long strides.

ℰ⊃ᑕ♃

"Remember me? The one with the red hair and the face? Everyone remembers *my* face. You stared at me like I was a fucking freak."

She leaned closer, placing the knife point under Roman's chin. One quick thrust and it would be over, but not yet, not yet. She rasped her words into his right ear, careful to say each word clearly and distinctly.

"All those mothers, all those children you murdered for the sake of profits…. I listened in that courtroom, listened to you *belittle* your despicable actions, heard you make a mockery of the miracle of our wombs. Oh, you were so very righteous, so blasé about it all. You murdered for the sake of *profits*, you miserable piece of shit! Well, Women Against Abortions no longer carry picket signs. We're rising up, taking physical action against contemptible scum like you. An eye for an eye. Now you die, scum, do you hear me? You DIE!"

She pulled back, saw his eyes widen. He'd heard; he was afraid. No more time. It had to be now. One stab in his stomach, then some below-the-belt surgery where it would count the most. As soon as he was aware of what he was about to lose on his way out, she could finish him with a new smile below the chin.

He moved beneath her, struggling, forcing her to lean back, regain her balance. Then something slammed her forward, twisting her about in the process. Her knife hand plunged down.

ꟾ

Thank God for Mack Daniels' night training! Even though she'd never imagined using a gun for anything but self-defense, stopping a murder was almost the same. She immediately rushed forward, arms straight and extended, both hands gripping the pistol, but Levine wasn't moving. In fact, Levine wasn't Levine at all… it was a woman, a redhead. That face… the one in the courtroom!

A shout from the restaurant; people running. She held position, alert to anything the attacker might do, but the redhead lay still on the macadam. Playing possum?

"Are you all right, Roman? Where are you hurt?"

He was struggling to stand, turning with her words, staring first at the motionless, crumpled form, then at her. She shifted to a one-handed grip, then swept away her head scarf.

"It's me, Roman, Andrea. They let you believe I was dead."

"Andrea?" Knees wobbling, he staggered backward, suddenly collapsing against the back fence and sliding down. "How did… your hair! This can't be happening!"

She approached the assailant, returning to her two-handed grip. "Here, help me, Roman. Roll her over. I want to check her bleeding. It's only a shoulder wound, so she'll recover, but she needs an ambulance."

"When did you start carrying a gun?"

"A week ago."

ꟾ

"Don't move, Miss. I'm a cop—off duty."

He held a flashlight in one hand and his service revolver in the other.

Andrea had already unloaded the clip, holding it in the palm of one hand while she dangled the weapon by its barrel. Once more, Mack's training was instantly in play.

"Officer, the woman on the ground used that Taser there, and was about to commit a murder with her knife, which I think might be under her. I stopped her with a shoulder shot from behind. I'm Andrea Robbins, a registered nurse. I doubt she's in any kind of critical condition, but might need immediate surgery. Call an ambulance if you haven't already done so. Here's my gun. My permit is in my purse."

The cop came forward, lowering the light somewhat, and took her gun. He identified himself as a police inspector, name of Bronson. Meanwhile, someone else was already straightening out the redhead's limp form.

By the time an EMS ambulance and two police cars arrived, the picture had become much clearer. Roman took the initiative once his shock had subsided, unable to take his eyes away from Andrea while he described the assailant as someone in the courthouse gallery. He'd heard her vehement words, heard he was about to die, repeated her claim that she was from Women Against Abortions.

He'd also contacted Ron LaForge, who was on his way.

Inspector Bronson just shook his head. "Wackos! We have lots of problems with that group. A few months back they torched a church." He stared down at the redheaded form being hoisted onto a stretcher. "Just curious, Nurse Robbins, but where exactly *were* you aiming when you shot her?"

"Right where I hit her, her right shoulder, up high. She had the knife in her right hand."

"You were aiming *there*, in the dark?"

"Anywhere else and she still might have plunged it into him or sliced his throat. I had to take a chance on spinning her... on spoiling her aim, if nothing else... except I didn't know it was a 'her' until afterward."

"Hmm. By any chance did you train with Mack Daniels?"

"Why, yes. How did you know that?"

ೱ೧ೞ

As soon as LaForge arrived at the scene, both victim and rescuer were off the stationhouse hook until next morning, when they'd appear with him for the unavoidable questioning. Ron was concise and to the point, as usual. *Nobody* had been killed, everything seemed just as it appeared, the Robbins woman had been properly trained and licensed, her actions had been honorable and in keeping with every citizen's duty to his fellow man. Roman Citrano had already identified the assailant as one of those women in the courtroom that very day. Ron had seen her there as well, the one with that blotched face. Emily Coe was an avowed ProLifer who already had a police record that included an acid attack and property damage. She *never* should have been allowed in that courtroom!

Ron took Andrea aside, jotting something she told him down on a pad. She nodded, took out her prepaid cell phone, and moved away a dozen steps.

Ron then turned to Bronson.

"Well, Inspector, I suspect the EMS crew knows who they have in their ambulance, but it would be best for all concerned that these two people here are *not* identified to anyone. My client has enough troubles already, and is slated for a federal witness protection program. Identification would be counterproductive, don't you agree? And then we have our markswoman here, Nurse Robbins, who fortunately did not reveal her name to the EMS crew. Your men? Well, that's another story, but *she* is also part of the larger picture involving the FBI and federal investigators. If you can turn the right screws, it may be possible to quash any breaking news a few hours from now about either of these people being involved in a scuffle here in Stella's parking lot. Silence means a lot, when it's used wisely, agree?"

"Can't guarantee that, Counselor."

"Understood. But I need you to try."

ꕥ

LaForge checked his watch, sighing. It was already 10:00 P.M. "Do you both think you can stay out of trouble until nine tomorrow morning?" he asked. "That's roughly eleven hours away." He eyed Roman. "I think you have some explaining to do."

Wisely, he left without saying another word. Nurse Robbins was *not* the woman who'd been shouting back her, "Yes!" from the courthouse steps about having dinner at Stella's. That was Sarah; he'd met Sarah in the Zorro Medical offices. Andrea Robbins was supposedly dead. Goldberg spoke as though she was; Citrano had been more positive. He'd seen the spot where she'd been buried, or so he claimed.

So much for sworn testimony!

ꕥ

"Andrea, I—"

It was as far as he got before the contours of his face were reshaped by a sharply delivered slap of her hand.

"That's for not being there when I needed you," she fumed. "When you *finally* answered my phone messages, I tried to tell you what had happened, and all I got back was blabber about you being a father. I've been kidnapped, drugged, locked up and nearly killed. If I hadn't been a nurse, I'd have been dead by now.

"I got away, but I was too dangerous to them, Roman. Too dangerous! I was alive, you see, able to point my finger and submit to any medical examination to prove what had happened. *Your* damned MAUs did this to me. They ruined my life. Now you tell me… did you know? About them taking uteruses? Were you a part of this… this abomination in the name of protecting women from backroom abortions? You *had* to know what Marcus Levine was up to. I didn't even know his name until I learned that he and Dr. Ram Singh are one and the same. He has a sister in New Jersey, Roman, did you know that? Did you?"

He brought a hand to his face. Even in the dark, she saw the blood. "Roman! Did she cut you? Where? Where?"

"I… it's…." He stared down at his midriff, soaked with blood.

"Oh, my god! Don't move." In a matter of seconds she'd torn his shirt aside. The slice was deep, crossing his body with an eight-inch gash that even then was oozing blood. "Why didn't you say something when the EMS was here? This is awful!"

"I didn't know. Everything is pins and needles. I can barely feel it even now."

"Come on, my car is over here. You're in for a few dozen stitches as soon as we can get you to an ER."

ꟸ

Regions Hospital was the closest; Andrea headed for it, thankful that she knew some of the staff there. With luck, they'd release Roman, once he'd been stitched up, and send him home in her care. Luck didn't arrive until much later. The hospital was known for its handling of trauma victims, and there'd been more than the usual that night. As a result, they didn't see Roman until 3:00 A.M., took their sweet time once they had him in an operating suite, and finally delivered their report as dawn was breaking. One of his *rectus abdominus* muscles had been partially severed, requiring internal stitches in addition to the forty plus used to sew him up. He'd be there a whole day before they'd release him, and then only if he felt he could walk unaided.

Andrea returned to the cabin exhausted. If only she'd known he'd been hurt before she slapped him, before she'd unloaded her torment, but no—her words came tumbling out before she could stop them. And the way his lawyer stared at her there in Stella's parking lot… surely *that* confirmed Roman's belief that she'd died somewhere in India after losing her uterus. He'd told LaForge she was dead because he truly believed it.

Damn you Roman!

Chapter Fifty-Two

Lake Minnetonka – The Cabin

ANDREA SHIFTED THE PHONE TO HER OTHER EAR. "SO THAT'S THE SITUATION, Chuck. I promised to tell you when things settled down, when things were under control, but until these bastards are brought to justice ...."

"So you save the guy's life and you're questioning whether or not you want to restart your relationship with him? Doesn't sound like the confident Andie I've known and seen take matters into her own hands."

"This is different, Chuck. I'm—"

"You already said you loved him, and you were all torn up about going to Philly and having it break up your romance. After what you've both been through, you gonna just walk away now? Sounds to me that he never stopped loving you."

"I'm not a whole woman any more, Chuck. I'm—"

"Whoa! If I lose a leg, am I less the man? So you had a hysterectomy. Make you less the woman?"

Regions Hospital

Andrea was due back any minute. Her damning words were still ringing in his brain no matter how he tried to think of something else. She'd never accept the truth now, never believe what he'd been through. How could she? Worse yet, she'd probably lump all those beautiful memories of their times together as simple lust, she the innocent victim, one Roman Citrano just out for a romp between the sheets. She'd been violated because of him, abducted, tormented, nearly killed, in her own words.

At least Sarah knew the real story, or most of it. She'd known from the moment he'd failed to show at the office; known when he turned up in India. The only difference was that she'd not known what he was going through. Still, *she'd* been the one who'd shown up with the bail money and stuck with him even when that bloody specimen was left outside the Zorro door. She'd probably had reasons of her own… she….

"Ready to go for a ride?"

Andrea was there in the doorway, with a wheelchair. He'd walked into the hospital bleeding from his wound. Now that he was patched up and fully functional again, he'd be wheeled back out? Who wrote these scripts?

"They allowed me to be your exit card," she smiled. "I've already signed for your body, so once we hit the front door, you can walk to the car. Feel okay?"

"With all this tape and padding, I can't feel a thing. Andrea, those things you said—"

"Shhh! Talking will make your stitches fall right out, didn't they tell you that? You should be sitting down before you say anything."

"I *am* sitting down."

"In my car, silly. Come on, get into the wheelchair and pretend you're sick. Want the top down?"

ཐཐ

They were off the elevator and into one of the main waiting areas when she whispered her need to visit the ladies room. The wheelchair was parked in a recess between building columns, leaving him sitting with more of his jumbled thoughts.

What's happened? Why the difference now, compared to last night? She's the woman I loved… love… nearly her former self, but it can't be just because she'd unloaded all her grief in that fusillade of angry words. Not her. Others, maybe, but not her. No, it has to be something else….

His thoughts were abruptly cut short by a group that had formed way across the open area, back near the elevators. They were mostly women, with a few men rounding out the twenty or so, but one man stood out—Josh Dunham! He was obviously the group's leader. The others treated him as such. He moved among them, handing out something that looked like a pamphlet.

"Okay, that took care of my hydraulic system," Andrea announced. She'd approached the wheelchair without his noticing. "You still okay?"

"No."

"No? What's wrong? Still have some pain?"

"That EMS vehicle last night. Did you learn where it was heading?"

"Nope, but they usually go to the nearest ER for serious things. Why?"

"Do you think they brought that woman here? The one who attacked me?"

"I can find out. Her name was Coe, Emily Coe. Admissions are right around the corner. Don't go anywhere."

A moment later, five of the group, including Josh, took one of the elevators. Those who remained sat down to wait. Of course! There could only be just so many visitors to a patient at one time, fewer if that patient was in a shared room, fewer still if in a ward. Emily Coe belonged to the WAA. No ward for her. And Josh? Was *he* involved with the WAA? A backer? Maybe a contributor? A goddamn *director?*

You should have suspected this, Roman. You always took him at face value, and he always made sure you did with his endless preaching. He never mentioned being actively involved in a ProLife women's movement, but there he is, handing out literature.

That red-haired woman with the face tried to kill you, no question about it. Was Josh in on that, too? Did he know how far she'd go? If he didn't, if he thought she was just there to scare you, then why the knife? Why any of it? Or did he simply turn his back on her, the way he did in quitting Zorro, so that he could claim ignorance?

Andrea's return interrupted his bitter thoughts. "Your hunch was right. They brought the Coe woman here because it was the closest trauma center. I was also right about her shoulder not being all that critical, but she won't be playing tennis for a few years. Maybe never. Was that what you wanted to know?"

"Yeah." He drew a long breath, turning the wheelchair away from the elevators. "Yeah, just curious. Now let's get the hell out of here. You and I have got some catching up to do… that is, if you want to."

She smiled. "I'm rather responsible for your welfare now, you know. I signed the release form, so what'll it be… your place or mine?" She turned the wheelchair and started for the entrance doors.

"How about yours this time? Mine's sorta off limits right now."

"Mine it is, Roman, but I have to warn you. I'm bunking in at a… at a friend's cabin. There could be another male there. We might not be alone."

"Whatever. We can talk on the way."

"You don't care if you have to share me?"

"Are you in love with this guy?"

"Not the way you think, but he really is cute. Kinky, too. Wears a mask all the time."

"A mask?"

"Mmm-hm. And he snores. Well, here's where your ticket to ride expires." They were outside, under the broad canopy that sheltered the Emergency Entrance. She pressed down on the wheel lock and came around with hand outstretched, ready to haul him up, but she was too late. He was almost on his feet, regaining his balance, trying to grin.

"A 'coon?"

"You got it!"

"Andrea—"

"Yes?"

"I love you."

"I know."

ᘓᘐ

LaForge nodded to himself. Roman was right about not finding any kind of safety in the Twin Cities area, or in Minnesota for that matter. The Feds had already reneged on any witness protection program unless they had more facts about the syndicate or cartel or whatever organization was behind the alleged EMBRYIA/AMBRIA mess. Marcus Levine wasn't even on their radar screen. Further, anything they used as a safe house was only safe if Roman stayed inside, a virtual prisoner.

But, "Marcus not on a radar screen" wasn't the same as, "Marcus, location unknown, status unknown." The syndicate still seemed like a shadow organization to the FBI, but they had Malovec behind bars, represented by a public defender, and sticking to his story that he never saw the people who hired him or gave him orders. He only saw their money. He could soon be freed on the technicality that he wasn't a citizen, since charges against him were all circumstantial and hearsay. The closest he'd come to confessing anything was his reference to rigging the BMW for destruction, and even that might be too weak to hold him behind bars. Nobody had actually seen him do it. He'd never actually identified the car by color or physical location.

There was little doubt that Malovec had been sent to the Twin Cities by his bosses, and even less doubt about his mission, so Roman would be safer anywhere else. The same was true for Andrea. Now that her ordeal was fully understood, she was as much a threat as Roman was.

They were now both sitting opposite his desk, waiting for his okay for them to disappear.

"Look, Roman… Andrea… don't tell me where you two are going or what you're planning to do. If you don't tell me, then I don't know, capisce? Just be damn careful, and keep in touch. I want a phone contact from either of you every day. Right now nobody knows about Andrea's return from the dead, so let's keep it that way unless she's absolutely needed, and that won't be unless the Feds get their act together or someone finds Levine."

"Right. Gotcha."

"Looks to me like you two have something pretty damn valuable going between ya, so cherish it. Take care of each other."

Roman carefully got to his feet. "Thanks, Ron. We'll be careful."

"One more thing," LaForge said, coming around the desk. "If you find Levine, *don't* do what you already have in mind, okay?"

"Levine? Who said anything about Levine?"

"You heard me. Now get outta here!"

Chapter Fifty-Three

It was their last lead, the only remaining address that might hold some final clues: a Research Laboratory at the Albert Einstein College of Medicine. Alicia confirmed receipt of numerous packages for Marcus from there. She'd told Andrea how Marcus often spent whole nights there, and weekends, especially Sundays. Students never went there on Sundays, and this was a Sunday.

The disheveled grad student smelled of stale beer and sweat, but as he pulled open the large laboratory door his aroma was quickly masked by the stench of untended animals.

Andrea gagged. "My god, I'm at the stinky end of the zoo!" She covered her mouth and nose.

"Yeah, even I bath twice a week. These buggers go months without even bein' hosed down," the shaggy-bearded student said. "The door should automatically lock behind you when you leave." He sauntered away, kissing the twenty-dollar bill Roman had stuffed in his hand.

ꙮ

Roman eased the door closed the final few inches, but the heavy lock still made a metallic *clank* that echoed inside the otherwise quiet room. Muffled grunts came from somewhere inside, perhaps beyond those heavy-looking glass doors at the end of the hallway. Light spilled from a side room door some fifty feet away, but elsewhere the lighting was spotty—no doubt a measure used to keep costs down. It made the atmosphere creepy, almost like being in a monstrous, dimly lit cave with thousands of huge bats clinging unseen overhead. The slightest sound, and….

"Who is out there?" The words were bellowed, coming through an open door from somewhere inside. *Marcus!*

Roman felt Andrea grab his arm and immediately put finger to lips, mouthing the words, "It's him!" Then he shifted to a whisper. "But we don't know if he's alone."

Suddenly, there he was, pushing a cart loaded with heavy-looking equipment. He stopped dead in his tracks, annoyance turning to surprise, then disbelief.

"Roman!"

Ironically, the single word was tinged with antagonism. Here was the man that turned two lives inside out, taking everything meaningful from them both. Where was the penitence, chagrin? Where was the innocent shrug, the denial that epitomized Marcus Levine?

There'd be no answer. Levine was no longer there; he'd suddenly pulled the cart back into the side room. Silence—followed by the sound of a heavy switch being thrown—then darkness.

"Andrea, your gun, give me your gun!" Roman pulled at her purse as he took three long strides towards the door, dragging her along with him, but the only lights came from two red EXIT signs, one behind them and the other at least a hundred feet away.

"Roman, we should get some help." Andrea had her left hand inside the purse, gripping the gun.

"No time. Can't let him disappear again." *That heavy switch was the main breaker, so the service panel is in that room somewhere. Only a few more feet to the door, so the panel has to be nearby.*

"Andrea, let me have the—"

The loaded cart hit him just below his sutures with such force that it sent him reeling and off balance toward the opposing wall, struggling to stay on his feet. Gone was his grip on the purse and anything resembling breath left in his lungs. Andrea was there in a flash, helping him as a shadow disappeared through those glass doors. The screeching and howling of baboons filled the corridor.

"Roman, are you… can you—"

"I'm okay, but I'm tired of getting my ass kicked. Just give me a hand."

"Here take this, too."

The gun gave him a renewed sense of power, even though he hadn't shot one since the beginning of time. It didn't matter. Time for closure.

"Come on. He's in there with the animals, but be careful. He knows the place inside out."

The stench inside was choking, more so because the inside air was hot and moist. Fans had probably been shut down for the weekend, mute testimony to how the animals were treated. Sounds of low grunts and barks came from the barely seen cages to the right and left of them. Roman's eyes were slowly adjusting, but his lungs were still struggling from the impact of the cart. Gun in hand, he led the way, moving cautiously.

"Marcus, we know you're in here!" It sounded trite, but it might provoke a response. No such luck. The grunts and snorts simply got louder. He'd started to release Andrea's hand when something hard knocked the gun from his grip. The weapon clanged against one of the cages. Something else reverberated with a metallic sound as well, like some discarded tool, perhaps a hammer? It bounced, brushing Andrea's leg.

"And now that you've found me, what do you propose to do about it?" Marcus was heading deeper into the massive room as he delivered the snarling words. A crescendo of primal screeches followed him. "Is that bitch the long-lost mother of your aborted child?" he taunted in a voice just loud enough to be heard. "The two of you found justification for a reunion, I see."

"You monstrous, callous bastard!" Andrea shot back. "Do you have any idea of what you've taken from me... from us?" The thing that had hit her shin was a heavy tool of some sort.

"I have an idea," she whispered, "but you need to keep him cornered back there. Keep him talking. Here, hold this." She handed over her purse and, before he could stop her, moved *toward* Marcus, disappearing into the murk. In two seconds she was out of sight, which meant she was back in among the cages, and yet there were no fresh howls or screeches.

Keep him talking. "Marcus, it's time you pay for what you've done. Everything comes with a cost. You should know that as well as anyone. Your trip to hell will be expedited by my hand or the hands of others... one way or another, it's over for you."

"Hah, by *your* hand, Roman? You haven't figured it out yet, have you? You're nothing but a pawn, a bit player has-been who never was important and never will be. Come on, do you know what I've become, how important I am to one of the most powerful organizations in the world? You can't touch me, but if you try, I will kill you. Have you ever heard of M99? Have you? It's a thousand times more powerful than morphine, used to subdue rogue elephants, but only with an antidote used a few moments later. I have it in my hand right now, but somehow I forgot to bring the antidote. Such a shame! You and your whore will both die if you come back here, so I advise you to save your miserable lives by going back out the way you came in."

Where's that damn gun! It hit this cage and skittered off in that direction, so it has to be here somewhere. Suddenly there was a hand on his shoulder, firm but delicate. "Come on, let's go… quickly!"

Andrea nearly dragged Roman through the double doors, turned and slipped the heavy iron tool inside the opposing door handles. Levine would be able to escape through one of the EXIT doors, but he wouldn't know that. He'd come charging for the double doors, only to find he was trapped inside.

She took the purse and dug inside, bringing out a small flashlight. "Roman, the light panel… it must be back there where he came from, turn everything on."

"But the gun, its back inside the—"

"We won't need it. Hurry. Do it NOW!"

Her words had almost the same effect as the Taser. He flicked the tiny LED flashlight on, then raced back to the side room. There! Three master panels, one with its door open. He lunged for it, throwing the top breaker and flipping every subordinate lever to the ON position. Then the adjacent panel. Finally, the third. The place lit up like a Christmas tree.

Andrea! He turned and charged back, relieved to see her still standing outside the reinforced glass doors, but appalled when he saw the iron tool in her hands. She'd withdrawn it! She was opening one of the doors. She was going back inside!

No!

But Marcus did not come charging through the doorway, and in moments Andrea reappeared, holding her gun. Inside, the baboons were setting up a collective din as shrill as if their cages had all been electrified. There were other sounds, too, of heavy metal cage doors flying open and banging against one another.

"What the hell?"

"I let them free. All of them." She'd already re-closed the door and reinserted the tool, her expression smug. "*They'll* know what to do with that monster."

As they stood together looking through the heavy glass, Marcus came into view. He was backing toward them. Several large alpha baboons were walking nearly shoulder to shoulder on all fours, stalking him, their close-set black eyes not turning away from his gaze. Not this time. Other, younger males were perched on top of cages lining the narrow walkway that led to the locked doors. They formed a gauntlet as if to corner a threatening predator.

Marcus was almost at the doors. As he turned just a bit to make his escape, one of the larger males lunged at him. With a single sweep, the flesh on Levine's cheek was stripped away, hanging, exposing muscles from the bottom of his eye to just below his chin.

"Andrea, you don't want to see this."

"Oh, yes I do! I *need* to see it."

Marcus spun, reaching for the door, giving it one, fierce, desperate but fruitless yank. He stood there, frozen, staring out, without any signs of emotion. Behind him was a figure taller than he was—an immense male wearing a collar none of the other males wore.

Nostrils flaring and lips puckered, the massive primate gripped Levine's deltoid and ripped an arm cleanly from its socket. A second, smaller baboon leapt onto Levine's back, reaching forward, digging his claw-like nails into the middle of the helpless human's forehead. In one vicious tug, Levine's scalp was peeled back. He dropped to the floor and was immediately covered by other males. As blood splattered over both window panels, the pitch of their screaming was unbearable.

"Seen enough?" Roman asked, pulling at Andrea's hand.

She let out a long breath. "Yeah… let's get out of here."

ꙮ

The electronic lock clicked loudly as the lab door slammed hard behind them, confirming the grad student's words. Locked or not, it didn't quite muffle a bellowing howl that froze them in their tracks. It had to be that huge baboon whose collar read "Aggressive – Handle with Caution

– 077648 Brutus." They'd both gotten a good look at it. His primal cry represented a deep-rooted emotion shared with the two *homo sapiens* he'd seen through those glass doors. It conveyed the painful pleasure associated with vengeance and the realization that it brings no true closure to the devastating loss of love and life.

In his case, a young female called Sophie.

ꕥ

Roman felt Andrea's added squeeze on the hand she was already holding. There, pinned on a bulletin board between the lab door and stairway was a copy of a recent published journal article by the department of Artificial Reproduction Technologies. Andrea quickly skimmed the title and ripped it free from its single tack. She looked suddenly pensive.

"Roman, you *do* realize that even though I no longer have a uterus that my ovaries are still producing eggs… at least for the near future?"

"Well, ahh… yes, I suppose, but—"

"And I'm assuming you still have viable swimmers down there, correct?"

"Of course." He smiled. "At least for the near future."

"So maybe you and I should consider… you know…." Her eyes locked on his, seeming to search for some sign of sincerity.

"What, a surrogate? Well, does that mean… yeah, of course!"

"Don't you think we owe it to each other?"

"Well, perhaps we could… no, that would be too much to ask."

"Roman, what's too much to ask? What is it?"

"Well, I was just thinking, I do know someone who might make a great surrogate, but… no, it *is* too much to ask. Besides, I'm not sure she's even willing to talk to me anymore."

"WHAT, you've got to be kidding! You'd really consider *her*?"

"Nah. On second thought, I don't think she'd have the stomach for it."

The End

Author's Notes

This author made a substantial effort to take *neither* a Pro-Life nor Pro-Choice position when using the abortion theme as a backdrop of this story. Neutrality on such a controversial topic is very difficult, but the prevalence of the procedure is undeniable and a reality that will not cease to exist in our lifetime. Regardless of your political or moral position, the reader should find support in the words and actions of the book's characters for whatever perspective they might have.

The Prologue is an accurate account of the author's personal experiences as a Research Associate while an undergraduate pre-med student at the University, working in the Human Genetics Research Laboratory at a Women's Hospital. This was the beginning of the scientific era in which *organ* culture techniques were developed.

The Animal Welfare Act was signed into law in 1966 which established acceptable standards in the treatment of animals for medical research. This includes the dis-continuance of toxic, painful inhalant anesthetics; (such as methanal/formaldehyde used to euthanize Sophie in Chapter 2).

In subsequent years at the University, the author also worked in the Chemistry Laboratory as a phlebotomist where he was responsible for collecting blood samples from newborns in both the Neonatal and Pediatric Intensive Care Units; (to run various blood tests and blood gases). The NICU had a separate room which incubated terminal neonates. *Rambo* in Chapter 6 was a real case.

After struggling to start his own Venture Capital Fund (where he actually considered the name 'Zorro Medical Ventures'), the author eventually joined a Med-Tech Venture Capital Fund in the Southeast designed to finance and create early-stage medical device companies. During that time, he reviewed and considered hundreds of new business plans, including one that incorporated the concept of utilizing "mobile abortion services."

In the 1990's, the author was an advisor to a new start-up company that developed disposable laparoscopic instruments to support a new procedure: *Laparoscopic-assisted Hysterectomies.* Otherwise known as "band-aid surgery," the company developed a procedure in which the uterus was vaginally extracted by inserting instruments through the navel and cervix. Surgeons became so proficient that they were able to complete the procedure within 15-20 minutes on an outpatient basis.

As Co-Founder and Director of one of the first Embryonic Stem Cell companies in the year 2000, procedures were developed by a group of the Company's scientists which used some of the actual tissue culturing techniques that were developed by the lab in Pittsburgh. This Company was eventually only one of 18 companies approved by the Bush Administration to pursue such "research." The Company was eventually sold to another Stem Cell company in Australia due to further political/regulatory restrictions in the U.S.

"Patient Consent to Release Products of Conception" was enacted by the Polking-horne Committee in passing the Human Fertilization and Embryology Law of 1990. In part, this was driven by the growing prevalence of women desiring to keep their placentas for religious, cultural or nutritional purposes; i.e. placental encapsulation. There are also specific laws now governing the use of fetal tissues resulting from abortion. A woman must consent for the use of her fetus in research or therapy. The Human Tissue Act of 2004 made embryonic cells exempt, but reinforced the need for consent in the donation and storage of aborted fetuses.

Although the author does not declare being either Pro-Life or Pro-Choice, he's been a proud member of the NRA for many years... just in case any radicals of either group get any crazy ideas about making an unannounced visit!

About the author

Rudy is best known as a medical device and biotechnology entrepreneur, inventor, and angel investor, with a history of starting new technology ventures throughout the U.S. and Europe. He's been privileged to have the opportunity to see the newest innovations in healthcare and work with some of the most brilliant researchers, scientists and physicians in the industry.

Authoring more than 50 patents, he has helped pioneer new companies involved in cardiology, oncology, orthopedics, neurosurgery and even embryonic stem-cell development. Through these efforts, he has become the recipient of many technology and business awards, including the Ernst & Young Entrepreneur of the Year in Healthcare and the Businessman of the Year Award.

Combining these experiences and opportunities, with thousands of hours of travel and long evenings in hotel rooms, he found the initiative to start writing a collection of medical thrillers based on true events, the first of which is entitled *Equity of Evil.*

CPSIA information can be obtained at www.ICGtesting.com
Printed in the USA
BVOW021630031012

302033BV00002B/188/P